Her
MOTHER'S
Mother's
Mother
& her
Daughters

Her MOTHER'S Mother's Mother & her Daughters

Translated from the Portuguese by Eric M. B. Becker

Maria José Silveira

OPEN LETTER

LITERARY TRANSLATIONS FROM THE UNIVERSITY OF ROCHESTER

Library of Congress Cataloging-in-Publication Data:

Names: Silveira, Maria José, author. | Becker, Eric M. B., translator.
Title: Her mother's mother's mother and her daughters / Maria José Silveira ;
translated from the Portuguese by Eric M. B. Becker.
Other titles: Mãe da mãe de sua mãe e suas filhas. English
Description: First edition. | Rochester, NY : Open Letter, 2017. | First
published as A mãe da mãe de sua mãe e suas filhas.
Identifiers: LCCN 2017036349 (print) | LCCN 2017048876 (ebook) |
ISBN 9781940953724 (Ebook - EPUB) | ISBN 1940953723 (Ebook - EPUB) |
ISBN 9781940953670 (paperback) | ISBN 1940953677 (paperback)
Subjects: LCSH: Mothers and daughters—Fiction. | Women—Brazil—Fiction. |
Families—Brazil—Fiction. | Brazil—Social life and customs—Fiction. |
Domestic fiction. | BISAC: FICTION / Literary. | FICTION / Contemporary
Women. | HISTORY / Latin America / General. | FICTION / Historical.
Classification: LCC PQ9698.429.I48 (ebook) | LCC PQ9698.429.I48 M3413 2017 (print) |
DDC 869.3/5—dc23
LC record available at https://lccn.loc.gov/2017036349

*This project is supported in part by an award from
the National Endowment for the Arts*

ART WORKS.
arts.gov

Printed on acid-free paper in the United States of America.

Text set in Caslon, a family of serif typefaces based on
the designs of William Caslon (1692–1766).

Design by N. J. Furl

Open Letter is the University of Rochester's nonprofit, literary translation press:
Dewey Hall 1-219, Box 278968, Rochester, NY 14627

www.openletterbooks.org

For my mother Galiana and my Aunt Sina,
Gali, José Gabriel, and Laura. For Felipe.

*Just as you see me now, I carry centuries within me:
numbers, names, a place among worlds and the
force of the everlasting.*

—Cecília Meireles, "Trânsito"

CONTENTS

Her MOTHER'S Mother's Mother & her Daughters

Inaiá (1500-1514) + Fernão; in the new region of Porto Seguro/ Bahia, near Monte Pascoal.

Tebereté (1514-1548) + Jean Maurice; in the region of the Cabo Frio/Rio de Janeiro trade post.

Sahy (1531-1569) + Vicente Arcón; on a farm near the boast of Bahia.

Filipa (1552-1584) + Mb'ta; on a farm in Bahia and a sugar mill in Recife.

Maria Cafuza (1529-1605) + Manu Taiaôba; between São Paulo, Rio de Janeiro, Bahia, and Pernambuco.

Maria Taiaôba (1605-1671) + Duarte Antônio de Oliveira; in Olinda and Salvador.

Belmira (1631-1658) + Wilhelm Wilegraf; in Olinda and Salvador.

Guilhermina (1648-1693) + Bento Vasco; in Olinda, Salvador, and the border between Espírito Santo and Minas Gerais.

Ana de Pádua (1683-1730) + José Garcia e Silva; in Sabará/Minas Gerais.

Clara Joaquina (1711-1740) + Diogo Ambrósio; in Sabará and on a farm in central Rio de Janeiro.

Jacira Antônia (1733-1812) + Captain Dagoberto da Mata; on a farm in central Goiás.

Maria Bárbara (1713-1290) + Jacinto; on a farm in central Goiás.

Damiana (1789-1822) + Inácio Belchior; on a farm in central Goiás.

Açucena Brasília/ Antônia Carlota (1816-1906) + Caio Pessanha; in Rio de Janeiro, Minas Gerais, and São Paulo.

Diana América (1846-1883) + Hans G; in the city of Rio de Janeiro.

Diva Felícia (1826-1925) + Floriano Botelho; in the city of Rio de Janeiro.

Ana Eulália (1906-1930) + Umberto Rancieri; in Rio de Janeiro and São Paulo.

Rosa Alfonsina (1926-. . .) + Túlio Faiad; in central Minas Gerais and Brasília.

Lígia (1945-1971) + Francisco da Mata; in Brasília and Rio de Janeiro.

Maria Flor (1968-. . .) + Joaquim Machado; in Brasília and Rio de Janeiro.

All right.

If that's how you want it, I'll tell you all the story of the women of the family. But let's take our time.

It's a sensitive subject, the family is a difficult one, and not everything in this story is wine and roses. There was, of course, love and happiness, battles and victories, great feats—after all, the women in this story helped to build this country, nearly from the ground up. But there were also madwomen, murderers, and a fair share of sorrows and tragedies. Great disappointments. A good many of them.

Remember, too, that whatever I tell you, it was you who asked me, this time, to recount the lives of these women. If at some point you think I'm passing over the men too quickly, don't come to me later accusing me of feminist bias. I'll tell you all right now that the lives of the men of the family are every bit as interesting as those of the women, and if I don't wade further into their exploits, it's only out of respect for your wishes.

And since it is almost time, let's begin our story where it began. With Inaiá, the little Tupiniquim girl, the origin of it all.

A
Shortlived
Romance

INAIÁ
(1500–1514)

In the crimson twilight of dusk cloaking the sea, when after forty-two days the sailors of the Portuguese armada glimpsed the first long, flowing seaweeds stretching across the dark green ocean, a clear indication they were nearing land, Inaiá's mother, standing on the packed earth of her village's ritual grounds, cast her eyes toward the first stars and knew immediately: It was time.

When the darkness blanketed everything and the sailors on the ship had gone to their bunks with their hearts in a stir, tipsy from the wine consumed during the anticipatory celebration of their arrival in an unknown land, Inaiá's mother turned over on her side in her cotton hammock and felt the initial pang announcing the contractions to come.

Early the next morning, as the sight of seagulls with their black feathers and white heads transformed the sailors' anticipation into a swell of euphoria and set the bells of the armada chiming, back at her tribe's village, Inaiá's mother stretched to her feet and resumed the previous day's chores beneath the turquoise sky.

During vespers on that twenty-first of April, the jubilant sailors, leaning over one another on the decks of the armada's twelve vessels, caught glimpse of a tall, round mountain at the exact moment Inaiá's mother stole away to the quiet spot in the forest that she'd chosen for that day, on the banks of a tiny river with crystal waters whose depths reflected the emerald green of the surrounding trees.

When the sky once again began to grow dark and each ship had dropped anchor, the sailors fell to their knees in gratitude at the sight of the thick forest just beyond a thin strip of white sand; the birds along the riverbank leapt skyward once again, startled at the sound of Inaiá's first cries.

Inaiá's father, a Tupiniquim warrior, cut the umbilical cord with his teeth. Privately, his heart leapt with joy because this time the child was a girl; it would not be necessary to remain abstinent in his thatch hut for days on end, protecting her from evil spirits. He would be able to join the group of warriors in their vigil on the beach, watching in wonder as the marine giants approached steadily across the sea.

Before the first rays of sunlight tinged the morning that followed, he was at the water's edge with the rest of the group, eight Tupiniquim warriors armed with bows and arrows. From there they observed the portentous approach of the twelve ships and caravels. Their eyes followed the tiny sloop nearing the beach, carrying creatures they'd never before seen. They wondered excitedly: what were those things?

The warriors on the beach numbered more than twenty—naked, strong men adorned with body paint and green, yellow, and red feathers, tensely clutching their weapons. They saw the signs exchanged between those strange creatures and heard their cries in a foreign, incomprehensible tongue that the roaring sea carried far away. The cresting waves kept the sloop from reaching the beach, but the warriors remained there the entire night, keeping watch while huddled around a tiny bonfire.

The next morning, nearly the entire tribe was on the sand to see the *caraíbas*, the prophets come from the East, the land of the sun. What they saw instead was the armada pull away to the north. At this, everyone, these warriors and a good number of the tribespeople who were now much too curious to return to their village, immediately decided to follow the ships by land or in tiny boats.

Little by little, they arrived to the place where the armada dropped anchor for a second time, a few days' walk from the village.

Even Inaiá's mother—who joined the expedition three days later—her child slung across her back, managed to arrive in time to see a cross erected on that first day of May. Two enormous pieces of intersecting wood raised skyward to the sound of music, chanting, and processions by those creatures with their strange white skin covered in fur, like animals. They were armed to the teeth, these strange men who, by fate's design, were welcomed as friends and brothers.

It might be said, then, that even if she didn't actually see a thing, Inaiá took part in the event that would forever change her life and that of her people.

Her tribe was enjoying a period of relative peace. The men hunted and fished. The women planted cassava, ground it into flour, and made *cauim* wine, wove ornate baskets and made pottery. They'd arrived at that fertile tract during their pilgrimage in search of the Land without Evil, and though there were occasional wars with other tribes, these were part of the natural order of things and did not otherwise disturb those days Inaiá and her sisters spent without serious worries. They bathed in the river, played with the forest animals at the edge of the village: they could identify each type of snake, sneak up on birds and marmosets, anteaters and sloths. They were capable of recognizing each plant and tree, and where it was safe to cross the river. They would help their mothers peel the cassava and they learned to make flour and cassava pancakes. When night fell, the girls would huddle next to the adults around the bonfire to listen to their stories and their laughter, to learn how to dance, make music, and play games.

Inaiá grew up with the belief that, above all else, people were supposed to enjoy life, and that we were born to find pleasure in each day. Melancholy and sorrow were sentiments that provoked great displeasure among the natives. They believed the gods were kind, and the idea of a life after death entailed a garden full of flowers where they would sing, dance, and leap around at their ancestors' side.

Inaiá also grew up listening to stories about the *caraíbas* who had arrived with the sunrise on the day she was born.

The events witnessed during those ten days in April and May were recounted again and again by the adults in the tribe, thousands of times, each individual adding a new point of view, teasing out another detail, as if the act of repeating these stories were a way to help them make sense of those stunning changes to their world by making them a part of their lives instead of a disruptive chaos. They passed the cascabels, mirrors, and beads from hand to hand—gifts from the white man. They placed the sailors' red caps on their heads and danced around, imitating the recently arrived visitors, their pirouettes, their way of walking and moving about.

A time or two, Inaiá caught sight of the *caraíbas* visiting her tribe or walking along the sands at the edge of the sea, next to the logs of Brazilwood trees that now filled the beaches awaiting the men's enormous ships. The hairy men weren't as imposing as she'd imagined when listening to the descriptions given by those who were present when they first arrived. In fact, in the flesh, those figures didn't impress the young Tupiniquim girls in the least. They would laugh out loud at the men's ragged clothing, which looked like a second skin hanging from bodies that were no longer all that white after months beneath the tropical sun, though they were still of a color Inaiá found unusual. She and the others found especially amusing the hairs that seemed to grow every which way and covered the men's hands, bodies, entire faces. They would laugh once again before trailing the sailors, offering them whatever they found along the way and receiving in return kind or impatient smiles, a flurry of gestures and the endless repetition of the same words used to express nearly everything. On occasion, they saw some who were better dressed, wearing colorful second skins—these, indeed, pleasing to the eye—and a headdress not of feathers but of fur, and a strange sort of shell covering their feet.

The adults in the tribe now spent a good part of their time felling trees of a certain red wood, trees the color of burning embers, those magnificent trees whose dye would be used to make the most fashionable clothes in Europe. The right to don this majestic color, previously reserved for kings and Church prelates, had been extended to all, and the demand for the tree's purple-colored dye had intensified. Those natives who possessed steel machetes, gifts from the *caraíbas*, were able to cut the trees with much greater speed, frenetically hacking away, proudly gathering rows of Brazilwood trunks in a few short hours. Had Inaiá lived a bit longer, she would have seen how, day after day, these trees with their metallic green leaves, yellow flowers, and red trunks—found everywhere in her childhood—slowly headed toward extinction.

What was Inaiá like, you ask?

Well. Inaiá was never especially beautiful. I realize you all would like it if this woman with whom it all began, this nearly mythological mother figure, were as perfect as in a fairytale. But she wasn't. If I said she was, it would be bending the truth, although any judgment is relative, of course, both because the standards of beauty of an indigenous tribe at that time are not the same as ours today, and because beauty has never been an absolute truth. There will always be those who consider what the majority finds beautiful to be ugly, and those who find beauty in what the majority judges to be lacking in it. But it's pure foolishness to try to idealize the very first woman in our family. There's no reason for it. It's enough to know that, in every way possible, the first inhabitants of our country attracted many a stare, as was noted by none other than the illustrious penman Sir Pêro Vaz de Caminha in the first document written about this new land. It appears he was unable to take his eyes off them, as he himself admits, and was incapable of concealing his fascination: "So young and so full of charm, with long hair black as night, and their privates so tiny, so slender, so free of hair that, after observing them at great length, we too felt no shame."

We'll never know for sure if all the women were so eye-catching—and if Caminha saw them from a distance or was able to examine them up close—but that shouldn't cause you to think that Inaiá was a beauty among beauties, because she was nothing of the kind. She was plump and of average height, a bit asymmetrical in relation between her torso and her legs, the latter being skinnier than some might like, her buttocks were simply average, neither large nor small, neither firm nor flaccid, her bosom ample but fated to succumb to the law of gravity at an early age, and her black hair was long and straight like that of all the native women, neither more nor less silky than all the rest. She had a flat nose, average black eyes, the same red mouth as her sisters, and a birthmark—this last detail a characteristic all her own—a dark triangle near the base of the nape of her neck that tilted left near its peak. But beyond this, not even Inaiá's personality was particularly exceptional. She performed daily chores eagerly and splashed about as she took baths in the river, and was as social and carefree as her sisters, as well-mannered and happy to be alive as they were.

After a time, she no longer trailed the groups of white men. She maintained a distance, along with her sisters, the whole of them laughing out loud. But their laughter was already different, something in their gazes had changed. That was when one of the men—a *caraíba* about her age by the name Fernão, with an extraordinarily white face nearly devoid of hair, with bright eyes that looked like little rocks made of crystal-clear seawater—cast his eyes on her, smiled, and began to repeat:

"Here, over here. Pretty girl, come here."

Inaiá went. She was twelve years old.

A smile on her face (she had never been so close to a *caraíba*), the curious Inaiá inched forward. She reached out to touch him, touched him and laughed, she smelled him, smelled him and laughed, his flesh was so white beneath that second skin and she laughed, his hair the color of falling leaves, she touched him and smelled him and laughed: Those eyes, yes, I want to see up close these crystals the color of the sea as it nears the sand, the sea without waves, the sea just after the day has begun.

She laughed, and laughed, and laughed.

Birds of a thousand colors flocked toward the heavens and the verdant trees slowly closed in around the two of them.

You might not believe it, but Inaiá was the first woman Fernão had known. The young man from Lisbon had no doubt laid his hands on a working girl or two on dark nights near the port, but on account of his tender age, his inexperience, or his innocence, he'd been content not to take it further.

While Inaiá continued exploring Fernão's strange white body, its every scent and its workings, he also explored the body of this young woman with the reddish skin, taking in her smell, her taste like the forest. The two of them stood there between the leaves, Inaiá laughing, always laughing, as was her radiant nature, and Fernão finding cause for laughter in hers, the two of them young, complete, at peace.

THE YOUNG FERNÃO, A "BRAZILIAN"

Fernão was a cabin boy on the crew of a ship that transported Brazilwood, whose sailors were, for this reason, called "Brazilians." This was his second time arriving at the coast of the Land of Parrots.

His first time there, he'd been little more than twelve years old, and it was also his first sea voyage. The son of tavern owners from the port of Lisbon, he grew up listening to tales of the high seas and their wonders, dangers, and riches. All he wanted in life was to one day travel to the Indies—or, better still, in the dream he dreamed every night and which he'd not confessed to anyone, to one day be part of a crew that would discover a new land where gold, silver, and diamonds were so abundant that they would make even the poorest of cabin boys rich. Where he would defeat one-eyed men with horns in a bloody battle, and where the women would be beautiful and affectionate and easy to talk to, their feet adorned with glimmering fish scales.

Fernão was practically still a child, but he possessed the savviness of those who grow up closely observing the world around them. At the tavern, it was he who demonstrated the most interest in serving the sailors, and after befriending them, they found him a post as a cabin boy on one of the ships making expeditions to that new land in search of the coveted Brazilwood. It was a ship belonging to the fleet led by Fernão de Noronha, and the young man from Lisbon knew that this was the best way to begin to live out his dreams of adventure and make his way to the Indies.

The ship's mission—like any other that set sail from that port with the same objective—was clear: bring back to Portugal as much Brazilwood as possible, as quickly as possible, and as cheaply as possible. To achieve this, the rules of the ship were strict and the discipline, military. The cabin boys were at the very bottom of the ship's chain of command, even beneath the sailors, and their lives were anything but easy. It was they who performed the most demanding tasks: they hoisted the sails, answered to the sailors, and were subject to all manner of mistreatment and punishment.

But the young Fernão considered himself lucky on that first trip. He loved the sea and never tired of watching it, wondering at it, learning more about it to predict its every shift and caprice. A tireless young man, he performed small favors for anyone and became the most highly sought cabin boy on the ship, covering every last inch of the vessel, and in no time at all he knew that ship as well as the tiny tavern where he'd been born. Not a single comment escaped him as he walked up and down the vessel, and he was soon taking advantage of the sailors' passion for betting to earn a few ducats by wagering when a small correction in the ship's route to the southeast might occur, for example, or which foods might be served as part of the following day's ration.

When the ship arrived in the new land, the young man grew ecstatic at the intensity of the light falling over the white beach, with the natives and their nudity, their feathers and body paint, the broad grins on the women's faces, the smell of the trees and sweet fruits, the exuberant vegetation, and a reality he had been incapable of imagining in his wildest dreams.

Restless despite hours of punishing work helping the natives to stack logs of Brazilwood on the ship, Fernão would lie on the sand, breathing in the fresh air and the varied smells he was slowly able to distinguish from one another. He thought that he'd found the land of his dreams, no other place could be so beautiful, not even the Indies.

With the ducats won placing bets during the sea-crossing, he was able to buy animals from the natives—one of the few things permitted each ship's crew—and bought a magnificent parrot, one of the most coveted new products in Portugal. A fantastic animal that, aside from the beauty of its green and red feathers, was able to speak and provide great entertainment for everyone. He also gained a handsome jaguar pelt after winning a bet with a sailor over the exact date they would once again set sail for Portugal.

On the return voyage, Fernão spent his resting hours teaching the parrot to talk, as many other members of the crew did with theirs. Some would teach the birds to exchange pleasantries—"Yes, me

captain," "No, seenhoree"—while others taught the birds vulgarities—
"Darling Lisb'n girl, give me your hand and other sweet parts"—and
others still, wishing to sell them for a fine price to high-ranking
clergymen, taught them prayers. It was great fun, and Fernão soon
discovered another way of earning a few extra ducats: capitalizing on
his natural talent as a parrot professor.

Soon after arriving in Portugal, he had already made arrangements
for a second voyage to Brazil. This time, however, fate did not smile
on the young man. Bad weather followed the ship nearly the entire
trip, food came in smaller rations than ever, and the cruelty of the
ship warden far surpassed anything Fernão had known during his first
voyage. For sneaking a few minutes of shut-eye, the cabin boys were
whipped until they lost consciousness, and Fernão no longer had the
same liberty to roam the ship as before. Worse yet, soon after the ship
arrived on the Brazilian coast, it was discovered someone had stolen
machetes and hatchets to trade with the natives. Fernão was one of
those accused, more on account of the ship warden's ill will than for
any real guilt. Prohibited from leaving the ship to walk along the coast
that he loved and considered more beautiful than all of his dreams,
Fernão, resentful and rebellious, had no difficulty deciding to desert.
When the ship set sail again for Portugal, Fernão and another ship-
mate, Cipriano, a burly Portuguese man known for his ability with a
harmonica, managed to leap into the sea and reach shore.

Soon thereafter, Fernão met Inaiá and befriended the natives.
However, Fernão and Cipriano, knowing that it would not be long
before more ships arrived, thought it better to distance themselves
from the area where they were certain to be pursued by subsequent
crews. They decided to continue on to the trading post at Cabo Frio,
a long journey made by canoe and days of walking.

They were joined by Inaiá and two of her sisters.

Who knows what reasons the women had for leaving their tribe.
They may have decided to follow the men for nothing more than the

thrill of adventure. Or perhaps they had been more or less forced. Or they could well have gone with the ambition of gaining access to the coveted objects of the white man. Though Fernão and Cipriano were mere deserters, they brought with them the possibility of contact with a world that had already become part of the natives' dreams and imaginations.

The Portuguese had built three trading posts along the lush coast, which had been transformed into a gigantic area for Brazilwood production. The consortium of so-called New Christians whom the Portuguese Crown had sent to explore the new colony sought the greatest amount of wealth at the smallest expenses possible—a process to which this country seems inescapably fated to this very day. The trading post at Cabo Frio was nothing more than a crude wood shed encircled by a fence of tree trunks carved to a point. The Portuguese had left a small number of their men there with a handful of bows and arrows and a couple of crates.

Fernão and his group received a warm welcome, but they chose not to settle at the trading post. They instead sought a clearing in the nearby woods, on a slope where they could glimpse a crystal waterfall where colorful fish plunged toward the rushing waters below. They built a hut of aroeira and jatoba wood, using dry Buriti palm leaves for the roof.

Inaiá showed Fernão which plants were edible, how to plant cassava, which types of wood were resistant to rot, and how to make fishing traps from the fiber of palm tree trunks. Fernão would carry fish, still writhing to break free, in his bare hands, and hunt capybara, tamarin, and armadillos. Inaiá would make cassava pancakes and nourish her man with hearts of palm, yam, pineapple, cashew fruit, pitomba, mangaba, imbu, jabuticaba, every sort of berry imaginable and every variety of guabiroba. She taught Fernão how to paint his body with the dark blue paint of the genipap tree and the yellow pigments of the pineapple bromeliad. At the riverbank, she would wash and arrange her hair, and she practically forced the young European to take a bath at least once per day as she laughed and played.

Fernão spent a good part of his time teaching parrots to talk and traded them with the men at Cabo Frio, who, in turn, would trade them with the ship crews that came to extract Brazilwood. Since they had deserted, Fernão and Cipriano had changed their names and the story of how they'd arrived there, telling others they had shipwrecked. If someone in those parts had ever doubted them, it was never mentioned. To ensure their safety, however, they avoided any sort of direct contact with Portuguese seafarers.

The starry nights were warm and pleasant. Fernão learned to play the natives' flute and composed original songs together with Cipriano and his harmonica to entertain the three sisters.

Within the year, Inaiá gave birth to a daughter. She called the girl Tebereté, and the father nodded his head approvingly.

Yes, they were in paradise. You ask me if they were in love? What is love; what was love then? I don't dare answer. But as to whether they enjoyed making love with one another; whether Fernão never sought out other native women because the thought never occurred to him; whether the two of them spent hours rolling about on the leaf-ridden ground, laughing and crying out; whether Fernão bathed in the river after being pulled in by Inaiá, who wanted to rid him of his foul odor; whether Inaiá thought of nothing but bringing him back to her hammock where they could further amuse themselves while avoiding the insects that lurked in the leaves—all this can indeed be confirmed.

If that was what love was, then yes, they loved each other.

Over time, Fernão's young and adventurous spirit led him to mull over the idea of setting out for the Kingdom of Serra da Prata, which he'd heard astonishing stories about from his Tupiniquim friends. He had even seen, in a hut belonging to a Tupiniquim chief, a rude chalice of pure silver that was said to have come from there. They also spoke of a trail, a path to the south, in use since time immemorial.

He surmised he could gather a group of white men and natives for his expedition, as long as they could obtain the necessary arms and munitions.

Fernão launched into preparations: he learned from the natives to make bows of jacaranda and *ipê* wood, adding sharp edges at either end of bamboo or—as he preferred—shark teeth, and to make sturdy clubs of hard rosewood and cords from the bark of the embauba. His curiosity endless, Fernão learned to craft weapons and traps and to identify medicinal plants. Inaiá explained the use for each plant and when night arrived she offered him *paricá*, a powdery aphrodisiac and narcotic similar to *rapé* snuff.

Fernão had begun to imagine himself as an owner of lush, virgin lands where crystal rivers hid treasures like gold and silver in their azure depths.

But there would not be time for so many dreams.

One dawn, after a night spent beneath a full moon, a sudden, piercing cry rung out. Inaiá was startled out of her sleep: it was the battle cry of the Tupinambá.

The group was small but fearsome.

Howling, yelping, and screaming, beating the ground with their feet, they attacked. Battle music streamed forth from their hollowed-out gourds, fifes, and flutes, their necks adorned with heavy necklaces made with the teeth and bones of enemies they had killed and eaten.

The young Fernão fell to the ground, struck by several arrows. A few short steps away, Inaiá died instantly when a poison dart struck her above the heart. Cipriano and his wives were killed inside their hut.

Howling and leaping back and forth, the group's chief raised his club to the sky and, with one fell swoop, victoriously brought it down on Fernão's dream-filled head.

Only the shots coming from the white men at the trading post, who'd grown alarmed with all the commotion, were capable of sending the attackers into retreat, frustrating the tribe's intent to take parts of the dead as nourishment for the return journey.

The warriors, however, did have enough time to snatch Tebereté and the other children, and to set fire to the huts and corpses, leaving them there to burn like incandescent torches beneath the warm sun of that new tropical day.

TEBERETÉ
(1514-1548)

The group of Tupinambá warriors had intended to attack the trading post of the Portuguese, but they had come upon Fernão and Inaiá's hut along the way, and it had proved irresistible. Attacks or ambushes from rival tribes were quite common at the time, and the assault on the trading post was part of an alliance between the Tupinambá and the French, who disputed the Brazilwood trade on the coast of this new land against the alliance of the Portuguese and Tupiquim.

It was a period of uncertainty.

The Portuguese and the French, all of them traffickers of Brazilwood, some within the law and others outside it, were constantly locking horns on the Brazilian coast. Each group had begun developing allies, natives from different tribes who, in return for clothing, hats, knives, and machetes were the ones to cut, saw, split, halve, and chop down the enormous trees and carry them to the ships on their bare shoulders.

Tehereté, a pudgy child only a year old, was presented as a gift to the Tupinambá chief, *morubixaba* of the entire region of São Vicente, because she was a special young girl: her eyes, a rare, nearly translucent green against her reddish skin, were reminiscent of the quartz of their labrets, the lip-plates used by the warriors as a good luck charm.

She grew up with the Tupinambá as though she were one of them. And though her childhood was spent among an enemy tribe, she grew up just as her mother had: full of laughter, frolicking in the rivers, games with the forest animals, an abundance of fruits, trees to climb, vines to swing on, joy, cassava, tasty food, flour. It was still possible to be happy in the Land of the Parrots, and Tehereté grew up strong and plump, with long, straight black hair, and her talisman eyes.

The first important event in her life took place soon after she entered puberty: her father brought home a white prisoner to be eaten.

When the warriors arrived, Tehereté was with the rest of the tribeswomen, young people, and children who followed the prisoner as he was paraded through the village. They threw stones at him, squeezed his arms so as to feel his fat, and howled: "Our food has arrived! Look at those arms! We are going to eat you, *peró*, you great big Portuguese man, but first you will make us laugh!"

That was their custom: the prisoner who would become the main dish in the tribe's next feast was welcomed with great euphoria and regaled so that he could fulfill each step of their ritual, which involved not only feeding the tribe, but entertaining it. It was a classic combination of bread and circuses, that most ancient combination so dear to humanity. Once the tribe settled down, Tehereté's father called her forth to tell her that she would assume the role of the wife responsible for fattening up "the Portuguese man." He pointed to a hammock. She was to take good care of him, watch his every move, feed him, and cure him of his melancholy so that the warrior's final days were not spent in misery. The *morubixaba* wanted his future dinner well-fed, fit for a feast, and in good spirits.

Proud, Tebereté drew close to her captive, marveling at his size and the importance of her task. She carefully removed his tattered clothing, lifted his arms to examine his armpits, stuck her nose close, and was overcome with nausea. She choked back her vomit and continued examining him. She pulled at his hair, peered inside his ears, and felt immediate disgust. She ran her hand along his skin, squinting to make out what lay beneath his body hair, and squeezed and pinched along his body to see just how much work she had ahead of her. She took stock of his buttocks and found them to be satisfactory. She liked the sight of his thighs and crouched down to see what was to be found inside the hard shells that covered his feet, but another wave of nausea, this time more intense, stirred her stomach. Tebereté was convinced that before she did anything else, it would be necessary to bathe the white man in the nearby creek to rid him of that putrid, rotting smell.

During this thorough exam, the captive, Jean-Maurice, pondered his next move. His ship had been attacked by two Portuguese vessels. Taken by surprise and without the means to escape while they were still anchored, the French squeezed into lifeboats and fled for the beach, where they were mercilessly slaughtered by the Portuguese and their native allies. The battle was the most violent Jean-Maurice had ever witnessed, leaving the beach full of bloody cadavers. By mere chance, he had managed to escape and run like a madman from the arrows and gunshots, finding refuge in the dense forest, walking for two days before being captured by the Tupinambá. When the natives seized him, he thought they would kill him right then and there; he was later overcome with surprise at being left with this young woman who was currently pulling him toward the river. It was his first voyage to Brazil, and though he understood nothing of what the natives said, he had a premonition of what fate had in store for him. He knew quite well that they were cannibals, he just didn't know the purpose of the young woman's careful inspection.

JEAN-MAURICE, THE "PORTUGUESE" NORMAN

Born in Normandy, there was nothing Portuguese about Jean-Maurice. But by a mishap of fate—or perhaps because he wore a Portuguese cross around his neck and did not have the same light complexion of the French, or *mairs* as the natives called them—the Tupinambás thought he belonged to the band of Portuguese, the *perós*, whom, for a variety of reasons, they had grown to detest. A pity, because had this misunderstanding been resolved by an interpreter, Jean-Maurice would not have become food for the natives. Two factors worked against the young man: first, his healthy physical constitution and tendency to gain weight, and second, Teber, eté's love for human flesh. And so, the immense pressure that the young woman placed on her father to kill the man quickly allowed no time for some interpreter to cross paths with the tribe and clear up the question of his lineage.

In some way, Jean-Maurice was fated for a tragic destiny. Born in Rouen, near the port, the son of a prostitute and a father he never met, he was raised by an aunt whose life was spent being poisoned day by day in a small textile factory, unable to give her unwanted nephew more than a blanket on the filthy kitchen floor to sleep on, endless threats about the punishment that a life of sin could bring a man, and rancor. That place could not rightly be called a home—and Jean-Maurice never did. Not yet eight years old, he abandoned Rouen aboard an illegal ship, or, more frankly, a pirate ship. It was on this and other similar ships that he grew up, a hefty young man with broad shoulders, perhaps a tad surly and a bit slow in the head, but able and knowledgeable about the sea and weapons—all in all, a good seaman.

He soon found himself highly sought-out in the port—strong, loyal, a jack-of-all-trades capable of fighting and killing to help his fellow sailors without a second or even first thought.

Jean-Maurice did not know how many lives he had taken in battles or beyond them, and could not even remember the first man he killed;

he only vaguely recalled the Portuguese man who, before closing his eyes for the final time, tugged at Jean-Maurice's shirt with unexpected force and, in the midst of death's delirium, asked him to take the cross he wore around his neck back to Lisbon. The unusual nature of the request moved Jean-Maurice to tear the silver cross from around the dead man's neck and, without another thought, retie the leather strap around his own neck, only to immediately forget the Lisbon part of the request in the heat of battle. The cross remained there out of pure apathy, dangling across his chest, and whenever someone asked him about it, he replied, "I have no idea!" And he truly didn't.

The last pirate ship he had sailed on set anchor along the Brazilian coast and had already been loaded with more than two hundred tons of Brazilwood, two thousand jaguar pelts, four hundred parrots, and a hundred tamarins—not to mention medicinal oils, pepper, and cotton—when it was attacked just before departure by several Portuguese ships carrying angry sailors who sought revenge for having lost, on that very same trip, one of their fleet to another group of French pirates.

So much blood was shed on the beach that day that it changed the color of the water. Of course, it takes enormous quantities of blood to dye the sea red, but I'm not exaggerating or resorting to metaphor here. That wasn't the first time such a thing had happened, and it wouldn't be the last. Many other beaches around the world have turned red during large-scale massacres, you can be sure of that.

From what we can tell, Jean-Maurice was the only one to escape, and even though he ended up dead regardless, at least his cause of death was a bit unconventional. Strictly speaking, I can't respond for him, but I'm fairly certain that, had he been able to choose between the two, he most certainly would have chosen to be devoured by Tebereté.

During his two-month long captivity, the young Tupinambá girl was like a dream. She fed him several times per day, bathed him in the river, and, with great care and several herbs to dull the pain, stripped him of all his body hair, leaving his skin soft and smooth. Later, as though trying to make up for the suffering she'd caused him, she would cover his body in honey, rock him back and forth in his hammock, and make love to him whenever possible. She would dance and sing for him and teach him games and new words in Tupi. She would comb his chestnut-colored hair, adorn him with feathers and other bodily decorations, and gently and lovingly stroke his skin, though she still paid great attention to the results of her work, the rapid accumulation of fat in the desired spots. She didn't leave him alone for so much as a minute, so attentive, caring, and skilled in her craft she was that she managed to cure the low spirits afflicting the young man, who, unfamiliar with the native ritual, had begun to believe in his own good fortune.

Jean-Maurice only became troubled when groups of noisy and excited old ladies circled his hammock and began to pinch his buttocks and thighs, smacking their lips. They would cackle and shriek in their wild, undecipherable language, forcing him to utter the words that Tebereté had taught him but whose meaning he hadn't quite grasped: "Look how fat and tasty I've become, perfect for your food!"

Whenever he took too long to speak or refused to repeat the words, Tebereté reproached him with a stern gaze.

At night, when neighbors from other tribes appeared in the village or when the tribe assembled to drink cauim wine and dance, Jean-Maurice was brought to the center of the village and put on display, to be inspected, smelled, and pinched. Shortly thereafter they would make him jump up and down and repeat ad nauseam the phrases he'd been taught, while the natives laughed and danced noisily around him, apparently having the time of their lives: "I am your food!" he proclaimed, "Look how I grow fatter and fatter!" If he made a mistake or took too long to say his part, an angry Tebereté would cast him a disapproving look.

When at last the day arrived for them to eat Jean-Maurice, Tebereté performed her task with zeal. That night, at peace, she made love to him several times in the hammock, though not to the point of exhausting him. At sunrise, she led him to the river and gave him a special bath with several perfumed herbs, later covering his entire fattened body with wildflower honey. But this time, to Jean-Maurice's surprise, when he pulled her toward him at the moment he felt himself growing erect after so much playful rubbing, Tebereté refused angrily, batting away his hands. Startled at her rejection, the captive took offense and began to sulk, unaware of the scale of the tragedy about to befall him.

With great pleasure, Tebereté combed the young man's hair one last time and adorned him with several necklaces made especially for the occasion. Later, placing a ceremonial rope around his waist, she led him to the ritual grounds, surrounded everywhere by the howling of the women and children who drew closer. There at the village center, the tribe was gathered en masse together with some guests; they had all painted their bodies in ways he'd never seen before, and had assumed poses that were unrecognizable to him.

It was there that Jean-Maurice sensed, for the first time, that the day had arrived for him to become their feast.

His first reaction was to try to wriggle free and run, but seeing how he was surrounded, looking around until his eyes met Tebereté's reproachful air, he decided to control his fear and his instinct to run. After all, he too was a warrior, courageous, a man accustomed to the idea of death and, since no escape was possible, he judged it better to die a hero's death so as to give this final satisfaction to the Tupinambá girl who had cared for him as no one ever had before.

And so, as the natives' hypnotic dance intensified under the effects of the cauim, and his warrior-executioner, possessed, spun around him like some colorful wild bird, raising his enormous club in the air and shouting Jean-Maurice's last rites. Jean-Maurice responded with the words Tebereté had taught him to recite. So concentrated was he on dying a proper death that he didn't even see the club as it was buried in his skull. He fell face-down without so much as a sound, an omen of the good times that awaited all those who had gathered to feast on him.

Letting forth a cry, toothless old women unable to chew the Frenchman's flesh ran to drink his blood while it was still hot, clicking their tongues. They then gathered up his brains so that nothing went to waste.

Tebereté knelt down next to her lifeless captive and quickly shed her ritual tears before slathering her chest in blood so that the child growing in her womb learned to recognize the taste of the enemy at a young age.

The Tupinambá immediately went to work: a staff was inserted into the dead man's anus to prevent the release of excrement; they later scalded him with boiling water to remove his skin, and then quartered him to roast and grill each body part. The dripping fat was gathered in a clay jar to be used later in cassava porridge.

Jean-Maurice, given his size and the quality of his flesh, no doubt provided a spectacular feast that stretched on into the night. Early the next morning, Tebereté, her belly full and her heart satisfied for having completed her task with such delicious results, continued chewing at one of the nose bones from the white hero, father to the daughter that now stirred in her belly.

Now, just look how interesting science can be. There was a time when anthropologists and historians thought that the anthropophagy practiced by the earliest Brazilian tribes served a merely symbolic and magical function: as they ate their enemy, the victors absorbed his strength and perpetuated the entire tribe's desire for vengeance through this group ritual. Today, however, archeologists and researchers maintain that cannibalism also served a nutritional purpose: during a period of population growth and scarcity, enemy flesh provided necessary protein to the victors. Of course, this interpretation may well be influenced by the excessive nutritional worries that loom over our modern times, but several arguments appear to support this theory, among them the natives' appreciation for the taste of human flesh, as was clearly the case with the ravenous Tebereté.

Following the death of Jean-Maurice, Tebereté was taken as a wife by Poatā, an iron-fisted warrior and tribal hero. When her daughter was finally born, the daughter of Jean-Maurice the heroic enemy, it was the tribe's shaman who chose her name.

He chose the name Sahy—water of the eyes, the tear.

For something terrible was in store for the tribe.

By some insidious, undetectable event, a dark cloud hung over them. Life's natural joy appeared to have been spoiled. A stain blemished the once radiant air, which now brought with it a series of threats.

Inside their tiny, dark cabins, the shamans sat reflecting, restless, troubled, and anxious, unable to see or understand what they saw but sensing, intuiting, that some great horror drew near.

But what? Where would it happen? What was in store for them?

Unrelenting, they performed their ritual dances, summoning the gods with their maracas, breathing in the hot smoke of dry leaves emerging from the eyes, mouths, and ears of enormous skull-shaped gourds. Then they burned more dry leaves, smoking more and more, asking, begging, and imploring the guardian spirits for an explanation that would never come.

Their world was slowly coming undone, a great evil was growing. But what was this evil, exactly? Where did it come from?

The shamans slept, still under the influence of the smoke. Their dreams were troubled, nebulous, cloaked in darkness. Even in the dream world, the spirits brought no answers, no comfort, no serenity.

Sahy grew up alongside her mother and Poatā, but life in the village had changed a great deal, and changed for the worse. The days were no longer so carefree and the nights no longer full of joy.

Tebereté would fight with Poatã because he had fewer machetes than his brothers. In fact, Tebereté picked fights with everyone. She felt uneasy, irritable, and the only person she didn't fight with was Sahy, whom every night she would tell the story of her white father.

The men had spent decades gleefully chopping down Brazilwood trees to trade them for machetes, fishhooks, scissors, and knives. The women too had developed a wild desire for the white man's tools and implements. They wanted more and more, as though infected with some sort of disease.

Curious, Tebereté began to follow the white men who were constantly appearing in the area, and was always one of the first to arrive on the beach when a new ship dropped anchor. One time, she convinced Poatã to join her, and together they stole a hatchet and three fishhooks from a *mair*, a Frenchman who had ventured out to do some fishing in a nearby river while he waited on the captain's order to board the ship. But Tebereté wanted a knife.

Whenever a ship entered the cove, hundreds of natives would approach and surround it, either by swimming or in boats. Banding together, they'd climb aboard, talking and gesticulating frenetically, tugging at objects, showing their own, begging. Women who'd barely reached puberty, full-grown women, old women with saggy breasts, all of them clamored toward the boat, stepping forward, grabbing; they wanted necklaces, they wanted machetes, they wanted knives.

The seaman batted them away like mosquitoes. One day, in search of her knife, Tebereté tried to grab a sailor by the clothes and pull him to a corner, but he pushed her away, irritated and impatient to rid himself of her hands and those of two old women, the three of them yelling things he was neither able nor wanted to understand.

Tebereté refused to let go and, exasperated, he violently shook her off as the two old women shrieked. Tebereté fell over a rusty old nail that had come loose from the ship's deck. Though it had pierced her skin, she felt no pain; she merely saw the nail and removed it quickly, slipping it into the folds of her labia before jumping into the sea. As soon as she returned to her village, she showed the nail to Sahy and made a special leather strap from which to hang it around her neck. Tebereté considered the nail a charm stronger even than her quartz eyes.

Little did she know, neither were good luck charms. There would be no more good luck for the Tupinambá.

Some days later, Tebereté fell ill. It may have been an infection from the rusty nail, or something else: at that point, several people from her village were succumbing to illnesses that the shamans, with their herbs, their smoke, their magic, were unsure how to cure in the midst of their bewilderment.

Sahy, meanwhile, believed her mother's illness could be cured with one extremely rare herb and, on the advice of a shaman, set out into the forest to find it.

She was sixteen at the time, and she never came back.

She was not present when death took her mother, who, burning up in agony, waited for her to return, the tears she shed more for her daughter than herself. Above all, Tebereté lamented that she would not be able to give her daughter the necklace with the nail that, as soon as she passed, would certainly be claimed by the two old women, the same old women who were on the ship at the moment she fell and who, for this very reason, considered themselves rightful owners of that strange iron ornament.

Desolate
Wildnerness

SAHY
(1531–1569)

On the day she was captured, Sahy had a dream: an enormous jaguar, young, beautiful, its paw capable of killing a man in one blow, runs through the forest, strong, majestic, bounding to and fro, in full control of her powers. But suddenly this vitality, this joy, this wonder and power begin to fade, and the jaguar continues moving forward, continues running, but soon stumbles, her strength gone, her radiance gone, she falls, she gets back up, she loses consciousness, her breath fails her, she rises to her feet, falls yet again.

She felt a burning in her side, her skin on fire, and when she woke, Sahy thought to herself that the jaguar was not her, but her mother.

Only when she fell like an animal into her captors' net later that afternoon did Sahy understand that the jaguar was indeed her, and that, had she paid closer attention to her dream, had she understood, she never would have headed off into the forest and would have avoided the fate that befell her.

From that day on, Sahy became a *marauna*, a person who pays close attention to dreams and has the ability to interpret them. And so she became inclined toward observation and reflection, dedicated to thought and not action, capable in some way of seeing the past with new eyes and predicting what was to yet to come.

THE CASTILIAN

Everyone referred to Vicente Arcón as "the Castilian," but no one knew for certain where he was born or what his real name was. The son of Spanish petty nobles, at the age of twenty-three he used his own sword to kill his wife and brother—whom he suspected of having an affair—in one of the outbursts of bloody fury that characterized his life. On the run from the law, he enlisted to serve on a ship embarking on a secret mission to discover the route to the mysterious Rio da Prata, the river named after a native king who dined with silver utensils at a table of pure gold, and who had life-size gold reproductions of all the flora and fauna of his kingdom installed in his palace gardens, so that they would reflect the sun and be visible for miles.

But the Spanish vessel shipwrecked in Brazil, on the coast of Santa Catarina, and if the Castilian managed to reach the shore, more dead than alive, it was thanks to his tenacity, his physical stamina, and the conviction that he had been born to conquer the sea rather than be conquered by it. These traits brought him near-legendary status in the new land, where he had decided to remain and build his empire. Molded as a hidalgo of insatiable ambition and intelligence, in fewer than ten years Vicente Arcón had under his control an army of more than five hundred indigenous warriors and dominion over the trading of enslaved natives in the region. He constructed an entire fort, where he lived with several native wives and hundreds of indigenous slaves.

In a short time, his weapons stock was larger than that of most provincial governors; he had several small-caliber cannons, harquebuses, swivel-guns and arbalests, spears, swords, cotton-padded jerkins to defend against arrows, and all the gunpowder he needed.

The Castilian would leave his fort to make periodic incursions to capture more natives and then sell them to the colonizers who had begun to settle in the country. He also built brigantines of cedar and perobawood, and traveled up and down the Brazilian coast selling his goods.

Vicente Arcón was not present among the group that captured Sahy. His men brought her back along with the other natives they'd captured that day, and the group of captives was piled up and tied down to the deck of the brigantine, headed for Bahia.

Tomé de Sousa, the first governor-general named by the Portuguese king Dom João III, had arrived in Brazil, bringing with him the first great wave of soldiers, artisans, servants of the Crown, priests, exiles, women, and children to settle the country. Dom João III's orders were clear: it was time to secure the new territory for Portugal. This included gaining control over the natives and transforming them into a source of manpower to build the future country. The demand for indigenous slaves increased.

The Castilian would have no difficulties selling a shipload of captives, but before arriving at his final destination of Bahia de Todos os Santos, he made his customary stop to visit a friend, owner of a farm on the Bahia coast. His friend was a Portuguese man who had family in Spain and a knack for good conversation. He was on very good terms with the Castilian, who, besides bringing him reliable slaves, also knew how to appreciate, as few did, his cured wild-game meat.

On this particular visit, after spending hours on good food, drink, and friendly jests, and feeling a bit disappointed because the cured meats had long since come to an end, the Castilian was about to depart when he had an idea. He walked to the brigantine, pulled Sahy from among the throng of natives, and delivered her to the Portuguese man: "I give you this native as your slave so that she might learn to make enough of your cured meats so I might take some with me." His friend took a liking to the idea and agreed.

It was no mistake that Vicente Arcón chose to leave Sahy behind. He did so because one night a few weeks prior, when the Castilian's boats pulled up along a bank and his men went off to hunt, the warm, humid night of the tropics led the Castilian to grab the first native he laid hands on among the hordes piled atop the brigantine deck. It was Sahy.

He took her to dry land, but, before throwing her to the ground, he felt her head touch his chest in the exact spot where his wife's head had before, against the same black, pea-shaped birthmark just below his left nipple. A sudden chill ran down his entire body: Sahy was the same height as his dead wife. She was also of a similar weight and shape, she had the same sized breasts, the same girth, the same passive manner of someone whose spirit appears to be far away, which provoked a powerful and peculiar arousal. Without warning, all of this caught the Castilian off guard and awoke in him the wild and terrible sensation that he once again possessed the body of his dead wife.

After this episode, he wanted to be rid of Sahy, and, at the same time, have her at hand when he found himself in one of those hellish moments when, on account of a similar pang of madness, he desired to possess once again the wife he had pierced through with his sword, but whose absence he nonetheless mourned.

For this reason, it was Sahy he chose to leave at the farm belonging to his Portuguese friend.

From that point forward, every time the Castilian passed through the region, a bounty of cured meats awaited him, and at nights in front of a bonfire, he would grab hold of Sahy, take her to his tent, and once again feel the touch of his dead wife against the same black, pea-shaped birthmark just beneath his left nipple.

For Sahy, the Castilian became someone to whom she would always be irreparably connected. She felt neither horror nor pleasure at this. She felt nothing at all. Ever since she'd dedicated herself to leading an interior life, always seeking reflection, it was as if everything that happened to her was happening to someone else, as though she merely saw and contemplated those events.

Each time the Castilian sought her out, Sahy would close her eyes and see the gently flowing brook that passed by her tribe's village, and listen to its soft murmur. Or else, she saw herself, as though she were lying on the jungle floor, staring up into the humid air trapped beneath the dense forest canopy, the leaves falling one by one, without a sound and without allowing the slightest passage of light amid the darkness. Sahy let the Castilian take her without drama, without a fuss, the same way she ate, breathed, drank, and relieved herself.

In her dreams she had seen that with each visit from the Castilian she would give birth to a son, all of whom would die as soon as they were born. She knew it was meant to be that way; she would wrap the dead infants in the mats she wove specially for this purpose, and bury them at the edge of the brook, along the left bank since all had been boys.

Something curious had happened to Sahy, and perhaps the only explanation for this was her existence as a *marauna*, a dream decipherer. She, who had dreamed of being a jaguar at the height of her freedom and power, had suddenly stumbled upon—at the exact moment that she herself was trapped in a net—the most tragic of traits common to all animals: their openness to vulnerability, the perverse potential to become prey, to be subdued by another. At that exact moment, so that she might know and feel in some way that she was more than a mere animal, she moved past the anger that she sensed would do no good and the sorrow that she knew to be useless, and soon reached a stage in which she always reached beyond, the stage where she could accept and contemplate the world as a passive observer of the infinite human capacity to inflict suffering.

Only after her daughter was born did Sahy step out of this state of mind, but not so much, not entirely, and only during those moments she sat Filipa on her lap to teach her daughter the things she knew.

Life on the Portuguese man's farm was quite hard for the other captives, but not for Sahy, who stayed in the kitchen and enjoyed an almost special status for her connection to the Castilian. She would slaughter the animals the men brought back from the hunt and, when she'd finished preparing the meats for curing, she would sit at the foot of a majestic cashew tree, solitary and still.

There she would close her eyes and see. She saw back to the beginning of her people, how they had come to that land where later the white men, too, would arrive. She could see what that land had looked like before and what her people's life was like there. She saw her brothers who were now working in the fields, planting seeds as the women of the tribe had done before, and she saw the hate swelling in their chests, or, worse than hate, their grief and their bitterness. Only in the act of clearing the forest in that way of theirs, separating out an area and setting fire to it, crouching down to observe the voracity of the flames devouring the forest, did they still seem to have some inner glow. The natives who watched over the cows and the steer, bizarre animals who had crossed the sea from distant lands and whose milk was much whiter and heaver than that made from cassava, these men led lives that were more in accord with their nature, free to roam the fields, but they were few in number. And even among them, anyone who sought to disobey the white man's orders, pausing when their body asked for rest, were whipped and bound and had their food taken away.

One night, there appeared a white man who was different than all the others. He was wearing a black cloak and his nose, the largest Sahy had ever seen, recalled the enormous beak of some bird. The boney angles of his deathly thin body exacerbated his resemblance to a smooth-billed ani. The way he looked at the natives was also different, like that of someone who had suffered a great personal trauma and who harbored a desire to see beyond the surface, to peer deep within them.

On Sunday nights, this man would come to talk with the slaves around the bonfire. He said that there was but one Tupã, the lord father of all, and that He had died on a cross like the one the man wore around his neck—just like the cross of Sahy's white father, the one her mother used as though it were a lucky charm. Now she understood that it was Tupã. The man told them that God was good and loved them all, and he would often stay for hours on end talking about the things that pleased this different Tupã.

He spoke softly and always in the same low, husky voice, often sounding as though he were repeating the same word. Sahy would close her eyes and see the freshwater brook, hear its soft murmur as it ran through her village; she saw her mother and her aunts and her sisters, she saw them all seated on the ground, weak, fainting like the jaguar in her dreams, and she observed them as she sat listening to the hypnotic voices of the priest and the water.

The priest would poke at her until she returned to herself and began to listen again, and his eyes bored into hers as though trying to see straight through her.

The priest did not like Sahy.

The poor Jesuit, who despite his oath to love all of God's children and the fact that he was there for this exact reason, to love the natives, *greatly* disliked Sahy. He found her to be sly, with those lifeless eyes that he found impossible to decipher. He thought she was indolent because she slept around the fire rather than listening to his words. He considered her wicked because she welcomed men to her mat without recognizing that a child of God should not do so.

He had the farmer's permission to catechize the natives on Sunday nights. He would gather next to them around the fire and begin speaking in his soft voice. That was when Sahy would close her eyes and have a vision of the priest, tied to the cross, as though he himself were the Tupã he was always talking about. The cross was carried away by the waters, but this time she didn't hear the sweet, soft ripple of the crystal-clear brook of her village, but the deafening noise of rough, violent waters, the piranha-infested waters of a rushing river that slowly turned red, then rosy, then red again with the blood of the priest tied to the cross-shaped raft as it was swept down the furious river.

When the priest would prod her yet again to listen to the words of his god, Sahy would open her eyes, but it was as if she hadn't opened them at all, because she continued to see the bird-like priest tied to the cross, rushing down the river, the water red, then rosy, then red again.

Only when the time for psalms arrived did the priest stop worrying whether Sahy had closed her eyes. As he felt his tenor's voice carry through the endless night, he forgot himself and Sahy and imagined himself in the kingdom of the Lord with all his flock. But it was then Sahy would open her eyes of her own accord because she wished to see the powerful sounds as they left the priest's mouth. She needed to see the movements that molded the air into sonorous waves so that she might learn and, together with the other natives, open her mouth, too, and let forth that sound that filled the night, giving it the palpable weight of the presence of great and impenetrable spirits.

Some days, the priest carried what appeared to Sahy to be a piece of some unknown type of corn husk where he drew some shapes with a tiny stick. He would ask the natives to repeat certain words over and over, and then he'd make a few more scribbles.

One day, Sahy asked him what those scribbles meant. He explained to her that he was drawing out words from their language, the savages', to remind him later of their meaning and show them to the others. Sahy then told him that he ought to write *mañuçawa*, the savages' word for death, for this was the best word to show the others. It was for reasons like this that the Jesuit priest disliked Sahy.

Or perhaps, too, because he thought it within her power to avoid Vicente Arcón, the Castilian, forgetting that she was merely a slave and that such things were completely beyond her reach.

Each time Vicente Arcón passed through, it provoked an argument that became increasingly heated between the hot-tempered slave trader and the Jesuit who wished to protect the Tupinambá. A Spaniard himself, the priest began to harbor doubts about Vicente's supposed origins. In a loud voice, he promised to ask for an investigation, he would not permit the slave trader to treat the natives like animals. So contagious was the Castilian's fury that it left even the Jesuit defenseless, rendering him nearly unrecognizable as he raged in a way entirely unbefitting a soldier of Christ.

On the Castilian's final visit to the farm, he slept with Sahy, who knew that a daughter had been planted in her womb that night, and that this time the child would survive.

Early in the morning, she saw the Castilian and his men heading for the priest's simple chapel. The previous afternoon, she had looked on as these same men, at the Castilian's orders, hammered two large pieces of cedarwood into a cross the size of a man. When she closed her eyes afterword, she saw the red- and rose-colored waters of the river thick with piranhas.

Neither the priest nor the Castilian was ever seen there again.

Among the baptized and unbaptized savages, there was mention that bits of the priest's black cassock had been found farther downstream. There was weeping, cursing, and vows of revenge against the

Castilian and his men. Their liturgical songs filled the damp night with a despondency that seemed to freeze the sound in the air.

Sahy continued canning meats for some time, though she knew the Castilian would never return for them.

When her daughter was born, Sahy's owner, the Portuguese farmer, had the new priest baptize the child with the Christian name Filipa, in honor of the Spanish king he so admired, and who would soon also be king of Portugal.

The first ten years of Filipa's life were spent on the farm, with neither great tragedies nor great cause for joy. At night, after finishing her work in the kitchen, Sahy would sit her daughter on her lap around the bonfire, close her eyes, and tell the girl in a dreamy voice everything she could see. She recounted what her people had been like in the beginning of the beginning. Where they had come from, and how they had lived. She spoke of the forest, its herbs, and its secrets. She told of the arrival of the white man who swore friendship yet offered anything but, of the cross that hung around the neck of the man the young girl's grandmother had eaten, and who had bequeathed her lighter skin than the others. She spoke of her tribe's decimation and the jaguar and all the other beasts that she knew so well. She spoke of the black bird-priest and the river full of piranhas and the strange god the man proclaimed was the one true god; she spoke of the slave trader who was Filipa's father and who had given her almond-shaped eyes and the scent of cured meats.

And so those first ten years went by, with mother telling daughter the story of her people and their suffering.

Until one night Sahy dreamed once again that she was a jaguar. But she was neither a young nor a powerful jaguar—she was old and decrepit, collapsed by the enormous trunk of a Brazilwood tree, where there soon appeared a blackbird who nailed her to an enormous cedarwood cross; this cross was not the size of a man, but of a woman.

On account of it being an old jaguar, Sahy committed her second major error as a dream interpreter, believing that the evil to come would touch only her. But even had she understood that the evil headed her way would also reach Filipa, what could she have done?

She woke early the next morning and went to the kitchen to help prepare a breakfast of tapioca pancakes with coconut, and the morning resembled all others in every way, it was neither less sunny nor quieter. But it was on this particular morning, identical in every way to the others, that everything would change, because on that morning, neither less sunny nor quieter than all the rest, Filipa was to be sold to the *mameluco* charged with buying slaves for a sugar plantation farther north, in Recife.

The buyer arrived at the crack of dawn and selected the youngest and strongest Indians, who, if they were still pagans, were immediately baptized by the priest at his side. When Sahy threw herself to the ground, offering herself to be taken along with her daughter, the *mameluco* looked into her nearly toothless mouth and declared that she wouldn't do.

That night, without her Filipa, Sahy sat at the edge of the fire one final time, closed her eyes, and saw the forest's darkness close in on the jaguar.

She never opened her eyes again.

It was said later that her death that night was the first of the great chickenpox epidemic that would kill more than fifty thousand Indians in Bahia.

FILIPA
(1552-1584)

Filipa shared her mother's privileged position at the farm belonging to the Portuguese man of the cured meats, and assisted only with the work in the kitchen.

The Portuguese farmer wasn't certain who the girl's father was, but because it was in his cautious nature to account for all possibilities, he decided to give her a Christian name—a Spanish one at that—just in case, and to treat her as he had Sahy. Except that the Castilian had not appeared once in the last ten years, and the Portuguese farmer soon began to ask what, when it all shook out, sort of obligation did he have to a murderer of priests? It's quite true that, beyond the good conversation and the praise heaped on his cured meats, deep down, just like everyone else, he harbored a terrible fear of the infamous Castilian. But ten years is a long time to harbor anything, even the most secret of fears, which, if they are not carefully cultivated, fade over time like everything else.

The only bit of news that reached him every now and then was that the Castilian was keeping a distance from the region to avoid any awkward situations, and so the Portuguese farmer thought it wise to consent when a slave trader said he would like to take the plump little daughter of an Indian and a white man. By all means, as money was one of the most welcome things as far as he was concerned. He could take Sahy too, if he wanted, and, if he didn't want her, he wasn't the one to blame for separating mother and daughter—and when it came right down to it, what was wrong with separating mother and daughter if they were both Indians? The savages, while he wouldn't say they had no feelings, for even he could attest they did, were like cattle: their suffering was of a lighter nature and would soon pass.

The fact is that Filipa, accustomed to canning meat and spending hours on her mother's lap by the bonfire, wasn't prepared in the least for what she was to find at the mill in Recife.

Things got off to a bad start on the journey north. Bound to the other natives, Filipa, who was unaccustomed to walking long distances, was practically dragged along by the others, her feet soon full of open sores, her legs cramping and pangs shooting up her legs, hunger—which she had never before known—piercing her stomach, and the thirst causing her throat to close up. This hell lasted for days, and she only survived because the slave trader, worried about losing a slave so quickly at the beginning of the journey, sat her on the back of a donkey carrying a load of salt.

When she arrived in Recife, nothing was left of the meaty girl who had departed Bahia three weeks earlier. She now looked more like a skeleton overcome with pain, and with a single thought in her mind: to run away.

On the day she first saw the sugar plantation, she was sure she had witnessed hell on earth as the priest had described it. Inside a cavernous shed, fiery stoves gave birth to fiery tongues that climbed the sides of enormous cauldrons, causing their boiling liquid to scream amid vaporous clouds; there was the deafening grind of wheels and chains, and an acrid smell that seemed to coat mouths and lungs even from miles away. All of this, along with the moans of the slaves forced into labor there, paralyzed the young Filipa with fear. Her job was to help separate the bagasse that the black slaves piled in the field behind the shed where the cauldrons could be found. This did not require her to enter into that devil's lair, but it did nothing to soothe her terror. The terror was not hers alone: many of the adult natives were incapable of entering the enormous shed. They would rather be whipped to death than ever set foot in there.

The Portuguese had developed a new technique for sugar production in the Azores, for which the Brazilian climate was ideal and the land spectacular. The Indians, the so-called "native blacks," excelled at clearing the forest to make way for sugarcane, but they were disastrous at the complex and repetitive work at the sugar mill, whose purpose they could not understand. Armed with the machetes and knives they received from the Europeans, the Indians had taken a great technological leap forward, but the operations of the sugar mill, an example of the most advanced technology of its time, proved too much for them. And so, the additional labor of African slaves was becoming increasingly necessary in order to make the colony productive.

MB'TA, THE SLAVE FROM GUINEA

Mb'ta came from Bantu people, born to family of farmers in a slave-trading village in Africa. He had barely turned eighteen when he was caught in an ambush as he was returning home from his father's rice fields. Mb'ta hadn't yet given any thought to marriage, nor had he fallen for any girls in his village. He had a few plans for himself: he intended to ask his father's permission to go live with an uncle who was a blacksmith in a village a half-day's walk away, and to learn this highly respected profession. He had simply been waiting for his brother to take his place next to his father, and he was certain that this time would soon come.

The young man had grown worried with rumors that men and women were being captured to be sold as slaves on the other side of the sea. And so, when one day a shiver ran up his neck and he sensed he was being followed, panic washed over him. Mb'ta was no warrior. He had not even undergone training to become a warrior. He'd always helped his father in the fields, dreaming of the day when he could join his uncle to learn his way around the foundry and master the art of ironmaking, forging weapons that his brothers, not he, would later take up. When he realized there were two or three men on his trail, he knew that, all alone, he had no chance. He tried to run, but it was no use.

His life underwent an abrupt and irreversible change. Mb'ta wished to die and ever since that moment thought of only one thing: running away.

After the hellish nightmare that was the sea-crossing in the hold of a ship, tossed amid a horde of other Africans speaking Bantu, Yoruba, and Hausa, Mb'ta landed in Brazil at the same sugar plantation where Filipa had been brought.

They spent years without really noticing one another, despite working in close proximity. And perhaps they would never have noticed one another had Mb'ta not lost the iron amulet he had worn around his neck, his last tie to his village in Africa. The same amulet Filipa found and hid, fastened around her waist beneath the thick cotton clothing worn by all the slaves.

Mb'ta found a way to approach the slave women to look for the charm, and soon came to Filipa to inquire, if she would pardon the interruption, whether she had seen an amulet that looked like this or that as she walked along the path that led to the stables. Filipa responded that no, she hadn't seen anything, because she had liked the tiny, beautiful iron fist even without knowing what it meant. Only later, whenever the opportunity arose, and because she had begun to feel a little guilty, or perhaps for another reason altogether, did she begin to look for the young man with his black skin like that of a shiny, polished fruit.

At night, when the slaves would gather around the fire, she began to notice the infectious rhythm coming from Mb'ta's drums. She couldn't take her eyes off him each time he stood up to wriggle his entire body in a frenzied dance that she found so foreign and, at the same time, so familiar. Mb'ta, for his part, had begun to take note of the young *mameluca* slave's attentions. There were few women at the sugar plantation, and nearly all were either Indians or the daughters of Indians and white men. The two black Yoruba women from the kitchen were older and already had husbands.

Dancing and beating his drum, he drew closer to Filipa, and suddenly she too was in the middle of the circle, swaying her body along to the beat, as though she had grown up dancing next to the Bantu man.

And so, their meeting was quite natural. Mb'ta savored Filipa's fragrant smell, an ancestral scent that directed his thoughts back to the meats seasoned for days over open fires in the houses of his village. Filipa liked Mb'ta's pitch-dark skin, where she would bury her face and once again feel protected as she had in Sahy's warm lap on those nights spent around the bonfire.

Just as natural was the way they began to obsessively plot their escape. They spoke in Língua Geral, the language of the first inhabitants of this new Brazil, who came from so many different backgrounds.

Filipa would say that she was an Indian, that her mother had taught her everything about the forest, that they would find some place near a river where they could build a camp. "And I know how to hunt," Mb'ta would reply, "I used to hunt with my father back in my homeland, and once even killed a lion with other men from the village." "And I know how to can meats," Filipa would say, "which is a delicious way to preserve game from the hunt. My mother taught me, no one here knows I can do this, but I can, and I know how to plant cassava and make cassava flour." "And I," Mb'ta would say, "know how to fish with a spear or a net." "And I know how to make a net," Filipa would reply.

Mb'ta would say that they needed to find a good weapon, at least one machete, though rope would also be good. "I can make rope," Filipa would say, "I'll work on it at night, in the dark, and hide it during the day. I've found a good hiding place." And she would laugh as she remembered the amulet, which she still hadn't found a way or the courage to tell Mb'ta about. "And I have a blade that I stole and hid away one day," Mb'ta would add. "I can make a handle for it, and a wooden spear, I can make these at night, too, and hide them during the day."

The preparations, however, had to be postponed because, by the time she finally noticed, Filipa had been pregnant for months. She still wanted to run away, she was an Indian, she insisted, and Indians gave birth in the forest. "But how will you run from the men," Mb'ta would ask, "how will you run from the dogs?" "I can manage," Filipa responded, "Let's go, Mb'ta, come." But Mb'ta, poor Mb'ta, convinced Filipa it was better to wait.

How was he to know that later everything would become much more difficult? How was he to know that the number of slaves who would later attempt to escape would be so great that security measures would be increased or—what was worse—that João Tibiritê was to arrive with his heinous philosophy that a runaway slave was a dead slave, because that was the only way they would learn?

But there was no way to know, and so they delayed their escape.

Maria Mb'ta was born. She had a birthmark, a dark triangle at the base of her neck, its peak slanted left. Filipa would gaze at the birthmark and remember the stories of her people that her mother had told by the bonfire, her with eyes closed. She thought about her people, whom she'd never known, and thought about the tranquil brook where she and Mb'ta would build their home.

Mb'ta made Filipa a necklace of tiny stones he'd found in the river and cut crudely with a nail he'd hidden among his belongings. Filipa returned the amulet to him without a word, as though she had just found it. Smiling, he tied it around young Maria's neck.

Life at the sugar plantation had become more and more difficult. The nights filled with drumming, music, and dancing were now only permitted on specific days of the week, holy days, or when some important white man made a visit. The work had grown more intense: the number of cauldrons had increased along with the number of slaves, who now worked in shifts so that production never ceased. Many times Filipa worked a different shift than Mb'ta, and days would pass without the couple seeing one another.

The plantation owner was an ambitious nobleman who'd left Portugal in the 1550s to start life anew in the land that was being built up from nothing. With a bit of luck and a great deal of cunning, he'd managed to build his sugar mill and, after production and a client base had stabilized, he sent for his wife and children. The house became more lively, and Filipa, having just given birth to her daughter, was assigned to help with the household chores.

It was the wrong job for the wrong person: how could she resist such temptation as, day after day, she visited the bedroom of the lady of the house?

With the fascination for new objects she'd inherited from her people, Filipa had accumulated various little trinkets over the year, which she stored in a hiding place whose location only she knew. Some things she had found, as she paid close attention everywhere she walked, but others she had carefully and artfully stolen from here and there. They were always things of little value, like hairpins that were bent out of shape, hairpins that had fallen on the floor, or rusty nails.

But no one escapes the inevitable. The day arrived when Filipa took a fancy to a cameo fastened to a bright-red velvet ribbon that the lady of the house sometimes wore around her neck when receiving guests. When the lady of the house took off the necklace, she would place it in a small jewelry box decorated with mother-of-pearl, a tiny box that made Filipa sick with the desire to stash it in her hiding place. When she found herself alone cleaning the bedroom, she always stopped to touch the box and open it. She didn't know what fanned the flames of her desire more: the cameo with the most beautiful red ribbon she'd ever seen, or the box with tiny, white, inlaid stones— which she wanted to show Mb'ta so that, who knows, he might make her one just like it.

Consumed by her desire, she decided one day to steal both. She hid the jewelry box between her breasts and walked out of the house, breathing a sigh of relief as she reached the yard, believing the worst was over.

You can imagine what the consequences were for her actions.

But what you have no way of knowing is that João Tibiritê had already been hired by this time as a slave-catcher to bring order to that "pack of lawless savages," and it was he who tied Filipa to the tree stump and tore at her skin with his whip, proclaiming at the top of his lungs for all to hear that, as far as he was concerned, whoever strayed once could very well stray again, but no one would do so a third time because he would be killed first, killed right and killed slowly, and he was of the opinion that the longer it took to learn a lesson, the deeper the branding iron would sear into the malfeasant's subsconscious.

Filipa listened to all of this until she understood—and Mb'ta, too. All the slaves had been summoned to witness the punishment of that *mameluca* thief. Mb'ta had been bound and tied inches from his wife so he could watch the blood run down her back. But was there any reflection on what had been said—and I'm not even talking just about Filipa, whose bold temperament wasn't given to patience and who thought everything had been the last straw on her haystack of suffering; but Mb'ta, too, who was always so sensible and cautious— did they reflect on João Tibiritê's words, did they study his character to see whether he made good on his threats? Not a chance! In one of these inexplicable and illogical bursts of temerity, the two slaves decided they could no longer delay their escape.

One week later, on a night with neither stars nor moonlight, they grabbed Maria Mb'ta and set off into the darkness.

MARIA CAFUZA
(1579-1605)

Maria Cafuza was not, in fact, a *cafuza*, as she was not the daughter of an African man with an Indian woman, but with a *mameluca*. But who cared about these details? Certainly not Filipa or Mb'ta. For them, their daughter was always Maria Mb'ta, and so it was until the day they fell into the hands of João Tibiritê, the same day that Maria was called *cafuza* for the first time.

If you're still hoping to find a good-looking member of the family, look no further. This girl, it's true, had a rare beauty, a combination of the best that could be found in all of the races that pulsed inside her. How can I describe her to make you realize just how beautiful she was? She was tall, with long legs, and golden-brown skin unlike any other. Silky hair the color of a blackbird fell in gentle curls over her shoulders. Lips that were ever so full, iridescent, almond-shaped eyes that alternated between green and violet depending on how the light struck them. A square chin and a silhouette so shapely that whoever saw her felt the desire to stop and admire her. And Maria's smile was certainly the most beautiful smile you've ever seen.

But after she became Maria Cafuza, she never smiled again.

And why should she? With the life she led, there wasn't the slightest reason for a smile, and nothing could uncloud the fierce drama concealed behind her perfect features.

All this is very sad, I know, but as I said in the beginning, I have no intention of glossing over the less savory aspects in this story.

Maria watched her parents die, tortured at the hands of João Tibiritê. She watched as João tore out her father's fingernails, rammed an enormous stick up his ass, gouged his eyes, and left him there bleeding on the ground. She watched as this same João turned to Filipa and began slowly cutting into her skin with an enormous, fine-edge knife, until her striped body was a stream of red flooding the piles of leaves that covered the ancient, pristine forest floor.

Maria Cafuza watched it all. She was five at the time. Later, João Tibiritê took her with him.

THE MAMELUCO FROM SÃO PAULO

The story of João Tibiritê could have been different, and his character might have been, too. But who can tell the exact moment when a gene is corrupted, creating a monster? Let's leave João for a moment and turn to his band of *mameluco* slave hunters, which included Manu Taiaôba, the son of a Portuguese settler and one of his three Indian wives.

Some of Manu's childhood was spent with relatives in his mother's village, some on his father's tiny farm, here and there, together with other little spitfires just like him. Then the Jesuits took him to their mission, baptized him, and tried to ensure he studied at their college and became a "good Christian," fearful of the one true God and capable of the repetitive work crucial to the economic order of the newfound colony. But the call of the forest, of adventure, and especially his blood was much stronger, and, a mere twelve years old, he ran away to join João Tibiritê's much-feared band.

The Paulistas, as they were called, were known as ruthless hunters of runaway native slaves, and would venture deeper and deeper into the untamed backlands in search of their prey. The João Tibiritê posse was one such group. They made incursions that would last for months on end and return with hundreds of natives they'd captured in battles and ambushes.

They would set out for their mission armed and ready; no one knew the landscape like they did, they were adept at hunting, fishing, and identifying edible plants, they could speak and understand any of the indigenous languages and Língua Geral, they had no difficulty facing the sun, rain, storms, thunder and lightning, they were hunters in search of jaguars and snakes, trained for war and adventure. A brand of men prepared for the circumstances they'd been born into and who lived to do exactly what they did: push further and further into the backlands and tame the land.

Manu Taiaôba, swift with his bare feet, his fine ear, and innate hunting ability, loved that life. It was as though he was born for it, and he spent hours dreaming and thinking of nothing else. He was soon devising battle strategies and logistics, and in a short couple years he became João Tibiritê's right-hand man, responsible for devising new, innovative tactics for catching slaves.

In that summer of 1583, João Tibiritê had captured a good number of slaves to take to Pernambuco, where he found a job as a runaway slave hunter.

An epidemic of runaways seemed to have hit the area, and he was the right man to put an end to it. Not everyone in his posse liked the line of work, but João thought it better to stay awhile to earn some easy money as he prepared to make the long journey back to the parts known as São Vicente.

As a result, Manu Taiaôba was present when João killed Maria's parents. Although he was part of João's posse, a group of adventurers accustomed to killing and who considered bloody victories their only reason for living, the strange and senseless violence of torture still caused Manu to turn away so as not to see the dismantled bodies of the black man and the *mameluca* woman. He had never felt this way before: a strange sort of pity filled his heart as he looked to their daughter, a skinny girl who looked as if she would fall apart when the captain snatched her up.

Ever since that day, Manu was present for each moment of Maria's life.

There were no women in João's posse, except for an old Indian witch-doctor who had begun to follow them one day and never left. When they arrived at camp the day Maria joined them, Manu called the old woman to her and told her to look after the girl.

Thanks to the old woman and the protection of Manu, Maria Cafuza survived. When she entered the camp, the young girl had already erased from her mind everything she had seen up until then, even how to speak. The only thing left in her heart was the crushing, oppressive, convulsive impulse to hate João Tibiritê. From that moment on, her only purpose in life was to be consumed by this hate.

She grew up in the midst of that posse, without speaking and as though she understood nothing, like a wild animal. She accompanied them on their journeys, witnessed their battles, all the while turning over in her head the only thought she ever had—her obsession, her fuel, her water, and means of breathing—to kill João. Crouching down, sneakily trailing behind and hiding amid leaves and branches, Maria Cafuza observed each and every move her private demon made.

What's curious is that João Tibiritê, experienced and observant as he was, never noticed Maria's stare as it fixed on him; he never suspected that the hand that held his destiny was but a few steps away. It never occurred to him that the mute child he had taken with him on a whim, whom he had raised among his posse, could one day represent some sort of threat. He had practically forgotten about her, the withdrawn creature who lived concealed in the forest bushes, more beast than girl.

And so he was completely surprised when, after a night spent drinking in celebration of the capture of an entire Carijó tribe, Maria, all of fourteen, stealthy as a rattlesnake, slipped into his tent and prodded him with the tip of her dagger until he opened his eyes to see his approaching death and assassin.

Then she plunged the dagger straight into his Adam's apple, then again into his heart, and one last time through his liver, exhibiting the ability and anatomical knowledge of someone who had trained for years without rest for no other purpose but this.

João Tibiritê's eyes flashed and he flailed about, but he was unable to cry out in horror and fear.

Manu was the only one who had seen Maria enter João's tent, had seen her leave, but he didn't interfere.

The following day, he assumed João's place at the head of the posse.

Just as Maria had obsessively watched João's every move, Manu Taiaôba watched Maria. The older the girl grew, the more bewitched Manu became.

Something interesting was happening there: the young slave hunter couldn't make out why he had begun to dream about Maria instead of battles, as he'd done before. The young man, brought up in the harsh reality of the wilderness, the rush of adrenaline in the midst of war, and in the sole company of other brutes like himself, knew nothing about feminine beauty. There was no beauty at all in that universe of crude men who wouldn't recognize a beautiful woman if they saw one. A person can only notice and understand what he has been taught to notice and understand. If he lacks the fundamental knowledge, some basic instrument to tell him what is and isn't beautiful, how can he take notice?

This was exactly what happened in the case of Maria's splendorous beauty: there was no one in the posse capable of taking notice. Only the old woman and Manu, without realizing exactly why, would spend hours on end staring at the young woman, and each time they looked, they felt something inexplicable and better inside themselves. And so it was the girl, rather than combat, who began to inhabit Manu's dreams. Manu asked the old witch to find him an herb to calm his mind, which was on fire, consumed with nothing but thoughts of Maria.

Each time Manu tried to draw closer, Maria would drive him away as she drove away the others. No one would ever touch her. All attempts to rape her—and there were many for the simple fact that Maria was a woman in such an environment—were thwarted by a vigilant Manu, who little by little made sure everyone in his posse understood that they were to leave Maria in peace, or they'd have to deal with him.

After the death of João Tibiritê, Maria felt something like disappointment that he could not come back to life so that, now that she had learned how, she could kill him over and over, until she, too, died, together with the hate she carried inside her.

Nonetheless, in some way something changed inside her—not by much, but enough that one night under a full moon, at the edge of a river, she let Manu approach her. He drew closer with such desire and such fear that it was nothing short of a miracle that anything happened there at all. But it did. Maria howled like a wild animal, but stopped when she finally understood that she wasn't howling out of hate or terror, but for some other reason she couldn't quite make out, but which she knew was not bad.

Her life, despite everything, did not change. Her uncontrollable hate for João Tibiritê, even after his death, left no room for any other emotion to occupy her mind and heart. She continued to lead her life in the same feral manner as before, at the side of the old Indian woman, trailing the posse wherever it went. On nights with a full moon—and only on such nights—she would go to the edge of some river and allow Manu to touch her.

Manu's devotion to her was almost religious. He always set up his tent next to that of the old woman and the young girl, and did everything in his power to ensure they wanted for nothing.

The leadership of the tactical, adventure-seeking Paulista took little time to assert itself, and soon his reputation for success replaced even that of João Tibiritê, as did his aversion to unnecessary violence. Manu Taiaôba was no delicate flower, but he had no sympathy for violence for the sake of violence: he was of the opinion that honorable death in combat was the safest way to resolve matters and that, while the capture of savages was a necessity, he could not say the same for violent forms of punishment, which only served to delay their forward progress.

In the ten years that passed, his posse marched many times from the backlands of southern Brazil to the sugar-producing region in Pernambuco, in the north. Maria became pregnant twice, and twice, with the help of the old woman, she aborted. She was unable to tolerate even the thought of putting a child into this world. Never that.

That was when a plan began to take shape in Manu Taiaôba's mind: to take Maria to the sugar plantation where she'd been born. Would she remember the time there when she could still speak? Would she recall memories of her parents that would rid her of the hate consuming her? His devotion to Maria caused his thoughts to wander in the hopes of finding something, anything, that would make life less of a burden to her.

They did, in the end, return to the old plantation. The Portuguese farmer who had hired João Tibiritê had already died, as had his wife. One of his sons had since taken over the mill, which continued to be a wildly prosperous enterprise. Under the pretext of talking over the idea of buying some land in the area, Manu requested permission to camp with his posse near the plantation.

They stayed for a while and Maria walked the land without any sign of recognition. She had merely become more given to contemplation:

she would sit down somewhere and stay there for hours, looking out toward some unrecognizable point beyond the horizon.

Until one cold and cloudy morning, she got up and she set off like a zombie toward the margin of the nearby creek; she began to walk faster and faster, as though following a clear path she could see in her mind.

Manu followed her.

Maria walked a good distance before stopping beneath a leafy jatoba tree, where she crouched down and began to dig furiously until she lifted out a small package bundled in an old and dirty handkerchief.

Shaking, she untied the tiny bundle of Filipa's treasures.

And then, her body no longer had the strength to hold back all the devastating, pent-up pain that she had carried all those years. As she fell to ground in convulsions, a terrified Manu felt he had committed an irreparable mistake.

But just look how life is full of surprises.

Maria Cafuza, this time without suspecting a thing, was pregnant. She'd barely gained any weight, her belly had hardly grown at all, and though she had a slight suspicion, she still lacked the certainty to take the necessary precautions. Perhaps her own arrival at the plantation of her childhood had lifted her thoughts to somewhere other than her body, and nature continued on its course without her or the old woman noticing a thing. But that day, there beneath the jatoba tree, everything happened at once: Maria writhed with painful contractions, without realizing that, as she died, taking that incurable pain with her, she gave birth to a daughter.

Had she known better, she would have killed her.

MARIA TAIAÔBA
(1605-1671)
&
BELMIRA
(1631-1658)

The city of Olinda—seated atop a lush hill flooded with green, with a view to the forest and to the azure sea—was, for many people, perhaps the most beautiful city in the entire country. And one of the largest, with its houses of stone and quicklime, brick and tile, its mother church with its three naves and many chapels arranged in such a way that the faithful could take few steps within its confines before feeling summoned to contemplate their souls. The streets were bustling with herds of animals passing by, with slaves—either savages or from Guinea—coming and going to fulfill their duties, the stores with their open doors and shelves full of goods, the streets paved in bright stone.

Manu Taiaôba looked around at it all and became dizzy. He had been to many villages and settlements and to the cities of Piratininga and Bahia, but Olinda left him with a nearly uncontrollable anxiety to run back into the forest. All the people and animals swarming through the streets, the harshness of the ground where his bare feet never managed to firmly grasp the cobblestones, the loud hum of conversations, oxcarts, animals, the nauseating mixture of the scent of sweat and food—it was all too much and too disturbing.

But he was there to negotiate the purchase of his land and would not leave until he had succeeded.

On the afternoon he had buried Maria Cafuza, the slave hunter swore to himself that he would never let his daughter grow up living the slave-hunting lifestyle that had done so much harm to her mother. He decided to settle down and buy some land in the region between Recife and Olinda, an estate where he had seen an enormous sugarcane plantation, a true beauty, where each sugarcane plant was uniform in size, packed in close, so nearly identical that they appeared to form a sea of green leaves as far as the eye could see. Manu knew nothing of planting sugarcane, but he was certain he could learn. Whoever among the posse wished to stay with him was welcome; whoever did not could strike out on his own, no hard feelings. The only thing Manu wanted now was to buy the plantation. He had seen a house of quicklime and stone next to the sugarcane fields: that is where he would take his daughter and the old witch-woman who had watched over Maria and who now watched over the child.

"Give her the same name as her mother," he said as he handed the premature child, still covered in fluids, to the old woman. "And find a place for this, it's hers." He handed her Filipa's treasure, the filthy cloth bundle full of tiny objects whose importance could only be appraised by someone like the old woman.

Yes, Manu knew the old woman could take care of everything. The old woman, whose name he never learned, or if she ever had one, had gone by simply "old woman" ever since she began following João Tibiritê and his posse, and though at that time she wasn't even old—she couldn't have been much more than twenty—she already had an old woman's way about her that seemed to have been hers since birth: the face of an old woman, the mannerisms of an old woman, the wisdom of an old woman. Daughter to an Indian man and a black woman, or perhaps a child of the forest—this, too, no one could say for certain—she was versed in incantations, she knew how to recognize medicinal plants, she could speak with the animals. If João Tibiritê allowed her to always remain close to his posse without bothering her, it was because the old woman had saved João's life the time he had been bitten by a venomous snake—it had been at the exact moment she had first stepped forth from the forest, saying she would cure him. And she did. Rumor had it she had ordered the snake to bite João to later gain his favor, but those who claimed this could never prove it, and since the old woman was a good person, it's likely simply coincidence that she had been passing through at that moment and had decided to stay.

For his part, Manu Taiaôba, in his old age, mulling over all that had happened in his life, was convinced that the old woman had joined up with the posse because she was predestined to care for the two Marias. He recalled that João Tibiritê had only decided to let her stay after Manu made him see that a medicine woman was a good thing to have around in a life spent in the forest and in battle, as had proved to be the case with João himself and the snake bite. Manu also recalled that he wasn't sure why he had said this to João, since he had no reason or authority to meddle in the decisions of the leader; he was merely just one of the gang at the time, João hadn't yet named him his right-hand man.

But it's just such inexplicable things that make life what it is, and if the old woman hadn't joined up with the posse then and there, neither the second nor the first Maria would have survived. If the most the old woman could manage with Maria Cafuza was to help her survive, in the case of the second Maria she was able to do much more. The two of them were inseparable. They were much more than mother and daughter could be, as neither had any obligation to the other; it was nothing more than pure necessity and a fondness for each other's company and doing nearly everything together.

The old woman was Maria's shadow and a bit of her soul: the old woman told Maria stories of the lives of Maria Cafuza and Filipa, taught her the secrets of medicinal herbs, explaining the cause of each shade of green to be found in the forest, she taught her about animals and their purposes, she showed the girl the course of the river-spirit and its waters, and, most importantly, she had taught her from a young age to peer deep inside herself to discover the source of her unique strength and power.

Maria Taiaôba had neither her mother's beauty nor her wild character, but she had inherited her father's strategic mind and his innate and even unconscious tendency to appreciate and seek out the unknown.

When she was a young girl, she would go with the old woman to Olinda and they would sit on a bench in the middle of the square and watch the people walk by. Maria would visit the churches, admiring the saints and the smell of burning incense; she walked along the sidewalks and admired the interiors of the homes through the open doors and windows; she would walk into stores and gaze at the shelves; she looked down from the top of the hillside onto the port, at the ships loading and unloading, the glimmer of the Capibaribe and Beberibe rivers, the azure spell of the Pernambuco sea. Maria loved all of that; her heart swelled with the beauty of the landscape and the old woman observed without any surprise that she was the exact opposite of the dark, troubled soul her mother had been.

Still a girl, Maria began to notice that something important was missing in her life: the ability to read. Sure of herself, she knew she could do anything and, after asking around and around, she found the house of a teacher where only young boys went to learn Portuguese, Latin, and arithmetic, but whose wife did teach young girls to read, write, count, and sew.

Twice a week, Maria and the old woman, departing the plantation on horseback, climbed the hillside to Olinda. Maria would go to her classes and the old woman would sit on a bench near the mother church, where she was approached by the women of Olinda eagerly seeking remedies for abscesses, nocturnal fevers, all manner of pain, and love potions. The old woman patiently attended to all of them, for this was her calling and she practiced it with great generosity.

The girl's father, Manu Taiaôba, watched his daughter grow up in a way unfamiliar to him, but which intuition told him was good and well. The plantation he bought sat on moist soil, and the land was good and fertile. Relying on native slaves, he soon began producing great amounts of sugarcane, which he sent to be ground up at Engenho Santo Antônio next to his plantation. As a creature of the jungle and an adventurer, however, Manu had begun to grow restless; at night he would hang his hammock far from the house, and during the day he practically never set foot there, not even on the veranda. His daughter would go fetch him in the fields or wherever he was and bring him food. There the two of them would eat together, Manu crouching while Maria sat on some fallen tree trunk telling him what she had seen in the city as he barely said a word—not for a lack of interest, but because he wasn't sure how to respond and because of the sound of his daughter's voice, that limpid tone that most certainly would have echoed Maria Cafuza's if the woman had ever spoken. It was as though only the sound of the girl's voice could bring him more peace than the placid murmur of the serene waters of a tiny mountaintop stream, and that was enough.

And so the day arrived when, watching as the time passed quickly and seeing how well off his daughter was at the old woman's side, sensing that the two of them no longer needed him, Manu felt free to seek out some other life more in accord with his temperament. He could raise cattle, animals that were becoming increasingly necessary for the colony's food supply, for the production of the sugar factories, and for transportation, which at the time was done exclusively via oxcart. He longed to roam the land with his cattle, opening new routes through the dark heart of the dense forest, and to return to the rough life he had known growing up, sleeping beneath the open sky, hunting for food, battling Indians.

He bought a small house in Olinda, where he left the old woman to take care of his daughter, along with some slaves and a few reliable men; he named another of his men foreman of the sugarcane plantation, and with part of his old posse he set off on a cattle drive toward the deserted backlands, toward the Rio São Francisco.

Later, he would always visit his daughter to listen to the sound of her voice, this sound that followed him day and night through the backlands and left him with something like a soothing warmth inside his chest. He would arrive in Olinda, negotiate for the cattle, and check in on the plantation, but he never stayed in the city for more than a day at a time.

On one of these visits, Maria, then seventeen, told him she was to be married.

Her suitor was Bento Diogo de Sá, born in the city of Bahia, the son of a Portuguese father, who had arrived in Brazil in 1550 to open a general store selling odds and ends and foodstuffs, and a Portuguese mother raised in the Orphans' Convent in Lisbon and sent to Brazil by Queen Dona Catarina along with other orphans to help populate the new land. A healthy and submissive young girl, Bento Diogo's mother served her one purpose: she fulfilled the mission given to her by the queen—in other words, she gave birth. Bento Diogo was the twelfth of fourteen children.

His father's small business established itself as one of the busiest stores in the city, a place that, most importantly, sold wine from Portugal and wine from Spain. While most of his brothers and sisters each had their own destinies to pursue, he remained at home, with the pretext of helping his father with the business. A handsome young man who was popular with the ladies, he, too, made a healthy contribution to peopling the colony, siring several children with *mamelucas* and Indians, all bastards, all raised without any assistance from him at all.

Lazy, but ambitious and lacking scruples, Bento Diogo had great plans for himself. Among them, that of becoming the king of the honey-wine made in the new country—cachaça. He maintained that anyone who didn't like cachaça was a fool. Cachaça was a wonderful alcoholic beverage that would bring Brazil recognition worldwide, it was the cheapest and the most accessible, the least susceptible to the unpredictable variations of sea and ship. This honey-wine, a true product of the new land, was extremely simple to produce and store, and easier still to drink. He would sow the widest sugarcane fields that had ever been seen and wouldn't use a single cane, not a single one, no matter how small, to make sugar, only cachaça, cachaça, cachaça, and he would fill an unseen number of barrels.

That's how he spent hours and hours, months and months, years and years, drinking with friends and planning out his grandiose empire, tied to the marvelous future of the Portuguese colony, the greatest and richest of all of them, as he never tired of saying.

After the death of his parents, Bento Diogo continued on for some years chipping away at the patience of his two brothers who spent hours working at the general store, telling anyone who asked that he was in the business of importing spirits. Until one day, pressed by his brothers who could no longer put up with his gambling debts, drinking binges, and boasting, he found himself practically thrown out of the house, forced to take some action and to try to survive on his own dime.

It was then that, already nearing the age of forty, but maintaining his fine figure and silver tongue, Bento Diogo set off in search of his empire.

He found it in Maria Taiaôba, in Olinda.

Watching her pass by, and asking around after her, the man from Bahia was quite impressed by this only child's coy grace and with her father's vast sugarcane fields. Losing no time, he put all his skill and experience into courting her.

Maria, for her part, who wasn't a silly girl in the least but who had felt, since birth, an enormous curiosity about everything, had for some time been hoping to find out what it would be like to have a husband. She wanted to know about the things the women of Olinda were always taking so much about, but up until that point, frankly, she had found her suitors rather dim-witted. She saw in Bento Diogo a boldness and a charm that she'd never seen before—and so she decided to say yes.

When Manu Taiaôba met his future son-in-law, he barely uttered a word or two in way of a greeting. Just as with everything else related to his daughter, he asked the old woman if she thought the whole idea was all right, and the old woman told him yes, everything was all right, that he shouldn't worry, that the man would have no opportunity to bring the girl any harm.

And so it went. After the wedding, Bento Diogo moved to the plantation and spent his days talking about his plans to make sure that all that sugarcane no longer went to the Engenho Santo Antônio, but rather to a factory. He already had it all figured out. "You'll see, Mariazinha," he'd tell Maria, "we're going to build an empire here in Pernambuco and you'll be the Cachaça Queen of Brazil. We'll go to Portugal and sell our honey-wine in Lisbon, and then move on the Spain. Did you know that those Portuguese colonists, those *reinols*, when they get off the ship here in Brazil, the first thing they do is drink our wine? And do you know why? Do you know the best thing about this wine of ours? It's that you only need a little bit, Mariazinha, and it will already whisk you off to heaven with all the angels and archangels. Are you sure you don't want to try some?"

Maria thanked him, but declined.

She didn't like cachaça, and though she did like something about her charming and loquacious husband's tirades, she was beginning to find it a bit exhausting to have a husband who did nothing but ramble on and on. She'd satisfied her curiosity as far as the bedroom was concerned, and even found it quite interesting, but she couldn't stay in bed all day and she had begun to note that her husband was of little use beyond the bedroom.

But Maria never came to truly worry about this because, in fewer than six months, right in the middle of one of his long diatribes about the great changes he would bring about at the plantation, Bento Diogo's heart gave out and Maria Taiaôba found herself a widow.

At the time there were some in the village of Olinda who remarked among themselves that the old woman had something to do with the unexpected passing of a man at the peak of his productivity. But the old woman need not have interfered. Blessed as she was with her premonitory gifts, the truth is that the she had merely assumed that things would unfold this way, and there was nothing to do but let time run its course, and she didn't need to lift a finger to prevent Maria from traveling further in the charming and unscrupulous opportunist's leaky canoe.

THE NEW CHRISTIAN REINOL

Duarte Antônio de Oliveira arrived in Olinda in 1628, at the age of twenty-three. From a family of New Christians, his parents had decided to send him, the middle child, to try his luck in that newly-forming country and where—if the good Lord so desired—he would be free from the harshness and austerity of the Inquisition. His father gave him enough money so that, arriving in Brazil, Duarte could construct a sugar plantation on par with the ones that were making so many people rich. The idea was for him to establish an alternative home for the family if the situation in Portugal grew worse. The father also placed family heirlooms and jewels in his son's luggage, which would be safer in Brazil than in Lisbon, where their confiscation was an increasingly frightening possibility.

The young Portuguese man was cultured, well read, a devotee of Camões—his copy of *The Lusiads* was always at hand and he could recite long passages from memory with ardor and passion. He felt as though he were living a hero's fate, taming the young continent and conquering a better life for his family. He exuded enthusiasm and dynamism when he arrived in Olinda and immediately fell in love with the exuberance of the tropics, their light, their colors, their smell, their lush vegetation, the flora, the sensual flavor of their fruits.

One day, following a guide on a visit to the sugar mills and sugarcane plantations in the region, he met Maria Taiaôba and the old woman along the road. Unconcerned with customs that had never been her own, Maria was not dressed in mourning clothes, and Duarte Antônio, seeing her with colored flowers in her hair and a basket full of yellow and red cashew fruits she had picked to make desserts, was fascinated at the sight, thinking he had come upon a Brazilian forest nymph.

That image of Maria Taiaôba must truly have been one of great beauty and power, for she would later fascinate a Dutch artist, as well, who would paint her exactly in this way, gathering flowers and fruits at the edge of a wood.

Maria began to serve as Duarte's guide, and few outings were necessary for her to likewise become charmed with the cultured and educated man from Portugal, as young as she was, as wonderstruck with life as she was, as in love with the country as she was.

Not long thereafter, the two of them were married.

The money Duarte brought from Portugal transformed the Taiaôba family's sugarcane fields into a powerful sugar-producing plantation. He succeeded in this with the unrestricted support of the old woman and under the supervision of Manu Taiaôba, who, little by little, for the first time in his life, would spend nights out on the veranda talking with an educated person such as Duarte. His son-in-law told him about life on the other side of the sea, the habits of the Portuguese, the royal court, what the kings of Portugal and the king of Spain were like, about business, what people wore, the importance of education, religion, the cruelty of the Inquisition. Manu would tell him about Brazil, the different kinds of forest, the friendly and unfriendly beasts that inhabited them, what to do when one came upon a river, what the natives were like, the differences between them, their way of life, their beliefs, and their arts.

When he had first arrived in Brazil, Duarte had worked as a scrivener at the Municipal Chamber of Olinda. He continued to exercise this public post during the first year he was building his sugar mill, which was an enormous investment not only due to the purchase and installation of the machinery, but also because of the necessity to buy more slaves. They required significant manpower to run the sugar plantation, and Manu Taiaôba's native slaves, though good for planting the sugarcane, were not suitable for the disciplined and difficult work demanded to manufacture the sugar itself—they needed to buy slaves who had come from Guinea, who were much more expensive.

In the year 1630, things were going well and Duarte had already abandoned his government post to spend his time exclusively overseeing the plantation, which was at full production when the Dutch invaded Pernambuco, sparking a war that would last sixteen long years.

Belmira, the first and only child born to Duarte and Maria, was born on the night of the Great Olinda Fire. No one slept that night in what was by then the enormous plantation house. They watched from a distance as the smoke and tongues of flames climbed higher and higher above the city. Even Maria, the baby in her arms, stood up to watch the voracious mouth of the fire as it swallowed the damp nighttime air hovering above the trees. The newborn Belmira cried uncontrollably the entire night, as though she could see the misfortunes that awaited a girl born and raised in the midst of war.

Throughout that entire day, they had given food, water, and shelter to those fleeing the city. People they knew came to the plantation, fearful and defeated, weeping over the bitter fate that forced them to abandon their homes, their furniture, cupboards stocked with food, and provisions of olive oil, flour, and barrels of wine. Tears, curses, hate, lives undone: this was the painful path that opened up before them and that would last for years of bloody suffering.

It was also there, watching the fire singe Olinda, that Manu Taia-ôba decided to enlist in the war against the Flemish. It wasn't that he harbored any special preference for Portuguese dominance since he led a lawless life; it made no difference to him—as far as he was concerned, the land belonged to those who had been born there, the Brazilians, and not the Europeans, no matter where they came from. But watching the fire devastate the city that even if he didn't love, he respected, Manu began to think the war did have something to do with him. However, more than patriotism or devotion to some cause, what inflamed his chest was his hunger for combat, and this time, combat on a much larger scale than any he had known before. A youthful enthusiasm swept over him. His son-in-law, who estimated his father-in-law was around seventy years old, even tried to warn him about the risk at his age, urging him to reconsider participating in something that would likely not differ much from any of his other experiences. The old *mameluco* flashed one of his rare smiles and replied that, if it was his fate to die that way, his daughter and his son-in-law could be sure that it would be great consolation to the old man to hear calls-to-arms and the sound of gunshots at the hour of his departure.

Old Manu Taiaôba was a minor military genius. But he had never had formal instruction, and knew neither how to write nor read; he had lived his entire life in the jungle, scarcely knew city life, and had trouble imagining what another country might be like. A talent for strategy and combat tactics flowed through his veins, the innate capacity to set battlepieces in motion, his gift for the art refined by years of experience. At that moment, he felt that his slave-hunter's body, sculpted along the intense journeys and the challenges of a life led beneath the stars, was still as agile and limber as a young man's. His passionate, rejuvenated mind once again dreamed of battles and hard-fought victories.

Early the next morning Manu and the most courageous of his posse, composed of *mamelucos* and Indians, joined the resisting army.

It wasn't long, however, before he became disenchanted with the white men's style of war, the war of the Europeans that he could already see was lost, and his enthusiasm and his dreams began to wane. From the outset, a disagreement had broken out within the Luso-Brazilian army over two very different strategies, and the rift only worsened over time.

One was the position of the native-born captains, men like Manu, familiar with the landscape and the climate, who defended the adoption of a Brazilianized combat-strategy, a war fought in the jungle, setting up an ambush precisely in those stretches of landscape unfamiliar to the enemy. They thought it was possible to undermine Dutch resistance by taking advantage of that which belonged only to those who lived on the land: a mastery of the climate and the geography, the stealth of the natives, agility and cunning on the battlefield.

The other camp was composed of the European officials who had arrived to lead the Luso-Brazilian army and who advocated for the only war tactics they knew: a battle over positions, great field battles, adhering to the precepts established by the European art of war. They expressed disdain at the military experience of those who lived in Pernambuco and considered war not only an art, but a science that had its own rules and principles, and which depended on discipline and order.

Except many of these rules of order had nothing to do with Brazil—that's what Manu Taiaôba said to his daughter and son-in-law each time he was given leave for a quick visit to the plantation. How, for example, are we going to use the cavalry and artillery the way they want? Here we have good horses, strong and resilient, but where are they going to run? How will they cover the dense forests, the sugarcane fields with their sharp stalks, the mangroves and the mud that can swallow an entire army? How are we to carry their heavy artillery along roads that don't exist? And the infantry, how will they cross the rivers, most of them without bridges or even passages, how, with their socks and shoes, dressed in uniforms made of miles of fine cloth? They don't even know how to tell an angry alligator from a complacent one and nearly suffocate in the heat, and what's more, their sweet blood attracts swarms of hungry mosquitoes like bees to honey.

Things deteriorated to a point that Manu lost his patience—so unlike him—as he recounted the folly of the Luso-Brazilian commanders. But the gleam returned to his eyes as he recounted his own unfailing tactic to lure the Dutch to the cane fields, where the thickness and uniformity of the sugarcane plants threw off their sense of direction; they soon looked like dizzied cockroaches and were stuck full of holes by the piercing stalks, they lost sight of each other and became easy prey for the surprise attack launched by Manu's men.

Disturbed with what he was seeing, Taiaôba decided to request a meeting with one of the commanding officials. After a long wait, he finally managed an audience with the *mestre de campo*, a veteran of the War of Flanders and other European conflicts. It's unclear which of the two men left that meeting more appalled and disgusted with the other.

To the eyes of the elegant European commander, the uncouth figure of the Indian hunter was frightening and an affront to decency. Though Manu had shed his beard, which he shaved before battle in order to apply war paint to camouflage himself in the forest, his light uniform of raw cotton was indecent in the eyes of the nobleman, his enormous bare feet a monstrous sight, and his voice, more often silent than engaged in speech, resembled an animalesque grunt. Everything about him was appalling to the official, who only managed to hide his repulsion because he understood very little of what Taiaôba tried to tell him. Taiaôba spoke in Língua Geral smattered with a few words of Portuguese, but the official didn't so much as bother to summon an interpreter because he had no interest in understanding what the old man was saying. According to his military code, based largely on his feudal nobleman's mentality, the ambush-style warfare advocated by the savage before him represented the total negation of all the ideals he had been taught to hold in high regard. The official regarded individual courage and loyalty as irreconcilably contrary to the cunning and shrewdness of this monkey warfare the natives wished to wage. The tactic of an ambush was for cowards and thieves, and the monstrous individual before him seemed only to validate his convictions. No matter how much he learned about the near-legendary battle victories of Manu Taiaôba, he was a man he would never allow to march behind him and whom he would never invite to sit at the same table, not even for a light meal of field rations.

Taiaôba, for his part, was also unable to conceal his aversion to the idiotic man before him. The peculiar European's insistence on following military orthodoxy in that unforgiving landscape, his inability to grasp what was so plainly visible to everyone else, this stubbornness that to some even appeared to be collaboration with the enemy more than stupidity, had begun to appear unacceptable in his eyes. Seeing the official's well-manicured hands, his nails as clean as if he had just scrubbed them, his mustache and hair so well groomed and waxed that it looked like a helmet, the old jungle fighter understood that any resistance would be futile. This fop—who was more worried with the presentability of his uniform and boots, and whose hands were in constant agitation, waving a spotless handkerchief near his face to fan himself and wipe away the sweat that poured in endless currents down his face—convinced Taiaôba that the war was ridiculous. At that moment, he decided it was better to return and watch over his cattle than to stand by as defeat closed in day after day.

That's what he thought, and that's what he did.

When, after successive defeats, the Luso-Brazilian generals were forced to surrender as he had predicted, Manu Taiaôba was already in the wide-open backlands far from the battlefield, raising his cattle. He learned the commanders had once again given the order to burn the sugarcane fields and other crops so as to leave nothing behind for the Dutch but scorched earth—but he didn't worry since he knew that his son-in-law, like many other landowners, would not obey the suicide order. Duarte, like many of his kind, had chosen to remain neutral and tend to his land, in contrast to those who had abandoned their plantations and fled for Bahia or other captaincies further south.

Duarte had thought through his decision to remain neutral.

No matter how hard he tried, he could find no reason to fight alongside the Portuguese and Spanish who, aside from not being native to Brazil, were confiscating the goods and livelihoods of so many of his people on the old continent. On the other hand, ever since he had arrived he had felt such deep kinship with the country that he considered himself a true Brazilian: he intended to build a life in that blessed land, to make his family a family of true Brazilians, born and raised and defending the interests of Brazil and not some foreigners, no matter who they were. His position during the war was, then, constant and well considered: he would collaborate with neither side, but gave shelter to all soldiers who were wounded or retreating. In the face of the threat of famine, he decided to plant more corn and cassava and reduce sugar production.

Maria Taiaôba approved of her husband's position. She considered it wise not to force a choice between the rule of two foreign powers, just as she considered it a good idea for her father to fight in the war, since that is what he liked to do and that was his calling. Maria carried peace in her heart, and in the midst of all that, it hurt her to witness so much suffering. She and the old woman were unrelenting in their work to provide food, water, and a few kind words to whoever passed by. They also set up a small shelter near the plantation entrance for treating the wounded with herbs and natural remedies.

When battles raged nearby, the two women would set out, baskets full of herbs in hand, to tend to the wounded. Maria also brought slaves wielding hoes to dig graves and bury the dead, whom the enemy had left to be devoured by the swarms of crows that circled the battlefields. Many times, they arrived too late, when nothing more than an acrid odor was left in the heavy, still air, the smell of rotting entrails disdained even by the satiated vultures that watched the women from a distance with something like an air of contempt.

With so many people passing by and even spending the night at Duarte and Maria's sugar mill, news of the war came and went from one side and the other.

Some told of the tragedies that swept the land, the devastating hunger, the scorched landscape, the landowners and slaves scurrying beneath the moonlight to bury sugar-making equipment and other valuables before they fled. Others told stories of drinking escapades of the Dutch, true walking distilleries, and how they became stuck in the mangrove with their heavy uniforms, only their heads visible; the natives need do nothing more than show up and bury them, with a thump of a club over the head. Others reported how African slaves took advantage of the disorganization wrought by the war to escape to the Serra da Barriga, some 150 miles away, where they built a village full of people called Quilombo dos Palmares. Still others spoke of what had happened with the *mameluco* Domingos Fernandes Calabar, some saying he was merely a guide and had been executed so swiftly because he knew too much, had known high-ranking sympathizers, since it was he who took the Flemish commanders to their rendezvous in the dead of night, and it was they, the sympathizers, who had ordered his killing, fearful he might prove unable to hold his tongue.

Conversation stretched into the night beneath a sky alight with the flames that rose across several points in the distance, transforming the warm backlands evening into a sweltering night of blood and suffering.

The war ended slowly as Portuguese resistance soon waned into a series of retreats. The flames covering the night slowly died out, the retreating soldiers growing ever more scarce, the sound of fighting growing more and more distant until everything grew silent across the land speckled with patches of scorched land, abandoned homes and sugar mills, solitude, sorrow, and hunger. Now only the Dutch passed by the plantation, their troops loud, rowdy, and often drunk.

Little by little, the news reaching the plantation began to tell of good things. News of the Dutch prince who had arrived, his energy, and the projects whose construction he had ordered. Recife would be modernized, transformed, it would be a real beauty of a city. Merchants would now have more freedom without the difficulties that the Portuguese monopoly had brought.

Months passed, and Maurice of Nassau soon became a beloved ruler.

Each time Duarte traveled to Recife, he returned full of enthusiasm. The prince wasn't constructing opulent temples dedicated to the glory of God, as the Portuguese had done, but had commissioned useful projects that improved the city and served to increase labor productivity. He had seen the plans for the Mauritian city, to be constructed near Recife, between the mouths of the Caparibe and Beberibe rivers, with streets, city squares, and canals. He had seen the palace and the botanical garden being built.

One night, after a trip to Recife, Duarte went to bed inspired, his head full of plans. Filled with affection, he had told his wife and daughter about his decision to bet on the young country's prosperity, and that important changes were afoot. Who knew, perhaps he would soon be able to send for his aging parents, from whom he had heard nothing in quite some time.

In the middle of the night, his moaning, tossing, and turning woke Maria. Distraught, she could barely touch his skin, which was burning with fever. There was no need to wake the old woman—when Belmira, at her mother's request, arrived frightened at the bedroom door, the old woman was already mixing her remedies.

This time, all of her wisdom was for naught: Duarte passed away three days later from some malicious tropical fever, which may have been malaria, or tertian fever, or something else entirely. He, who had loved this land so much he could only see its beauty, had succumbed without a chance to its maladies.

Belmira was at her father's bedside when he died. The girl who had been born and raised in wartime was quiet and had sad eyes. She was very attached to her father and his romanticism. By the age of eight, she could recite passages of Luís de Camões from memory, just as her father had taught her, and she collected the flowers and leaves she gathered on walks through the forest with the old woman and her mother in a thick album her father had given her. She would glue the leaves to the pages and in her careful handwriting take down the names the old woman taught her. During several conversations, she had told her father that she wanted to learn to cure people of their illnesses. Duarte, who treated her as an adult, said he thought that was wonderful; this young country had its own unique illnesses whose cures ought to be found here, where the old woman sought them.

Her father's death left the girl so inconsolable that Maria was forced to overcome her own pain to tend to that of her fragile and pale daughter. Just like the fine porcelain of the East Indies Company, the very last present her enthusiastic husband had bought her in Recife, Maria knew that her daughter, too, could crack under the slightest pressure. There are those who grow stronger when faced with adversity, but the majority does not. The majority clams up, unable to overcome their dread when they see themselves forced to confront the misfortunes fate has in store for them.

After her father's sudden passing, Belmira began to think her dream of curing illnesses was a useless and empty one. One of the few things that still made her happy, however, was to walk with her mother and the old woman through the dark forest. There, they would gather up herbs as Maria picked fruits to make sweets and vibrant flowers to adorn her hair and her daughter's in an attempt to once again bring, in some measure, a bit of color and light to her melancholic daughter's cheeks.

One June afternoon, as they returned from one of these walks, they came upon a group of Dutch artists and scientists who had arrived with Prince Maurice. The vision of Maria so adorned, which years before had captivated Duarte, is said to have also fascinated the young artist Albert Eckhout, who asked Maria's permission to paint her with her basket full of fruits and flowers.

Perhaps it truly is her, perhaps it isn't, but even if Maria Taiaôba was the figure portrayed in Eckhout's famous painting *Mameluke Woman*, this doesn't mean she looked exactly like the woman who appears in Eckhout's portrait: no matter how realistic the Dutch painter's life-size paintings of the people of this land were, no portrait corresponds entirely to the model the artist has before him. Portraiture is not photography, but rather the expression of what he who paints sees or is capable of seeing.

One thing is certain, however: the golden-brown complexion and the sharp nose, the soft-sloping lips, the almond-shaped eyes of a woman who finds cause to laugh in the situation before her, are all Maria's. The curly hair, no—Maria's hair was straight and jet-black—but the necklace and teardrop earrings of pearl and gold could well have been those Duarte had given her, part of the family jewels he had brought from Portugal. The white satin dress was also not hers— Maria certainly had her share of dresses of silk, velvet, and satin, which she'd sewn herself, but she would never have worn them for a walk through the jungle. It's possible the painter transformed simple, white cotton fabric into shimmering satin in order to obtain the density and luminosity he sought.

Whatever the case may be, the friendship between the three women and the Dutch was a fact. The young Dr. Pies and the naturalist Georg Marcgrav were particularly astounded at the old woman's wisdom and Belmira's album full of plants.

Many times the doctor and Marcgrav would set off with Belmira and the old woman through the woods and along the riverbanks. Belmira and the old woman would show them the male papaya tree, sage, achiote, and all manner of herbs and plants. They showed the men unknown specimens of animals like the scarlet ibis, the oronooco eagle, and the many snakes that slithered about. At the edge of rivers that ran crystal clear, they showed the men fish of varying sizes and colors, and from a distance pointed out several species of alligator. They would pick fruits such as pineapple and pitomba and give them to the Dutchmen to eat. Seated on tree trunks at the edge of creeks, Dr. Pies and the old woman spent long hours discussing venoms and antidotes, medicinal plants and their therapeutic properties.

Though it was evident the men had done considerable research, traveling along the coast and through the countryside of Pernambuco, even crossing the Rio São Francisco, and had also spoken with many other native-born Brazilians to gather incredibly rich material that allowed them to complete the first two publications with systematic classification of the flora and fauna of the tropics—published in Holland in 1648, *Historia Naturalis Brasiliae* and *De Medicina Brasiliensis*—these books contained, without a shadow of a doubt, the contribution of the duo, the young girl and the old woman.

Deep within Belmira's heart, the scientists' attentions managed in some way to alleviate the pain of her father's absence; when they left, in 1644, they carried with them the album full of plants that Belmira had given them, along with the promise that she would write them whenever she discovered some new plant.

The widowed Maria was now responsible for looking after the sugarcane plantation herself. The foreman, a trusted advisor to Duarte, stayed on as her right-hand man, but it was she who would negotiate the price of sugar with the Dutch of the East India Company, and it was she who made all the decisions. Intelligent and observant, she was a quick study and no fool. She soon discovered that she liked doing business and that she knew how to do it well. Her style wasn't to assume great risks or bets, but rather to play it steady and safe. She didn't earn enormous sums all at once, but she was always bringing in earnings, and in no time she had managed greater profits than those of the old sugar-market negotiators who considered themselves smarter than the rest. Maria became known for her pragmatic approach to business, her kindness toward others, and her straightforward and honest gaze.

At the plantation, the slaves considered her a fair and just woman, and her sugar mill had one of the fewest cases of runaways during the chaos that set in with the war.

In the city, however, the respect all maintained for her was, frankly speaking, due much more to her money than to some recognition of her virtues.

During the war and the Dutch invasion, many women had taken on roles that had previously been reserved for men, but not all of them had Maria's intelligence and good sense, or her grace and beauty, or her youthful exuberance.

There were scheming and envious women who had always existed; they thought Maria was this and that, they found her daughter to be very pale and therefore judged her to be malnourished, and they thought that the old woman, whom they never hesitated to call whenever they needed, was, regardless, a witch—and once a witch, always a witch. Whoever cast spells for good could also do so for ill. And how else do you explain the death of Maria's first husband, that charming gentleman and skirt-chaser whom no one could resist and, in fact, no one did resist—he knew many a bedroom throughout Olinda, those belonging to both single and married women.

Of course, there were also many men who wished to take advantage of the still-young Maria, be it in the bedroom or in business, and they became livid when they realized that the widow's naiveté was something that existed only inside their heads, for in both these matters Maria Taiaôba was a remarkable woman. Natural and free, as she had always been, if someone spoke of her sensuality, and if she were in the mood, she would allow things to proceed to a tryst in the woods, but not any further. Twice a widow and more concerned with her daughter's well-being than her own, she had no wish to think about another marriage so soon.

When war broke out again, plans were made to launch an insurrection from Bahia, before the Luso-Brazilian troops began to make their way back north toward Recife.

These events swept into the thick of Maria and Belmira's lives.

First, the news arrived of the death of Manu Taiaôba, who had died in the jungle, fulfilling his wish. Following orders, the old warrior's right-hand man buried his leader in the same place he had buried Maria Cafuza, and then brought the news of his death to the old man's daughter.

Soon thereafter it was the old woman's turn to tell mother and daughter that she had grown very tired and needed rest. By her count, she'd fulfilled her mission, having raised three generations—mother, daughter, and granddaughter—and had taught them everything she could; they would have to forgive her, but she had no desire to witness yet another war.

She explained in great detail how they were to bury her and, a few days later, when the old woman made no appearance in the morning, Maria knew she had died.

The year was 1646, war was raging, and for the first time in their lives, Maria and Belmira found themselves alone.

A SOLDIER NAMED WILHELM

Wilhelm Wilegraf was born in Amsterdam, which was the center of European commerce at that time. His grandfather, a brilliant naval engineer, had been one of the men responsible for the construction of the frigate, a new type of warship that brought the Dutch great fame in the seventeenth century, making it possible for them to threaten Spanish and Portuguese dominion over the seas. Wilhelm was the youngest child of a rich and powerful family of Lutherans; his father had been one of the celebrated commanders of the Eighty Years' War against the Spanish empire.

Wilhelm's older brothers were large-scale merchants: their ships, which sailed from Amsterdam full of European products, would pass along the African coast to load up on slaves, then head for the Antilles or the Brazilian coast, where the crew would sell both the products and the Africans on board, only to load the ship once again, this time with sugar, before sailing back to Europe. Returning to their port of origin, they completed their tour of the "most lucrative trade under the sun," as the English were fond of saying.

Wilhelm wished to follow not the example of his brothers, but that of his father: he embarked on a military career. On his first mission, he enlisted to go to Brazil, this magnet of tropical light that represented an irresistible attraction for Europe's young men.

Wilhelm arrived in Brazil in 1646, when the Dutch once again found themselves practically surrounded on the coast. Soon after setting out for the first time, and after spending a few days in smaller skirmishes in the jungle, Wilhelm and his group passed through the Taiaôba estate, where he remained after falling prostrate, burning with a fever common among the recently arrived European soldiers. Given the family he came from, his commander thought it better not to force him along, but to leave him to the care of the widow and her daughter, people he knew to be neutral and who, besides, enjoyed a reputation for their knowledge of natural medicine—especially the young girl, who appeared to have inherited the knowledge of the late old woman.

And so, the young soldier fell under the care of Belmira and her natural remedies. Whoever lived at the sugar plantation or simply passed by—native-born slaves or those from Guinea, overseers or field laborers, people from Recife and Olinda, cassava planters and peddlers, soldiers and commanders, fugitives and combatants—knew exactly what would inevitably follow upon seeing Wilhelm and his caretaker. Maria Taiaôba was, above all, overjoyed, believing the situation might provide an end to her daughter's sadness and that unknown evil that had seemed to corrode her soul ever since her father's death.

Given the resurgence of war, the sugar plantation's economic prospects had once again become uncertain: the price of sugar continued to plummet in Amsterdam and, what's more, the factory's production had been seriously compromised. The men Maria trusted most felt the itch to join the ranks grow stronger and stronger. Many slaves, too, longed to fight, others tried fleeing for the runaway slave colonies; supplies were becoming scarce and the suffering of all was greater by the day.

Maria had her friends, the Dutch and the Luso-Brazilians, and, as before, she was at peace with her neutrality. But she was not at peace with what she saw before her. Without Duarte, without the old woman, without her father, she felt that the world was too full of suffering. At night, peering into the distance as the sky was filled with the flames of burning sugarcane fields, she began to think that perhaps it was better to leave behind the mothballed factory and head for Bahia, as many others were doing.

She gave up on the idea when her thoughts turned to Belmira, in whose eyes a tiny light had begun to shine. Even after he had been cured, the young Dutch soldier sought out the plantation during his leave, and when together the young man and woman forgot about the rest of the world. They couldn't stray far from the plantation grounds on account of the war. All the same, Belmira would take Wilhelm on long walks. In the beginning, she tried to teach him the young country's language and show him the plants and animals she had previously shown the scientists, thinking they would also interest Wilhelm. But it wasn't long before she noted that the soldier's interests were not of the scientific variety. His only desire was to know the tiny thickets of the gentle Brazilian girl's body, the delicate flowers of her face and the moist fauna of her caves and hideaways.

As far as Belmira, sweet Belmira, was concerned, she too yearned for nothing more than to faint with love into her handsome Dutchman's warm and gentle arms.

But love in times of war is, by its very nature, a temporary ceasefire. April 1648 arrived and with it the first Battle of Guararapes, which would change the course of the war, marking the beginning of the advance of the Pernambucans. It would also change the course of Wilhelm's and Belmira's story.

The Dutch went to battle with an army of nearly five thousand men, Wilhelm among them; the Army of the Restoration, as the Luso-Brazilian forces were known, numbered just more than thirty-five hundred, of which two thirds, to the army's good fortune, were home-grown soldiers—native-born, *mamelucos*, Indians. The Dutch forces were superior, in numbers and in combat skill, but the Luso-Brazilian forces had their familiarity with the land in their favor. Setting out from the mangroves, the jungle, and the hills, they went on the attack quickly and with great agility, bounding and dodging about in a way that, to Dutch eyes, appeared chaotic, but which in practice allowed them, with great success, to bedevil the sharp aim of the well-trained and well-disciplined Dutch battalions. The Brazilians gained the first significant advantage in the bloody hand-to-hand combat, leaving more than five hundred of their enemies dead, among them the young soldier Wilhelm Wilegraf.

When the time for Wilhelm to return seemed to draw out too long, Belmira went to look for him on the hillside battleground. Her pain was so great when she found the lifeless body of her young beloved that this time her only refuge was to escape to an inner world, hers alone, where Wilhelm still lived, where her father still lived, where the old woman still lived, and where no one knew the meaning of war.

Not even the birth of her daughter could bring her back. Her breast milk was scarcely enough to feed the infant girl who, like the newborn Belmira, wailed all night long. But her grandmother detected in the pitch of her crying a sliver of hope: it was no cry of lament inherited from her mother's deep sorrow, but an angry cry of revolt. Revolt, Maria Taiaôba thought, would be easier to handle.

Less than a year later, the two armies clashed again at Monte Guararapes. To this day, legend has it that a beautiful long-haired woman with alabaster white skin, dressed in blue and cradling a child, was seen walking among the wounded on the battlefield, surrounded by light. Many say it was Our Lady of Light. Others contend it was not, that the Holy Virgin was seen instead at the Battle at Monte das Tabocas and even at the first Battle of Guararapes, when she gathered the enemy's bullets in her miraculous cloak and distributed them among the Pernambucan fighters. But in this second battle there was no apparition, and what they saw was not Our Lady. It was Belmira, carrying her daughter, hoping for a bullet that might kill her in battle, just as it had Wilhelm.

This was the last straw for Maria Taiaôba. She understood that it wasn't right to allow her granddaughter to grow up in the midst of war as her daughter had. She also thought that a change in their situation might spur a reaction in Belmira and bring her to her senses, or that she might find in some other place a remedy for the sadness that her herbs had been unable to cure. She did what many had done in those years: she buried all the tools for sugar production, packed only necessary belongings in trunks, chose her most loyal slaves, freed the others who hadn't gone off to fight, and set out for Bahia.

Maria Taiaôba named Wilhelm and Belmira's daughter Guilhermina, a combination of both parents' names. With her light skin, red hair, and great big brown eyes, the girl appeared to have inherited her grandmother's natural vivacity and determination.

When they arrived in Salvador, Bahia, Maria Taiaôba rented a house on the Ladeira do Lava-Pés. On account of her business prowess and practical spirit, she soon discovered a way to recover the family's finances, by renting out her African slaves. The price of manpower had increased dramatically in light of the difficulty of finding slaves from Guinea after the Portuguese had lost some of their African colonies to the Dutch: one of the most lucrative forms of business at that time was renting out slaves. Maria used her native slaves to cut Brazilwood, which was still one of the most coveted products in the land, even if ever more scarce.

When the war in Pernambuco ended in 1654 and Portuguese dominance was restored, those who had abandoned their sugar plantations began to return to them. Meanwhile, many of these had been confiscated by the Dutch and sold to Brazilians who were interested in acquiring them for a low price and maintaining production even under Dutch rule. This situation, wherein sugar plantations had duplicate owners, gave birth to the famous "war of the sugar plantations." Who had a right to these lands: the old owners who had abandoned them, many following the orders and counter-orders of the Luso-Brazilian commanders at various stages of the war, or the new owners, who had maintained production in the pandemonium that set in amid the war's many battles?

Maria Taiaôba's plantation had also been caught up in this war, the difference being that Maria had abandoned it when the war was nearly over and, in reality, had no thoughts of returning. She feared her daughter's condition would deteriorate if she returned to the site of so much suffering. Additionally, Maria was doing well in Salvador and had managed to increase business. All the same, she had no desire to simply give away the land that had belonged to her father. Besides this, like everyone, she would happily receive an increase in the capital she could then invest in her business. Once again, her pragmatic spirit resolved the question to the satisfaction of all. Rather than wait for a decision from the restored Portuguese government—which, as could be expected, did not wish to raise the ire of either the new or the old owners and, as a result, took decades to arrive at a decision—Maria Taiaôba made a quick trip to Recife, where she met the old farm-hand who had appropriated her land. There they arrived at a private agreement that, even if not ideal, at least gave Maria the ability to expand her business in Bahia.

She also used the trip to dig up the belongings she'd buried before fleeing. Among them, a durable trunk holding the tiny mother-of-pearl jewelry box that had been inside Filipa's tattered cloth bundle.

The war in Pernambuco had made Salvador the port par excellence for those who fled. The city on the hill, with a view to the Bay of All Saints and every bit as beautiful as Olinda, was one of the fastest-growing in the country. It was said that, when it first began colonizing, the Portuguese Crown had bestowed its favor upon Salvador, sending colonizers and money, furnishing slaves and other goods, drowning it in privileges so that it would grow quickly and steadily.

After returning to the city with the money from the sugar plantation, Maria Taiaôba bought a tavern on the Ladeira do Bom Jesus. Behind the tavern, she built a house with a large yard, where daughter and granddaughter could spend the days beneath the shade of the trees.

Belmira's alienation was Maria's personal heartache. Maria sought out doctors, medicine women, priests, everything. One priest told her that Belmira's illness was the devil's work: she suffered from an inferno caused by hellfire that, instead of devouring her body, had filled it with woe. He blessed her and made several attempts to exorcize the girl's private demon before admitting that his powers were inferior to those of the Evil One. The city doctor—an old Portuguese man—bled her with leeches: his diagnosis was that Belmira's veins and body were stopped up, obstructing her body's humors, causing them to become agitated and disturbing her corporeal harmony: hence her apathy, her aloofness, weak appetite, lack of a voice.

It was all in vain.

Maria considered selling everything and heading for Portugal, where she could find both her husband's family and more advanced medical practices to cure such grief. But then she remembered her conversations with Duarte, and how he used to say that the cures to the new land's illnesses were not to be found in Europe, how the Brazilian maladies demanded a Brazilian cure. Was Belmira's illness Brazilian, or not? Maria didn't know its source, but it made her daughter weaker and weaker, paler and paler, sending her further into her internal abyss.

Maria would take Belmira to the beach, to walk on the sand with Guilhermina, who was already displaying a strong personality, with sudden fits of rage that saw her throw herself to the ground like an animal. Maria, who had initially felt relief when she realized that the girl's crying wasn't out of sadness, began to worry that her granddaughter might have inherited the devastating rage of her great-grandmother, Maria Cafuza. Observing mother and daughter, one of them as pale and silent as death, the other with hair like fire, a face full of freckles, running and screaming along the sand, she asked herself what she should do.

Fortunately, life goes on without giving a second thought to questions like those, and slowly Maria's tavern became one of the busiest in the city. Intellectuals, poets, and musicians gathered there in soirées that stretched on into the night; they played cards and backgammon, and the checkers and chessboards were in high demand no matter the hour.

Maria Taiaôba never followed any religion or heeded anyone who would tell her what to do or impose rules on her. With the old woman at her side and under her father's protection, she had learned to live differently, more freely than was typical, trusting herself and her instincts. Her experience heading up to the plantation and selling her sugar had greatly enriched her knowledge of life. Duarte, an educated husband, had also taught her a great deal, and she was perhaps one of the most learned women of her time in Salvador. She wore fabrics from the court, her house boasted the best furniture and comforts, her table abundant with food and wine. She had enough money to live well without needing to work, if she wished, leaving the slaves to work for her, but her independent, energetic spirit drove her to assume the management of the tavern herself. Her intelligent and free-spirited way fascinated many men, and though she had no thoughts of remarrying, she had no qualms or hesitations when the desire struck to share her bed.

As a result, it was nearly inevitable that the men of Bahia fell for her. Just as inevitable was the hate she inspired in women. Not that these women were saints or anything, for they certainly were not. Travelers passing through at that time never tired of expressing shock over the licentiousness of the men and women of Bahia and Brazil, and more generally, of the uninhibited sexual habits of that era, even in the convents. At that moment, the country had many more men than women; women no doubt found this numerical disproportion quite convenient, and things began to really heat up.

But while people in Olinda had known Maria Taiaôba since she was a child and knew the reasons for her unusual behavior, in Salvador no one knew who she was, and her manners were even more perturbing because of their mystery.

It could indeed be a disconcerting thing to see the three free-spirited and independent women pass through the streets—Maria, at the fullness of her forty-something years, Belmira, in the ethereal beauty of her madness, and Guilhermina, in the obstinate vigor of her youth—walking up and down the hills of the city, leaving a trail of curiosity and fascination.

People would look, remark, and sometimes even follow the women to the beach.

As was the case with Antonio de Sá, the son of *reinols* and the warden of the jail in Salvador, married to the daughter of hot-blooded Castilians and father of three.

As a matter of fact, it was on account of his wife, who would go on and on about this family of women from Pernambuco, that poor Antonio began to pay attention to the trio and above all the beauty of Belmira, who to his eyes seemed an otherworldly creature, without knowing that she in fact was. He began to frequent the Taiaôba tavern, and, considering himself a poet, started to pen verses about a muse who was no longer the olive-skinned Andalusian figure of his wife, but a woman from Pernambuco with the complexion of an angel. His wife couldn't read, but as she watched the pages of scrawled-out poems pile up on the table, she was unable to contain her curiosity; certain as she was that they were all intended for her, she asked a friend to read them aloud.

But as she listened to her husband's, a poet whose greatest fault may have been an excess of realism, description of his muse the Castilian woman's blood boiled, and not a single doubt remained in her mind regarding her rival's identity. She raged through the streets, knowing that she would find Belmira and her daughter on the deserted beach where they always walked in the sunset hour, even when Maria was unable to accompany them, as fate would have it that day.

Seeing Belmira sitting in silence, as she often did, and the ruby-haired girl nothing more than a dot on the far end of the beach, the Castilian woman attacked without a moment's hesitation, clawing tooth and nail, pulling Belmira by the hair, biting her arms, and screaming obscenities. When Belmira made no move to defend herself and, in truth, seemed up close to be an extremely sick and fragile individual, the Castilian woman quickly regained her composure, but the harm had already been done. She left the beach muttering threats, but now these were half-hearted, as though she had suddenly been drained of all her hot air, just like a deflated balloon.

For a few moments, Belmira did not move from where she lay on the ground. But the violence she had suffered was the last straw.

Before Guilhermina could return from her race to the other end of the beach, Belmira got to her feet and very slowly walked into the waters of the emerald sea, as though she were wading into the deep, glistening eyes of Wilhelm, her handsome soldier.

Guilhermina walked home without knowing where her mother had gone. Maria was overcome with the feeling something terrible had happened; her fear was confirmed the next morning when she was summoned after Belmira's body had been found on the beach.

At the funeral, Maria Taiaôba could not understand why a woman with olive skin whom she'd never seen before wept endlessly at her side, before embracing her and begging forgiveness.

Without her mother to provide a silent counterpoint, Guilhermina became even more unruly than before. Perhaps she was merely a hyperactive and spoiled child, unused to discipline or boundaries. With great effort and patience, Maria nonetheless ensured that Guilhermina at least learned how to read, write, and count, though she never managed to make her sit still long enough to listen to even a bit of poetry, unless it were one of the more abrasive verses by The Devil's Mouthpiece, Gregório de Matos, who regularly appeared at the tavern to provoke laughter in both grandmother and granddaughter. But if there was one thing that the girl liked—and did she ever like it—it was the sound of the drumming and chanting coming from the slaves' quarters. She had a pretty singing voice and her energy made her one of the liveliest singers on nights when the slaves would host celebrations.

The young girl also took no time to discover liturgical music and the melodies played on the organ, an instrument whose intensity left her in awe. She also found the spot in the church where the sound of the organ could best be heard, and she made a point of always sitting there, near the altar boy, a handsome brown boy who, as everyone in the city knew, was the priest's son.

THE BASTARD BENTO VASCO

An attractive boy with brown skin, and well-muscled, Bento was the son of a Portuguese vicar of the Church of the Outeiro and his slave Domitila, a black woman from Angola, freed by the priest after their son was born, and who likewise grew up free. The two lived in a house at the rear of the church and assisted the priest in taking care of the house, the church, and celebrating Mass.

Easygoing and with an inclination to keep the peace, Bento had, from an early age and with his father's blessing, learned and dedicated himself to the art of making miniature sculpted saints. His unique style, even though not yet mature, had begun to earn him certain fame and led to a demand for his work from churches and homes in cities throughout the country.

He also acted as altar boy during Mass and, kneeling before the altar, he first came to know Guilhermina by her voice, which stood out among the chorus. Later, without realizing it, he began to look for the girl with the fire-like hair, and soon his gaze, as though of its own free will, began to linger longer and longer on Guilhermina, her hair, the nape of her neck, her face—a gaze that was particularly inappropriate for church or for an altar boy.

As was customary at that time, when the faithful donned their best clothes to attend Mass, Guilhermina also wore her Sunday finest. She was neither religious nor baptized, and she knew very little about God, sins, or saints, but for her, going to church on Sundays was like going to a party with music and singing, and she dressed accordingly in dresses of velvet and silk. Bento Vasco soon fell under her spell.

The young girl had also begun to linger a bit and return these ardent gazes, raising her voice a decibel, as though to step closer to the boy and, with the warm touch of her voice, caress the young man's muscular back.

Soon the two began to meet at the slaves' gatherings to dance the lundu. The fieriness of Guilhermina's long, flowing hair fell across Bento's dark, muscular chest, and they could see nothing besides one other. With time, the lundu made the leap from the celebration grounds of the poor to the soirées of the wealthy, the dancers' bodies fusing in pulsing, lascivious movements, but for now, it was still a black people's dance that white society considered in poor taste.

Oh, how certain people take offense at the happiness of others! The love between Guilhermina and Bento, now plainly acknowledged, more open and free, flaunted before everyone's eyes, was not easy to swallow. Certain things seem to assume colossal proportions if left to grow in the light of day. The contrast caused by the young girl's angelic white hand resting languidly over the wiry blackness of the young man's arm seemed to hover threateningly over the city.

It was as if Bahia and Brazil weren't made up of blacks and whites and every combination thereof. As if the young lovers were partaking in some behavior entirely unknown and unseen before, rather than merely repeating the actions of the majority ever since slave ships had brought the first people from Africa to the young country. As if a black boy and a white girl courting in plain sight were scandalous, even though everyone else did it behind closed doors.

The priest barred Guilhermina from the church and removed Bento from his post as altar boy. Guilhermina, obsessive in her admiration for organ music, felt like a victim of something she could not understand and which, even if she had understood, she would never have accepted under any circumstances.

The scandal she raised outside the church door after she had been barred from attending Sunday Mass was recorded in the annals of the colony as one of the most severe cases of possession by the devil ever witnessed. Her screaming, the brute hate lashing out from her ember-like eyes, and the way she threw her body to the floor over and over, the stream of profanity and her kicks against the church door, her scratching of the door with her fingers, her nails digging into the solid wood until hot blood ran down her wrists, her fiery hair like a hurricane, her rage at full combustion and her wild howl—it was the vision of a tiny apocalypse on the church steps that morning.

After this, accused of possession by the devil, she had no other choice but to flee. Had it been up to her, she wouldn't have left at all, and she only did so under the influence of Maria's natural remedies. Maria helped pack her granddaughter's things onto the horse-drawn cart with which she, Bento, and four slaves, five Indians, and two black house slaves (one of them pregnant), chosen by Maria for their strength and loyalty, set off for a faraway destination.

Guilhermina was sixteen years old.

Maria Taiaôba only heard from her years later. At that point, Maria was living with a young Bahian man, Juvêncio, the son of Brazilians who had an open mind and a broad smile, and who was much younger than her.

Juvêncio was always at the tavern and, little by little, with the aura of adoration that overtook him each time he saw Maria, his brown skin, wide smile, taut muscles, and soft guitar-playing soon found room in Maria's heart as well as in her bed. He moved in with her and helped her manage the tavern. He was a simple young man, but he had a generous heart and made Maria happy. The tavern was at the center of both of their lives. Maria felt at ease there, with her friends, with the young Juvêncio and his guitar, and with the nights that stretched to dawn fueled by heated political discussions, poetry, and singing. All the city's important events were held at the tavern, and Maria Taiaôba's house—much the way her plantation had transformed into an important and neutral place for meeting and catching up on the news during the war for Pernambuco—itself soon assumed, quite naturally and unexpectedly, an important place in the cultural life of Salvador. Amid the languor of colonial life, it was important to have a place where people could gather to talk and trade information, and Maria had a talent for surrounding herself with diverse and open-minded people.

After receiving news from her granddaughter, she began to plan a trip to visit the girl. One afternoon, far from home, in the forest where she still enjoyed gathering fruits and flowers for her sweets, she began to think about her approaching visit to Guilhermina, how she would meet the girl's children, see the life she had built for herself (would she be the same as before? Did she make the desserts Maria had taught her to make? Was she happy?), when the sky grew dark and a heavy rain began to fall.

Arriving home completely soaked, she thought to prepare some of the remedies she often made to warm body and soul, but feeling tired, decided, *It can wait until tomorrow.*

In a few short days, pneumonia killed her at the age of sixty-six.

Juvêncio sold the tavern, the house, the furniture, and the slaves, and set off to find Guilhermina, for that had been Maria Taiaôba's final wish.

GUILHERMINA
(1648-1693)

On the afternoon Guilhermina and Bento fled the city of Salvador, her head resting on Bento's shoulder, her mind regaining its calm but still a bit muddled from her grandmother's concoctions, Guilhermina slowly shook herself awake and thought back on fragments of her childhood. She remembered the cattle drive arriving at the plantation that had belonged to Manu Taiaôba, the swirling river with the heads of cattle, their horns knocking up against one another, the stir of hooves and mooing, and she smelled the sweet and acrid scent of cow dung. She heard the voice of an old man in a leather hat as he sat at the top of the large staircase leading to the porch, telling stories from the cattle drive.

The old man told how Manu Taiaôba, many, many years earlier, had discovered a way to teach the frightened cattle to cross the violent, rushing rivers of the backlands. How he had placed a cow skull on his head and jumped into the river, swimming and pretending he was a steer and showing them the way across. "It was your great-grandfather who invented this strategy," he would tell her, "and today, everyone does the same."

In her dream, she laughed, proud of her great-grandfather, but soon she thought to herself that no, it couldn't have happened that way, she hadn't known Manu Taiaôba, she hadn't known the plantation, she hadn't known the old man with the leather hat—I didn't know my father, I only knew my grandmother, I only knew Maria Taiaôba.

For a second, she stirred about confusedly in her dream, but soon she realized: *Of course, it was my grandmother who told me.* Calm washed over her again and she saw herself on the beach, running far from her mother, the waves drawing closer and washing over her feet, and Belmira sitting there, still as could be, staring off into infinity, and then suddenly there was no one and then the sea washed her mother's dress up on the beach, and then her shawl, *Mother!* she cried, *Mother!* . . . and Bento pulled her closer, *Shhh . . . shhh . . .* don't worry, everything will be alright, Guilhermina, everything will be alright, I'm sure of it.

But how could Bento know!

Bento didn't even know where they were going. They had already been in the horse cart for hours and the roads were becoming worse and worse, increasingly narrow, difficult to navigate with all the tree stumps and branches that lay along the shallow dirt clearing. Soon they would have to abandon the cart and continue on foot, but only after resting to allow Guilhermina to regain her strength.

When night fell they stopped in a clearing and slept through to the following morning. Bento had never imagined he'd find himself in such a situation, but before they left Salvador, a friend had advised him to settle down in a place where no one knew them, somewhere they could start a new life. It was better to follow the paths through the backlands and not along the better-known roads along the coast where, had the people of Salvador wanted to, they could have come after them.

They abandoned the cart, unhooked the horse, and set out on foot. Their guide was an Indian who knew the region. When possible, they would walk along the river so as not to become lost, and to have water and fish at hand.

Guilhermina had already recovered her strength and was easily able to keep a steady pace, leaving Bento trailing behind. She liked the cold humidity of the dense, dark jungle, where the thick, tall trees with their bushy canopies kept even a sliver of light from seeping through. It was a source of peace to follow the guide's footsteps through that unknown darkness; it composed the perfect dramatic setting for her personality and temperament. Later, she barely noticed the heavy swarms of mosquitoes tirelessly circling them, buzzing and leaving bites that slowly clot in the steam rising from the forest floor.

Their clothes often became soaked as they crossed muddy swamps; made for city life, Bento's and Guilhermina's shoes didn't last long, and their feet suffered from the sticks and thorns. Their Indian guide taught them how to walk by flattening the soles of their feet against the ground and turning their toes a bit inward to reduce fatigue. They passed through regions thick with jaguars and saw earth overturned by their claws, great big gouges in the earth as though hacked out with hoes; they rubbed linseed oil into their skin so that the scent would keep the beasts at a distance.

They hunted as they could, fished, ate hearts of palm and wild cashew fruit. Their mood improved dramatically each time they found a monkey to roast.

After a few days on foot they entered a region of hills and mountain ranges. Their guide warned against making noise, hunting with shotguns, or even lighting a fire: they had entered territory belonging to the Tapuias, fierce warriors with long flowing hair like a woman's. Fear caused the group to quicken its pace, limit their stops to rest, and eat less. When they arrived at the edge of navigable rivers, Bento and the slaves built improvised rafts they took as far as they could.

They wandered until they came across a troop of cattle-ranchers; their conversations with the cattlemen led Bento and Guilhermina to an idea. They asked their guide to take them to a region that served as a cattle crossing, at the basin of the Rio Doce, not far from what would later become the border between the states of Minas Gerais and Espírito Santo.

When they arrived at a clearing in the middle of a valley, Guilhermina thought it was a good spot for them to settle down. Bento agreed. They built a house out of logs, with a beaten earth floor and a thatched roof, and hung hammocks and selected wood for a table and stools. They constructed a corral and planted the cassava they'd brought with them.

Looking out upon the vast earth around him, Bento realized that raising cattle would have its advantages; cattle are a product that have no need to be carried; the cows and steer bear their own weight, simply requiring that someone show them the way. During long drives, however, one or more of the cattle would sometimes tire out or grow weak from lack of food or water. If Bento and Guilhermina were to establish themselves along the cattle-driving routes, they might end up with some of these ailing cattle, nurse them back to health, and slowly build up a small herd of their own for food or to sell down the line. From their doorstep, they could also sell the foods they planted to the cattlemen who passed by.

And that's what they did, and life followed its course.

They went about clearing some more land in the floodplain and succeeded in obtaining corn seed from the travelers who passed through, and even planted sugarcane. They sold what they had or traded for what they did not at the tiny stand they constructed at the edge of the road. Soon they began to make *rapadura*, a luxury in those inhospitable backlands: the sweet taste of the hardened block of sugar energized tired bodies and brought a bit of warmth to the chest during early morning cattle drives.

The first ailing livestock the couple managed to recuperate resulted in Guilhermina's discovery of her talent for raising cattle. From the very beginning, it was she who took charge of the animals with the help of the slaves. She had a special method for reviving the weakened cattle and was so devoted to caring for the cows and calves it was as if they were her own children. At times, she found herself thinking that the dream she'd had of Manu Taiaôba's cattle drives had, in reality, been a sign as to their future endeavors.

Guilhermina was tall, strong, fearless, and possessed such natural authority as she performed the farm work that no one—neither man nor beast—tried to test her. She began to wear men's clothing to better perform fieldwork, and the male cowhands treated her as though she were one of them, despite knowing quite well that she was their boss and a woman.

Guilhermina found peace in those wide-open spaces and their solitude.

Though it had been difficult for her to accept the rules of society life, it was easy for her to accept the laws of nature. She loved the dense forest, the wild animals, the heavy rains. She especially enjoyed the storms that brought lightning and thunder; she loved the rushing rivers and winds. In Bento's eyes, his wife was also a force of nature, a sister to the storms, the long cattle drives, and the strong river currents.

Theirs was a solar life: they rose before the first rays of sun shone through the morning fog, they would rest when the sun had reached its peak, wrap up their work as the sun set, and sleep soon after darkness set in. They sometimes received travelers and other outsiders. Like others who were peopling the colony, Guilhermina and Bento gave lodging to all who passed through; this was their only contact with the outside world. Travelers were scarce in the region, but whenever they did come by, the farm's door was open at any hour of day or night, and slaves were at the ready to serve them a hot meal. They sold provisions to anyone needing supplies for the road, but the meals served upon arrival were part of the hospitality, a necessity, a custom they observed in that era of endless distances and few villages.

They would have cattle dealers pass through and, at times, even an entire expedition, a tiny town on the march, raising a ruckus and a constant din that left Guilhermina feeling uneasy, at risk, and often she would seek refuge among the livestock, leaving Bento to see to the roadside stand and conversation.

There were only two things that Guilhermina longed for: Maria Taiaôba and organ music. But she knew it was unlikely she would ever have either again. All the same, she continued singing more than she ever had, and Bento bought a fiddle off a cowboy to provide accompaniment. All who passed through grew wide-eyed with her singing, and soon a legend was born of a woman with fiery hair who sang like an angel of God and belted out songs that were so melodious and beautiful they appeared to cast a spell over the livestock.

Bento was able to resume making his saints in peace, selling his statues to the cattlemen, who resold them when they reached the cities and were soon bringing him orders. In addition to the tiny statues, he sculpted altarpieces, but his talent was most apparent in the tiny images of women saints. These, his tiny saints, were strong; they had a formal and rigid posture characteristic of the religious art of the time. The only difference in Bento's images was the subtle, more real sensualism than most baroque models, and a more vibrant color palette, even if he was limited to tones of red, yellow, and black, a detail imposed by the limited varieties of pigments to be found in the surrounding forests.

The region was rich in soapstone, also called panstone and used for kitchen cookware. A bluish-green or gray color, it was a soft stone uniform in texture, and was malleable like wood. Bento began to sculpt smaller pieces from this stone, pieces that gradually became more refined, more harmonious, tiny blue-green and gray jewels.

It was a life of isolation and endless horizons, and both Guilhermina and Bento were comfortable that way. Indeed, Guilhermina was happy, her world, at Bento's side, was the livestock, broad horizons, the music coming from the bull's horn, and her singing filling the vast fields that opened far beyond what the eye could see.

She became pregnant twice but lost the children; when the twins Jerônimo and Romualdo were born, she was nearing twenty. Soon after, she became pregnant again, but the girl was stillborn.

Guilhermina didn't know what to do with the twins. She had accepted her natural role—just as animals gave birth, so did people. But, beyond feeding them and providing a favorable environment for them to grow, she wasn't sure what more was demanded of her in relation to her sons. The two boys were very different from one another, but they were always a mystery to their mother: she didn't know how to interact with or what to expect from them.

Their father, for his part, left their fate to God. He, too, was distant from his boys but, beyond feeding them, he considered it his duty to give them something of a religious education. To that end, he began to construct a small chapel on a little hill next to the house. He threw himself into the project with such enthusiasm that he spent all his time working there on his saints, the altar, and the altarpieces, practically forgetting about the boys' education.

When the chapel was ready, it provided one more point of admiration among those who passed by the farm. It was small and had a single wooden cross hanging above the altar. All the numerous and varied statues, however, were small, delicate soapstone images of women saints. Until his death, Bento continued making saints for the chapel, filling nearly all its walls and creating a curious effect like a gray and blue-green cave peopled with miniatures, a strange sky overrun with tiny women saints.

One afternoon, Juvêncio arrived at the farm carrying the inheritance Maria Taiaôba had left to Guilhermina, namely a large sum of money. There were gold coins stored in a leather chest, along with some jewels—those from Duarte's family—and the mother-of-pearl jewelry box with Filipa's treasures. Guilhermina and Bento weren't sure what to do with it, and decided to leave it in a corner of the room, inside the same trunk.

Juvêncio declined when invited by Bento to stay. Having fulfilled his promise to Maria Taiaôba, he was determined to roam across the mining region, where it was said many people had discovered precious metals. He promised to pass through whenever possible.

Of Guilhermina and Bento's two children, the first to go out into the world was Jerônimo. He left to accompany a band of cowboys who had stopped on their way to Sergipe, farther south. For more than two years, he had nurtured hopes of going after the so-called herbs of the backlands, various plants and roots utilized in cooking and medicine. Once he had arrived in Sergipe, his idea was to continue on to Sítio do Uma in the state of Pará, from there to São José do Rio Negro. He carried a hand-drawn map by a priest from one of the religious missions in the Amazon; his plan was to continue on to the destination marked on that map, which was a present he'd been given from a dying man two years earlier.

The twin boys had been little older than twelve when a *reinol* who had become lost arrived at the farm, dehydrated, malnourished, on death's doorstep. He had wandered about the jungle for months; the other fifteen men from his expedition had expired along the way. They had set out from the port at Espírito Santo for Caminho dos Currais da Bahia, a land passage stretching through the backlands up to Salvador, but their guide gave so many orders to take wrong turns, they only learned later that, in order to avoid the attacks of the Tapuia, they had set off in the opposite direction from their destination. The original plan had been to follow the Rio São Francisco to Pernambuco, where it was said precious metals were to be found. Along the way, however, they had encountered a lone traveler, a priest who said he was part of the religious missions along the Rio Negro. The priest told them of riches, more guaranteed than gold, in a place much farther north where he had been and for which he had a map. These riches were the aforementioned "herbs of the backlands," discovered with the help of the tribes of the North, and included several types of plants such as cacao and clove, and other sources of oils and balms. The Europeans thought that these could substitute Eastern spices, whether in medicine or food, and they were paying a fortune for them. The priest could not stop talking about how he would grow rich with this map leading to the herbs worth more than gold or silver, and which were easily sold, how he had already planned the whole thing out. He spoke so much and with such swagger that he began to fill the heads of that group with ideas, and some began to think it wasn't right for a man of God to have this type of ambition. In the end, one of them arrived at a dispute with the priest and killed him. The map, as the group soon discovered, truly was in his bag, drawn entirely by hand and drawn well, though few of them there knew how to read it. By punishment or by coincidence, the first to die on the expedition was the man who had killed the priest, and one by one they all began to die until only the wandering Portuguese man remained. Sensing his own death approaching, he wanted to perform the benevolent act of giving the map to someone who, having gained possession of it by gift rather than theft, might use it without any guilt or fear of revenge.

That's how, before dying, he gave the map to the two brothers. But the man's story had left an impression on only Jerônimo. Romualdo, not so much. Jerônimo had the dreamy, romantic temperament of all adventure-seekers, but Romualdo had inherited his priestly grandfather's mystic side, and though his father had given him little education, his calling seemed to be religion. For some time, he had been gathering information from this or that priest who passed through, and his future plans included the Jesuit college at Piratininga. Soon after Jerônimo set off with his map, Romualdo decided it was time he too left, and off he went.

Each of the brothers took with him a portion of their great-grandmother's coins.

Their parents never heard from either of them again.

The twins also never met their sister, Ana de Pádua, who was born a few months later, after another complicated pregnancy for their mother. As with the twins, Guilhermina's daughter was a mystery to her; a child was something whose sense, meaning, or purpose she was unable to grasp. As she had also done with the twins, she left her daughter in the hands of a house slave, the same woman who had accompanied her pregnancies since she and Bento fled Salvador.

Now that his chapel was complete, Bento was able to focus his attentions on his daughter. He taught her to read and write, as he had the boys, and taught her the rudiments of religion.

The girl didn't like cattle and never accompanied her mother on her chores. She would stay with her father, helping him with his sculptures—but she worshiped Guilhermina.

When her mother arrived home at the end of the afternoon, covered in burrs and dust, she would wash up in a nearby stream. This was Ana's favorite part of the day, when, fascinated, she helped Guilhermina wash her long fire-like hair. Guilhermina always wore her hair up as she did her chores, wrapping the long strands around her head several times and securing them beneath a leather hat. Later, she calmly unfurled them before Ana, as though they had all the time in the world, slowly and carefully massaged her mother's hair with oil from coconuts, which she rubbed between the palms of her hands before sliding them along her mother's voluminous tendrils of hair. She felt the softness of the curled waves and their beauty as they shimmered beneath the golden, late afternoon sun. She would comb it until each strand shone, and watched as the color transformed beneath the setting sun. In such moments, her mother would let out her voice and fill the clearing with the fullness of her powerful singing, and there the two women would remain until the first stars or the light of the moon could be seen.

Then, upon waking one morning, that fire-like hair of Guilhermina's, which she had never cut and which, when untamed, reached her feet, was white. It happened without any warning or explanation.

Ana's and Bento's jaws dropped and Guilhermina also marveled at herself, but no one grew sad because her long white hair was as beautiful and extraordinary as it had been before.

Immediately, Bento began to add a new characteristic to his statues of female saints: though he lacked the proper pigments, he found a way to scrape the soapstone until it resembled Guilhermina's white hair, and he also began to let this hair fall until it reached the saint's feet.

It's a pity that so little remains of the work of Bento Vasco. With his growing technical skill, the frivolous levity of his earlier work gave way to figures that were more world-weary, and the long white hair of the women saints gave his sculptures a particularly seductive aspect.

As a strong storm set in one late afternoon, a cowhand came to tell Guilhermina that her favorite breeding cow had escaped the corral. The two immediately set out on horseback in search of the runaway. A jaguar had been seen prowling the region and killing livestock, and Guilhermina didn't want to lose the pregnant cow. Armed beneath the violent storm, the two heard the growling of a jaguar and desperate moaning as they approached a familiar hollow in the forest. They drew closer to see the terrified cow lying on the ground, giving birth, the jaguar directly next to her.

Perhaps under the effect of the lightning and thunder that reinforced the violence and cowardice of the jaguar's attack on the defenseless cow, or for God knows what reason, the bloody scene seemed to have driven Guilhermina mad with rage and, in the blind fury of an irrational attack like none she had ever experienced since that scene in front of the church door in Salvador, she instantly jumped from her horse and advanced unarmed on the jaguar.

Woman and beast leapt at one another in a scene of pure horror, and as strong as Guilhermina was in her uncontrollable fury, the jaguar—by its very nature a hundred times stronger—had in no time clawed open her jugular.

The cowhand who had accompanied her would repeat, for the rest of his life, that he never understood why his boss had done that. Paralyzed with fear, he only managed to shoot the jaguar milliseconds after it had already killed Guilhermina.

Woman and beast died side by side beneath the electric storm that illuminated the birth of the calf, which survived together with its mother.

That night, Guilhermina's body lay across the long wooden table in the main room of house. Ana carefully cleaned the blood from her mother's body, unfurled her long white hair and arranged it, lock by lock, curl by curl, until it covered her entire body down to her toes.

The next morning, they buried her behind the tiny chapel.

IMPROBABLE
SPLENDOR

ANA DE PÁDUA
(1683-1730)

Unlike her mother, Ana had inherited more of her father's complexion and had a tiny, thin frame and brown skin. Fragile only in appearance, she was bold and courageous, not as much as her mother, but enough to be considered a strong woman. Her name had been chosen by her father, who had also chosen those of the twins. Ana's had resulted from a promise made to Our Lady of Pádua, the saint of Bento's devotion, at the hour of his daughter's difficult delivery.

When the cowhand recounted how her mother had died, Ana was the only person to say that she did, in fact, understand why her mother attacked the jaguar with her bare hands, for if she had been there herself, she would have done the same. Despite her tender age, it was she who arranged Guilhermina's body atop the long wood table, and wrapped her in her hammock when the time came to take her to the prepared grave on the hillside.

Bento found himself adrift following the death of his wife, the force around which he had constructed his life at the farm. A man without larger ambitions, an artist who lived for his saints and for Guilhermina, he felt empty and alone now that she had died.

It was Guilhermina who had overseen not only the livestock and the crops, but also the slaves. Not knowing what to do with them, Bento decided to grant them their freedom, an action whose perhaps unexpected consequence was of great worth to him later in easing the solitude of advanced age; the freed slaves did not depart, but rather built mud huts with thatched roofs on the surrounding land and continued to work for him in exchange for calves as payment, as other farmhands did. Little by little, a tiny village began to develop, at its center the tiny chapel constructed by Bento on the hill next to his house. Bento became a sort of patriarch for the outpost, which he named Pouso da Capela.

News began to trickle in that gold had been discovered, the information received more trustworthy and euphoric with each report. It was said that a mulatto had dipped his trough into a stream to gather water when he noticed tiny grains the color of steel; everyone thought this unusual, because no one knew what sort of metal it was. But they did know that the mulatto ended up selling these grains to a trader who had no idea what he was buying, and who sent them to Rio de Janeiro for examination only to receive news that they were the finest gold. They said that in the mining region there were plenty of streams just like that one, and all you needed to do was dip a trough into the water and pull it back out to find it full of gold.

The number of travelers passing by grew as they continued toward the Rio das Velhas and the Rio das Minas dos Gataguás. They passed through quickly, often not stopping for more time than necessary for a quick rest.

At her father's side, Ana watched as the number of travelers increased, and she took a liking to it all.

She was always the first to bring water to the outsiders and to strike up a conversation. Unlike her mother and father, she enjoyed others' company and was eager for news.

One of the many who passed by on his way back from the region near the Rio das Velhas was Juvêncio, Maria Taiaôba's former companion. At his side was Baltazar, who'd recently arrived from Portugal, impelled by his fever for gold. Somewhere around forty-five years old, Baltazar took a liking to Ana de Pádua's youthfulness, her dark-skinned beauty, and silky black hair, and asked Bento for the young girl's hand, that Bento might let her go with him to Sabará so they could be married by the first priest they could find.

Bento saw no reason to refuse. His daughter was reaching a marriageable age and it wouldn't be easy to hunt up a husband in those parts, unless it were in a similar situation with a traveler passing through. And the Portuguese man had accompanied Juvêncio, who was at least something akin to family. When he finally saw that Ana seemed to like the idea of setting a new course for her life, Bento gave his blessing.

For Ana, it was as though things had been pre-ordained and were merely following their natural course, in the same way a river did, or the weather, or time. There was no rhyme or reason to think the issue over: if Baltazar had stopped there, was in need of a woman to help him settle in the country, and he wanted it to be her, what was there to argue? It was only natural for Ana to go with him. The only obstacle that could have gotten in the way was if she had been too attached to her father or the farm, or if she had been too shy. But no—Ana wasn't shy at all, and though she loved her father, what she most wanted was to leave that place, to know others, to see the world. Whether it was at Baltazar's side or someone else's, the girl of fifteen asked no questions. Her restlessness and youthful curiosity were much greater than any fear.

Had it not been for Juvêncio and his Indian slaves, the journey to Sabará would have been a disaster. The heavy woods and roads nearly did Baltazar in, since he understood nothing about the tropical land where he'd arrived with the intent of becoming rich. Baltazar arrived at his destination with a fever, feeble and weak, and Ana de Pádua spent her first few months of marriage tending to her husband's illness.

After he'd recovered, Baltazar, a merchant by origin, showed little enthusiasm for the hard work of mining, but soon saw an alternative path to instant wealth. Gold was the only truly abundant thing in the region, and since no one eats gold, drinks gold, or sleeps with gold, the enormous scarcity of basic necessities in the region would affect the camps that, with the hordes of people arriving daily, were rapidly transforming into villages. Everyone wanted to dedicate themselves to the extraction of gold and no one thought to lose time planting crops or guaranteeing the essentials for survival. In this gap between ambition and necessity, Baltazar's offerings found great demand in the greedy hands full of gold, gold which ultimately ended up in his hands, but without his having to wear down his body in the rivers next to those swaggering, brute men whose skill in this area—this point he was not foolish enough to ignore—was much greater than his.

He opened a lodge with a home in back, and with a few coins and some of the jewels that had belonged to Ana's grandmother, purchased slaves for planting cassava, corn, and sugarcane; he organized a network of cattle-drivers and livestock sellers, and sold literally everything for its weight in gold: food, drink, tobacco, clothing, anything at all.

For Ana, the lodge was a dream, with all its people coming and going and stirring about. The toughest labor was performed entirely by slaves, and her husband, in the beginning, showed her great tenderness and never made unreasonable demands. Hers was a bustling, energetic life that fit like a glove.

But in a region infested with men without women and where having a woman was a prize, especially a young woman who was more white than black, Baltazar began to suffer from that deadly illness called jealousy. As in every mining region, the majority of the adventurers preferred to leave their wives, if they had them, in their cities of origin. And so, disputes over a skirt-tail—a black woman's, an Indian's, or whatever combination—were a natural part of the raucous gold-mining nights. Given their rarity, white women, or those who appeared to be, were coveted like jewels of unparalleled purity.

This was no place for jealous men. And after Ana's first pregnancy resulted in a stillborn son, Baltazar's disposition only made matters worse.

That's when restrictions were placed on Ana's activities: she was not allowed to go to the lodge during the busier hours; she couldn't leave the house unless it was with her husband; and when she left, she had to cover herself with a long black shawl that concealed her from head to foot.

But Ana was young, cheerful, extroverted, and Baltazar was soon of the opinion that his restrictions weren't strict enough. He turned to physical aggression. He would whip Ana with an enormous leather belt that left her back red and swollen. It no longer mattered after some time whether or not she had given Baltazar reason to be jealous, since a life of an aching back and broad leather belts inevitably sent Ana looking for an escape.

She found it in a man who had come from São Paulo—one younger, better looking, and richer than Baltazar.

THE PAULISTA JOSÉ GARCIA

José Garcia e Silva came from a family of explorers who had set out from São Paulo. His father, Manuel Garcia e Silva, had participated since a young age in the expeditions that preyed on Indians to be found in the Jesuit missions of southern Brazil. Such expeditions were highly attractive to the Paulistas, who could find hundreds of natives at a time, settled in villages, already pacified and adapted to white society, practically ready and waiting, so to speak, to be kidnapped and sold as slaves. There were other Paulistas who preferred to take it upon themselves to enter the service of His Majesty, via contracts to pacify and settle contested regions of the colony, receiving as payment a portion of the prisoners they took and land, positions, pensions, and commendations. Manuel Garcia e Silva was different. He liked to work independently and keep his distance from the men of the Crown.

For Manuel, the backlands spelled mystery and adventure. It was the force of the rivers and the beauty of the mountains, the constant battle against nature. In the backlands, there was the possibility of gold and precious gems, the certainty of finding native slaves, the adventurous lifestyle of rugged men.

Twenty-two times Manuel Garcia e Silva set off into the backlands, on trips that sometimes took up to two years each, in search of Indian slaves for plantations, the chattel whose work the Paulistas considered "the best remedy against poverty." Manuel's life was a constant coming-and-going, seeking, capturing, and selling slaves. But the backlands also meant insidious fevers, delirium, infection. Territory rife with jaguars and other wild beasts. Savages and the unknown. The backlands could be the death of you and, on his final trip there, Manual Garcia was killed, victim to poison-tipped arrows. He was sixty-nine.

As for himself, José Garcia took part in his first expedition when he was still a child, little more than twelve years old. He went not with his father but with an uncle, Bartolomeu Bueno da Silva, on an expedition to the land of the Goyaz Indians. José and a cousin, named Bartolomeu after his father and a bit older than José, were part of the infamous expedition of Anhanguera the Elder—the Old Devil, the legend himself—who set the rivers aflame with alcohol and terrorized the Indians.

Some years later in 1722, when this same cousin, Bartolomeu Bueno da Silva, managed to organize an important expedition to return to that region in search of the gold he knew existed there, he invited José Garcia to go with him. But Garcia, already a bit out of shape and soft from the life of luxury he had been leading in the mining region, thought it best to decline. Had he accepted, perhaps the cousins would have together been better able to remember the route they had taken the first time as boys, thereby avoiding the three long years the expedition of Anhanguera the Younger spent wandering lost through the backlands before it finally reached the gold of the Goyaz Indians.

The explorers who joined Anhanguera's expedition were part of a long line of Paulista slave hunters, and they continued their taming and conquest of the new land. By that time, however, they had the benefit of being better equipped, with leather boots, clothing suited to their task, and well-trained riding horses. It was these explorers who would be the first to arrive in that region, and the first to discover the gold in the mines. They considered themselves owners of the place and did not look kindly upon outsiders, such as the Emboabas—as they called men invading from Bahia, Pernambuco, and especially the old country—who had begun to arrive in large numbers.

José Garcia was among the first to arrive in the region surrounding the Rio das Velhas, and was shocked as he became richer with each passing day and with startling speed. Barely a day over thirty, he began to feel the itch to settle down. An itch, in fact, that he had begun to feel one afternoon after seeing a young woman in a black shawl pass through the streets, which were muddy after a summer storm. Having nothing to do at that moment, and provoked perhaps by the forbidding black shawl, or a desire to irk the Emboaba who ran the town lodge (everyone knew the young woman was the Portuguese man's wife), José Garcia dismounted his horse and, in a display of utmost courtesy, carried her in his arms across an enormous mud puddle.

The young woman lowered the shawl from her face and flashed a grateful smile. Remaining just out of sight, José Garcia decided to follow her to a distant point along the river and there, hiding behind a termite mound, he watched her undress to bathe. Whether because it had been ages since he'd seen a woman undress with such gracefulness, or because this scene only increased his resolve to irk Baltazar, or else for no other reason than the chemistry that makes the world go round, José Garcia never again managed to get Ana de Pádua off his mind. And because word traveled fast in that tiny little world of theirs, he soon learned of the beatings Baltazar inflicted on his wife.

Ana, too, had already taken note of the Paulista, famed as one of the richest men in the entire region, with hundreds of human chattel—Indians and blacks—and inclined to freely spend the fortune his slaves unearthed for him in the mines. With the swagger common to his people, José Garcia rode through the streets at a gallop on his handsome Bahian racehorse, kicking up dust and drawing attention. Ana had heard all about him: how he had begun building a two-story house, the first in those parts; how his horses' saddles were adorned in gold and precious crystals; how he put on huge banquets for his guests, serving roasted chicken and suckling pigs, pacas, and deer seasoned with sumptuous glazes, cornbread and maize loafs, sponge cakes, and flowing casks of imported wine that lasted until sunrise.

José Garcia would send messages to her through his slaves. Ana de Pádua responded by begging him not to think of her; her husband was capable of anything. José Garcia replied that he, too, was capable of anything, and told her to set a day and time for him to take her away from there. Ana de Pádua, gently protesting, begged him to stop, for her husband would certainly kill her if he suspected anything.

In the meantime, the animosity between the two factions disputing the riverbeds only grew. Groups on each side were meeting constantly to discuss every little development in this dispute, and the tiniest quarrel, no matter how insignificant, assumed the proportions of an unpardonable offense. On the one side stood the Paulistas, superior in number and otherwise, who considered themselves the natural owners of that section of land; on the other side was the greed and boldness of the adventure-seeking Emboabas, who arrived prepared for anything, worsening an already tense situation that soon gave way to open confrontations. One of the first was José Garcia's killing of Baltazar.

Ana and Garcia had met fleetingly one afternoon on the distant banks of a stream. The Paulista asked her to go with him, insisting she should not worry about retaliation from Baltazar. Ana neither agreed nor disagreed. She wavered, unable to arrive at a decision, not because she wished to continue to endure Baltazar's abuse, but because she felt her fate was beyond her control, the river of her life subject to rushing waters it seemed would take her to unknown depths. Ana was not one for tragedy. She enjoyed the pace of everyday life, the little things that change here and there without our realizing that a new world is slowly taking shape without our lifting a finger, without theatrics, without great surprises. Ana was a courageous and decisive woman, but only when it came to small things within the limits of the world she knew. Whereas she became paralyzed in the midst of important events, or when faced with the unexpected, unable to decide what to do or where to go. It hadn't been so when her mother died. But in that case Ana decided to take control of the situation after a still greater change—her mother's death—had already taken place and life had returned once again to the way it more or less had been. Only then had she been able to say that she understood exactly why her mother had taken on the jaguar bare-handed, *that* Ana would have done the same, would have acted with determination, courage, and all the rest. And so she was able to see to her mother's burial. But in the midst of the whirlwind, in the eye of the actual hurricane, she would hesitate, confused.

Ana stood motionless before the unexpected direction her life was taking. That night, Baltazar, drunk and without any apparent reason, removed his leather belt and told her, "Today you're going to get to know the buckle, and we'll see if that doesn't quiet you down," before beating her as never before, as though he had guessed it would be the final time. Garcia's spies heard Ana's hoarse cries and took little time to report back to their boss.

Baltazar didn't have so much as the time to stagger to his feet when José Garcia and his band of men burst into the inn like a horde of wild beasts. But at least he knew why he was about to die; José Garcia told him why, just before shooting him in the head: "A coward who beats his wife deserves to die on his knees."

Without waiting for the last of Baltazar's life to trickle out of him, Garcia destroyed everything inside the inn, and without giving Ana time to verify that her husband was in fact dead, ordered her to grab her things and took her with him to his home.

But Baltazar was dear to his people, and the Emboabas, furious at his execution, and perhaps more furious at the sight of so many broken, unusable goods, considered the incident yet another act of despotism on the part of the Paulistas. Stealing the Portuguese man's wife was one thing; but killing him was another matter entirely. Challenging Baltazar to a duel, like an honorable man, could have resolved the issue to everyone's satisfaction, but invading his inn with a band of criminals to kill him in cold blood and then lay waste to everything was an affront. Given the existing animosity between the two groups, Baltazar's death was just one more reason for things to grow ever more heated.

As tensions and confrontations reached an all-time high, word was that the Paulistas were of a mind to rid the region of all the Emboabas, and that Baltazar and his lodge were merely the first step. Rumors began to circulate that the Paulistas were preparing a full-scale massacre of the outsiders, and that they had sworn to steamroll every last one of the Emboabas, their families, and their children. When the Emboabas heard all these "diabolical rumors," as the Paulistas would later call them, the outsiders felt threatened and banded together, deciding it was better to launch an offensive than suffer an attack themselves. They had more weapons and ammunition than the Paulistas and by that time outnumbered their rivals.

First, they attacked the town of Sabará. Their Indian allies shot flaming arrows at the Paulistas' homes, nearly all built with thatched roofs, and they were soon reduced to crackling bonfires, forcing the inhabitants to flee, including José Garcia. Ana de Pádua, at a gallop on the back of a horse that was more frightened than she was, thought she should find Juvêncio and ask him to take her back to her father's house in Pouso da Capela. But José Garcia had other ideas, and decided to send her south to stay with his parents in São Paulo. War had broken out, and he wanted Ana safe.

After a journey that took more than three months, Ana arrived at the town of São Paulo de Piratininga with the help of slaves and her husband's most trusted men. She wasn't feeling well after the recent undercurrents coursing through the river of her life. To make matters worse, José Garcia's relations—his sister, nieces, and cousins—greeted her with distrust and hostility. She felt entirely alone. They lived in an enormous house two stories tall, with walls of stucco and a tiled roof, on the same street as the Church of São Francisco. She thought the city looked sad; it was filled with abandoned homes, homes whose owners preferred to live on their plantations outside the city or who were off waging the campaign against the Emboabas.

Inácia Benta, sister to José Garcia, had lost her husband to fever. But being a daughter, wife, and sister to explorers, she persevered and continued earning a living by selling Indian slaves. Her business was to lend small sums to those organizing incursions into the backlands, receiving in return half of the slaves found on each trip. It was good business and she, too, had grown rich, without the help of her brother. As a result of her wealth, she treated Ana de Pádua badly in the beginning. She found her sister-in-law's lineage lacking for the family's standards. She asked Ana where her parents had come from, and Ana would speak of her great-grandmother's trunk and a Dutch grandfather, but none of this touched Inácia, who thought Ana's color compromising, darker than was suitable. She told Ana that the Garcia e Silvas were a family of certifiable Old Christians, without a drop of Moorish or Jewish blood, and that she hoped it would stay that way.

Ana spent hours alone sitting on the windowsill, waiting for news to arrive from the mining region.

News did arrive, but it was not good. There were reports of villages rising up against each other and bloody confrontations spreading everywhere. The Emboabas had appealed to the governorate general. The governorate had sent troops from Rio de Janeiro to stop the fighting, but it had sided with the outsiders. The Paulistas, inferior in numbers and arms, had been forced to retreat.

Whenever a messenger arrived, members of the family—almost all women—gathered to hear the news. Ana stood in the back, but she could clearly hear everything that was said and the murmur of indignation that the news provoked in the others, since the messenger nearly always brought news of defeat.

The Paulista women, long accustomed to receiving news of their husbands' and adventurous relatives' victories as they tamed the backlands, were shocked at their unjust and unexpected change of fate. "The gold belongs to us, and us alone!" they protested, heartbroken. "We were the ones who discovered these mines. We're the ones who have a right to them."

"Somebody needs to teach these Emboabas a lesson," they raged. "God Almighty, how can such a thing be happening?"

"And what about the help these outsiders are receiving from the government in Rio, this government of Portuguese usurpers who want control of our riches?" still others protested.

When news arrived of an absolute massacre in the middle of the woods, in a spot that became known as Betrayal Grove, the women, furious at what they'd heard, marched out into the streets. They implored the whole town not to leave unanswered the horrible deaths of their countrymen, who had trusted the abominable Emboabas and laid down their arms only to be massacred with untold cruelty, countrymen whose memory would live on through future generations.

The horror! Shameless cowards! Revenge will be ours!

Ana de Pádua was pulled along through the streets, and suddenly saw in this uprising one last sliver of hope amid those solitary undercurrents coursing through the river that was her life. From that day forward, she became one of the most ardent defenders of the honor of Paulistas, leaving her sister-in-law and nieces in awe of her ardor and enthusiasm in the defense of José Garcias's interests. With that, she was finally accepted into the family.

After successive defeats, the Paulistas returned to São Paulo, but to their great misfortune, they were welcomed with disgust and scorn. José Garcia was not among them; wounded in battle, he was recovering his health at the home of allies.

The women, unwilling to accept the bloodshed and the loss of their wealth, demanded retaliation and revenge. They gathered in one another's houses and stormed the streets in large groups, shouting and exhorting the others: "We cannot let the Emboabas think they own this country! We will take back what's ours! We will avenge our dead!"

Ana and her sister-in-law were two of the leaders who went from house to house, dragging women out to the streets and stirring up the small town as never before. So great was the commotion that no one thought to tell them to go back home. On the contrary. Roused to action by the two women, humiliated by defeat, irritated with the loss of their mining sites, the Paulistas gathered in the Palace of the São Paulo Chamber of Deputies, whose doors were open to the people, and decided to organize an expedition to Minas to force the outsiders to return their farms, their mining sites, and their slaves.

One sunny August morning in 1709, an expedition of some thirteen hundred set out from the Pátio do Colégio in São Paulo, the leaders on horseback and the rest on foot. They were joined along the way by groups from several towns throughout the state of São Paulo: Itu, Paranaíba, Sorocaba, Jundiaí, Moji, Taubaté, and Guaratinguetá. But yet again, fate was to conspire against them.

After a difficult march lasting more than four months to the town that today is São João del Rei, they found the town protected behind a wall, ready to rebuff their attack. Attempts were made to arrive at a truce, but the confrontations continued without respite for eight days and nights, leaving many dead and wounded on both sides, without delivering either victory. The two sides locked horns in battle after battle, until the news arrived that troops were on their way from Rio de Janeiro, sent by the governorate general in support of the Emboabas, and the Paulistas were forced to return home yet again.

And so, a pall set in over the Paulistas, and the war for the gold mines that had been discovered in the Portuguese colony two centuries after the Portuguese had arrived came to an end.

José Garcia, still recovering from his wounds, did not participate in the failed revenge campaign, and Ana only saw him after it all had come to an end, when he was finally able meet her again in São Paulo.

He found Ana very much adapted to domestic life. She had learned to sew, to do needlepoint, and make candied sweets. She had found two books in a trunk at the house that had left her entranced: the *Mysteries of the Passion of the Christ* and the *Exemplary Novelas* of Miguel de Cervantes. Though she had learned to read with Bento Vasco, this was the first time she had picked up and read an entire book. She also enjoyed taking her nieces to the Rio Agongabay, and to lie beneath the shadows of trees to admire the golden wheat fields of the farms on the other side of the river as the little girls played in the tall grass.

She had begun to go to the churches, too. Her rather incomplete religious education had been administered by her father in his tiny hillside chapel. Visiting the churches of São Paulo, Ana became fascinated with the structures that, though hardly sophisticated for the time (the village in the middle of the fields of Piratininga was not a rich one), were by any account larger than anything she'd ever seen, and they cemented her love for the churches she would later watch being built in Sabará. She was captivated by the pomp and ritual of Mass, the clergymen's fine vestments, the extreme formality of it all, the cloying smell of the incense and especially, especially, with the inebriating music of the organ.

For the very first time, Ana understood something her mother used to tell her. At moments when everything seemed to grow quiet after her powerful voice carried through the open fields near the river, when the trees, the birds, the waters, and the wind appeared to go silent out of reverence for the extraordinary voice they had just heard, Guilhermina, without turning to face her daughter, perhaps so Ana wouldn't see the sadness written in her features, would say: "My girl, you will never truly know what music is, or the power it holds, until you hear the sound of an organ."

As she listened to the sound of the organ, the memory of her mother's voice intertwined with the music and Ana cried, not exactly out of sorrow, but with emotion at the beauty she had been blessed to witness that day, in that church, in that city. Ana became a religious woman and a mystic for aesthetic reasons.

José Garcia, on account of his battle wound, now walked with a limp. He had managed, however, to keep ownership of the majority of his mines, in no small part because, important man that he was, the governor-general considered it more convenient to leave José at peace rather than further embittered, beyond the humiliation of defeat, over a loss of wealth. It required effort to bring peace to the region, which certainly included measures to avoid raising the ire of men of Garcia's caliber.

He had barely arrived in São Paulo when he told Ana to pack up so they could return immediately to Sabará and reassert their mining rights. And that's what they did.

The return trip was easier and more comfortable than the one Ana had made when she fled the burning village. It was the dry season, the weather mild. The three-month-long journey—familiar to Garcia, who knew how to avoid dangerous or risky stretches—was made without anxiety or fear. If on earlier trips her haste and agony on account of the war had made her unable to appreciate the beauty along the way, this time Ana was able to calmly take in the endless mountains covered in virgin forest and the vastness of the open fields that stretched as far as the eye could see. Lying in her hammock at night at their well-protected camp, she listened to José Garcia tell of his adventures and to the singing of the slaves; when the time came to rest at high noon, she rested near tranquil or turbulent rivers, waiting as the slaves prepared a lunch of fresh fish with porridge as she cooled off at the edge of the peaceful riverbed.

Ana enjoyed comparing her life to the course of a river, a body of water that had always held an irresistible fascination for her. As an explorer, José Garcia considered rivers a natural and invaluable roadway. He knew that without them the Paulistas could never have traversed the backlands and conquered new territories.

Seated atop a riverbank, in the cool shade of the intertwining canopies of a few tiny trees, Garcia began to tell Ana how the explorers' incursions were always made alongside rivers, which was the safest way to avoid becoming lost, dying of hunger or thirst, and, at least from one side, avoiding surprise attacks. He explained how advantageous it was that the rivers of São Paulo ran through the flatlands,

far from dangerous waterfalls, and were easy to navigate, which made
the explorers' advance through unknown lands considerably easier.
But there are rivers and then there are rivers, he would say. There
were good rivers and bad rivers. There were those that allowed easy
navigation—calm, serene—and you can trust those, he told her. Others, not so much—those were wild rivers that concealed gales, eddies,
and maelstroms, and were full of waterfalls and other traps: dangerous
tree trunks, debris, stretches of pestilent waters that breed disease.
There are still others under the control of hostile tribes, who are ready
to cut short your journey and your life. And then there are the inop-
portune angry, moody rivers, subject to attacks of rage or weakness
depending on the weather.

The Rio Tietê, he often repeated, had always been a benevolent
river, and even when navigating it became difficult, you could rely
on it. It was a remark that local tribes certainly wouldn't agree with,
since for them the Tietê had always been a river of slavery, a river of
cruelty, the river that carried their predators into the backlands and
carried them out dragging miles and miles of Indian villages in chains
behind them.

The Rio Paraná, José Garcia went on, that was a bad river. It had
no waterfalls, but it was treacherous, with dangerous currents and
shifting winds. That river called for an abundance of caution.

That's how, listening to her husband talk about the rivers, Ana
began to like José Garcia. Before that, he had been an unknown, a
man who had changed the course of the waters of her life, but who
remained someone she barely knew. Then, on their long journey, she
allowed herself to be seduced by his self-assuredness and the experience of a man who knows his own value and the value of what he
finds in his path.

The late Baltazar, being an outsider, hadn't known anything about
the land and had tried to overcome this lack of knowledge and his
insecurity with aggression and arrogance. Ana hadn't been happy with

him. Even early on, because she felt no admiration for him, she could see his faults, his haughty ignorance. She remembered one instance in the first days of their trip from Pouso da Capela to the region surrounding the Rio das Velhas, when, dying of hunger, he discarded a sour but edible tamarind in favor of the sweet but laxative gel of the aloe vera plant, despite protests from the Indian slaves. Still nearly a child, she had thought that because he was older and more experienced and was from the kingdom—imagine that!—he certainly knew more than everyone and must have had his reasons; but when night arrived and she saw him trembling and sweating, doubled over with uncontrollable diarrhea, Ana understood that he was no better than anyone else. The disdain she slowly began to feel for her husband no doubt contributed to the tragic end of their union.

But with José Garcia, she had gotten to know the other side of the same coin. The knowledge and confidence of the seasoned explorer was seductive, and she was happy to have such a man at her side. Besides which, he wasn't old like Baltazar; he wasn't young, either, but he was handsome, elegant, a man with skin the color of wheat, a neat mustache, and a pair of eyebrows that met above his eyes like a dense forest.

Ana de Pádua was happy.

When they arrived in Sabará, they resumed their life in Garcia's large, reconstructed house. Gold seemed to spurt forth like water from their mines, and when their first child, Gregorio Antonio, was born before they'd lived a whole year together, José Garcia was already a fabulously rich man. As were a great number of those living in the area.

The wealth and the splendor coming from the mines were soon reflected in the villages. The governor-general had convinced a Paulista—the Paulistas were the only ones who knew the region well at that time—to open the Caminho Novo das Minas, a new road connecting the mining regions directly to Rio de Janeiro. It was a dangerous road, but it allowed the passage of men and beasts, bringing not only more and more Emboabas who invaded the region, but also more and more goods to attend to the growing demand of the newly rich. Caravans of mules, hauling every sort of commodity, began to replace the backs of Indian and black slaves as the mode of transport for supplying the burgeoning market. They came from São Paulo, they came from Rio, they came from Bahia, and their arrival provoked great agitation and excitement across the villages and farms. They also brought scores and scores of African slaves to work in the mines and slave women for the private little courts of society women.

The lives led by the gold prospectors were, frankly, lives of leisure. While the slaves toiled in near-subhuman conditions, these "respectable men" gathered for banquets beneath the refreshing shade of the leafy trees on the banks of the crystal-clear streams: tablefuls of vegetables, roasted chicken and suckling pig, chicken stew, succulent fruits, jaw-breaking sweets made with generous amounts of sugar, wines imported from the royal court. They never missed Mass or the rosary and, to emphasize their deep faith, they parted with huge sums to ensure their churches boasted the same riches as those of the mother country; altars of pure gold, statues from the most refined artisans, sumptuous works of architecture. They sought to imitate the Portuguese nobility, importing fabrics to make clothes unfit for the tropical climate, building eye-catching houses, hiring artists, buying expensive jewelry. Some even announced their passage through the streets with trumpet-toting slaves; others transformed their riding saddles into small works of luxury and art.

Euphoria and excitement hung over the city.

At home, Ana reigned over her court of slaves. She was surrounded by black women in her bedroom, in the rooms of her home, on the streets. They fanned her, dressed her, served her food, and brought messages and news back and forth.

If you were to see them today, the group of ladies seated on the veranda, talking, laughing, nibbling on tropical fruits and finger foods—and, of course, if you ignored the fashions of the day—you would think you were watching a group of friends enjoying themselves. Evidently, this was mere appearance. There was a clear and unshakeable hierarchy among them; each woman knew perfectly well where her place was.

A greedy spirit when it came to gossip, Ana soon formed a powerful network of information in the town where the homes, with the comings and going of slaves and their rooms without doors, were constantly exposed to strangers' eyes and ears. She knew of all the political intrigues and bedroom secrets, the disputes and sworn enemies, the fornicating priests, the First Communions that cost a fortune, the Capuchins who hid gold beneath their cassocks or in hollowed-out statues of the saints, the slave women who hid gold in the curls of their hair. She knew of the gentleman who took black lovers, whom they made to parade around wearing nothing but silver and gold necklaces. She knew of central government decrees and the arrival of government officials.

Ana knew everything.

Sometimes she would comment on these matters to Garcia; others she kept to herself. Her network of informant slave-women was her private pleasure, her unique form of power. Ana was a pioneer in the great modern addiction to information. That pure delight of being well-informed that has developed to an unimaginable degree and which is ever more common, giving way to those who, like Ana in her time, feel their endorphin levels rise merely at knowing something—anything at all—before and in greater detail than others, as though such a thing gives them a sort of special and ineffable power.

Whenever José Garcia's friends visited, Ana would sit in her high-back chair in the living room, a beautiful and apparently challenging bit of needlepoint in her hand, and, when she thought the time right, would contribute to the conversations surrounding the situation at the mines that stretched late into the night.

The war may have ended, but resentment of the central government and the Portuguese remained. There was gold in abundance, it was true, but the gold belonged to that land, and still the Portuguese Crown demanded a fifth of all gold extracted. With the new road leading directly to Rio de Janeiro, the central administration no longer depended on the Paulistas to show the way to the mines, and had severely tightened its control over the region and also, principally, collection of its part of the gold-mining tax.

We won't call the meetings that took place a conspiracy, because they weren't. They were merely conversations between friends who shared the criticisms that come only naturally under any government. But it's also best not to forget that these were the first people to settle the Captaincy of Minas Gerais and they had certainly, without knowing it, begun to plant the seed of independence that would later spread throughout the region, which by no coincidence was the stage for the War of the Emboabas, one of the first struggles in Brazil against Portuguese dominance.

Ana, privy to all the news and gossip in town, didn't take long to discover that José Garcia was an unfaithful husband. He had not one, but many women, slaves and free women, and many bastard children. Ana understood that this was just how things were in this region of riches and adventure, but she didn't like it one bit, and the jealousy nearly killed her. When she allowed her sense of humor some breathing room between bouts of despair at her husband's betrayal, she would ironically claim that it was the late Baltazar taking revenge from beyond the grave, and that she had been infected with his same fatal disease.

She tried everything she knew and everything she had been taught in an attempt to stop Garcia from ever looking at another woman. When they made love, she would utter the rite of the host into her husband's mouth, "*hoc est enim corpos meum*," to consecrate him the same way the priest consecrated the body of Christ during Mass, an incantation of sorts that others had guaranteed would be effective at deterring her husband from seeking another woman's body. She repeated the prayer of the Sorceress of Bahia, Antonia Nóbrega, whose fame had spread even to Minas with those who had come from Bahia: "José Garcia, I enchant you and enchant you again with the wood of the holy cross, and with the thirty-six philosopher angels, and with the enchanting Moor, that you might never leave my side, and that you might share with me all your knowledge and give me all that you have, and love me more than any other woman." She performed the wine spell, taking Garcia's semen from her own vagina after sex and mixing it secretly into her husband's wine, which he drank from a silver chalice he had ordered from Portugal, unlike the more common tin cups from which Garcia refused to drink.

Since none of this worked, Ana decided that she could at least put an end to her husband's extramarital fornicating inside their home, and sold all of the family's female slaves between the ages of ten and forty, leaving only a few old black women and male slaves for the housework. The flock of women who remained around her saw their joy greatly reduced. Ana was no longer so happy herself, and the old black women hardly shared the same cheerful mischievousness of the young girls who had surrounded her previously with their laughing, their mischief, and their jokes.

Ana had three children. A year after the birth of Gregorio Antonio, Clara Joaquina was born. Two years later came Bernarda Bárbara, who died at three months of age and was buried at the mother church, in the company of Sabará's finest. Her tiny casket was made of pure gold, and her little body was covered with jewels before being lowered into the grave. After that, Ana never became pregnant again.

From a young age, Clara Joaquina was a sickly and difficult girl. She cried often, demanded everything, and considered herself the center of the world. She would throw tantrums, quarrel with everyone, pinch the slaves, and she hated her older brother, her father's favorite. Gregorio Antonio, on the contrary, was an easygoing boy, but he sought to keep his distance from his sister. They were raised by different nursemaids and had separate circles of friends. Even so, Clara Joaquina never left her brother alone—she was always after him, pestering him, sowing rumors about him. She sought to pit him against their mother and father, she accused him of everything, scratched him with her nails and pulled his hair.

When Gregorio turned twelve, José Garcia sent him to study in Lisbon. He had relatives back in the kingdom, of pure Old Christian stock, as Inácia Benta used to say, who would look after the boy.

Ana appeared to have inherited the same perplexity in the face of the expectations placed on her as a mother as experienced by her own mother, Guilhermina. Both Clara Joaquina and Gregorio Antonio owed their upbringing more to slave women than to their parents. There was an unbridgeable distance between Ana and her children, a mutual ignorance, a void filled with a lack of intimacy, a space of dread and hesitation, and, for this very reason, perhaps, a degree of indifference.

Ana knew what kind of person her daughter was, but she never understood what to do about it. She saw her daughter's troublemaking and the tiny cruelties visited upon the slave women, the poor people of the town, animals. She saw through the innocent act Clara Joaquina put on before her father, to her selfishness and her intrigues. Yes, Ana knew all about that. She just didn't know what more she could do other than to go around undoing her daughter's harm.

If Clara Joaquina struck a slave, Ana sought some way to compensate for this mistreatment. She once convinced José Garcia to free two slave women, a mother and daughter whom Clara treated with particular cruelty, to the point of leaving whip-scars on the girl's face.

If Clara told her father that Dona Gertrudes's son, who also studied in Portugal, had written his mother a letter in which he said Gregorio Antonio spent his life drinking in the taverns of Coimbra night after night, Ana advised José Garcia to consider his daughter's words untrue, because they were—this bit of news did not, in fact, concern José Garcia's son, but rather Dona Gertrudes's own nephew.

If Clara told some well-respected woman in Sabará that her husband went to visit his lovers in his travels to Vila Rica, well, Ana didn't so much as try, because she knew that there was no way to undo that kind of harm.

When her daughter married Diogo Ambrósio, a wealthy cattle dealer from Rio de Janeiro, Ana thought it might perhaps straighten Clara out. The marriage of eighteen-year-old Clara Joaquina was arranged between her father and her future husband. Much older than his bride, Diogo Ambrósio was however welcomed by her because she sought with their marriage to increase her wealth and prestige, and to achieve her dream of moving to the most important city in the entire colony.

Less than a year after her daughter married and years before her son would return after graduating law school at the University of Coimbra, Ana de Pádua disappeared. Her disappearance was much discussed by everyone for quite some time. But it was, in fact, a quite simple story.

Ever since she had discovered Garcia's infidelity, Ana focused practically her entire life and thoughts on her husband's fornicating. It was, in a sense, a sort of occupation at which she spent her days: as soon as she learned of a new affair, she immediately set out to meet her rival, tell her off, and clarify a few things about what the other woman could expect from Ana in the future.

It was as though she believed that a healthy dose of the truth could remove any danger. Many times it did: the fear she instilled in her rivals, generally young women, with her combination of insults, threats, and a brief description of what, going forward, life would be like as lover to the husband of the powerful Ana de Pádua, could curb the seduction of Garcia whose charm, let's be frank, was already in visible decline and whose wealth was not and never had been an exception in those parts.

On one of her betrayal raids, accompanied by two slave women and a trusted male slave, Ana mounted an ambush at a ravine where she knew her infamous new rival could often be found strolling. There, lying in wait, she began to think about her life. She thought about her father, whom she had never again sought out and of whom she only received news from travelers who told of how Pouso da Capela was growing and how old Bento, with his gentle manner, had become a patriarchal figure respected by all. Her father had sent some of his statues of saints, making her cry because of their beauty, but also because they so closely resembled her mother.

She thought about her faraway son, a stranger to her life, living in a city overseas and doing things she couldn't even begin to imagine. She thought about her daughter, whom she also hardly knew despite living side by side for many years, with her troublemaker's personality, her propensity to inflict suffering.

Finally, she thought of the way her life's river had become a river of troubled waters that did nothing but constantly carry everyone around her far away, as it was also doing with her husband, and how it had transformed her days into a sequence of the same trivial things that seemed to lack meaning, lack substance, lack purpose.

She thought of God, who was also something distant, whose significance she also struggled to understand.

The news that before had been so enticing to her, the unfolding of even the most insignificant event, no longer brought her the least bit of pleasure, since she could no longer count on the merry mischief of the young black girls who used to surround her, but only the melancholy wisdom of the old black women. The stirring of her river's waters no longer captivated her as before, after she had been contaminated by the obsession to possess her husband for herself alone, of clutching onto him as though she could wrench out the answers to her anguish from inside him, as though this would return the meaning and beauty to the river of her life.

The storm struck suddenly and without warning. Lighting, thunder, raindrops that battered the ground as though they wished to pierce straight through whatever they crossed on their descent. Ana gave the order for the three slaves who had accompanied her to leave their hideout and return to town as fast as they could. Only she stayed behind, watching the river flow, hypnotized by the hard raindrops that landed quickly and violently in the demonic river-waters as though they were made of pure metal. So she was alone when she was struck head-on by a bolt of lighting, electrocuting her with a single, instantaneous blow.

She, along with her horse, died instantly. They tumbled down into the ravine and Ana's body, or what was left of it, was lost to the river.

Without a body, there was no funeral.

Garcia ordered the house covered in black sheets for a period of mourning that lasted seven weeks. He ordered five hundred Masses said for Ana at the Church of Nossa Senhora dos Martírios, which she had helped to build, and a hundred of these Masses were sung to the sound of the organ she loved so much. These were the most expensive Masses, and José Garcia paid the parish right then and there, with bars of the purest and finest gold.

CLARA JOAQUINA
(1711-1740)

A band of cattle men drew close to the city.

The celebratory ringing of the herd's lead cow could be heard from a distance, and the noisy approach of pack mules could be seen, surrounded by handsome horses at a regal gallop.

The men arrived in high spirits, knowing they would be received well.

At the front of the group came the "godmother," a brown mule with a distinguished look and a natural elegance, harnessed with style and trained to guide the animals that carried all kinds of goods. Following closely behind were several groups of horses, each with its own point man, each marching sprightly and at a careful distance from the others so that they would neither trip over one another nor disturb the order were something to happen along the way.

At the back of the procession rode the owner of the caravan, Diogo Ambrósio, mounted upon a splendid black horse trimmed up with a shiny silver harness. Imposing atop his steed, a red wool cape tossed over his shoulders, his hat dangling gracefully against his back, his high boots of white leather and silver-handled dagger in his boot-leg, he was a man fully aware of his importance. His farmhands and cattle-handlers marched at his side, all of them with the haughty air of men who considered themselves braver and more masculine simply because they held the mysteries of the backlands and because they knew the well-being of the people across several towns depended on them.

As they entered the city and passed through the square, Diogo Ambrósio nodded his head in greeting to Clara Joaquina, who was leaning out the window of the family's two-story home.

That first time he entered the town by that street, he had also nodded toward another window on the opposite side—that belonging to Idalina, daughter to Dona Gertrudes. But he only ever looked to that window once. That very same day, Clara Joaquina made sure a message made it to Diogo informing him that Idalina was already promised to a student at Coimbra, and that the only young woman in town who was worthy, skilled in the home, and available was the daughter of José Garcia, owner of several mines and farms, the pretty girl who lived in the large house on the corner of the square.

The wealthy cattleman understood perfectly. Only the disillusioned and humiliated Idalina never understood why Diogo Ambrósio didn't nod to her window as he left the city, but toward that of her neighbor, the unbearable Clara Joaquina.

On his next visit, Diogo brought Clara Joaquina gifts from Rio de Janeiro: a pair of topaz earrings, a church dress of black velvet with blue taffeta sleeves, a mantilla of Spanish silk, and flat-heeled shoes from Valencia adorned with silver buckles, highly valued for their cork soles. And then he made the necessary arrangements with José Garcia.

On his third trip, he brought a beautiful white camel-hair wedding dress, decorated with the Portuguese lace.

Their wedding was a simple affair and took place as demanded by the groom's life on the road, but there was a Mass sung and the union was celebrated with great pomp and much incense per the bride's demands, followed by a banquet served at the estate of José Garcia and Ana de Pádua.

DIOGO AMBRÓSIO

The fame of the wealthy cattleman from Rio de Janeiro, who insisted on rubbing elbows with his men, had spread throughout the mining region.

Born to a family of near-nobility that had been granted a land allotment by the Portuguese Crown, Diogo's father was intendant to the governor of the Captaincy of Rio de Janeiro who, sometime around 1600, had the rather creative idea of constructing purely out of Brazilwood what was to be the world's largest ship. This governor, whose name was Salvador de Sá, was an enthusiast of the new land's riches, and intended to prove with this ship-building endeavor the excellent quality of the tropical woods and the colony's extraordinary potential. Diogo's father was the young man charged with supervising the selection and felling of the trees and the transport of the lumber to the shipyard built on Ilha do Governador. It was there where, during nearly four years of work, Indian carpenters supervised by specialists from Europe prepared the giant galleon, christened with great jubilation and pride the *Eternal Father*. It was a highly successful endeavor, and when the galleon pulled into the port of Lisbon it was cause for wide-eyed admiration for its light-weight construction that much improved its maneuverability, and for its durability and ability to carry large loads.

Upon the success of the ship, those who contributed were generously rewarded by the governor. Diogo's father was given a land allotment near Rio de Janeiro, close to the city of Campos. There, his children grew up amid a sugarcane plantation, a chicken farm, and more than three hundred domesticated Indian slaves, purchased with the inheritance belonging to his wife, a daughter to Spanish nobility. Diogo, the fourth child in a family of nine, was fascinated from a young age with the great distances that stretched across the backlands, and saw the sale of goods to the fabulously rich mining region as a way to establish his independence from his brothers and create his own wealth.

His ambition was to be wealthier and more important than his father. He made a point of overseeing everything himself, and a life spent in the backlands and on journeys with his mules and a few trusted men was the kind that best suited his adventurous and enterprising temperament. What's more, he highly valued the prestige he enjoyed as a wealthy cattleman.

Diogo Ambrósio sold every type of commodity he carried at a hefty price, and he was an important buyer of products from the tiny localities along the way that, little by little, he slowly organized to suit his own vision and necessities. The way he saw it, if a farmer in Pouso Alto grew cassava and produced all the flour Diogo needed, another in Mato Aberto, the next stop over, ought to provide him with corn, another with tobacco, and yet another in Carapinha, on the other side of the hill, with sugarcane candy. Diogo Ambrósio was also the supplier of medicines, letters, messages, and news from the outside world, duties conferring a certain importance that reinforced his condescending view of the people of the smaller villages and towns.

He considered his marriage to the young heir to rich mines yet another excellent deal, a deal that would add gold and more prestige to that which he already possessed.

He never even suspected the surprises that the capricious Clara Joaquina had in store for him, not by a long shot! And she, for her part, never imagined the series of disappointments she would face from the very outset of her married life.

The first disappointment was the trip across the backlands to the house where they would live. For the village girl, who knew only the celebratory aspect of the troops' arrival and whose travels had been few and far between, and those being little more than short jaunts to neighboring villages like Vila Rica and Congonhas, the rhythm of the mules and the horses began to bother her after just a few hours. Her body ached, her stomach contracted with hunger, and much to her distress, the troops encountered a disgusting throng of black flies that first afternoon. Swarms of whizzing insects suddenly burst into the middle of the troops, circling the heads of the horses, sending the animals into a wild, unbridled gallop through the fields as they tried to escape the biting and buzzing pests. Clara Joaquina would have been thrown by her skittish horse had Diogo Ambrósio not grabbed her by the waist, rescuing her from the animal's desperation. There began the first of a near-uninterrupted series of fits of yelling, crying, and complaining.

There were attacks of nerves when burrs stuck to her skirts and socks, and she screamed without restraint each time they passed through the tall sedges that sliced her skin like broken glass. She feared crossing swollen rivers and hated the frequent mud sloughs where animals got stuck up to their bellies, their distressing whinnies heard leagues away.

Given her girlish inexperience, her dresses and shoes suited for city life, and her complete inability to find beauty in nature, Clara Joaquina's life soon became a living hell.

At night, Diogo would set up his young wife's hammock in a clearing he'd ordered his men to open as best they could, using extreme care to hang the burlap mosquito net so that it safely covered the hammock all the way to the ground, sealing it off like a tent. All the same, Clara Joaquina couldn't sleep with the constant attacks from mosquitos, the caterpillars creeping across the ground, the spiders descending like acrobats through the air. Before going to bed, a female house slave who had accompanied her as part of her dowry would rub her down in tobacco juice to remove the ticks that anxiously stuck to her tender, sweet, and soft young skin. After lying down, she would order the girl to stay close, practically forcing her to sleep standing up next to her hammock to scare away any critters. She would wake up time and again throughout the night and her screams, in turn, would wake the entire camp.

She would scream at night because she felt the sticky crawl of a caterpillar along her arm or because she saw bats clasping onto the slave's skin; she would scream in the morning when she found her shoes infested with giant ants. She screamed in the afternoon each time she saw a gigantic anaconda basking in the sun at the edge of a tiny island in the middle of a river they would have to cross. Or when she felt the acute, intolerable pain of a wasp bite after the insects were attracted by the scent of her fear. She would panic every time it stormed, leaving her soaked and trembling with cold. Her husband would order her slave servant to rub the bites with sugarcane liquor and salt, and prepare hot lemon juice to keep her from growing weak.

At first, Diogo Ambrósio tried to be patient, explaining to Clara Joaquina what life was like in the backlands and how he wouldn't expose her to any real danger, but Clara Joaquina seemed to harbor an irrational dread of the jungle.

Diogo became even more diligent in his attempts to establish little habits that gave structure to this sort of life, as he and his men often did. As though familiarity through repetition could bring a bit of predictability to the unknown and create the monotony necessary to provide stability from day to day, balancing out the frequent surprises they'd encounter. There was a time to march and a time to rest; they observed some basic mealtime rituals; they made sure to create the necessary conditions for a good night's rest.

When they arrived in familiar resting places, whether at some friend's farm or a ranch where they'd planted crops for their return, Diogo Ambrósio tried to improve his wife's mood by organizing rustic banquets from the harvest: young cassava, sweet corn, beans, hearts of palm. He had his men roast meat from the hunt—monkey meat prepared several different ways, paca meat, deer meat, partridge. He offered her ripe bananas, juicy oranges, watermelon sweet as sugar. Desserts with sugarcane syrup and boiled cassava that melted in their mouths.

Diogo did what he could, but he grew increasingly irritated with the woman he'd taken as his wife, whom he accused of being "softer than cornmeal mush."

Clara Joaquina's second major disappointment was the village where they settled down. One of the reasons, or, better yet, the true reason she had wanted to marry the cattle dealer was her belief that, since he was from Rio de Janeiro, her fate as a married woman would be to live in the famous town that floated through the heads of young girls from the rural mining villages. But no, the house in Rio that belonged to Diogo Ambrósio's family, where they went above all for religious holidays, had been practically abandoned since the invasion of French pirates who, in 1710 and 1711, had pillaged the city. On the very day the pirates began their invasion, Diogo's aging mother had gone to the baptism of a friend's grandson. But terrorized by what she saw and by the escape she'd had to make with her two daughters at her side, she swore she would dress in black for the rest of her life and never again return to the ravaged city.

Her son Diogo, for his part, raised on the farm, had nothing urbane about him, and he didn't particularly like the city; the house where he intended to live with his young wife sat on his portion of his father's allotment, seven leagues from the tiny town of São José do Matosinho. On top of this, it was much simpler than José Garcia's house in Sabará; a man who spent most of his time traveling, Diogo had little concern for creature comforts.

And now we've arrived at the third and most crucial of Clara Joaquina's disappointments: her disappointment with her own husband, whose imposing figure and elegance when mounted on his handsome steed disappeared the very same moment his feet touched the ground. When mounting his wife, he no longer had a trace of this horsebound elegance and gallantry. Whenever the mood struck, he would pull Clara Joaquina any which way, pushing her up against the wall, lifting her skirt only as high as was necessary and, without the least interest in seeing an inch of her naked body, penetrated her, panting, panting, and then that was it. Everything ended suddenly, and without so much as looking at her, he would pull up his pants, fix his shirt, and leave the bedroom, leaving her where she stood, her skirt only barely wrinkled.

Now what? Clara Joaquina asked herself after the first time. *Is that it?*

Poor Clara Joaquina!

Poor Diogo Ambrósio!

Diogo had realized that his marriage was a mistake during that first fateful journey when, after his wife's continued screaming, he came to the conclusion that he couldn't stand her. He even thought about returning her to her family, but decided against it when he remembered the mines he would inherit. Anyway, he had married her for the gold and the children he intended to sire. Those were the reasons he needed a wife, and despite her irritating daintiness, she at least seemed to be healthy. He decided he would leave her at the house on the estate to give birth and raise their children. That was the life Miss Cornmeal Mush would lead, and that was that.

When Clara begged him to take her to Rio, he resolutely denied her requests without giving an explanation for his motives. In fact, he barely spoke to her. When she began to insist, he told her once and for all that she wasn't to try his patience with such things, he wasn't about to take her anywhere, because it was clear that she couldn't handle the trip, and even if she could, he couldn't handle another trip at her side.

Then he mounted his horse and rode off.

Clara Joaquina became a sort of prisoner, and her life a private hell on the deserted farm.

Diogo didn't bring her news of her family, either, thinking he'd avoid any further arguments or hassles. He didn't tell her about her mother's death until several years after the fact. When he told her how her brother had returned from Coimbra and was now taking over her father's businesses, he regretted it as soon as he saw the hate flare up in Clara's eyes.

Diogo would scarcely arrive from one trip before setting off again— when possible, the very next day. There were so many reasons that Clara Joaquina no longer knew for certain why she was filled with hatred each time she heard the sound of the troops gathering in the dark early morning hours and Diogo Ambrósio raising his gruff voice above the din of whinnying, horse hooves, and barking dogs, to offer up a prayer to clear the way before them as his folded hands traced a cross in the air:

"Saint Michael the Archangel, defend us in battle. Be our protection against the wickedness and snares of the devil. May God rebuke him, we humbly pray; and for Thou, O Prince of the Heavenly Host, by the Divine Power of God, to cast into hell Satan and all the evil spirits who roam throughout the world seeking the ruin of souls."

On such dark mornings, Clara Joaquina wished for her husband's death. She wished him death by a rattlesnake, or crushed to death by the giant anaconda she had seen that distant day on the tiny river island, his bones popping and piercing his skin. Or shot through with arrows by the Tapuia Indians and left to bleed out in the open air, his rotting corpse devoured by ants and caterpillars.

Every day, the whole day long, Clara Joaquina tried to imagine a way out. Her only contact with the world was through the slaves and Diogo Ambrósio's right-hand men. There were also the other residents of the tiny neighboring village and the few travelers who would pass through the farm and request lodging.

"I need to think," she would say to herself. "There must be a way out of this hellhole. I need to think of how to get back at Diogo and get out of this place."

She thought about asking some traveler to help her flee, but she knew no one would dare because everyone was certain armed men would pursue her.

She thought about asking them to carry a message to her father, who she wasn't even sure was still alive. Not to her brother, though, no, she'd never do that—she preferred to die. But, unlike her mother, she didn't know how to read or write correctly beyond signing her name. When her mother had sent her to study with Maestra Catarina, where she should have learned to sew, play piano, and to read, write, and count, she had instead preferred to sit at the window, observing the people passing through the streets. Or spend her time drawing pictures. She liked to draw women wearing fancy dresses and shoes covered in jewels.

She still drew every now and then, but her once harmonious figures began to morph into tiny black monsters, small and deformed figures she drew in charcoal because when he traveled, Diogo Ambrósio often forgot to bring her the pencils and paper he knew she liked because he didn't see any importance in it at all.

She stored her precious pencil stubs in her family's tiny mother-of-pearl jewelry box, given to her by her mother when she married—a jewelry box she found very ugly, very old, and not very interesting, but which for some inexplicable reason she did not throw out. Of all the things inside that Ana had told her belonged to her grandmother and great-grandmother, she only kept the jewelry. The old piece of red ribbon, the dried flower, all of this she tossed.

Unable to count on the support of the slaves, who were faithful to their master and felt no sympathy for her or the air of superiority—which she never lost—that led her to disdain everything and everyone around her, she had only the five slave women she had brought with her from Sabará. But even these women, though they performed their duty as expected, lacked any sense of dedication or love for her.

Clara Joaquina suffered from the most complete loneliness a person could feel—a cold, hard loneliness that was impenetrable from a place where no one felt any sort of affection for her.

The figures she began to draw became more and more horrendous, monsters who began to coil around one another, who hung from trees, hid behind trunks, all of whom had the face of Diogo Ambrósio.

It's difficult to pinpoint exactly when the couple's life became an invisible and silent war, a going around and around in the poisonous air filled with a more potent smell of rot greater even than that in the backlands.

In the case of Diogo, perhaps it had truly begun when it dawned on him that his wife was avoiding having children, the only reason he had to justify his marriage. This discovery had been more significant than catching on to his wife's ill-fated attempts to have him murdered.

He began to take her at whim, up against the walls time and time again on the days he spent at the farm. For him, this private war with Clara Joaquina soon became a substitute—perhaps the only one possible—for a marriage that had been hopelessly doomed from the beginning. In a certain way, he enjoyed guessing at his wife's next move, the traps she tried to set for him, her plans for the next attack, each little surprise.

In the case of Clara Joaquina, her hate for her husband became her sole and most precious activity. She tried poisoning him, but he refused to touch any food or drink she put before him; on the few nights he spent at home, he preferred to eat and sleep with the hired hands in the bunkhouse. She put venomous snakes and crab spiders in his clothes, and loosened the saddle of his handsome steed. But without the support from any of Diogo Ambrósio's men, nothing she tried would work.

Being pinned up against the wall grew increasingly painful, and as her tactics for avoiding pregnancy were dubious and hardly scientific, she ended up losing that battle, too. When she finally became pregnant, she felt too weak to opt for an abortion with nothing more than the aid of her female house slaves.

After the birth of their first child, Alencar, Diogo offered Clara Joaquina a truce, but she wouldn't hear it. She was obsessive and unrelenting in her intentions: she would get revenge and leave that place.

Between the months of May and August, there was a large open-air market in Sorocaba, a region of wide, green grazing fields where herds of mules and livestock marching north from Rio Grande do Sul on their way to Minas Gerais would stop to rest.

Cattlemen like Diogo Ambrósio would go to the fair to purchase animals and hire additional help. They also went there to unwind when the town saw itself overrun with every sort of people—horse doctors, horse trainers, men selling toys and trinkets, circus performers, gamblers. It was a time of celebration and card games, and the cattlemen made the most of it.

Many business deals were done there, too, and men spent fortunes at the cabarets, the casinos, and the circus shows. As far as Diogo Ambrósio was concerned, it was paradise.

That same year, however, there was an unexpected guest at the Sorocaba Fair: the smallpox. Diogo Ambrósio was one of the lucky ones chosen by the nasty illness. The only reason he survived was because he was a man whose body was prepared to fight off threats. After enduring the many bloodletting sessions supervised by a doctor from the South, he was able to return home for an extended rest like none he'd ever had before.

He didn't stay in the big house with Clara Joaquina, but out in the bunkhouse, under the care of the old slave woman who had been his own nursemaid.

One afternoon, a commotion broke out among the farmhands, followed by an uproar and yelling that ended in graveyard silence when Diogo Ambrósio rose from his cot to whip one of the hired hands, running him off and telling him to never return to the farm.

In the he-said-he-said that followed, Clara learned, to her unimaginable surprise, that the situation was a result of the man being caught looking through the window into her room. Surprised by her husband's wounded sense of honor, Clara had finally found the weak spot where she could bury her knife.

She could barely contain her excitement at this discovery; the eruption and scale of her enthusiasm grew and grew, rising through her chest and up through her skull until it escaped. It kept her from sitting still, she had an irresistible need to move about, to rub her hands, to walk back and forth to the window, open it, close it, open it and close it, until the euphoria no longer choked her or overflowed now that it had greedily saturated the hollowness of her pathetic existence.

"It will be easy! Oh, how easy it will be. Now you'll see!"

Each day acquired an unfamiliar excitement as she dedicated herself to preparing the much-sought revenge that was finally within reach.

Of course, it was out of the question to seek out a slave to take her against the wall. It would have to be a traveler or, better and perhaps easier yet, one of the farmhands. If the first man who had been whipped and sent packing had tried something without her having suspected a thing, without her even knowing who he was, there must have been others with the same daring and desire.

It doesn't matter whether Clara Joaquina was beautiful or not, if she was eye-catching or not, if she was anything at all or not. What's important here is that she was a woman among so many lonely men. A woman who wasn't a slave, or an Indian, or the daughter of an Indian with a white man, or a black woman—but a woman with light-colored, clear skin, a woman who wore a gown with a full skirt and fancy shoes. For these things, strange as it may seem, Diogo Ambrósio made sure she never lacked: dresses from the cities, shawls from Portugal, shoes from Valencia. Much could be said of him, but Diogo could not be accused of not seeing that the mother of his children dressed well.

Yes, children plural, because after the truce following Alencar's birth, Diogo Ambrósio had returned to waging his phallic crusade against the contraceptive methods of the time, and their daughter Jacira Antônia was born; a girl with curious, dark eyes that shined and looked all around in an attempt to make sense of the world. In the same way Alencar resembled his father physically, the girl resembled her mother, except for her deep, dark eyes and a dark triangle near the base of her neck whose peak inclined ever so slightly to the left.

Like Alencar, Jacira was raised by the slave women, though much closer to her father, who worshiped his daughter. If Clara Joaquina resented her son for his physical resemblance to his father, she also resented Jacira for her emotional connection to her father. Unlike their mother and her brother, however, Alencar and Jacira adored each other, especially Alencar who, as the eldest, considered himself his sister's natural protector.

Clara Joaquina, the taste of revenge on her tongue, methodically laid her trap. She began to pay attention to her husband's farmhands, men who, to her eyes, were disgusting and dirty like beasts. But she would have to choose one of them and, who knows, if she looked closely, perhaps she could look past the layer of clay, mud and other crude materials that seemed to stick to them like a second skin, a skin hardened during the days and nights, suns and moons, rains and putrid odors characteristic of the pestilent backlands. Or if she wasn't able to see or feel a thing, to at least evade the hot breath on her face coming from the rotton depths of these men who were the very models of ugliness.

But could it really be worse when she was with that miserable wretch Diogo Ambrósio? This time at least, she wouldn't feel the bitter taste of hate, merely the sickening nausea and euphoria of revenge. And so, she saw no reason to take her time choosing. It could be any one of them, it didn't matter who. Anyone. Except for those Diogo trusted most, the most servile, those who she knew would die for their boss.

Except for these men, anyone would do. Anyone at all.

And it ended up being one of the new men, hired at the Sorocaba Fair, who was dying of boredom, waiting for Diogo to recover so they could once again take to the road.

It was all too easy. Except that it didn't happen against a wall, for there were no walls in the patch of forest they ran off to, and the methods of the man from Sorocaba were less vexing than those of her husband. A bit more gentle and a tad more attentive, though Clara Joaquina didn't linger on these differences.

She only wanted to get over with it. To get over with it all.

It was perhaps because she was so thrilled at discovering how to wound her husband that she made such a terrible mistake afterward, thinking that everything would end with her husband's tragic embarrassment. Or perhaps that she simply forgot to think things through. Or perhaps she thought that once again someone would simply be run off or even killed, but only the hired hand in question, and that her husband's honor would be washed clean with the blood of the offender and not that of the woman who brought shame upon him.

Poor Clara Joaquina.

Only her girlish inexperience—though at twenty-nine she was no longer a girl—or her lack of life experience due to all those years spent isolated and alone, could explain how she couldn't see that this story could only end when she, more than anyone else, paid for her husband's wounded honor.

When Diogo Ambrósio drove his knife into her chest, after he had done the same to her lover, she was surprised, it's true—but after the disconcerting realization that her blood was soaking her blue taffeta dress, somewhere deep down, she truly didn't care. She felt victorious as she had never felt before. She had achieved what she wanted, and this was, honestly honest, completely honestly, all she cared about.

In an absurd finishing touch, during this final moment of her pleasure, when she saw her daughter's tiny face appear at the bedroom door with its curious little eyes, Clara Joaquina had a few final words for her husband as the dark blood spewed forth, in a flicker of extreme cruelty and without so much as thinking or caring that what she was about to say might be the noose around her own daughter's neck:

"Have you ever thought why your girl looks nothing like you? I'll tell you. She's a bastard. She's not yours."

Then she died with an icy smile on her lips, with the conviction that, yes, in that final moment, her magnificent revenge was complete.

Diogo Ambrósio's initial reaction was to also get rid of the little girl right then and there. But the deep love he felt for her, perhaps, or perhaps because he thought too much blood had been spilled for a single man's honor, or because he realized the cowardice and stupidity of such a gesture—whatever it was made him drop his knife and he instead punched the wall repeatedly in blind rage, that same poor wall against which he had made such an effort to conceive his children.

When he was himself again, he snatched the girl, and, nearly out of control, mounted his horse like a blind man. Still wild with rage, he placed her on the back of his saddle and broke into a full gallop, not to the closest village but to another, several leagues away and far from the roads he often traveled.

He took her to a village where a corporal named Jesuíno lived, a poor fellow who owed money for some goods Diogo had sold him.

Arriving in the middle of night at the mud hut he had visited before, he jerked the sleepy girl to the door.

In a dry, steady voice, he told the bewildered corporal, who had come out when he heard the approaching sound of horse hooves, that from then on he was to forget his debts and forget, too, that it was he, Diogo Ambrósio, who had left the young girl there.

Without further explanation, he turned his back and set off once again.

JACIRA ANTÔNIA
(1737-1812)
&
MARIA BÁRBARA
(1773-1790)

Poor and feeble, Corporal Jesuíno's only stroke of luck was the day he killed a rattlesnake that had nested in his commander's kepi, saving the man from certain death. In return Jesuíno had received a runaway slave girl whose owner had resolved to sell her at all costs after breaking her pelvis and rendering her practically useless.

Not that killing a venomous snake deserved a second thought in that era. In everyone else's eyes, the corporal had only been doing his duty, and the fact that he killed a rattlesnake—a common occurrence, after all, since there were more snakes than anything else in that village, which itself was nothing more than a clearing in the middle of the woods at the end of the world—wouldn't have caught anyone's attention were it not for the commander's dream the night before. In the dream, a rattlesnake slithered through one ear and, before crawling out the other, rattled around every last corner of his terrified brain, which was swollen like a big old ball. When he woke up in agony from his dream with his head pulsing with pain, the commander woke his wife, well-versed in prophecies and witchcraft, who without batting an eye ordered him to do two things early that morning: the first was to slather his scalp with a special concoction she had immediately begun to prepare that morning with ingredients from her personal pharmacopeia; the second was to find a way to perform two good deeds in one, in the name of Saint Benedict. They couldn't be two separate good deeds. They had to occur simultaneously.

Late that morning, at the small border post around which the tiny village had sprung up, the commander, driven insane by the tortuous pain attacking his brain and by his inability to hit upon a way to fulfill his double mission, decided to go out for some fresh air. That's when it happened: the commander reached for the kepi, the rattler readied its attack, and by some miracle the poor *cabo*—who was generally oblivious to what went on around him—looked and saw, and still more miraculously grabbed his blunderbuss and pulled the trigger. Not only did he pull the trigger, but he shot the snake right in the head. A truly inexplicable and authentic miracle. The comandante's hand remained suspended in mid-air, paralyzed.

It was at that moment, too, that the owner of the crippled runaway slave girl showed up, offering her for a pittance to whoever wanted to do him the favor of taking the useless creature, or else he would have to beat her to death as she deserved.

At that moment, the commander saw a clear signal from the heavens to perform his double-good deed, one for the corporal who had so spectacularly saved his life, and the other for the slave owner, from whose shoulder he was lifting a burden. What's more, he secured the man's goodwill should he need his help one day. So he paid a pittance for the black slave woman and gave her as a present to the corporal.

Then, feeling quite satisfied with himself and considering his day won, he headed home to finally rest now that the swelling in his head had begun to recede, leaving the startled corporal the owner of a black girl who could barely walk.

Seeing no other alternative, the new slave owner took the hobbling woman to his hut and there, walking with the crutch he made for her out of some wood from a mango tree, she lived long enough to bear him five children and serve as an adoptive mother to Jacira Antônia.

Ever since Jacira had arrived on the back of her father's horse on that morning lost to time, she had always been a serious girl who rarely smiled. The world, as she saw it, ought to be confronted with seriousness, if not distrust, and that is what she did with her big dark eyes.

At the edge of her parents' bedroom door, on that fateful day, she had been spared from seeing the bloody wounds on her mother's body. From where she stood, she saw only her father's back. But she no doubt noticed that something very wrong was happening there, and when her father pulled her up violently and hoisted her up onto his horse—her father, who had always looked upon her with affection and treated her so kindly—she felt that whatever this *thing* was that was wrong, was also wrong with her.

She never figured out what had happened or what to think of it all. Meanwhile, the trust the girl of three had placed in her father caused her, unconsciously and without even understanding why, to accept her new life in some way. In the beginning, she was certain her father would arrive at any moment and once again set her upon his horse and gallop away. As time passed, she made a conscious effort to abandon this hope, but in the depths of her soul and until the day she died, that hope was to continue, a tiny flame that burned with the same unbearable desire to hear the hooves of a galloping horse, returned to take her back home.

At fourteen, Jacira was spindly and boasted few attractive features. Yet when one Captain Dagoberto made the settlement his last stop before setting off on an expedition into the country to find lands that

would bring him wealth and importance, it was the corporal's adopted
daughter whom he thought to take with him to start a family. It's
true that the captain's options were limited, but it's also true that he
could have soldiered on alone. But again, don't romanticize a simple
calculation made by a pragmatic man. What he saw in Jacira—and
he was right to see in her—was an inner strength, an energy that was
not easy to find in others. The girl had a confident stride, a reflective
gaze in her big dark eyes, a sure sign of intelligence and learning,
and she was always busy: sweeping the house and the porch, fetching
water from the river, stirring the coals in the oven, washing clothes in
a stream, feeding the chickens and the pig, shucking corn, preparing
food—food that was simple but abundant, thanks to the initiative of
that very same girl, who had substituted her crippled mother in practically everything. Dagoberto sensed she would be a good acquisition
for his ends and went to communicate his decision to the corporal,
who evidently responded positively, as expected, and simply said: "I'm
very honored, dear captain."

As for Jacira, marrying the captain or any other man was all the
same, since at that time and place these things were considered com-
monplace, as they had been in her mother's and her grandmother's
time, much as one accepts a rainy or a sunny day, or the arrival of
night or day. But setting off on an expedition—that indeed was an
unexpected bit of news and it left her slightly agitated and feeling
something she had ever felt before—an inner restlessness that she
couldn't put her finger on and which, for the first time in a long time,
kept her body from sleep that night, her eyes wide open in the dark
of her corner of her family's hut. It wasn't a bad feeling, on the contrary. It was good to feel the subtle itch of curiosity, that unfamiliar
agitation breaking into a slight smile that she found silly, but which
stubbornly loomed on her lips, expectation opening tiny wings inside
her chest.

CAPTAIN DAGOBERTO

Dagoberto da Mata had come from the far away Captaincy of Ceará in the Northeast, where his father had settled along the Rio São Francisco, becoming a rich cattle rancher. The fifth child from a large family, Dagoberto decided to strike out on his own and left for Rio de Janeiro, where he thought of enlisting to tame the backlands in service of the king. His passion for gambling, however, led him to give up on a military career, taking nothing with him but the nickname "Captain."

He was a just man, clear-headed, magnanimous, with an impressive ability to read people's faces to decipher their character and emotions, a talent that was evidently at the root of his formidable skill in gambling and which also brought him to choose Jacira as his wife.

Despite his love for gambling, it was not his only or his greatest passion: the young man from Ceará had always aspired to conquer new lands. The exploration and conquest of the unknown territories were his sirens' songs. In the beginning he had thought to do this exploring in the name of the king, but during the conversations he had over the months of travel between Ceará and Rio, he became convinced that he could do everything he wanted for himself.

His gambling in Rio served to multiply the banknotes his father had given him as an advance on his inheritance and to build the necessary capital to buy slaves, animals, arms, and supplies. Preparations lasted nearly a year, and only came to an end in the village where he was making his final arrangements—where he met Jacira, and asked Corporal Jesuíno for her hand.

On the exact day he turned twenty-five, Captain Dagoberto da Mata set out to conquer his dream of venturing into the rugged backlands to put down roots.

That same day, in the chill of a foggy morning, Jacira left with her husband the Captain, each of them on their own horse, accompanied by twenty mules carrying provisions, supplies, and munitions, four mulatto foremen, and thirty slaves (twenty-five men, five women, all of them black). They were heavily armed, and full of enthusiasm as they headed toward the Captaincy of Goiás, a place that was still little-explored, and where it was said there was much gold and plenty of good land.

After more than eight months of traveling, they came to a field near a river with lead-colored waters, lush trees, and fertile soils of humus. They had arrived in the deep backlands of Goiás; an imposing jatoba tree lifted its branches skyward in its stubborn desire to touch the bright blue cloudlessness. They had been camping in that spot for a few days when the Captain told her that it would be the spot where they would build their house and sow their crops. Whether there was gold close was anyone's guess, but the soil was good for farming, and that was the Captain's priority. There weren't any Indians for miles and the local tribe wasn't violent, and didn't seem to pose a threat. The Captain and Jacira would settle down here. The next day they would begin to clear a plot for the house and the crops.

Jacira was filled with peace as she listened to the news. She had also liked that spot. A short distance from there, the river broke off into a separate branch until it reached a pool of water that, it seemed to her, would be very useful. The land was indeed good and their crops were sure to grow. She would plant rice, beans, cassava, and corn. Lots of corn. Dagoberto had been advised by Paulistas he'd come across in his travels to bring corn, whose kernels were easier to carry on long journeys than cassava cuttings. They would raise cattle. Jacira knew the Captain also had plans to grow sugarcane. They would irrigate the land with water from the nearby river. They would build a gristmill. There she would have their children; her belly had already begun to show signs of the first. Yes, that would be her land, her home. She was at peace.

The time passed quickly, and within four years the house, with its five bedrooms and a beaten-earth floor, was at the center of a small plantation. The sugarcane was profitable. The gold the slaves had found in nearby riverbeds—it wasn't much, but it also wasn't a pittance—was dried in cow leather and stored in tiny leather bags that Jacira had sewn, which the Captain stored in a location known only to the two of them.

Jacira had become her husband's right hand. He respected her and treated her with great consideration, admiring her tirelessness and the authority she wielded calmly but without hesitation. On cold country nights, they would sit around the copper pot where the Captain leisurely tossed corncobs that slowly transformed into burning embers, consumed in the fierce and corrosive red flames. It was at such hours that the Captain would tell her of his plans in slow, thoughtful sentences and wait for her opinion, which, without his fully realizing it, he had come to consider essential. Her eyes fixed on the embers, where it seemed she saw beyond the crimson incandescence, Jacira would deliberate as long as she needed. She would only offer her opinion when she thought she had something important to add, otherwise she merely assented: "Good thinking, my Captain."

When the Indians, who until then had been friendly, began to adopt more hostile attitudes, neither of them considered it grave. Since they had first settled there, the natives had been a constant presence, sometimes looking at them from a distance for days on end, sometimes disappearing for months at a time, other times one or two would sneak up close to nab a piece of clothing from the line, a round of ammunition or something of the kind, either out of curiosity or for fun, Jacira imagined, since they always did this in broad daylight, darting joyfully about, drawing attention to themselves.

Nearly all the other farmers who had recently established themselves in the area around the same time or a little after Jacira and the Captain were violent with the Indians, trying to drive them far from lands the farmers now considered theirs. The Captain was one of the few who had given orders to his slaves and hired hands to leave the tribe alone. Not because he was especially virtuous, for, like everyone else, he too thought there was little difference between an Indian and any other beast, but rather as a question of style; the Captain was more accustomed to dominance through the force of one's character than with violence and disorder. As for Jacira, she also thought it only natural that Indians were considered more closely related to beasts than to people. Her generation of Brazilians, after fewer than two centuries had passed, had forgotten entirely who their ancestors were. Besides not being considered fellow human beings, the Indians incited fear and—worse yet—disdain. Were you to tell Jacira that she had Indian blood running in her veins, were you to tell her about Inaiá, Tebereté, and Sahy, her deep dark eyes would light up in shock.

At that time, everyone thought that was the ways things were: the white man in command, the slaves doing the work, the Indians and animals in the forest. Jacira never thought to question this as she sat around the burning embers on chilly nights. It wasn't worth thinking about. But just as she didn't mistreat animals, she also thought it wrong to mistreat the savages. Besides, much was said about their vengeful spirit, and this, yes, was often the topic of conversation when sitting around their copper pot: tales of revenge, cruelty, and savagery that served as warnings against the foolishness of provoking them.

The danger gradually became noticeable. First, the episodes even seemed like nothing more than horsing around, the deeds of snot-nosed little kids. In the middle of the night, they would wake up to the panicked whinnies of the horses or the terrified grunting of the pigs, who had been tied in groups of two by their tails and chased around by the Indians. Or it was the large mortar found full of manure the next morning, the irrigation ditch gone dry, the river's course altered upriver, the gristmill jammed, small animals missing.

Soon men brought news to Captain Dagoberto that the farm of Senhor Jahudehir had been attacked, some fifteen leagues away. His head and that of his wife, two foreman, and five black slaves had been mounted on the pointed fence-tops protecting the fields. When her husband returned home that night, Jacira was mute as she listened to the news.

Jahudehir had never been easy to get along with. He was well known for the violence he inflicted on the Indians, the way he burned their villages and their crops in his zeal to chase them to the ends of the earth. The local tribes, which weren't violent, saw themselves forced to respond to the attacks of Jahudehir and his men, but this business of attacking a farm and killing families was something new entirely. In addition, the latest news they'd had of their avaricious neighbor was that he had emptied rat poison into the natural well where the Indians got their drinking water.

Captain Dagoberto announced that, early the next morning, he would set out with five men to gather more information with the other neighbors and stock up on ammunition. Jacira was to be careful and keep the slaves close to home. No one was to wander far and they ought to always walk in pairs, guns in hand, even if it was just to retrieve water from the well or the nearby channel.

He would return as soon as possible.

Morning greeted them with a tense and threatening silence. There was an unfamiliar and palpable weight in the air, a warm mass condensing around a nucleus of cruelty and danger that hovered heavily, quietly above them. The animals, also much quieter than usual, stood at attention, their senses sharp and alert.

Jacira ordered a group of slaves to reinforce the doors and windows with wooden crossbars. She sent another group to make sure the animals stayed close together. A third group she sent to bring back every stick, rock, and whatever else might be employed as a weapon. The black women were to continue their work in the kitchen.

It was early afternoon when the group in charge of protecting the animals came to sound the alarm. They had seen Indians armed with arrows stirring in the bamboo trees. Jacira ordered them to immediately sound the bell warning everyone to come inside the house. Within minutes, the slaves came running from every corner of the yard and arrows skidded onto the veranda, as though the two movements were part of some strange choreography. The doors and windows were quickly bolted. Jacira gave the order for them to fire from the two rifle holes in the front and back doors, warning them to aim carefully because they couldn't afford to waste the little ammunition they had.

She was certain of one thing: the Indians lacked numbers. She knew that there were more women and children to be found in their villages than men. There was no doubt the women would not be on the front lines. Sitting there locked inside her house, Jacira couldn't be sure of how many were outside. But judging by the howling and the quick glance she took before closing the last window just before the tribe attacked, she was certain they were no more than two-dozen men. At her side, meanwhile, were twenty male slaves and five women who were also capable of mounting a defense. She would send some of them to stay with the children in the large, windowless middle bedroom, and the rest would stay to help as necessary. The Captain would be back soon, she only needed to hold out until he arrived with more men and more weapons.

The savages' strident howling, the sound of their clubs beating against the doors and windows, the desperate panic in the slaves' eyes were only interrupted by the gunshots coming from the holes in the doors, shots that, in reality, had not been much more effective other than to frighten the Indians. As the attackers had already reached the building, they were outside the line of fire except for when they passed directly in front of the holes in the doors where the bullets escaped.

Jacira's composure was admirable, but she knew they would not last long that way. That's when her eyes fell over the stove; a simple idea came to her when she saw the large copper pan forgotten in the hearth.

"Light a fire to boil the animal fat," she immediately ordered her two quickest slave women, and within minutes the crackling flames were spitting forth scalding bubbles that began to burst from the pan like the fiery mouth of a tiny erupting volcano.

"Let's go," she said. "Fill the ladles carefully and throw them on the Indians through the openings in the doors and windows. And you two"—she turned to a pair of male slaves—"pay attention, and when you see they're close, open the wickets quickly and throw the pans right in their faces."

Immediately grabbing spoons and frying pans, the slave women began to pour out the boiling slime on any Indian who came near the gaps in the doors and windows, following Jacira's orders: "Get them in the eyes and hands. Don't waste time on other parts of the body."

The cries of pain and surprise multiplying outside filled the house with joy. They soon realized that the unorthodox tactic had rebuffed the Indians' attack until the Captain returned.

With her extraordinary composure and a triumphant smile on her lips, Jacira sat in her chair in the middle of the living room and savored her bizarre victory.

After that day, once she had felt enormous satisfaction at discovering her own strength, something inside Jacira changed. Something subtle, deep down, something that not even Captain Dagoberto, an astute reader of others, realized at first. Something that might have been translated as an almost natural passion for power and the conviction that to obtain it, she would find the right path, by stealth or by force.

Thanks to the energy of Dagoberto and Jacira, the plantation grew into a source of enormous prosperity. The number of slaves and cowhands, who were paid in money, products, or livestock, also grew, and day-to-day operations entailed a great hustle and bustle. The livestock soon stretched further into the backlands, and the fields of corn, sugarcane, and cotton also expanded—the land was endless and open, and Captain Dagoberto's property continued to spread through the uninhabited expanse. In his travels to Rio de Janeiro, he had managed to double the size of the allotment he had originally asked of the Crown. And there was barely any more talk of Indians.

Jacira oversaw the production of cassava and tapioca flour of an unrivaled whiteness, and of marmalades and guava pastes prepared with enormous quantities of fruit and sugar, which the slave women stirred without rest and for hours at the stove, in large copper pans that were black as coal on the outside and shiny like gold on the inside. At the foot of the giant clay ovens in the covered sheds behind the house, more black women stirred the mixture until it began to thicken and slowly erupt in viscous and noisy, plopping bubbles. Packaged in tiny wooden boxes before they could cool, they soon made their way to fill customer orders in Rio de Janeiro and Bahia. The sweets produced at the Jatoba Plantation had become famous.

Jacira also ordered a shed constructed for housing looms and increased the quantity of cotton planted, sending the slaves to spin the cotton into thread and stitch white clothing for everyone on the plantation.

When the storehouse became full, Dagoberto would send one of his foremen out with a barren of mules to the stores of Rio de Janeiro.

Over time, the couple also began expanding and repairing the old mud house with its beaten-earth floors, whose furniture consisted of the hammocks, boxes, and trunks they'd brought with them, and a single long table and two matching wood benches they'd made soon after they had arrived.

Dagoberto brought a bricklayer and a carpenter from the regional capital, Vila Boa de Goiás, and constructed a large house made with bricks and roof tiles, a house with many bedrooms and an enormous veranda, with ceilings more than twelve feet high to ensure the house stayed cool. They no longer had a beaten-earth floor but one of long wooden boards. Later, he sent for two beds with ornamental headboards from Rio de Janeiro, lace curtains for the living room, and a blue taffeta curtain with red and yellow tassels for the bedroom. He also bought silverware for special occasions.

Captain Dagoberto was a man of refined tastes and ideas that were ahead of his time.

In the trunk full of things they had brought with them, there were two packs of cards, a backgammon board, and silver chalice monogrammed with an interlacing D and M. In his first trip to Rio, Dagoberto brought Jacira a wrought-silver snuffbox and two silver cups with a new monogram, now with a J between the D and the M, a monogram that from that moment on Dagoberto would have printed on the leather trunks and everything else on the plantation. On other trips, he brought her a four-foot-long gold chain, an ivory cameo, a silver basin, and a blue-silk mantilla she never let out of her sight and which she took to the grave, wrapped around her head.

From the beginning, Jacira learned a great deal from her husband. Dagoberto introduced her to life's three great pleasures: the bedroom, the snuffbox, and the foot-bath. All of them had come as a surprise. He also taught her more useful things. Dagoberto passed on all of his knowledge, his ideas, his enterprises, and his aspirations to Jacira, both through his daily conduct on the plantation and the easy con-versations they had around the fire in the copper pot, a custom they maintained even in the new house. When night fell, a slave woman would bring the copper pot and a basket full of corncobs, which she placed at the side of Dagoberto's high-backed chair on the raised veranda built above the cellar. It was there they would sit and admire the sun setting across their lands, which stretched on and on, and lay out plans and dreams. Jacira would discreetly wonder at the whiteness of Dagoberto's feet beneath the clear water of the foot-bath.

Dagoberto also taught Jacira to read and write. This, however, hadn't been intentional. It hadn't occurred to him that this ability could be useful to his wife, but rather to his children, whom he made sure knew how to do both. Jacira was always close by during these lessons and easily learned to read and write as she looked on. When he discovered that his wife already knew how to read, Dagoberto nodded approvingly: "Well, well!" he exclaimed and began to make lists of books his foreman was to bring back from Rio.

Neither Dagoberto nor Jacira had been brought up in the Church. They considered themselves Catholics, however, and over time their religiosity began to grow. Colonial society breathed Catholicism in a rather unorganized yet effective manner. Traveling priests often passed by the plantation to do a bit of proselytizing, and many of the slaves and hired hands were baptized. Slowly, with the increasingly frequent visits from the priest of the nearest village, visits which sometimes carried on for days, the couple ended up constructing a "room of the saints," where they placed a few statuettes, among them two tiny female saints of blue-green soapstone with wavy white hair flowing to their feet. For some unknown reason, Jacira had been overcome by an unfamiliar emotion when she saw the saints for sale by a cattleman who had passed by the plantation, and she immediately bought them. From that day on, she had considered them the most beautiful pieces on her tiny altar, these almost miniature saints, made, the cattle driver had told her, by an old man, who was by now deceased, in a tiny town the people called Pouso da Capela. At the feet of the two saints, she laid a branch of a blessed palm from Palm Sunday that the priest always brought for protection against thunderbolts, lightning, and storms.

It was a happy marriage, Jacira and Dagoberto's. Without great displays of affection, as the era demanded, but nonetheless with great attention and care for each other and the tranquil pleasure of being together. They had nine children, of which only five survived: four boys and a girl.

Their surviving daughter was named Maria Bárbara, and was born when her mother was thirty-two. But can we really call someone a survivor if she doesn't make it to the age of eighteen?

Maria Bárbara was a slender girl, almost frail, like her mother, but she had a sweet and lively temperament. The slave women who helped raise her called her Birdie on account of her voice and persistent cheerfulness. Her story, however, is quite sad, though perhaps a bit banal for her time and circumstances.

As an adolescent, she fell in love with Jacinto, Captain Dagoberto's foreman. In reality, he was Dona Jacira's foreman, since at that time twelve years had passed since the death of Jacira's husband, though she made a point—as she had done when he was still alive—of referring to him in everything, as though the Captain were still alive. Jacira had been widowed at thirty-six, leaving a hole nothing could fill until one chilly dawn when, after yet another endless night spent opening the bedroom windows and passing the hours peering, hypnotized, into the dark, she decided to dedicate the rest of her life to making her husband's name the most important in the region. She hadn't left the bedroom ever since the morning Dagoberto had suddenly fallen dead, practically at her feet, as they were making the rounds of the sugarcane fields four weeks earlier. That is, until the morning she made her decision, when, to everyone's surprise, she emerged from behind the bedroom door with her customary serenity, her hair done up in a bun, wearing the black mourning clothes she would wear the rest of her life.

That morning, she had summoned all the men and women on the plantation, those who had been welcomed into the family, the hired help, and slaves, and gathered them in the large yard. Looking down upon them from the veranda, as Dagoberto had always done, she spoke: "All of you know that the Captain is dead. This is a fact that I would give my life to deny, but I cannot. But here on this plantation, which he built and which belongs to him, he is not dead and never will die, not as long I'm still here. Everything will continue on exactly as when he was with us. No one will change anything, not so much as a blade of hay. You will all continue to belong to the estate of Captain Dagoberto, and be the men and women of Captain Dagoberto, until the day I die."

And so it was. The plantation still belonged to Captain Dagoberto, the cattle were still his cattle, the sugar mill, the cotton fields, the goods, and the hired hands, all his. The place at the head of the table, where Jacira never allowed anyone else to sit, was his, the chair on the veranda next to the copper pot, the left side of the bed, all of these places were left empty and would never be filled by anyone else; they would always belong to him, her Captain.

Jacira was careful to ensure everything ran as it should. She replicated her husband's gestures and his approach; she more than simply replicated them, in fact, she adopted them as her own. She would set out early in the morning, as the Captain had done before her, to make the rounds of the plantation and the innumerable tasks its maintenance required. She did everything as she had learned to do by watching her husband day after day. She used the same hat as her husband, which she had managed with particular deftness to make sit firmly on her smaller head, and off she would go in her widow's attire, made of lightweight fabric to make riding easier, spending entire days surrounded by the Captain's men.

Are you surprised that a woman could exercise such power and authority in that era? Well, you shouldn't be. In every era, everywhere, there have always been women whose power rivaled that of men. They've always existed, and they are anything but rare. By this point, you've no doubt noticed that the women who peopled this land during the first two or three hundred years, the ones who traveled to the most remote backlands to live on the frontier, in a country that was just getting its start, couldn't afford to be weak and submissive the way some people would like to portray them. They had to take care of themselves; if they didn't, they wouldn't survive the inhospitable conditions in which they lived, often passing months without their husbands at home, forced to fend for themselves in many cases, and see to the conditions that would guarantee their survival. Of course, there have always been all kinds of men and women, weak and strong, craven and gullible, intelligent and limited, good and bad, powerful and impotent. But you all can be certain of one thing: the women who lived in the vast, unforgiving, magnificent backlands in the early centuries of this country's history could be many things—but silly and fragile they were not.

It fell to Jacira then, with her team of foremen, to wait for visitors at the edge of the property to guide them up to the plantation house, per the standards of courtesy and hospitality that Dagoberto had always made a point of observing. If the visitors were important, the meals they were served, as during the time of the Captain, were comparable to real banquets. When it came time for visitors to depart, it was she who once again led the convoy, accompanying them to the edge of the property. When it was neighbors who visited, she would receive them, as Dagoberto had done, taking snuff in her hammock on the porch, where she administered the courtesies her husband often had and gave her opinion on the subject matter at hand.

She soon found herself busier and busier. In a few years, she became the most powerful plantation owner in the area. What couldn't be obtained through persuasion she obtained by cunning or force—that was her secret motto, the motto that lent a victorious little smile when, as night neared, she would sit in her chair on the porch, her feet soaking in the warm water of the foot bath a slave woman regularly refreshed. There, next to the empty seat of her late but eternally present Captain, she would toss corncobs into the copper pot and tell him, without uttering a word, about all she had achieved in his name.

Dona Jacira's manner and imposing attitude were well known and were a topic of conversation miles away, together with the wealth of Captain Dagoberto's plantation. Even in the regional capital, Vila Boa de Goiás.

Everyone knew of the absolute loyalty Dona Jacira demanded of her employees, but they also knew that she didn't hesitate to do her own part whenever necessary. The story of what happened with one of her cowhands, Manuel Damasceno, who killed a man over a gambling dispute and was immediately arrested by an officer of the civil guard, quickly became a legend. As soon as she learned about what had happened, Jacira set off at a gallop, trailed by her troops to the village of São Francisco. São Francisco was the closest village to her lands, and though it was small, it boasted a church and a jail.

They entered the village kicking up dust and causing a commotion with their combination of horses, spurs, whips, dogs, and men. Within seconds, they filled the small open field that served as the town square, and Jacira ordered one of her men to dismount from his horse to call the officer to the jailhouse door. A good man, the officer had a peaceful and calm manner.

"Good afternoon, Officer," Jacira said.

"Good afternoon, Dona Jacira," he responded.

"I've been informed, Officer, that Your Honor mistakenly arrested one of Captain Dagoberto's men."

"You've been informed correctly, Dona Jacira, but there was no mistake about it. I had every intention of arresting him."

"Oh, is that so, Officer? May I know your reasons?"

"Manuel Damasceno killed a man over a card game, Dona Jacira, and this I cannot permit in my village."

"If he killed him, the other man is already dead, Officer. It's not by arresting one man that one brings another back to life."

"I may not bring him back, Dona Jacira. But I will bring him justice."

"Justice is for God to decide, Officer. And when it comes to my men and my things, that's up to me and my husband. But, to make this brief, Your Honor must know I've come to fetch Manuel, since he is one of Captain Dagoberto's men and is sorely missed."

"That I cannot permit, Dona Jacira. The lady will forgive me, but with all those arriving here in the village, how much can a single man be missed?"

"A great deal, Officer. And all these people you see here with me came for no other reason than to bring him back with us."

"Only if you kill me first, Dona Jacira."

"My dear man, why this stubbornness?"

"It's not stubbornness, Dona Jacira. It's authority. I'm here to arrest anyone who disturbs the order and send him to trial in the capital. And that's what I'm doing."

"I see, Officer, that the gentleman is a man of authority. But the greatest authority in this region is Captain Dagoberto. Perhaps Your Honor hasn't yet heard."

"This comes as news to me, Dona Jacira."

"Well, that's no fault of ours, Officer. If you're in need of a lesson, we're only too happy to provide it. You need only wait."

Maintaining her elegance, Jacira circled her horse around and ordered her men to retreat, but the officer knew his fate was sealed. Distressed, he thought over his next move. From the very beginning of his conversation with Dona Jacira, he had seen he'd reached a dead end. He stood still, his thoughts fading away and leaving a void in their place. For a moment, he had the sensation that he had left his body and was looking down from a distance on some rooftop at his solitary figure standing at the jailhouse door, watching as the widow and her men departed, kicking up so much dust it seemed a twister had blown through town.

The officer was unmarried and had no children. He had arrived there a little more than two years earlier, sent by the Civil Guard's provincial command to oversee the region along with five soldiers. Just think about it: five soldiers against the Captain's band of rough-and-tumble men.

What a mess he'd gotten himself into! A cold sweat ran down his face as the adrenaline remaining from his confrontation with the Captain's widow began to fade.

When he slowly regained his thoughts, he became convinced that he had no other option than to release Manuel Damasceno. His decision made, he walked back to the cell, unlocked the door, and muttered: "Get out of here already, you miserable wretch, and I don't ever want to see you here again. I'm warning you."

Later that day, Jacira was surprised to see Manuel Damasceno walking toward the plantation, kneeling at her feet and kissing her hand, thanking her and invoking all the saints that they might protect her. But Jacira was not satisfied.

That very night, a group of ten men, each of them carrying in his saddlebags a large bundle of dry sugarcane, entered the town, this time without kicking up dust or making any noise as you'd expect from a group of their size, or even from a single man—they were trained for this after all, and could slip undetected through the cool night air as they carried out their orders. They circled the jail with the dried sugarcane, kicked down the door to check whether anyone was in the cell. There was no one, and since there was no one in the cells, even the soldier who acted as night watchman had gone home to sleep. Lucky him! The Captain's men threw more of the dried sugarcane inside the cells, lit them on fire, and left as quietly as they'd arrived.

The first people in the village to wake with the crackling fire and the smell of smoke could do nothing but keep the fire from spreading to other homes. The jail was already consumed by the furious flames, their rage redoubled at being called to work on such a peaceful, easy night.

Many miles from there, from her chair on the porch, Jacira finally allowed a tiny victorious smile to form on her lips.

"That officer has likely learned that you're the one in charge here, Dagoberto."

This was Dona Jacira's life after her husband's death: to command, to plot, to emerge victorious. Which, nevertheless, did not diminish the attention and love she lavished on her children. She wanted to raise them, the boys, in the image of the Captain. And Maria Bárbara, in that of a little queen.

It was not, therefore, out of cruelty that I'm about to tell you what happened. Rather, it was an error so common to so many mothers who think they know what's best for their children, better even than the children themselves do. Hers was a tragic error that she would bitterly regret for the rest of her life.

JACINTO, THE FOREMAN

Strong, good-looking, and intelligent, Jacinto was also what one called a "pardo" at the time, a mulatto who was born free. On account of his skills and the affection the Captain's family had for him, he earned the post of deputy foreman when he was still a young man. The son of a cattle driver from Bahia, a man who was neither rich nor poor, Jacinto's family had settled down along the road to Goiás. From a young age, he liked to linger at the Jatoba Plantation each time he and his father would pass by, and many times his father left him there to pick him up on his way back. Jacinto became best friends with the Captain's sons and the love of Maria Bárbara's life.

Ever since they were young, the couple would go off on long walks, or on horseback, their eyes bright, their faces tanned by the sun, their bodies exuding vitality with each step.

But Jacira had other plans for her daughter. She wanted to marry her to someone as kind and as important as Dagoberto. Let's be fair: it wasn't out of pure material interests that she intended to choose her daughter's husband for her; it was because she wanted to see her daughter as happy as she had been. Love had come to her in a way so natural and so sure that she thought it ought to be the same for everyone, especially for her Maria. Which would no doubt happen were she to find a husband worthy of her, like Dagoberto. A clear thinker, learned, kind—qualities that for some reason, whether for his lack of education or his poverty, or perhaps even the color of his skin, she thought Jacinto seemed to lack.

As soon as she noticed the friendship between the two transform into something more, she did not hesitate to transfer the foreman. First, she sent him to oversee the most distant pastures, which meant he was rarely present on the plantation. When she noticed that the distance only left her daughter more excited and happy each time she saw him, she called him aside and informed him she would no longer be needing his services. Since he had been welcomed to the plantation with Dagoberto's blessing, she told him she would accord him the respect of speaking frankly: he was to leave the plantation, once and for all, and forget Maria Bárbara.

Jacinto obeyed the first of her orders, but the second and third he ignored. It wasn't difficult for him to find work at a neighboring plantation, and since he would be caught by day, he began to secretly visit Maria Bárbara at night. The young woman could barely wait to hear his soft tapping on her blue bedroom window, asking her to open it and let him in for the night.

This constant commotion drew attention in the end. Aware that someone was stealing up to the plantation in the dead of night, Jacira ordered her men to prepare an ambush and shoot any intruders on sight, since whoever was sneaking around like that could only be a thief or troublemaker.

No one can say for sure whether Jacira suspected the intruder was Jacinto. And nobody could question her order, since anyone who sneaks onto another person's property, no matter who he is, is probably doing so without the best of intentions. And perhaps, just perhaps, had Jacinto not been wearing a hood, or fled like a thief when given the order to stop, Jacira's men would have recognized him and his fate would have been different.

But fate is never different.

The order had been given, he was wearing a hood, no one recognized him, and they had truly thought he was a thief. And there he died, beneath the blue window, a bullet to the heart.

Maria Bárbara's heart also suffered a fatal blow that night.

Not even the birth seven months later of the child she was expecting brought the least bit of color or happiness to her face.

She died of pneumonia less than a year later, without having forgiven her mother or having spoken to her ever again.

During endless days of mourning and regret, Jacira would sit on the porch for hours and hours, looking out over her lands, whose emptiness once again seemed immense. She tried with all her might to revive the happiness she felt after the birth of Maria Bárbara and Mariano, her handsome twins, and the euphoria that struck Dagoberto, who considered twins a sign of abundance and who finally had himself a little girl. On his first trip to Rio after their birth, he bought a piano for his daughter, a tiny, well-tuned piano that would also hold up well along the way, ideal for beginners, as the owner of the store had told him. He wanted her to learn to play as soon as she grew a bit more and her tiny fingers could master eighty-eight keys of ivory and ebony.

Dagoberto loved music. He'd had a baritone's voice and was fond of repeating that music was a gift his mother had passed on to all her children. Jacira didn't know it, since when it came to family she couldn't remember anything beyond her father's and mother's first names, but she also had a talent for music in her veins. It came as no surprise, however, that at least three of her children had a gift for music, especially the eldest, Antonio, and Maria Bárbara, both of whom had perfect pitch.

Antonio was a baritone like his father: his voice, however, had a deeper and more melodious timbre, as well as an acute and fatal sadness. During his adolescent years, a kick in the head from an angry horse had nearly killed him, knocking him unconscious for several days and leaving him entirely deaf in his right ear. On account of this injury, or perhaps on account of his submissive temperament, Antonio never stepped out of the shadow of his parents. If prior to the accident his voice could often be heard in a duet with his father, after the incident he practically went silent. Later, he took the most pleasure in sitting with his left ear turned toward his sister at the piano. In such moments, his face lit up with a rare, tender expression and Antonio would close his eyes as if dreaming sweet, easy dreams.

It was Antonio who saw to the instrument's maintenance, and after some time studying its workings, he was a consummate tuner and connoisseur. When Dagoberto died, no one even considered the idea that his eldest child might assume command over the plantation. His roles had always been secondary and changed frequently; his lack of initiative left him no place of his own in the running of the plantation. At the age of thirty, Antonio married Maria Ambrosia, a young woman who had come to live with the family and who was as timid as he was. They went to live in a house that Jacira ordered built for the couple on a plot of the plantation's land near the grazing fields. There, after the death of Maria Bárbara, Antonio began to build instruments similar to his sister's piano. Without the right materials, though, he managed to create instruments that emitted unknown sounds, some of them pleasing to the ear, others disturbing. Several of these instruments can be found today in the Museum of Image and Sound at the Institute of History and Geography of Goiás.

Maria Bárbara was a self-taught piano player. Sometimes, travelers who passed through the plantation would know how to play and taught her a thing or two. Her dream was to go one day to Vila Boa de Goiás, or to the capital of what was now the Viceroyalty of Brazil, to study piano more seriously. Their brother Feliciano, who had been living in Rio de Janeiro since the age of sixteen, dedicating himself to business affairs, would write to her with encouragement, telling her of the many good family girls who played well, but none of whom, in his opinion, could match her. Her plan with Jacinto was to flee to Rio, where her brother would no doubt help them.

Her twin brother Mariano, a close friend to both her and Jacinto, had promised to help them as he could. After their deaths, unable to forgive his mother, whose guilt he considered clear and unredeemable, Mariano abandoned the plantation and went to live with Feliciano in Rio.

Back at the plantation, Jacira had only her youngest son Justino left, born two years before Dagoberto's death.

Jacira made an effort to evoke the plantation of years past, when Maria Bárbara played her piano, Antonio, his eyes closed, would dream at her side, and Mariano, leaning against the instrument, also drank in the melody. Above the piano hung a portrait by a young painter who Dagoberto had brought from Rio expressly for that portrait: Jacira sitting down, wrapped in her blue silk mantilla with her gold chain and cameo necklace, holding the twins on her lap; Dagoberto behind her, cutting an elegant figure in his dark suit, hair parted down the middle, his arm resting on the chair-back, the other on Antonio's shoulder as Feliciano kneeled at his side, the two boys in festive attire. Justino had yet to be born. The colors of the portrait, once so vivid, now appeared to have a mist hanging over them, permanently depriving its subjects of their splendor and sharpness.

Jacira remembered the boys' cries of joy when they were little and the happiness in her daughter's eyes, eyes that never again looked her in the face after that terrible day, the memory of which cut her anew like an eternal wound. The day her daughter told her with eyes full of tears: "I hate you, and I will never forgive you for what you've done." She remembered her daughter's blue bedroom window, which opened up onto a trellis of jasmine whose sweet, piercing perfume would wash over the room. It was next to that window that Jacinto had fallen. Some days later, no longer able to stand the smell of the jasmine she herself had planted, Maria Bárbara walked over to the trellis as the sun set, at the exact moment when the flowers exhale their heaviest scent, and tore the plants up by the roots, one by one. It was that very same night—or perhaps not, Jacira couldn't remember anymore—that her daughter ran to the imposing jatoba tree where the Captain had decided they would settle down so many years ago and tried to unearth it, too, her nails digging into the hard bark with such fervent and unnerving despair that Jacira wished she could die in Jacinto's place rather than see her daughter suffer. Maria Bárbara had to be torn away from the spot, her hands covered in blood and wounds so deep they would never heal fully, or didn't have the time to do so.

Jacira would also think back to Mariano, who from a young age could always be found at his twin sister's side, as if the two were one. Her son Mariano who, on the same day his sister was buried, mounted his horse and, looking back on his mother standing there like a silent statue on the porch, rode up alongside her and, rather than offer the consoling words of goodbye Jacira had hoped for, had looked straight at her and spit.

Afterward, the bulk of Jacira's days were spent with these memories. They were wounds she knew she would carry with her until she was in her casket and covered with earth. They were indelible moments she could never erase but which—this much was in her power—she could keep from ever happening again. Keep them from happening with Damiana, the precious creature who had remained from Jacinto and Maria Bárbara's union, the union she had so stupidly tried to thwart.

Her granddaughter was what gave purpose to Jacira each day, surpassing even her efforts to preserve Dagoberto's memory.

Albeit with some delay, news of what was happening throughout the country always arrived at the plantation. Travelers passing through brought news of events in the other provinces. The cattlemen who went to Rio and Bahia were also important sources of information, and they also brought the books she requested. Later, her son Feliciano's long letters gave her a direct connection to the capital and its unsettling developments.

That's how Jacira had learned about certain decrees, like the one prohibiting the installation of mills and factories in the colony, or another that ordered the immediate collection of all unpaid taxes. She was quickly informed when, in Minas Gerais, talk of a rebellion spread everywhere—in the streets, throughout the taverns, out to the roadside farms. Later, she learned how all of it ended, the sedition of Minas, the hanging of one of the rebellion's leaders, the ensign Tiradentes, and the jailing of all the rest. In a long letter, her son Feliciano, a man with modern ideas who closely followed the debate over independence, described the flag that the conspirators had already designed and which circulated in several places throughout the country, and which bore phrases in Latin.

Feliciano wrote her about what had happened in France in 1789, and how in Rio people were saying that equality, fraternity, and liberty were the basic rights of everyone, "including us, mother, including the Brazilians." Many people even declared openly, he told her, that the French had done well to kill the king and Marie Antoinette.

Jacira read these reports attentively, but thought it all had little to do with her. Faraway from everything, isolated from the rest of the country, dedicating her life to her lands and the goods they produced, such great issues were quite vague in her mind. Her relationship with her farmhands was one of hierarchy, built on economic power and tradition, not violence. As far as the slaves went, she felt that their dependence on her was greater than her dependence on them. How would they survive without someone like her to put clothes on their backs and the food on their plates?

Strictly speaking, she saw herself as a sort of mother figure to them all, a mother who provided the basic means for survival and who, when forced to punish them, punished them like a mother would, a just punishment she administered for their own good. On the plantation she, like Captain Dagoberto before her, never permitted violence against the slaves like that at other plantations. When a neighboring farmer warned against the danger of runaway slaves, she would respond that if a slave truly did not want to work for her any longer, he wouldn't be missed much were he to flee.

Nearly ten years later, news arrived of insurrection in Bahia—the Tailor Revolution, an uprising caused by a shortage of food in the city. People told of how a mob had attacked slaves carrying enormous quantities of meat on Holy Saturday, destined for the commanding general in Salvador. For the first time, Jacira heard talk not only of independence from Portugal, but the proclamation of a Brazilian republic, the end of slavery, and free trade.

When Prince Regent João VI of Portugal, and his mother, Queen Maria the Mad, fled Napoleon and disembarked in Rio, Feliciano's letters conveyed the sense of euphoria that had taken hold of the city despite the chaos provoked by the rapid increase in its population, which swelled quickly on account of the fifteen thousand Portuguese who followed the royal delegation. As far as Feliciano, who traded in foodstuffs and other odds and ends, was concerned, the arrival of the Portuguese was a blessed and promising gift from the heavens. He described in great detail the stupendous public works the king had ordered and how life for everyone was about to change for the better, as though a tornado of miracles had swept the city.

There was only one thing Feliciano's long letters never spoke of: Mariano. As soon as his brother arrived in Rio, Feliciano wrote Jacira telling her that Mariano had arrived and had accepted his offer to live with him under one condition: Feliciano was never to give her any news of him since he considered her, like Maria Bárbara, dead to him. Feliciano had given his word and, as a result, this would be the first and last time he would ever send news of his brother, a promise he kept to the very end.

As the years dragged on, the production on the plantation began to change naturally, despite Jacira's speech about how everything would remain the same, despite her Captain's name being always on her lips. However, without her realizing it, it was as though this name she repeated constantly had become a rare sort of sweet candy on her tongue. A candy that didn't melt from outside to inside, but from the inside out, slowly devoured from the core by the most powerful and invincible being of all—time, the force that both carries everything and takes it away, never to return, and which had left in its place a thin, empty shell with the name of Dagoberto. Without her realizing it, Jacira began to set her own wishes aside, and the winds of change slowly swept across her land.

Since she seemed to have a greater inclination and skill for looking after the cattle, the cattle began to take over, soon assuming priority over the sugar mill, the cotton fields, and the crops, all of which continued to grow, of course, but on a smaller scale with fewer slaves and fewer workers. Those on the inside perhaps failed to notice these changes, but beyond her lands, Dona Jacira became better known for raising cattle—the biggest in the region—than for her crops or her sugarcane. From her porch at the end of the afternoon, she'd look out upon her river of white horns crowding into the enormous corral with a satisfaction that could not be put into words.

THE RE-ENCOUNTER WITH ALENCAR AMBRÓSIO

On that distant morning lost to memory, when Diogo Ambrósio killed his wife and left Jacira on Corporal Jesuíno's doorstep, his son Alencar, then nine years old, had recently set off for the Jesuit School of Rio de Janeiro at his paternal grandfather's urging. Visiting him later, his father told him merely that his mother had died and that he ought to forget his sister because he would never again see her. At that moment, the young boy was unable to question his father or demand any sort of explanation. But he always had an intuition that his sister was still living and he knew that, when he was able to, there would be some way of finding her.

With his mother's inheritance and his father's money, and his paternal grandfather's contacts, Alencar Ambrósio, little older than twenty, entered the slave trade. The notable increase in demand for slave labor in the gold mines transformed the trafficking of black chattel into the era's multimillion-dollar business.

The rich men with business in the ports of Rio de Janeiro and Bahia had created an extraordinarily lucrative system of commerce: ships would carry tobacco, sugarcane liquor, and other products produced in Brazil to Africa, and return with slaves. Without the permission of the Portuguese or protection from a naval fleet, these ships were easy prey for ships belonging to pirates or to other countries. But the profits from the sea crossing were so great that they gave birth to the greatest Brazilian fortunes, greater even than those earned in the gold mines. And so the Ambrósio family would quickly become one of the richest of Rio, and Alencar a venerable old patriarch.

After 1808, when England began to apply pressure to end the Atlantic slave trade, and up until 1850, when the traffic of slaves was effectively outlawed and put to a definitive end, several decades passed during which Brazil's slave-trading elite mounted startling fortunes. Alencar Ambrósio's sons and grandsons would later transform their grandfather's ships into true warships, capable of fending off attacks from pirates or the English Navy. They would also continue, as their grandfather had done, to diversify the family business, becoming coffee farmers, bankers, and ship owners.

All the same, the old patriarch Alencar Ambrósio never forgot his sister.

He didn't wish to reopen his father's wound while he was still alive, but after the old man's death he began his long search for her. He dispatched one of his men to discover what had happened to Jacira Antonia, but no one at his father's old plantation knew where Diogo Ambrósio had gone when he set off at a gallop on that terrible morning, his daughter of three on his horse with him. No one, not even the slave women, had heard Clara Joaquina's fateful lie just before she died; nearly all of them believed that Jacira's father, acceding to madness and jealousy, had killed his daughter as well and buried her in the woods.

And so Alencar had sent one of his men to continue the search together with his maternal grandfather's family, with whom his father had broken entirely. The descendants of Paulista explorer José Garcia, however, had never heard anything of the whereabouts of Ana de Pádua's daughter, much less her granddaughter.

The man returned without making inroads. Many years would pass until Alencar decided to adopt another approach: he ordered his man to cross all the towns and villages within a day's reach from the old plantation. The search was slow, full of false leads, but in the end they discovered where Jacira had spent her childhood and whom she had married.

After that, it was merely a question of time.

One afternoon, at eighty years old but strong as the giant trees of the backlands, Alencar announced himself, together with one of his sons, at his sister's plantation.

The likewise old and powerful woman received her visitors from her hammock on the porch. She was seventy-four. At her side was her youngest son, Justino, and her granddaughter Damiana, already twenty-two.

Jacira could not hide her trembling as she listened to the words of the imposing old man with hair and a beard that were completely white. She didn't know what to make of that patriarchal figure with his city manners, so different from her own. In her memory, she had preserved the sound of her father galloping away and the names Diogo Ambrósio and Clara Joaquina. A dark room, filled with mist. Nothing more.

No brother. No tenderness or memory of affections once traded, no remembrances good or bad. Nothing.

But there on the porch of her own house, her great big dark eyes became even rounder as she attempted to rescue some resonance from inside herself that could explain the attention and the emotions being directed her way.

Alencar told her who their parents had been and how, from a young age, he had sworn to find her some day. But he couldn't provide what might have been the only motivation and interest on Jacira's part to return to the mysteries of the past: the motive for her tragic abandonment, what reasons her father had for leaving her, so small and fragile, to the care of complete strangers. Alencar did not have an answer for this. Alencar wasn't even sure how their mother had died: his father had told him it was of natural causes; with time, however, he heard vague, foggy rumors of a revenge killing. But he had made no attempt to verify this; he had no interest in stirring up that mystery. What was done was done, he thought, and there was no way to change history now.

Unfortunately, what he did not know is that there is never a way to change history, whether in its entirety or in part.

The story had already been lived. It was over, completed. More impossible to change than the most immovable of mountains since, if there is something that is absolutely unalterable in this world, it's the past.

Suddenly feeling as helpless as when her father had left her on Corporal Jesuíno's doorstep, and even more so than when her husband had died thirty-four years earlier, Jacira closed her eyes and asked herself, as she hadn't done for nearly a lifetime: "Dagoberto, what should I do? What does this man want of me?"

No, Jacira had not liked learning this part of her first three years of life, years that had been closed off in a heavy and unbreachable darkness.

She did not like knowing that, along with her father, her mother, and her former life, she had lost a brother, too. She wanted that old man with his white hair and imposing figure to leave her in peace. Seventy years is an irrecoverable mountain of time. She did not wish to relive what had never been, she had no desire to nurture memories of an impossibility.

The sooner that man went away the better it would be for everyone.

Justino and Damiana understood perfectly their mother and grand-mother's desire to avoid rummaging through the past. What's more, they were young people who, due to the influence of Feliciano and Mariano, detested the slave-trading vessels, ships whose fame for unthinkable horrors had already spread across the country. Especially Damiana, who maintained a frequent correspondence with her uncle Mariano and considered herself widow to one José Batista, a young teacher whom she would later meet through her uncle and who had died two years earlier. The three of them were enthusiastic abolition-ists who, together, would do what they could to bring slavery to an end.

They didn't like this relative standing here before them, nor his air as though he owned the world.

Alencar and his son gave them a card with their address and left the plantation, disappointed with the cold reception, frustrated at the chilly façade they encountered, and the impossibility of reinventing the past. But since Alencar was not a man to give up on his plans, much less this one, which he had obsessed over his entire life, he left convinced that with time it would be possible to overcome the indifference of his sister and her children and reaffirm the family ties he had always valued so much.

In Jacira's case, meanwhile, this encounter did irreparable harm, reopening a wound she thought she had put behind her.

The overwhelming effort to remember her past, provoked by her brother's visit, seemed to have drained her of her strength. Worse yet, it was as if she had been abandoned all over again, on that doorstep where the terror and panic induced by the episode were once again visited upon her after so many years, after an entire lifetime.

"My god, seventy years later and I've still not erased these things from my memory?"

Her brother's visit brought back the tramping of the hooves galloping away, a single deafening sound in her head, sweeping across the dark night, rousing her from sleep, leaving her weak, panicked, entirely alone.

Jacira's strength slowly seeped away through those terror-filled nights when she was transformed once again into the trembling little girl left on a dark doorstep, watching her father gallop away.

Panicked and entirely alone.

Until the inevitable morning not long thereafter when a slave woman found her cold and stiff in her twin bed, the muscles of her mouth slack in death's hollow silence, her body on its side facing the left half of the bed, the place belonging to Captain Dagoberto, empty for so long.

DAMIANA
(1789-1822)

In a tiny, dark, humid cell, barely able to breathe the thick air, enveloped by the sickening smell of sweat and rot, her ears flooded by the sound of the clubs beating one more body down into the earth, Damiana asked herself why. Why had her life always been filled with misfortune, and why had she not perceived from the beginning that there could be no other end but this? Even before her birth, her fate had been riddled with a continuum of tragedies, which had brief interruptions, small respites filled with joy, but these were only respites, soon followed by more sadness and suffering.

She was loved, this was impossible to deny; from a young age, she had always known the company of an almost excessive tenderness and the watchfulness of a grandmother who sought to spare her the least bit of suffering. Then there were the uncles, all of them, who treated her like a precious stone, each one of them protecting her as they could, above all Uncle Mariano, who had been like the father she never knew.

But what good had all that love and protection been? Had it prevented the murder of her father?

Had it prevented the misfortune that marked her life?

Had it prevented the melancholy desperation that resulted in the death of her mother, whom, as a result, she never came to know?

No. It had prevented nothing, nothing at all.

In her pestilent little cell, Damiana could not explain or understand how or why everything around her seemed to end in terrible suffering.

Just look at her mother and father.

Just look at João Batista.

A young school instructor, a professor of mathematics and literature, and a friend of her Uncle Mariano, she had barely turned sixteen when he first showed up one day at the plantation with a letter from Mariano in his hands. He had long hair tied back and dark eyes, and a mind brimming with courageous ideas, enthusiasm, and desire, those vigorous gifts of youth. He was there to spend some time on the plantation at the request of Mariano, who wanted live reports of his niece.

From her cell, Damiana arrived at the conclusion that she had loved him at first sight, and that he had also loved her as soon as he set eyes on her. João, with his new ideas, his eloquence, and his ardor; she with her curious spirit, her rapt ears hungry for his words; he with the books he brought and a knowledge that his body seemed unable to contain; she with the desire to learn and understand the world; he with his twenty-two years, his charm, and his savoir faire; she all of sixteen, with her golden-brown skin with its scent of wildflowers.

João Batista had been received with full honors at the plantation and there he stayed for two entire months. On days with blue skies and golden afternoons, they rode horses together through the fields, strolled through the woods, sat side by side at the edge of a waterfall, identifying each little sound—the water, the leaves, the birds, and the small forest creatures. João Batista would pull paper and a pen from his pocket and begin to write. He wrote short texts about liberty, equality, and justice. Texts that spoke of Brazil, of independence, of the common humanity shared by all men, including slaves. João Batista read French writers, translated the works of Enlightenment philosophers, and was an abolitionist. In Rio de Janeiro, together with Mariano, he was part of groups that met to read censured books and discuss follies committed by the Crown. He also took part in the city's nightlife, with its music and drinking, and alongside Mariano, an incorrigible bohemian, he sang, played, wrote his own songs, and was a bit of a celebrity in Rio.

Damiana was the most ardent listener the young man had ever encountered. She developed a passionate interest in everything, she wanted to understand, to learn more. When João Batista proposed, Grandma Jacira gave her blessing, tamed by remorse. They made plans to live in the capital, where life seemed so rich and full of possibilities. He would go before her to make preparations and would come back for her when everything was ready.

Two months later, however, Mariano returned in João Batista's place. Somber, exasperated, in mourning. He would not set foot on the plantation—where he had sworn never again to tread as long as his mother still lived—so he sent someone to fetch Damiana and bring her to the neighboring town where he was staying, so he could give her the news that João Batista had been killed in a street fight. It had been a fight over nothing, an argument over a gambling debt, pure stupidity and pent-up frustration that boiled over, mindless violence. A knife raised to the sky and then a purposeful blow. A fallen body and, suddenly, right there, almost without time to realize the immense consequences of the events, a heart that stopped beating.

Another death in Damiana's path.

Back on the plantation with her letters from João Batista, she would try to face her fate without losing hope. She was like that, she had an ability to accept life no matter what it brought her way; a gift for not transforming the past into a burden, but rather a locked safe where she forever guarded the treasure of her inextinguishable light. She understood that it was a privilege to have known the love she had known, and so she took up the ideals of João Batista; she wanted to write as he had. At that point in this story, her interest in modern ideas appeared to multiply by two. She had her Uncle Mariano to guide her, to send her the books that João Batista read, to tell her about everything that was happening in the capital, to help her become a person with the ability to make her life mean something. She seemed to possess a source of invincible, internal vitality.

Ever since the death of his twin sister and Jacinto, Mariano had felt responsible for his niece: she was the daughter tragedy had placed in his hands. His plan had always been to remove her from under Jacira's influence, but he knew that he would never be able to simply send for her. Neither he nor Feliciano, his oldest brother, had married; for different reasons, the two had opted for the life of two court bachelors. If they had married or if Feliciano hadn't died so young of a heart ailment like their father, perhaps they could have both looked after their niece in the capital. But alone, with his penchant for the nightlife and free love, he felt unfit to care for a young girl. He traveled often and rarely stayed put. He had a passion for visiting the different regions of the enormous country and falling in love with its women, staying as long as he could wherever fate smiled upon him.

Following Jacira's death, Mariano began to visit the plantation again, but nothing about the rural life interested him. He found it too limited, as well, for his niece's restless mind, and the plan to take her away from the farm became a sort of obsession. To accomplish this, the only solution he saw was to find another husband for Damiana, another friend who could bring her to Rio as a wife, established, protected.

To this end, then, Mariano once again sent a friend to the plantation: Inácio Belchior, a Portuguese businessman from Porto.

It was strange that Mariano, so experienced, so urbane, would have let himself be deceived so easily. Especially since Mariano wasn't exactly enamored of the Portuguese and knew of his niece's nationalist ideals.

But that's how the human race carries on, stumbling, taking wrong turns and false steps. Inácio—a big talker, flatterer, false to the core, eager for adulation—had the gift of recognizing at first glance just how to please his interlocutor. From the outset he insisted on affirming to Mariano that, in fact, he was nothing more than a legitimate Brazilian born in Portugal by mistake. He adored the new land that, deep in his heart, he felt was his true country, and said all the things Mariano wished to hear, and at length. He did so with even greater persistence after he became aware of his friend's origins, the stories of the powerful Dona Jacira and her young granddaughter, her only one, and principal heir to her grandmother's lands. It was just such land—splendid and sublime land, with its prestige and unique ability to confer upon its owner, whoever he was, the status of an important and eminent person in the viceroyalty—that was practically the Portuguese man's sole secret ambition.

Damiana welcomed Mariano's friend out of curiosity, and accepted his courting with interest, though without passion. With kindness and goodwill, so to say, but without butterflies, without anxiety, without any of the great emotions that had come with the love she felt for João Batista. Her wish, which was no secret and had been openly declared to anyone within earshot, was to live in the capital, to behold the marvels of the big city, to make friends, participate in reading groups, go to the theater. And write.

The two were soon married. Damiana's dowry was generous: namely, the extensive lands Belchior so coveted. In formal arrangements, Justino, Damiana's youngest uncle, would continue to oversee the couple's lands as he was already doing, since Inácio only wanted the lands for the prestige they lent and had no desire to take on the life of a plantation owner, which would certainly have resulted in his dying of boredom.

Damiana was twenty-six when she finally made it to Rio. Predictably, she fell in love with the city, its bustle, the constant sounds, the impeccably dressed women, their elegance, the city life so different from the malaise of life on the plantation. Her Uncle Mariano served as her guide and mentor. He introduced her to the city and to his friends. He took her to the theater, to the operas that the queen, Carlota Joaquina, had ordered to be brought from Europe. He was right to sense that Damiana's true place was in the city; during her first year there, it was as though she were discovering a new world. She fell in love with it, a laugh never far from her lips, happy at her uncle's side.

The teeming capital was a sight to behold. The ports were open and busy, dozens of ships were always anchored at the docks, the activity never-ending. Merchandise was unloaded and shipped out. Visitors were constantly arriving in Rio; scientists and artists from abroad came in search of the tropical wonders that were the talk of Europe. There was nearly always a party, or joyful and elegant reception, the city's social scene at fever pitch.

Damiana's friends were Mariano's friends: young artists and intellectuals, Brazilians who sought changes suited to the country, which is beginning to see itself as a nation. Meetings mixing literature, politics, and music swept the nights in the imposing house where Damiana went to live with Belchior. They recited poetry, discussed philosophy, and began to talk of raising the funds needed to continue publication of a newspaper that defended the cause of Brazilian independence, as the *Correio Brasiliense* did. Printed in London and smuggled into the country, it was to cease publication due to a lack of funds. They discussed the events in Recife, the disputes between Brazilian manufacturers and Portuguese merchants, the movement for separation from Portugal; revolts had begun to sprout up everywhere. They followed each incident as it unfolded, ecstatic when news reached them that a republican government had been established in Pernambuco; they grew worried when they learn that João VI had sent his entire army to quelch the rebellion. They wore armbands to express their mourning when the principal leaders of the rebellion were hanged in the public square and their bodies mutilated with excessive cruelty, as had happened before with Tiradentes. They helped to circulate an underground manifesto against Portuguese tyranny.

At these gatherings, Inácio Belchior maintained his façade of charm and friendliness for a time, but he slowly grew weary of these meetings. Worse still, he began to worry about what sort of influence his wife's friendships might have on his ambitions to become a member of the royal court.

Damiana couldn't be sure of the exact moment when things began to truly deteriorate, but their dispute over what to name their daughter was perhaps the first of many she remembered with clarity. Even before they had married, she had come to an agreement with her husband that when they had children, he would pick the name in the case of a boy, and she in the case of a girl. As soon as she learned she was pregnant, Damiana was certain she would give birth to a girl, and told her husband that she would give her the name Açucena Brasília, the name of a flower, a Brazilian name, a name for a true daughter of that country. It was also the name she had chosen with João Batista for the first of many children they intended to have, but she left this part out, not in the spirit of keeping secrets, for this was not in her nature, but out of discretion, as she considered that her history with the professor was hers alone, a history she did not wish to share with anyone.

Inácio hadn't complained about the unusual name; either because he didn't believe that their child would be a girl, or on account of his habit of flattery and falseness, he pretended he liked the name, too. When Damiana, full of enthusiasm, would speak of her daughter, already referring to her by name, he feigned an agreeing smile. So it came as a great surprise when, after Damiana gave birth and the doctors confirmed it was a girl, he told her that their daughter would be called Antônia Carlota. Outraged, Damiana argued they had already agreed that she would be the one to name any daughters, that he had never expressed any opposition to the name over the previous nine months, and that he knew she did not want their children to have Portuguese names—their daughter had been born in a country that was rich, new, magnificent, and ought to have a name characteristic of that country. Belchior, for the first time ever, ordered her to stay quiet. He screamed that, in his house, he was the one who gave the orders and that their daughter would be called by the name he chose and there would be no more discussion on the matter.

To the consternation of Damiana, who had believed in the story he had always repeated about being nothing but a true Brazilian born overseas by mistake, Inácio registered and baptized his daughter with the Portuguese name. While it's true that their marriage began to come to an end at that moment, their dispute did not: the girl's mother and her friends continued calling her Açucena Brasília, and her father and his friends called her Antônia Carlota.

Damiana had begun to catch on to her husband's duplicity, his miserly *arriviste* character disguised beneath the mask of charm and flattery he used to please whoever served his interests. She had noted how he barely contained his disdain for Mariano and his intellectual friends, how he treated her with irritation and impatience. In fact, Inácio had resolved to let his true feelings be known. He recriminated Damiana for leading a life unfit for a family woman and accused Mariano and his group of being a bunch of good-for-nothing leeches. He didn't agree with the ideas circulating through the house; he found them much too revolutionary, too independent, a country of mestizos, after all, ought to proceed with caution, ought to look to the example of countries in possession of a more elevated culture. He could no longer stand Damiana's interest in literature, which he considered the fancy of a rich heiress. If in the beginning he had pretended to read his wife's poetry and other writings, heaping praise upon them, by now, whenever he read them it was only to make them the subject of his mockery.

Only the fear of the lowly merchant in the face of the symbolic weight of the lands belonging to his wife's family managed to curb more aggressive behaviors. With time, however, to the extent he began to increase his own circle of important relations, he gained confidence, as though he had finally managed to perform a psychological transplant on himself of the prestige he so coveted; with each day that passed, he began to consider himself the true owner of the family lands, since, if Damiana was his wife, he—by law and by fact—was the true property holder, the owner, the principal.

His objective was to obtain the title of baron, the coronation of his influence and power. Doors had begun to open to him thanks to his wealth and status as an owner of great tracts of land. He formed friendships with influential nobleman, and performed favors that began to attract the attention of the king.

The proof of his importance came with an invitation to the coronation of King João VI after the death of his mother, Queen Maria the Mad. Inácio felt as if nothing could hold him back. His participation in the sumptuous court procession that followed the king from the majestic Mass to the Arch of Triumph, erected expressly for the occasion in the palace square, was a milepost in the psychological life of Inácio Belchior: from then on he felt more powerful than his wife, capable of doing to her whatever he pleased.

His audacity had no end. Damiana was soon being called frivolous, a mere society lady. Her friends, a bunch of shameless louts. Her poetry, the work of a child. Her habits, licentious.

Damiana, however, did not lower her head. She didn't know how to, she hadn't been brought up for that. She had always been free and did as she pleased, and she would continue to do so. Her initial surprise with the changes in her husband soon morphed into a determination to leave, to live only with her daughter, to divorce. She decided to write Mariano, who was traveling, for there was no one better than her uncle to help her with how to proceed.

Meanwhile, as often happens in such cases, things quickly got out of hand. One night, when he arrived at home to find friends visiting his wife, Inácio practically kicked them out of the house and, in a burst of rage, waited for Damiana in the bedroom and struck her across the face. Damiana, her eyes full of tears but sure of herself, announced her decision to immediately ask for a divorce.

This was her tragic error: to make her intentions clear to her husband.

Don't be surprised: divorce was possible in Brazil. It was, in fact, almost always a result of the wife's request. Though Catholic doctrine considered marriage an indissoluble bond, the ecclesiastic tribunals of each diocese had the freedom to rule over separations and annulments, and the civil tribunals would then oversee the division of goods among the separated parties. The problem was when the husband did not accept the divorce out of what he considered humiliation, or because he did not want to divide the couple's assets. Which was exactly the case with Belchior.

For him, the divorce would mean the worst of his fears: the loss of part of his goods and a risk to his obtaining the title of baron. It had never occurred to him that his wife could think of such a thing. It was a threat and a humiliation that he would never allow, and which brought out all his demons and eradicated whatever remaining scruples he still possessed.

After a sleepless night, he decided to act quickly. It was essential he take advantage of the fact that Mariano was not in the city. He sought out the intendant-general of the Rio police, a personal friend, and filed a complaint accusing Damiana of being a libertine, an atheist, licentious and a spendthrift, unfit for society. He, an honorable subject of the Crown, a merchant belonging to the Order of Christ, and owner of land in the province of Goiás, no longer knew what to do to preserve the honor of his house and his daughter. He accused Damiana of being dangerous, of threatening his life and seeking divorce, which would amount to dishonor and ruin for him and his young daughter. He did not want to create a public scandal, but wished to punish the adulteress who organized republican meetings in his house, in his own house, the house of a loyal and honorable subject of the king.

He also sought out the archbishop and other important friends to denounce her and bring his plans to fruition. The friends of his wife and Mariano were mostly artists, without great political or religious authority, and Inácio took advantage of this fact in the execution of his plan. He could also count on his own friendships and money to convince everyone of his wife's dishonor and his own despair, and the need to take all precautions, and quickly, before the situation deteriorated further. With neither difficulty nor delay, he obtained false witnesses to attest to his wife's calamitous state. The intendant-general, the archbishop, and the prelate found it advantageous to agree; it was imperative that something be done, and fast.

Damiana, ignorant to her husband's machinations, was caught by surprise. The same night of the argument in which she had naively announced her decision to her husband, her daughter became sick with a bout of fever, and so she spent the following days and nights by the crib, having neither time nor the mindset to tend to her own concerns, much less speak to her friends. She wasn't the least bit prepared for what was about to happen to her. She wasn't at all alert enough to realize the trap her husband was setting when he asked her to go with him to the convent to speak with the Mother Superior. Inácio insisted, practically imploring her, he swore it was the last chance for them to arrive at an understanding, that she owed him that chance. He said that a slave woman would watch over the girl, that she was already better, she no longer had a fever.

Damiana, exhausted after many nights of keeping vigil and without the will to continue arguing, decided she would lose nothing by going to the convent.

When she arrived at the convent she was led through several dark hallways, then was asked to enter in a tiny cell; after they closed the door behind her and locked the door, she began to grow perplexed. At first, she had no idea what was happening. She spent the next few moments thinking about the strange behavior of the Mother Superior when welcoming visitors to the convent.

Then, a chill ran down her spine.

But she did not give in to fear, for what did she have to fear? She came to visit the convent at her husband's request; the whole thing was strange, true, but such things are always strange, the Mother Superior was bound to provide some explanation.

She began to understand the situation little by little. At first, as a small insinuation that she quickly discarded, chiding herself: "You're stupid, stupid, how can you think something so stupid? Inácio and the Mother Superior will arrive any moment." But as more time passed and the niggling idea lingered, and once she decided that she had effectively passed an unusual amount of time there, she began to scream. Her terrifying cries echoed down the long, hollow corridor. She received no response.

Just silence.

Damiana had no idea how long she had stood there screaming, how much time she spent there committed to the terror to end all terrors, that of not knowing what awaited her. The clear light entering through the tiny window near the ceiling began to change tone, to turn yellow, then a dark orange, when she heard the sound of an iron door opening and, filled with hope, she screamed louder: "Help! Who's there?" But there was no response. Only the faint sound of footsteps along the corridor with its towering ceiling and the small slot in the solid wood door that opened to pass through a tray with a cup full of water, a piece of bread, and a bowl of soup.

Damiana's screams had no end.

Her voice seemed a constant font of despair, terror, and a search for answers.

Still later, when darkness began to take over her tiny cell, she again heard the noise of an iron door opening at the end of the hall, and again the sound of footsteps approaching. The small window in the door opened again, and through it the cavernous mouth of the archbishop himself appeared to explain the situation. At her husband's request and by unanimous decision by the relevant religious and civil authorities, she was there to repent for her dissolute lifestyle and her licentious and corrupting habits. The length of her reclusion would depend on, above all else, her repentance and good behavior. He hoped to grant his blessing for her to return to a peaceful life at the side of her family, as soon as she accepted her role and destiny as a wife and mother in accord with the laws of the Church and society.

When she would accept her situation, cease screaming, and calmly commit herself to that period of rest and reflection in the convent, which is what everyone expected of her and with the greatest speed, she could be transferred to a larger cell in the company of other cloistered women.

Damiana, however, never accepted the situation and never stopped screaming. As she grew increasingly weak, her screams became briefer, her voice hoarse, but she could still be heard down the long corridors. She did not accept or resign herself at any point, not even for a fraction of a second, to the convent life; no matter how futile, she never lost an opportunity to try to flee, however small.

Ah, Damiana!

Why?

When people face such unexpected blows and intolerable losses, they try to relive over and over the moments that led up to the tragedy, the actions that brought them to that point, in a desperate attempt to understand that which cannot be understood. They don't do it out of the irrational hope that they might still change things, or out of the longing to torture themselves, or to make themselves pay for something they did or didn't do, as though they were ultimately as responsible for their predicament as their tormenters. No, that isn't what drives them to do this, but rather the absolute human need to understand what happens and why it happens, where they are and how they got there. It is the all-consuming need to uncover some thread of logic, no matter how tenuous, on which to stand and rise above the incomprehensible, the unacceptable, the madness. Because if such a thread does not exist, then only one thing remains: unadulterated terror.

Damiana relived her final days at home over and over in her head. She saw the abominable image of Inácio Belchior invade her mind, repeating the same words, making the same gestures. She saw herself also repeating the same gestures and words. Time and time again. She tirelessly sought the thread of logic that could help her rise above it all and save her from her fate.

After a time she was transferred to a cell that was slightly larger; at least the window was larger and offered a wider view. But the convent's walls were tall, its doors thick, its locks impenetrable. Her attempts to escape were rather amateur, fruitless, and only led to tighter vigilance that made the limits of her confinement even more unbearable.

Many times the thick, humid air became difficult to breath and caused her to faint. When she woke up she would begin again to scream, to cry, to hurl threats. She would spend days without eating. She grew thinner until she was nothing but bones, she grew weaker, suffered hallucinations.

She demanded they give her pencil and paper to write. She wrote to her uncle, to friends, but soon realized that her letters were never sent. The only option that occurred to her was to throw her letters, her poetry, and her denunciations through the convent window. She would write, write, and throw the pages to the wind. Sometimes with a certain destination in mind, sometimes folded, but generally without an address, pages released to the wind, that it might take them wherever it would.

She did not know this, for she could never climb high enough to see, but her tiny window did not face the street, but a thicket. It was there that everything she wrote fell and became lost amid the leaves fallen from the trees, one more leaf of paper among so many others, a leaf different and whiter than the others, the pencil marks its veins, leaves that were more desolate and awful than any other, but as abandoned as the others, without a single hand to find them. They gathered there one by one, day after day, until they formed a mountain of unimaginable loneliness, stuck in the mud that came with each rain shower.

She wrote at length to her daughter Açucena. These letters were hopelessly sad, a bit illogical, a pale reflection of the absurdity of her situation. Sometimes, when she was lucky, she was able to dip into the past and write her daughter with memories of her former life: the never-ending plantation, the cattle, the jatoba tree, the great big porch where Grandma Jacira had sat for her ritual footbaths. When she could, she also dipped into the age when she arrived in Rio and held the illusion that the city could be hers, and she would write about them. When her captors wished to punish her for bad behavior, however, they would transfer her to another cell, the worst in the convent, a horrific cell whose tiny window opened not to the forest, but onto the tiny cemetery where they buried the homeless and slaves.

It was a hell to end all hells.

The dead were still buried at the church at that time, something that would only change after Brazil's independence, when modern modes of hygiene gained sufficient influence, resulting in laws that determined that cemeteries would be constructed on the edge of the city, obeying basic notions of public health. But at that time, burials took place in the same churches belonging to the parishes that the deceased had frequented while living and where, while they were still alive, they had tread over other graves. Dona Maria, the Mad Queen, was herself buried there, in the very same Convento da Ajuda.

But those dead who did not belong to a parish, the slaves abandoned by their owners in alleys, those from Africa who had died in quarantine before they could disembark from the slave ships, or indigent mestizos—these were buried without a proper funeral, without any thought, in any old place that could be found, such as the woods behind the convent. These corpses, without caskets or even burial shrouds, were thrown into the shallowest of graves and covered with only a bit of dirt. If some limb or other remained exposed, it was beaten down with heavy wooden clubs, forced back down beneath the dirt.

In these shallow graves, the decomposition of the bodies produced noxious gases that posed a health risk, carrying disease through the tiny convent windows. One's sense of smell eventually adjusted and no longer noticed these pestilent aromas swirling all around, miasmas that hung like dense clouds in the cells, causing nausea, headaches, and nightmares.

The dark of night was worse. Damiana would summon all her strength and determination so that her thoughts, at least, could flee that place. It was then, if she was lucky and managed to allow her mind to abandon the suffocating darkness of her cell, that she could see the city entirely light up, the candles and the street lamps burning on every street, and in even the poorest houses, a light in each open window and every door. She saw the streets bursting with flowers, the stones carpeted with sweet-smelling herbs, rosemary, chamomile, basil. The princess approaching from the port, the princess was arriving in Brazil, daughter to the Austrian emperor, the princess who was a lover of the arts and natural sciences, the new wife of Dom Pedro, Carolina Josepha Leopoldina Von Habsburg. The princess treading over the herbs that were placed there so that she might tread over them, and tread she did and wave and smile from beneath a golden canopy, the princess was completely taken with Brazil, she saw right away that it was a magnificent country with sufficient greatness to warrant independence, and she tread over the herbs with her ankle boots with heels and a sweet, tantalizing smell began to rise from beneath her soles, a pungent, sweet, and asphyxiating smell, a smell that began to suffocate her, the princess was about to faint, she was about to faint in the tropical heat beneath the resounding bells, the salvos of cannons and fireworks, and from among the fireworks a louder sound rises then wells, and Damiana, overcome with horror, soon recognizes it, the thudding of the clubs beating the corpses back down into their graves, and then she watches as the half-buried bodies rise up from the earth, and the living dead torment her through the walls to the beat of the deafening thuds of the wooden clubs.

She opened her eyes, unable to breathe, once again overcome with terror.

It was one more night she would spend without sleeping and given over to complete despair.

Don't think that Damiana was the first or the only woman to be imprisoned in a convent. This method of getting rid of one's wife was often used at the time, when a husband did not want a divorce to divide up their property, but lacked the courage to kill her outright, or merely wished to teach her a lesson, so to speak.

At first, no one knew where Damiana was.

Only Belchior made sporadic visits to the convent, but she refused to speak to him. She allowed his visits in the hopes that he would bring their daughter, too, and she barely listened to what he said. During the two years she was confined, he brought Açucena to see her mother on two occasions, and this to not displease the Mother Superior, who insisted it would help Damiana to mend her ways.

Belchior told anyone who asked that Damiana was being treated for her nerves, and that she had been advised by her doctors to rest and avoid visitors. To his friends, he would say that she was at the plantation in Goiás. To her uncles from Goiás, he sent false news.

Mariano had departed on a long trip to the south of the country. It was a trip he had been planning for many years, a longstanding desire: to visit the provinces which, it was said, were practically a country unto themselves. And so the troupe of amateur artists, three musicians—all of them from wealthy families like his own, one of whom belonged to a family of dry-meat barons from Rio, a young man with a tenor's voice and several acquaintances in the land of the pampas who acted as guide for the group—set off on a "gallant excursion." Mariano was the oldest, the most bohemian, and the most generous among them. He ended up involved in many stories, including a wild and amorous exchange, losing his head over a country girl from the Azores whom he mooned over for quite some time. He only returned to the court more than two years later.

He had thought it strange that his letters to Damiana remained unanswered. He even wrote directly to Inácio Belchior asking after his niece, and received a cold and formal response assuring him that everyone was doing well and that Damiana, thanks to the Good Lord, was recovering from a treatment for her nerves, and for this reason had been unable to write. But he was not to worry, as the doctors had assured him it was nothing grave and Belchior was seeing to her well-being, down to the very last detail. The brothers from Goiás also sent Mariano the same news: Inácio had written telling them that Damiana was treating her nerves and assured them that she was making a full recovery at the hands of the best doctors at court.

The news of such a lengthy treatment began to worry Mariano, and he decided to return to Rio. His passion for the Azorian woman had subsided, leaving him once again able to exercise normal logic, and he resolved to abandon the life of a "conquistador of the South." The very same day he arrived in Rio, he set off for Damiana's house and, from the beginning, found himself faced with Inácio's evasiveness and subterfuge.

It took him some time to discover the entire shocking truth. Only then, with the influence of his cousin Ambrósio, whom he felt the need to seek out, and with the threat to break down the convent doors, did Mariano finally obtain authorization to visit Damiana.

But it was too late.

He found her sick in body and soul. Something—perhaps tuberculosis, perhaps some other fever—was burning up her body and lungs.

It was difficult for Mariano to completely grasp what had happened. Damiana was no longer in any condition to coherently explain her years of captivity. She seemed confused about the facts, mixing them up, muttering absurdities that he couldn't understand. Mariano was scared and perplexed: his niece had been so strong, so fearless, so sure of herself. What had happened? How had she fallen so low? She looked like a tattered ragdoll, light as a feather, something he could carry as though she were a tiny pillow that no longer held its form. Which is what he did. He pulled her to her feet and then, carrying her in his arms, immediately took her away, and after everything that had happened, after all those years, no one, neither the Mother Superior nor her acolytes, dared stand in the way of his resolute steps, not even to ask him what he thought he was doing. They were relieved, in a way, that someone had assumed responsibility for the cloistered woman who had only brought them problems, and who had been growing sicker by the day; they were content to send an urgent notice to her husband.

Mariano took her to his small bachelor's house.

There, in her uncle's living room, was a watercolor of her done by the painter Chamberlain, a visitor to her old house and former gatherings. Mariano spent hours staring at the portrait where Damiana appeared in all her vigor: her golden-brown skin, her full lips, her above-average height, her hair pulled back in a bun. Her vitality seemed to spill over the faint tones of the watercolor. She smiled with her entire body and eyes; she smiled with her soul.

Mariano could not forgive himself.

The fetid air of the convent, her refusal to eat, the tumult of her incomprehensible suffering, all of this would have been too much even for someone as strong as she was. But the fatal and decisive fact seems to have been her complete isolation. Mariano was certain that, had she been able to write him, to tell him everything from the beginning, she would have been able to overcome Belchior's cruelty. Mariano could not forgive himself, it was inadmissible to him that he had not been there for someone he had always considered a daughter, at the precise moment she most needed him.

Belchior arrived at Mariano's home: tense, fearful, feigning worry but quite relieved upon seeing that Damiana's weakness and incoherence would make it impossible to contradict his story. Instead of waiting for the moment he was to become a widower, he had since become the sole owner of all his wife's property. He brought Açucena by the hand, the little girl with the wide eyes who, in truth, barely knew her mother.

In his attempts to explain things to Mariano, Belchior insisted without once vacillating upon the story about Damiana's nerves, her attacks, the danger she represented to the safety of all, especially herself and her very own daughter, Antônia Carlota, who one day . . . no, it was too painful to remember. Inácio Belchior lied without shame or remorse: she was sick and could not be accounted for, she had no control over her actions. He had felt forced to act as he had, for the good of his wife, because this was what everyone counseled him to do, from the archbishop and the prelate to the doctor who had seen her on the occasion.

"Who was this doctor, Belchior? Give me his address."

"No, that won't be possible, he's no longer in the city. He returned with the king to Lisbon, he was the doctor to the royal family, the best around."

Mariano couldn't say why, but he didn't believe a thing Inácio said. Damiana's terrified expression when she refused to see her husband confirmed his suspicions. He didn't know what to do to repair the guilt and pain he felt wash over him.

More than ever, the city found itself in a frenzy. On account of the events in Portugal, King João VI had returned to Lisbon, leaving his son, Pedro, as prince regent. But the tense climate had persisted, as had the conflict between the orders sent down from Lisbon and the interests of Brazilians. The only thing on everyone's lips was the need to declare independence once and for all. Rumors flew back and forth. The country leapt headlong toward its defining moment. The city was electric.

Damiana died two days after the declaration of independence.

The city commemorated the declaration with enormous fanfare, every lamp was lit, the town glowing from end to end. Fireworks exploded, church bells rang, people gave speeches and danced in the street, groups of musicians played alongside them. Everyone proudly displayed ribbons of yellow and green on their arms or on their clothes, the colors of a free Brazil.

Damiana's was a modest funeral. A few friends. Inácio leading Antônia Carlota by the hand. Her uncle Justino, who had come days earlier from the plantation to see his niece, was also there.

The city was overrun with joy and everyone was happy; there was no room for sorrow or private dramas.

Back at home from the cemetery, Mariano walked directly to his bedroom closet, where he grabbed two pistols. With all the calm in the world, he crossed the city streets just as he was, the two pistols in hand, heading straight for the house of Inácio Belchior.

He was completely at peace.

Completely at peace with what he was about to do.

VICIOUS
MODERNITY

AÇUCENA BRASÍLIA/ ANTÔNIA CARLOTA
(1816-1906)

More than her four names, which didn't even sound so strange on her, but rather had a certain ring to them, what was most notable about Açucena were her laughing eyes, her grin that seemed to leap forth from her round, brown face, and her hands, especially her hands, which had a warm touch, a quality of transmitting something vibrant and strong that attracted other people. The touch of her hands sowed peace wherever they roamed, leaving behind a sense of well-being that was not unlike the physical relief felt after a massage.

With those hands, she made sugared sweets that always provoked the same reaction in whoever ate them, the same near-verbatim appreciation, as though each person saw what the others had, as though they had closed their eyes in ecstasy and rolled their tongue around the corners of their mouths in an attempt to conceal an irrepressible desire to find some remainder, no matter how small, of the sweet and then let forth a sigh borne from a state of pure bliss, a twin to the frank expression that always accompanied it: "Mmmmm . . . God almighty, this is the best sweet I've had in my entire life."

She also created delicate flowers out of bird feathers, of various shades of green, blue, yellow; flowers that appeared so natural that they were often accidentally destroyed when some overzealous slave woman put them in vases full of water as though their vibrancy and texture demanded the same care as fresh flowers. These flowers were highly coveted by those who passed through the city. They were presents Açucena would give to her visitors and friends and which many—without her knowing it, though had she known it she would have found it amusing—then resold.

Açucena Brasília was small, plump, and had a natural tendency for dressing up: she wore bright colors and a whole assortment of earrings, necklaces, bracelets, and rings—every day, no matter where she went. And everywhere she did go she left a trail of laughter, the rustling of silk, and the jingle of jewelry. She was the most ardent fan of the sugared fruit-candies she made, and it was common to see her with tiny white grains of sugar melting in the corners of her mouth, full of satisfaction. That had been her personality as a girl, and remained once she became a woman. Exuberant, luminous, attractive, like a crystalline font of joy and affection.

But her life, we can all agree, got off to a difficult start. She had a good-for-nothing, calculating, criminal father. She couldn't even say she had known her mother. And having two names—no, not two, four, four names, well, just think about it, such a thing could have easily been too great a burden for anyone. But not for Açucena.

Luckily, her life also had an easy side: her generous and level-headed great-uncle, who raised her giving her total freedom and who was—of this she had no doubt—a much better father than Inácio Belchior ever would have been. He taught her how to read, write, and see the world on its lighter side, a talent which was also in her genes—the capacity to always see the bright side of life, and if necessary, of turning it upside down to laugh at its split seams.

It was only when he was on his deathbed that Mariano asked

Açucena—herself already a mother of two children—if he had told her how he'd killed her father.

He had not, she responded.

And so her great-uncle told her how, as the streets throughout the capital had erupted in euphoria to celebrate the newfound independence, no one had noticed him as he walked along, two pistols in his hands.

Not even the friends he encountered on his way to the house of Inácio Belchior noticed, all of them unable to contain their joy, all of them hugging him. They insisted that he join them in that exuberant commemoration of public joy, but not one of them took note of the guns he carried, not one of them mentioned his late niece, not one of them asked where he was going at a festive time like that.

He told her how he knocked at Inácio's door; Inácio, too, had gathered with friends on that historic night, important Portuguese merchants titillated with recent events, confident there was no threat posed by the heir to the Portuguese throne who would now lead the Brazilian government. On the contrary, business was certain to thrive under those new circumstances. Also present were some of Inácio's aristocratic friends, who likewise felt safe on account of Emperor Pedro I's royal blood, all of them drinking champagne to ring in the new era, when Mariano knocked on the door and Inácio Belchior himself answered, because most of the slaves were also in the streets celebrating.

When he saw Mariano, Inácio was overcome with fear. He became even more so when Mariano handed him one of the pistols and calmly asked him to come out into the street so he could kill him. But he wouldn't kill him like the mouse of a man he was; he was granting Inácio the right to die like the man he had never been.

Mariano recounted to Açucena how he had been calmer at that moment than he had ever felt in his life. He was certain that he had never been calmer, the day his blood ran as cold as it ever would.

Inácio, caught by surprise in the presence of his friends, didn't have so much as the time to think of a way out of the situation. His standing and his honor had been summoned, there on the front step, elegantly invoked by the words Mariano made a point to pronounce with complete levelheadedness so that everyone heard him. Under everyone's gaze, there on his own doorstep, Inácio could not simply turn and run, as he surely wished to his very core he could do.

"The duel, right there in front of his house, was quick and painless for me," Mariano said. "No effort or emotions were wasted on my part when I shot your father. As I have already said, I had never been calmer my entire life. I've always been a good shot, and it's important to recognize that the option Inácio had was to die as a man; that of escaping my bullet was not up for discussion."

His composure still intact, Mariano continued to say he then walked into the house bathed in lamplight and went straight to the girl's room; he lifted her from her bed and carried her away in his arms. He was certain that he would be able to do for her what he had failed to do for his sister and his niece.

"And you did, Uncle," she said to him, squeezing his hand. "You most certainly did."

In the midst of the festive chaos that had overrun the city that day, Mariano knew he had some time, but not much, since Inácio's friends, once recovered from their initial surprise, would certainly seek to have him jailed. In reality, he had already prepared a place to flee to, a place where he would not be found, a plantation that was at his disposal as he needed it. It was one of the plantations of the famous Ambrósio cousins (and there, at Mariano's deathbed, the two of them—great-uncle and niece—had to laugh).

The famous Ambrósio twins.

That was how they jokingly referred to the cousins. There could be no doubt: the two sides of the family couldn't stand one another. And the Ambrósios, mind you, had even done quite a bit, done all they could to help, had practically saved Mariano from prison, had seen to all the papers so that Antônia Carlota—their side of the family referred to her by her Portuguese name because they considered it more aristocratic, more fitting than Açucena Brasília—would receive the entire inheritance that rightly belonged to her. They continued running her father's business on her behalf. The cousins had made the plantation available to them until the law forgot all about Mariano and his crime, after which she and her uncle then moved to a tiny village near the border between Minas Gerais and São Paulo.

But, notwithstanding their generosity and all their elegance and pomp, the Ambrósios had been slave traffickers, owners of fleets of slave ships—and they still were then, clandestinely, even after it had been outlawed. They marred the name of a great young nation, and Mariano and Açucena could not accept that. They felt a great debt to their cousins for the favors they had done them, but they could not accept their activities.

Of course, Mariano and Açucena had always had slaves, just like any other family of their standing. And just like any other family of their standing, they also had never done any hard labor. The difference between them and the others was to be found in the way they treated their slaves, and above all in their views of slavery, in their understanding that it was intrinsically wrong, that it ought not exist. But to demand that they release their slaves would have been to demand that they live beyond their time. They freed a great many slaves, it's true, and after some time—and well before any law was passed—they began to free the elderly and the newborns, they gave refuge to runaway slaves, all of it. But it's also true that they still kept slaves at work and at home, though they truly believed they were treating them as equals. Was such thinking contradictory? Without a doubt. But, without the contradictory consciousness of these early abolitionists, it's likely abolition would have taken longer than it did to come about.

In the tiny village where they went to live after they left the plantation, Açucena arrived having barely emerged from adolescence. There, her lovers were numerous and her affairs made her notorious. Like her great-uncle Mariano, she too gave no thought to marriage, but had, as far as anyone could tell, all the men she wanted. She gave birth to five children, of which only three survived.

Her first love was a widower nearly twenty years her senior, a comendador from a family of barons from Ouro Preto. Entirely besotted with her, the comendador was her instructor in the art of lovemaking and some choice Latin phrases that, like many Brazilian men of his time, he had incorporated into the daily lexicon when he studied in Portugal at the University of Coimbra. He and Açucena lived in different cities, and for three years she refused all nine of his marriage proposals, made yearly every Easter, Advent, and Christmas, until one day she not only refused his proposal, but informed him that he should not bother coming to see her anymore. The one thing Açucena took from him was the habit of inserting Latin into her conversations, which she did out of pure irony, to add a bit more wit to her already clever remarks and biting commentaries. Now and then, off she'd go with her *sine qua non*, her *modus vivendi*, her *quantum satis*, and her *dura lex sed lex*—in the living room, the kitchen, the church, past a ring of people dancing the lundu, making everyone laugh, even those who had no idea it was Latin.

She loved to joke around with her friends, and would do anything to surround herself with the sound of laughter.

Her second love was a young military man who was passing through the village. They had one of those affairs that people tend to describe as torrid and short-lived.

Her third, the most enduring because it demanded even less of her, was with the priest, and lasted some three years. It was also one of the most tranquil relationships, with its falsely clandestine encounters once or twice a week, with its lack of demands on either party, free of great demonstrations of jealousy, possessiveness, or quarrels. Falsely clandestine because—and of this there could be no doubt—everyone in the village knew about them, and only pretended to be unaware. Açucena also had an affair with a young slave. A tall, muscular, sheepish young man. But I can't say for sure whether this affair took place during the time of her rendezvous with the priest, or just before or after. It must have been just before, since after the priest, Açucena finally met Caio Pessanha, a man from the Northeast who had fled the Revolution of Pernambuco in 1817. With him, she finally married.

Caio was an adolescent at the time of the struggle in Recife. He'd barely turned fifteen, but had become involved body-and-soul in the movement for independence. He was at the side of Padre José Inácio de Abreu e Lima when Padre José set out on a trip to Bahia carrying letters in his rucksack written by the insurgents to explain the goals of the new republican government—a trip on which they were captured and the priest executed by a firing squad. Caio, little more than a boy, managed to flee, and after wandering around for some time in the backlands of Bahia and Goiás, turned up at the plantation belonging to Açucena's great-uncles.

Later, when things calmed down in Pernambuco, Caio resumed his studies in Olinda and continued his commitment to republican ideals. He was ardent, effusive, an admirer of the French Revolution, and a Mason. Seven years later, history repeated itself in Pernambuco, and once again it ended in tragedy, with the Republicans declaring the establishment and secession of the Confederation of the Equator. Caio was among them. And once again, troops arrived from Rio de Janeiro, invading, setting fire to Recife and laying waste to the city. The military's forceful reaction, which resulted in the imprisonment and execution of the movement's leaders and the execution of the insurrectionist Frei Caneca before a firing squad, forced Caio and other revolutionaries to flee wherever they could.

That was when he decided to return to the middle of the country and work to spread his ideas. He became an educated and politicized peddler of revolution who used his salesman's charm to spread Republicanism. From that point on, he was tied to many of the rebellions and revolts throughout the provinces that made those years an era of great political agitation.

At the very end of one beautiful May afternoon, Açucena felt her heart stop beating for a brief but unforgettable moment as she watched a distinguished man arrive at the village mounted atop his horse, accompanied by two black men also on horseback. The man's long hair was pulled back, his mustache carefully trimmed, his coloring seductive, dark. Caio Pessanha elegantly dismounted and introduced himself and the splendid black mare on which he'd arrived, whose name was Republica; and his two black aides, free men, Constancio and Belizário, with their mules, Liberty and Fraternity. He also presented his trunks full of wares, which served both as his disguise and his means of income. The unexpectedness of his manners and loquacity filled Açucena with surprise and joy from the beginning.

Mariano knew Caio, and welcomed him in grand style to his home.

Açucena bought two magnificent silk sheets and several necklaces, bracelets, and rings. She purchased two of the books he had brought. She bought linen bed sheets, woven by seamstresses from the Northeast, two silver chandeliers with finely worked details, and a carved bone-fan and wallpaper depicting a country scene. She bought, to tell the truth, a good part of the stock brought along by the journeying salesman, who stayed for dinner. Then it was Caio's turn to be introduced to the delights of Açucena's candied sweets and, hours later, her bed. Ultimately, he made the village the resting spot where he would always return during the best years of his life. They had two children: Socrates Brasiliense and Diana América.

The likelihood is quite high that Açucena was the subject of much commentary for her love affairs and strange manners, so ahead of her time was she in that tiny countryside village, though nothing can be said on the subject with any certainty. Because if it's true that an omniscient narrator supposedly knows everything, it's also true that in literature, as in every other discipline, there's an appreciable distance between theory and practice. A narrator knows many things, it's true. If it were the opposite case it would be impossible to tell you this story—but to be frank, narrator and omniscience are separated by a considerable gap and heavy dose of exaggeration.

Whatever the case, whether the liberties her heart took subjected her to gossip or not, this in no way hindered her from being considered by nearly everyone as a sort of blessing for that village.

This was the case for several reasons, all of them quite concrete.

As soon as they had come to live there after those several years spent on the Ambrósio plantation in Minas, where Mariano taught Açucena nearly everything she knew, uncle and niece had been a breath of fresh air to the tiny moribund village. They lived well and without worry off the inheritance from Inácio Belchior's import-export business, managed for Antônia Carlota by the Ambrósio cousins, and from part of her lands in Goiás. They had arrived with money and slaves; not many, but enough to bring life to the small town.

Out of a tiny house on the edge of the emerald mountains that surrounded the village, they made a magnificent two-story home—the first seen in those parts. And after the house on the foot of the mountains, they helped to renovate the church and built a gazebo in the village square. Mariano liked to build, to draw out plans and watch a building being erected. But it was Açucena who had the idea of giving her slaves the opportunity to learn a profession and encouraged them to dedicate themselves to their apprenticeships, for one of the rewards for whoever became a master craftsman was freedom. They had slaves who built mud houses, there were carpenters, blacksmiths, tailors, certified artisans who would learn and teach each other, even as a sort of strategy toward their own freedom, since they knew that their capacity as a master craftsman would be more quickly recognized if they managed to train others who they could even leave as substitutes, ensuring their own freedom did not create hardship for Senhor Mariano and Senhora Açucena, who were deserving of nothing but appreciation and gratitude.

With their skilled slaves, they had transformed the town into a center sought out by everyone in the surrounding area, a situation that brought welcome progress and activity. Those from outside the village came to order furniture from the local carpenter, suits from the tailor, keys, nails, and door knobs from the blacksmith. The town was becoming known as a small hub for craftsmen that had grown out of the enormous yard belonging to the large home on the mountainside, and this was good for everyone.

Another reason people came was for Açucena's magical hands. Not that she was a healer, but her natural talent with her hands led her to clean a wound here, apply pressure on an aching spot there, examine an old man who could no longer leave his bed, and by the time she realized it, her fame as a curer had spread far and wide. She would effortlessly set a broken bone, eliminated back pain brought on by years of hard labor, relieve the swelling on a wounded hand. As she conversed with those she healed, she would apply pressure to a certain spot, gently pat others, run her hands through their hair, caressing them with an affectionate manner and contagious laugh until suddenly the person no longer wanted to leave her side, and was soon feeling better than ever before. With her hands alone, Açucena cured bodies and lifted spirits.

For all these reasons, the town residents showered her with thanks and affection. Her easy-going, happy, and charitable manner threatened no one and, on the contrary, left others inclined to take her in and protect her.

Mariano was also pleased with his new life. One of the main activities in the village was card playing, and along with the modest orchestra and band he formed, where free blacks were allowed to play next to whites, he didn't need much more than that to enjoy himself. They would gather nearly every night to rehearse and play in the house with its blue window-frames. On Sundays, they gathered in the square where he had paid for the construction of a gazebo especially for his little orchestra. They also played during religious processions.

Açucena sometimes paused to reflect that her religiosity owed much to the music and incense found at church and during processions. In that town devoid of theaters or balls, the closest thing to a grand spectacle was the singing at Mass and the nighttime processions beneath the enchanting candlelight, accompanied by the melancholy sound of the band and the anguished voices of women singing. Açucena loved these processions so much that she took it upon herself to organize them, and the town's processions became the most famous in the entire region. Not only for their beauty and the profusion of colorful arrangements of candles and the spectacular wooden candelabras, not only for the quality of music, but also, without a doubt, for the fact they were some of the few processions throughout the country where the little angels could be black. The village priest, who did everything Açucena asked, could not deny her that request, and so she made her little black angels, the children of slaves and free men, the best dressed in the entire region.

When the little altar boys appeared at the church door dressed in red robes and white surplices, gently swinging silver censers to send the perfumed smoke of the incense skyward, and Mariano summoned the first chords from his band, Açucena's heart warmed as she sought the best spot from which to appreciate the colorful, melodic procession that marched down the street.

Açucena's other joy was dancing the lundu. She would dance in her living room or around the slaves' bonfire, she would dance anywhere. Plump as she was, she nonetheless possessed a sort of levity, a certain grace and a sway in her hips that provoked a fair bit of admiration.

Her demeanor and her sensuality were to everyone's liking and rejoicing, and she gave life to each dance. When Caio was present, the couple's dancing left onlookers with their chins on the floor.

Caio Pessanha was always coming and going on his trips as a traveling salesman and revolutionary, along routes and intervals Açucena knew well. But one day he was taking longer than expected and that morning, Açucena suddenly awoke with the certainty that she would never see him again. And so, when that very afternoon she saw Constancio arriving alone on his old mule Fraternity, she called her children so they would be at her side when their father's faithful companion said whatever it was he had to say. Socrates was twelve, Diana ten. What Constancio had to tell was that Caio and Belizário had died on the roads of Bahia, ambushed by thieves, and that he, Constancio, was the only one who had managed to escape with his life.

Constancio also told them how, in reality, they had gone to that region charged with a risky mission, carrying ammunition to a runaway slave colony that was under threat, whose leader was an old comrade of Caio's. The situation was growing more dangerous each day because the price of slaves had increased ever since the trade was outlawed, and the plantation foremen went after the runaways like madmen. It was a tense journey, requiring they travel at night and hide with their cargo by day; they had tussled twice with soldiers they encountered along the way, but everything had gone quite well. Their mission complete, they had begun the trip home, at ease, their guard down. Perhaps for that very reason, feeling the danger had passed, they were too at ease and had forgotten that lately the roads had been the site of attacks by fugitive criminals who made their living by ambushing travelers. Frankly speaking, they were quite careless. "Senhor Caio only thought about getting back here to you, Senhora 'Çucena," Constancio told her. Then the rest was what it was: the men didn't have so much as the time to react, and Caio was shot right between the eyes. Belizário survived for a few more hours, which was worse because, wounded there in the remote scrubland waiting for death to arrive, with the sun beating down on his head, the shadows of vultures circling around him in his desperation, and without a single drop of water to alleviate his parched throat—his was a painful death. At least Caio had been spared this: he died before he had time to realize death was upon him.

An icy cold swept over Açucena, and a sharp wound took root deep within her. She realized that a part of her life, too, had also come to an end out on the road. The best part of her life, no doubt, the part where she had known love. But she also knew that in every way and notwithstanding everything, it was merely that, a part. Her life and her children would have to go on.

Three years later, death arrived for old Uncle Mariano. It arrived without much fanfare, in the form of a disease common to the elderly that left him only two days in his bed, days Açucena spent at his side, alleviating him of any pain or affliction. It was during these days that he told her how he had killed her father, Inácio Belchior.

After Caio, Açucena had other loves, but none of them lasted long.

Magnólia Liberta was born of one of these loves, a young musician who led Mariano's band, Justa Independência, after the old man's death. Açucena was certain that her love for processions had something to do with the mysticism and piety that influenced Magnólia's life. As a young girl, Magnólia was the most beautiful angel, her blue satin dress shimmering in the lights. Her wings were the largest of them all, enormous angel wings made from little feathers that seemed to make her fly, thin as she was, with her sandy-brown curls and her voice that left no one with a dry eye. She was the one who coronated Our Lady in the month of May and led the Procession of Our Lord during Advent.

Something of the emotion of these moments that she lived with such intensity must have left a deep mark on her childish heart, for

Magnólia never wanted to perform any other role. Her life—all of it—played out in the peaceful village streets of light-colored stone, along the route to church, and back to the house on the mountainside. She was easygoing, serene, and projected an inner peace.

When she was little, she liked to cover her head with the big copper pot from the kitchen until it hung over her face, and would delight in the reverberating echo created by the bewitching sound of her voice.

When she was a young woman, she wrote sonnets, sonnets that spoke of the natural beauty that surrounded her and mystical loves. These she kept in an album with a thick cover, between pages littered with dried leaves and flower petals.

Later, already grown, she would gather slaves and neighbors in the oratorium in the evenings to sing the third mystery of the rosary, prayers, litanies, and hymns. As she listened, Açucena was filled with admiration for her daughter's voice, which emerged strong and crystalline above the choir's, as though the other voices existed to create the base from which her voice could rise triumphantly. She also learned to make Açucena's candied sweets and her feathered flowers, except she didn't make the flowers from feathers, but from soft fabrics like silk, velvet, and satin. These were every bit as beautiful as her mother's.

From the house on the mountainside, Açucena watched her children grow, each pursuing his own path: Socrates went to study in Olinda, as his father had, and earned his law degree, and there he stayed, marrying a woman from Pernambuco and maintaining close contact with his father's side of the family. Diana, at thirteen, set off for Rio to live her own series of tumultuous love affairs. Magnólia continued living with Açucena, never straying from her tender care. Açucena also raised Diana América's first child, Dionísio Augusto, a freckled boy with red hair, and was a decisive influence in the life of Diva Felícia, her granddaughter.

In the village, she continued to be the center that radiated good news and generous acts. Over time, her hands were increasingly a source of wisdom and relief, touching everyone with her great circle of affection. She was part of the village heritage, and people came from far away to see her.

There, from her tiny kingdom at the foot of the mountains, Açucena lived a long life and saw a great many things. She saw the arrival of abolition and danced the lundu in the square with all the black people of the village. She saw the declaration of the Republic, and to celebrate, she opened a bottle of French Champagne her granddaughter had brought her on a recent visit. She saw the dawn of the new century and the birth of her great-grandchildren, Dionísio's children with a mulatta woman from right there in town, and had continued to live in the same house. She also saw the births of Diva Felícia's children. And finally, she saw the birth of her great-granddaughter Ana Eulália, and it was that same year that she allowed herself to depart from this world after ninety joyful years.

She died peacefully, in the most natural way possible, as though closing her eyes to enter into an extended slumber as she chuckled at the stories one of her great-grandsons was telling her.

The entire village took part in her funeral procession. Family businesses closed for the day and everyone, before leaving their homes, locked their doors and their windows, a strange thing to see in that time and place where even at night no one locked anything. The children dressed up as angels, and flower petals littered the streets along the route of a procession that included men, women, youths, and children on foot, on mules, in carriages, on horses, as they followed the casket to the cemetery. The band founded by Mariano led the way, inspired as they played their final homage to the venerable village matron.

Hers was a funeral that the people there would never forget.

DIANA AMÉRICA
(1846~1883)

Just look how life repeatedly escapes our control: despite the objections of her mother and uncle, Diana América adored the Ambrósio cousins. When she turned thirteen, she asked her mother to let her go live with them in Rio de Janeiro.

Sweet and affectionate until the moment things or people did not conform to her wishes, Diana had a fragile constitution, subject to colds and illnesses. She became a rather cunning and obstinate young woman, capable of bending even the emperor to her will if she judged it necessary.

With such characteristics, when her daughter turned thirteen and asked to go live at her cousins' house because she wanted to live in the capital, Açucena was not especially surprised. By nature, she was the sort of mother who never intended to rule over her children's lives: in fact, she thought that anything was possible, and made no judgments, everything had a right to happen beneath the sun, a belief that certainly played into her own longevity. She merely looked deep into her daughter's eyes and said: "If this is what you want, my daughter, very well, follow your path in peace."

Diana América arrived at the home of her uncle Teófilo Ambrósio, who had become the family patriarch and had promised his grandfather, Alencar, to always care for Jacira's family whenever they should need it.

Dom Teófilo not only understood, but admired his grandfather's dedication to the memory of his younger sister and his determination to repair the injustice that had been done to her. Like his grandfather and later his father before him, he too seemed not to comprehend that Jacira and her family had, by themselves, returned order to their lives and in fact needed neither the Ambrósios' condescension or protectionism. Convinced by his own power, pride, and will, Alencar had believed that the Ambrósios were responsible for their cousins and had instilled that same belief in his family. And only this belief, which owed much more to blind arrogance than reality, was capable of explaining the great effort they put into their task.

Diana eventually filled them with considerable regret for their concern, but at the beginning she was warmly received by her uncle and his family. She immediately began her studies with her cousins' French tutor, and she adapted to the festive and high-spirited rhythm that defined the lives of the wealthy during the Empire.

Rio de Janeiro was, at that time, the great slave trading port of the Americas, with the highest concentration of slaves in the world since the Roman Empire. It was, in some sense, an African city, a black city. Barefoot slaves filled the streets to perform their daily tasks; during working hours, few whites had something to do in the streets, and even those who weren't sufficiently wealthy to own several slaves had at least one or two they rented out to others to earn a living that way. Leisure was a refined virtue cultivated by the whites and a sign of status and prestige, since if work was done by slaves, then work, by definition, was beneath them, a necessary evil that—thank

God!—was the domain of black people. The repulsion Brazil's slave society had toward work was noted by every foreigner who arrived in the country.

Despite all this, Rio was the remarkable city it always had been, with its mountains, sea, and dazzling light. It was a festive city, energetic, bustling, with soirées, parties, and balls—everything possible happened there in the capital of the Empire.

From the beginning, Diana captivated the Ambrósios with her musical skill (she had inherited her family's perfect pitch) and practically took the gorgeous grand piano, somewhat abandoned in the living room, for her own. For some time, she showed her tender, sensible side, and soon learned all the necessary manners of an elegant *mademoiselle* in Rio society, *très charmante*. She would go on outings with her girl cousins in the elegant coaches with a driver and a valet dressed in charcoal livery with red trim. They made their way down the raucous Rua do Ouvidor buying dresses imported from France, *bien sûr*, girdles and silver petticoats to make their skirts more voluminous, white shawls from China and mother-of-pearl fans that had arrived on the *dernier bâteau*. These were necessary so that the girls could prance about at court balls and other musical soirées throughout the city, where the piano-playing talents of the "Ambrósio niece" came under increasing demand.

Diana was truly an exceptional pianist. At the age of five, she was already playing several songs on the small upright piano belonging to her uncle Mariano, her first teacher. In Rio, with the opportunity to approach her studies more methodically, she quickly grew into a respected musician at the salons and was considered one of the most original performers, with a whimsical, memorable style. She was even invited to play at a concert of non-professional musicians sponsored by Emperor Dom Pedro II and the young Princess Isabel, her same age, who gave her enthusiastic applause.

Diana's first few years in Rio were spent in complete awe. Given her restless temperament, however, she wanted more. She wanted to take advantage of the best of everything she knew, enjoying the luxury of her uncle's lifestyle without renouncing the liberty afforded by her mother's. It wasn't long before disagreements with her uncle and his family began to crop up, but Dom Teófilo, in his role as family well-doer, sought to tame as best he could what he saw as the young girl's rebellious streak and which, in his eyes, confirmed that the other side of the family required his steady hand.

A rupture, however, became inevitable, and for a rather good reason. Everything has its limit, after all, and when Diana became pregnant after meeting a young English student on holiday in Rio, it was the last straw. Her uncle told her that if she did not marry she could not have her child there, having a child out of wedlock would bring shame upon the family, something that was completely unacceptable in polite society. But marriage was the last thing on the minds of Diana and the young Englishman, who, frightened at the passion of those exotic people, took the first ship back home.

Diana also went back home, where she gave birth to her son, Dionísio Augusto, at Açucena's side. But it didn't take long for her to see she didn't like her new role caring for a child. She spent days exhausted, refusing to leave her bed, in what may have been her first bout of neurasthenia. She missed the exciting life in Rio and wanted to hear again—oh, how she wanted to hear it!—the pure tone of that grand piano. The upright piano that had belonged to Uncle Mariano, and had been hers as a child, now seemed to emit a tinny sound, with no force, no luster. She dreamed of going to Europe, where she would meet great composers and learn what could not be self-taught.

In Rio, Dom Teófilo, a fervent and sincere devotee of music, missed hearing her play. He also missed the prestige of having a talented niece to show off in the salons of the court. When Princess Isabel herself, greeting him at a soirée, asked after Diana and expressed her eagerness to hear her play once again, Teófilo Ambrósio resolved to forgive his niece. He sent her a conciliatory message, offering to welcome her back, as long as she did not bring the child. He imposed other restrictions as well, but promised to send her to study in Europe, as soon as her instructor thought her ready for such an undertaking.

Diana accepted his offer, but during this second stay at the Ambrósio mansion, she was already quite changed. Her radiance and vivacity appeared somewhat diminished, perhaps the result of motherhood, perhaps because she lived so far from her son. This despite her decision, which she made rather lightly, to leave him with Açucena. She considered him not so much a bastard son, but a younger brother, beyond her responsibility.

She buckled down on her piano lessons, and was no longer as enthusiastic about strolls through town or grand balls. Her piano instructor, meanwhile, an elderly German woman of an inflexible seriousness and an eagle-like appearance, possessed a tyrannical mastery of classical piano and was incapable of understanding or appreciating, much less accepting, her student's heterodoxy. Diana played with great originality, in plain opposition to her instructor's orthodox approach; inevitable, then, were the increasingly frequent disagreements between strict instructor and undisciplined student, whom she was supposedly there to help spread her wings. The result of this tension, beyond the stream of tears that fell from Diana's eyes like waterfalls, was the permanent delay of her teacher's approval for her trip to Europe.

The photo she had taken in a photographer's atelier on the Rua do Ouvidor dates back to this time. Her entire body is in frame, as was common in those years to accentuate women's fine attire, her hand resting on the back of a chair. She appears young, elegant, *très jolie*, but those who look closely can inevitably see in her eyes an undisguisable dejection, something that appears to be consuming her from within.

There is another photo, taken a short time before, of the entire family, shot by a photographer whom Dom Teófilo called into their home. Pictured are her uncle and his wife, Dona Carolina, their two daughters, Isidra and Irismara, both a bit younger than Diana, along with four slave women posing in the corners. Dom Teófilo's three sons do not appear in the photo, since they were already married, lived in their own houses, and were not present at the time. There are many other portraits of the entire family; it was a craze at the time to leave visual records for posterity using this new and revolutionary technology. Photography was admired by all, even the emperor, who had imported a similar contraption to take his own daguerreotypes. But in the photos restricted to the family, Diana is absent.

There is yet a third photo of Diana, taken many years later, when she was already married. She is sitting on a stool in front of her Essenfelder grand piano—this instrument truly all hers, a wedding gift from her husband. The photo is not dated and so it's impossible to know exactly when it was taken. It may very well be an effect of the technology at the time, when it was necessary for subjects to hold their pose for a minute and a half to obtain a perfectly in-focus photograph, but the fact of the matter is that Diana, her hands resting on her lap instead of on the keys of her magnificent piano, wears a gaze full of nearly unbearable sadness: it is an extraordinarily beautiful photo, but no one can look at it for long without averting his eyes from that disturbing, melancholic abyss.

Dom Teófilo's wife, Carolina, was the first to suspect that Diana's unstable emotions, her crises of reclusion in her bedroom, her refusal to come out for days at a time, were perhaps not solely the fruit of her niece's rebellious spirit. She had always thought her niece very thin, tending to eat little and poorly when she did. Dona Carolina dedicated herself to her house and her children, and Diana's temperament and emaciated figure concerned her a great deal, especially because she worried they might be contagious. For that reason, she paid close attention to her niece's moods and frequently sent her to the family doctor, who mostly prescribed rest and fortifying tonics.

It was Dona Carolina who asked Diana one day if she didn't want to visit her mother to deliver a tiny mother-of-pearl jewelry box that had belonged to the family of Dom Teófilo's great-grandmother, Clara Joaquina. Her daughters thought the old jewelry box very ugly, but she couldn't bring herself to throw it away. Diana agreed; she would take the jewelry box to Açucena. Subject to brief health crises, her piano playing had suffered as a result, and Diana had come to realize that her dream of studying in Europe was, even more so now than before, nothing more than a chimera.

Back when she had returned to Rio for a second time, it was her uncle's intention to marry her with one of his relations—his two daughters were already betrothed—but Diana had absolutely no interest in suitors. Unaccustomed to having his wishes and orders contested, he found his niece increasingly difficult and, may her father forgive him, there were many occasions in which he did not refrain from expressing his regret for having taken her in a second time. With the country at war with Paraguay, her uncle, engrossed in new business ventures, seemed to have less time for family life. Even if he had been able to devote more time to reigning in Diana, she had stopped listening to him some time ago. She wanted to stay in Rio and so she would stay, *n'importe quoi*.

The city was electric. The cafés along the Rua do Ouvidor were awhirl with news, and Diana had begun to frequent them without her cousins, who were barred by their father from doing so. She began to form friendships with people beyond the Ambrósios' circle. Thrilling reports began to arrive from the front, along with the debate over freeing the slaves to fight in place of their owners, and the murmurs surrounding a conscription law. There were also discussions around literature and the arts. There was music, and excitement in the air. Poets recited their poems, composers performed their music.

It was in one of those cafés that Diana met the young Hans G., a poet with gleaming green eyes and wild hair as blond as wheat. He cut a sharp figure and looked possessed each time he climbed onto the table to recite his translations of poems by Goethe and Schiller, in addition to his own compositions.

Diana could barely contain her ecstasy and delight when she saw him for the first time, that blond Adonis standing on the table, showered in applause, who seemed to recite his poems for her alone, his eyes fixed on her, his words a bridge that would forever tie him to her. It was then she first told herself what she would later tell him over and over, consumed with ardor: "You're absolutely sublime, Hans! Absolutely sublime!"

That night, he climbed down from the table and walked straight over to her:

"May I ask your name, senhorita?"

"Diana."

"Like the goddess."

"Like me."

A mysterious man, Hans spoke little of himself. He was certainly younger than she, though Diana never managed to learn his exact age; even putting together everything she managed to find out about him, she never found a precise answer. His parents had immigrated to the southern state of Rio Grande do Sul, and were part of a group known as the German Legion, invited by the Brazilian government to come to Brazil. This group included intellectuals, professors, and journalists who had participated in the Revolution of '48 in Germany, even going straight to the front lines, where Hans's father was wounded and nearly died. But Diana didn't even known his full name—she only knew him as Hans G., since that's how he signed his poems and introduced himself to everyone. At the age of thirteen he'd left his family in the south and had been trekking around the country ever since. He was merely passing through Rio, as he would always do in life. He had told her from their very first meeting that his destiny was to write and know the world, this portent of unimaginable wonders, with its battles and glories, its comedies and tragedies, its heaven and its hell.

The two of them lived in rapt ecstasy for a period that, at least to Diana, seemed to pass much too quickly. When Hans told her the time had come for him to leave, she implored him to stay a bit longer or else let her depart with him. But Hans was resolute as only the very young can be. With his steady green eyes and his hair fluttering in the wind, he desired to move on, tossing his black cloak between his body and Diana's, and he was clear:

"I don't want to stay and I can't take you with me. I've always said this was my life, that it was my destiny to be solitary, a wanderer and adventurer. Just me and my poetry. There's no room for anyone else at my side. Not even for you, sweet Diana. Farewell."

These words were daggers that Hans's green eyes shot mercilessly into Diana's impassioned heart. When she discovered soon thereafter that she was once again pregnant, she didn't have the energy to even think about what to do. She gave up life in the cafés. She gave up the piano. She gave up her dream of studying in Europe once and for all.

This was the ideal moment for Teófilo Ambrósio to take control of his niece's life. A friend, Caetano Acioli da Fonseca, a partner with the English on various enterprises in Brazil, had always been in love with the young pianist and had already requested her hand in marriage several times. A widower several years her senior, he presently agreed, as though it were a mission, to marry her and assume paternity for the unborn child. He was a solitary man, without children, and was gratified at the possibility of having the young woman he loved and her child at his side.

Diana let herself be swept up by events.

Soon after the birth of her daughter, whom she named Diva Felicia, she had another attack, much worse than earlier ones, and suffered from intense fatigue. She couldn't sleep at night, had little appetite, and spent her days practically locked in her bedroom with the curtains drawn, because she couldn't stand the sunlight and the noise coming from the street and the rest of the house. Her slow movements and speech, her extremely pale complexion, all attested to her deep exhaustion. She was diagnosed with neurasthenia and recommended total bed rest as treatment.

From that point on, for several years, Diana spent a good part of her time at a clinic in the mountainside town of Teresópolis. Those were times when she didn't even have the energy to visit her mother's house. Only when she finally began to recover did she go and complete her convalescence in Açucena's mountainside home. It was there that she managed to recover and summon the strength to return to Rio and try to pick up the pieces of her previous life.

The pieces of her previous life.

They weren't many. But among them was the Women's Abolitionist Club.

In the time when she had frequented the cafés on the Rua do Ouvidor, Diana had begun to take part in club meetings, and this was one of the activities she picked up whenever she returned to Rio; there, she felt useful, and was invigorated by the small risk she sometimes thought she ran. The women distributed manifestos against slavery, organized small parades with speeches in public squares, and, to raise funds to purchase the freedom of slaves, they organized artistic shows that featured Diana's piano playing as their grand attraction.

But in fact, it was her participation in a more secretive venture that brought the color back to her face: a clandestine network that supported and aided the escape of slaves, arranging for documents, transport, and information that could neutralize any plans for their pursuit and recapture.

Her husband, Caetano Acioli, was an ally of the British and had long defended the necessity of a free labor force so that Brazil could transform itself into a new country, more prosperous and more closely aligned with European ideals. Being the last country in the world clinging to slavery was a shameful designation he sought to erase from our history. He knew of his wife's abolitionist activities, but did not investigate the matter much; notwithstanding his own convictions, he surely would have judged much of what she did—even setting aside the clandestine network of which, evidently, he hadn't the slightest clue—as hardly appropriate to a woman of her standing. He knew all too well, however, that attempts to curb Diana's wishes would be fruitless; besides which, what he most desired was to see a bit of vitality in his wife's features, and for this the abolitionist club and the piano were the best medicine.

As far as the Ambrósio family goes, they certainly knew of Diana's ideas and considered them part of her rebellious spirit, but they were far from imagining that these ideas had resulted in some sort of practical application. They mocked and ridiculed women's clubs in general, the abolitionists in particular, as futile gatherings around imported tea, where women poorly controlled by their husbands spent their afternoons. Little did they know that these clubs—especially the club to which Diana belonged, whose most important sources of information were the very salons the Ambrósio family attended—had already, among other things, managed to limit the success of many of the plans to pursue runaway slaves that had been articulated at their gatherings, between puffs of cigars and jokes and sips of the best Port wine.

The one person who knew the details of her participation in these clubs was her mother, Açucena, who was also part of the network that aided runaway slaves. If someone were to search her lands at the edge of the emerald mountains, what they would find, in all likelihood, were runaway slaves living in the tiny farmhouses and working the land.

Diana's brother, Socrates, from whom she periodically received letters with news, was a militant abolitionist lawyer in Pernambuco. He had the custom of sending his brother-in-law, Acioli, boxes of cigars stamped with the likeness of the abolitionist Joaquim Nabuco.

But the moment would always arrive when these thrilling periods of Diana's life in Rio, the house full of people, the whimsical sound of the piano revived, her trips to the cafés on the Rua do Ouvidor, the coming and going from club meetings, would be interrupted by lengthy periods of silence at the clinic in the mountains of Teresópolis. Periods that began to make themselves known when, suddenly, she took longer to emerge from the bedroom for breakfast or stayed sitting for hours on the veranda with her blank eyes circling the garden, where she no longer strolled to pick camellias, the symbol of abolition, with which she liked to decorate the living room. Or when she would sit at the piano and play her favorite pieces, each movement played at *piano* and *pianissimo* cast a pall over the house. Or when she called to little Diva to sit on her lap, and, taking her face between her hands, fixed her gaze with its incurable despondence on her daughter's green eyes, the same gleam in her eyes as Hans G., until the girl, growing frightened, began to cry or kick her legs, running away in tears from the stranger who had begun to take over her mother's body.

Caetano Acioli's wife had always been an enigma to him that he felt incapable of deciphering. He had and continued to love her, but throughout the years of their unstable matrimony his love grew into something closer to compassion than anything else. At first, he'd tried everything to make her happy, and there were moments in which he believed he'd succeeded in bringing her a bit of serenity. When, however, she began to suffer from increasingly grave attacks of neurasthenia, an illness that at the time physicians felt powerless to combat—today, perhaps, her case would be diagnosed as a masked form of depression—he found himself forced to accept the situation. He understood then that his happiness, were such a thing still possible, would come merely from his adopted daughter, whom he loved as he'd never loved anyone before.

The summer her daughter turned twelve, Diana was in a tranquil phase of her life. The weather in the city that year was terrible, with torrential rains, mosquitos, unbearable heat, and an epidemic of yellow fever that had begun to spread. As he did every summer when Rio became a boiling cauldron of epidemics and disease, Acioli had made plans to take his family to their mansion in the mountainside town of Petrópolis so as not to expose them to the risks brought on by Rio's climate. But that year Diana said she preferred to stay in Rio, where there was much to be done. She had been hired to help with an important plan to aide a group of slaves who had fled Bahia. She also planned to visit her mother and son, Dionísio Augusto, whom she hadn't seen in quite some time; she missed her mother's house, Açucena's caring manner, and her sweets. When she went, she also wanted to bring Diva, who loved spending time at her grandmother's.

The plan to help runaway slaves for which she was supposed to provide cover was, in reality, very simple, like many others that were taking place at the same time. The idea was to divide up a large convoy of many slaves along several different routes as they fled, dispersing their pursuers and weakening efforts at recapture. Her role was the same as always: to be on the lookout for some important piece of information during any conversations at the Ambrósio home to which she might be privy.

Since it was summer, however, her uncle's family was not in Rio, and her only chance to learn something was by visiting the enormous Ambrósio & Ambrósio commercial offices in the city center. The offices were also half-empty, but, as with any office worthy of the name, if there were any movement being planned, it would be the ideal venue for conversations, offhand remarks, and other useful information. Besides, it was also an opportunity for her to get out during those languid, rainy summer days.

And so, on her way to the offices in the city center, she passed without giving it much thought through streets with open sewage, swarms of mosquitos, and the acrid stench of filth. Even though she considered herself well-protected by closing the little window of her coach, the disease-carrying mosquitos did all they could to find their way to her sweet-tasting blood.

Diana América did not make it back to visit Açucena and her son as she had intended.

She died of yellow fever before she could reach the end of that abrasive summer in Rio.

Ah, so you want to know if the information Diana uncovered in the offices of Ambrósio & Ambrósio was useful in planning the escape of slaves? I suppose I could say it was, couldn't I, and give a *beau final romantique* to the turbulent tale of Diana's life. But no—while I may leave some things out, to lie in order to soften this tale or smooth things over, that I won't do. And so, unfortunately, the answer is no. On that occasion, with nearly all of her contacts far from the city, she was unable to gather any information of real use, and the worst is that a good number of the slaves who fled were recaptured.

But remind yourselves of at least two things to ease your frustration: at that moment, slaves were very expensive and, therefore, not punished for their attempts to flee as they would have been some years earlier; what's more, abolition was just around the corner. Five more years and that was it—everyone would be celebrating in the streets.

DIVA FELÍCIA
(1876-1925)

All right. Now let's talk a bit about Diva and just how beautiful she was. Though nothing's indisputable when it comes to beauty—personal preference will always result in a "but" or a "not so much" to just about anything—Diva was worthy of standing among the most beautiful women ever seen. Ah—this she most certainly was! She had green eyes, with the same gleam in them as her father's had, ever so slanted and crowned by a pair of eyebrows like perfectly drawn black velvet, and her lashes were so long and thick that, were they any longer, they would have likely impaired her vision; her high cheekbones and perfect nose could easily be used as a model for any plastic surgeon today; her full lips and slender neck may well have been what Audrey Hepburn sought to imitate years later. All this, and a body with the most harmonious proportions and golden skin, a color alone that ensured its owner eternal beauty.

Fortunately, she had a happier fate than her equally-beautiful ancestor, Maria Cafuza, and unlike Cafuza, Diva was fully aware of her uncommon beauty; she simply didn't know if it was a good or a bad thing. When her mother, in all her sorrow, would sit her on her lap, holding her face between her hands, peering at her in such a way she seemed to want to disappear inside her daughter's eyes, the young girl felt a sharp pain and a confusing mixture of guilt and anguish for making her mother wish to fall into a deep, dark abyss. She would cry, kick her legs, and close her eyes in an attempt to stop her mother from disappearing. However, when it was the slave women or her father looking upon her, their faces reflecting the happy harmony gained from contemplating some beautiful object or scene, she felt at peace with herself, capable of transferring this happiness to those she loved.

It was her grandmother, Açucena Brasília, who one day explained the reason for this internal struggle and how to deal with it: "You, my dear, like everyone, in fact, just to a greater degree, hold the power to inflict pain or bring joy. This often doesn't depend on us. It depends on the eyes of the beholder, and in such cases little can be done. But there is one thing that you can do, and that depends on you alone, which is to choose what you wish to cause more of: pain or joy. And after you choose, you should dedicate yourself to this choice. That way, you'll be able to better control these two feelings that, wanting to or not, everyone causes."

Diva, actually, chose more of everything. She chose to also call attention to the beauty of the things around her, things that were so mundane, so common, so within reach, things we see with such frequency that we take them for granted. Revealing the beauty in everyday things: that was why she began to take her camera into her grandmother's yard and photograph the corncobs half-removed from their husks, the bunches of bananas, the jatoba berries, the numerous and undervalued dried flowers of the central plains. She photographed vegetables, took close-ups of flowers and fruits, and saw to developing and enlarging the prints in the darkroom she had built in her house, emphasizing the characteristics of each subject and revealing surprising forms no one had ever noticed before, despite or perhaps because they'd been seen over and over.

If today photography is an expensive art, just imagine back then, when it was rare to boot. But being the sole heiress to a millionaire father has to be good for something, and Diva's passion began when her father gave her a camera for her twelfth birthday, the same year Diana América died.

Diva Felícia's life, like the turn of the century in which she lived, was full of novelty and excitement.

To begin with, she was the first woman in her family to regularly study in a school. She had her tutor—who only spoke French with her—but she also attended a girls' school for some years. She was also the first to travel abroad.

After her mother's death, her father took her on a long trip to Europe. They traveled by boat, passing through Italy, England, and France, where Diva remained for four years, studying art and, especially, photography and lab techniques. At one point her father asked whether she didn't wish to live in Europe, but she responded that no, she wanted to return to her land, the country where she had been born.

She found everything in Brazil to be more striking, more vibrant. She loved the landscape, the breeze, the smells, and above all the light, which was a bit excessive for some, but for her it was an intense source of pleasure. She loved the light, whose different shapes and intensities she knew how to appreciate and admire. She would say that, like Goethe on his deathbed, her final words would likely be: *mehr Licht*, more light!

Why yes, she did also speak German, having learned from reading Goethe and other German poets in the original. She had been captivated during her travels through the Rhine Valley and the romantic roads winding through Bavaria. She never learned of her biological father's German heritage, but it was as though some ancestral element had filled her with admiration for the German language and culture, and she had the great ability to soak up the sounds of the language like a sponge, and effortlessly assume the characteristics of that people so distant and different from her own. Caetano Acioli never revealed the identity of her biological father, because the reality was he didn't know either, and even if he had, he would never had said so. He considered himself the true father of the girl he loved so much, whom he had watched being born and raised as his own, without hesitation and without question. The only person who could have revealed the identity of Hans G. was Açucena, but Diana had never told her mother where he was from. She told her, of course, that he was a poet—"a sublime poet, mother, absolutely sublime!"—and enthusiastically compared him to Goethe and Schiller, but she must not have thought it important to mention his nationality. At any rate, even had Açucena known, she also would never have said anything, for she wholeheartedly respected Acioli's choice, and she also considered him her granddaughter's true father. In the case of Diva, the most interested of all parties, it never occurred to her that Caetano Acioli might not be her real father.

She returned from Europe at the age of seventeen with an ecstatic love for Brazil and its people. She enjoyed walking through Rio, stopping to appreciate the way the light cast down over the homes, the buildings, the monuments, the squares. She would walk along the beaches, soaking up the luminosity of the sand and sea. She would sit on a bench in one of the city squares for great lengths of time, marveling at her city and everything she intended to do there.

She'd had the luck of arriving at a moment of fevered enthusiasm and great change, when Rio de Janeiro was a hotbed of passionate ideas. Princess Isabel had just signed the Lei Áurea, abolishing slavery, and celebrations spread throughout the city, an effusive commemoration of the arrival, even if belated, of a new era. The shoe stores on the Rua do Ouvidor, full of freed slaves giddily spending their meager savings on the footwear they'd dreamed so long of and could finally use, were a spectacle in themselves, swaddled in a euphoria that no one could hide.

And why should they? The city was full of elation, the city was rejoicing, the city laughed out loud. From the balconies of their homes, residents would toss flower petals that coated the streets and sidewalks. People would parade through the streets, in carriages or on foot, in groups whose joy went round and round. Musicians gave impromptu concerts on the streets and in the squares, dancing left and right to the pulsing drumbeat of the newly freed.

There was no better time to be in the country's capital.

Soon thereafter it came time for the protests and impassioned cries of the Republicans. At any given moment one could hear voices on the streets singing "La Marseillaise," the anthem adopted by the radical Republicans, as enthusiastic young students marched through the streets.

One afternoon, Diva was eagerly following one such group, when everyone stopped so that a handsome young man with coffee-colored skin, his mustache carefully groomed, could climb atop a crate to deliver a speech with passion and charisma:

"We want a people's republic," he said, "a republic of popular protests, a republic with liberty, equality, and universal rights for all citizens. This is the republic we desire!

"We don't want a republic that seeks balance, where power acts as a moderator, a republic of compromise, a republic where the highest virtue is the exercise of power.

"We want a republic that allows the collective exercise of freedom. Not merely a governable republic, but an ungovernable republic, should it be necessary, should this be necessary to make ours a republic of the people."

Roundly applauded by the captivated onlookers, the young man was hoisted on their shoulders as they continued their march, everyone singing with great emotion: "*Allons enfants de la patrie . . .*" Farther up ahead, the march came to another stop and the young man once again climbed atop the crate to offer another eloquent speech.

"The perfect homeland is not a motherland, with its feminine traits of sentiment and love, and it is not a fatherland with the masculine traits of power and force. The perfect homeland is a brotherland, a nation of citizens with equal rights.

"The good Comtean dictator, the one who leads the masses, where is this dictator? Such a dictator does not exist."

He ended his speech exhorting the public in French.

"*La Republique doit être un gouvernement?*" he yelled while the crowd responded, "*Nooooonnn . . .*" He continued, his voice resounding: "*La Republique doit être le peuple!*" To which the group responded wildly, "*Vive le peuple!*"

Diva Felícia, full of joy and enthusiasm, followed the group a little longer, singing along to the anthem that stirred her as few others had. She wanted to go on listening to the inspiring words of the young, visionary defender of the republic.

It was not possible that day, but in the days to come she would indeed have other chances to listen and applaud him as enthusiastically as the others. Or perhaps more enthusiastically still, because her presence was soon noted, and it was not long before he approached her and introduced himself. His name was Floriano Botelho, he was an engineer, and believed that a republic was the only way to civilize Brazil, to make this land a country that lived up to humanity's noblest ideals. He was twenty years old and had just arrived from Paris.

Floriano was an idealist, a visionary, tireless. He was part of a republican club and described in great detail his dream to transform Rio and Brazil into a city and country that would provoke awe in all who visited.

The republic that soon arrived, however, was a devastating disappointment for the passionate young man. He had placed such hope in a new, egalitarian, modern country of brotherly love that the republic that actually came to be, beginning with its very proclamation—uninspiring, vague, and disunifying as it was—left a bad taste in his mouth. How was it that the republic of his dreams had been proclaimed by a group of military officers? After chanting "Long live the Republic" a few times in the middle of the Campo de Santana, the officers had then abolished cabinet posts and set out on a military parade throughout the city. Where were the people? Where was everyone? Whose hands were it that held the fate of the country? It was said the parade made its way through the streets of Rio in complete silence, with the old and cantankerous Marshal Deodoro wearing a look of displeasure, his coloring a bit green—it was said, no doubt the result an attack of shortness of breath.

Floriano could not accept that.

But the fact is that the republic was what it was.

Everything that followed later was one more bucket of cold water on the young engineer's revolutionary fire.

The spirit of speculation that overtook the country's elite, the accumulation of wealth at all costs, the massacre at Canudos, the terrible events of which news arrived daily via the newspapers, the creation of a modern market of stocks and backroom deals—all of these novelties that were swept in along with the Republic filled Floriano with disgust. He never tired of repeating that the republic of the military and the elite was not his republic.

He decided to leave politics behind.

It was at that time that the couple decided to marry. Diva took Floriano to meet her grandmother. It was at this time, too, that she took the photo of her grandmother that she would later set aside as her favorite. Seated on her wicker chair, adorned with necklaces, bracelets, rings, her silk dress and shawl, a smile on her face and surrounded by her sweets, her flowers, her friends, and the black women she'd freed, Açucena was the image of a self-proclaimed queen, the manifestation of a rich and well-lived life. Aunt Magnólia is also in the photo.

Standing next to her mother, with her diaphanous air of sanctity. Missing is her half-brother, Dionísio, who was never there at the same time as Diva. He refused to accept her as a sister, just as he'd never accepted his mother. He considered himself rejected by them, and paid them back with still greater rejection.

When they returned to Rio, Floriano's disappointment had already lost a good part of its intensity and, almost without noticing it, which is generally how these things happen, he drew closer, little by little, to the positivist technocrats of the new republic. When he was invited to work with Mayor Pereira Passos on the reurbanization of Rio, he could not refuse. The mayor, also an engineer and urbanist, was a family friend of Floriano's and knew the young man had studied in Paris and had seen close-up the monumental reforms of the French capital under the much-discussed Baron Haussmann, reforms that would serve as a mode for those Pereira Passos had in mind. He needed young men like Floriano around him, and he spared no arguments to win over the young man.

Rio suffered from narrow streets and a heavy concentration of the poor in old mansions in the city center, where its precarious sewage system was considered a serious public health threat. It had become increasingly impossible to tolerate the urban chaos that had taken hold, principally after abolition, when the newly freed slaves abandoned the plantations and sought refuge in the cities, where they lacked for everything. The port had also become unfit to handle the growing volume of commercial transactions.

The order of the day was to modernize the port, bring about basic sanitation systems, and complete an urban-reform project.

All this might appear well and good, but the problem was that the military men and the technocrats, who preached progress above all, would bring about this great urban transformation using methods that allowed little room for ifs, ands, or buts. The mansions in the city center were declared public enemy number one, and the order was to summarily "raze them to the ground." This was followed by decrees granting the mayor exceptional powers to disappropriate and take possession of homes without any sort of judicial process, much less indemnification. The poor were literally thrown onto the streets.

The terror of modernity quickly took hold in the name of the works that were moving full steam ahead. Progress and civilization were noisily moving in, waging fierce battle against the tumult, disorder, and "the rabble and their filth."

Floriano, at the very beginning, earnestly asked if it weren't possible to employ methods that were less authoritarian, less disastrous, to relocate these residents. He was told that there was not; there was no time to lose with such discussions, what had to be done had to be done, no matter who it affected. In the end, it was all for the common good, and everyone would later understand and give thanks for the changes that needed to be made by any means possible in order for Brazil to become a country that inspired confidence and acceptance from the rest of modern Western civilization.

And so they built wide avenues, like the grand boulevards of Paris; they erected gorgeous buildings that were to serve as splendid display windows onto the new capital of the new republic; they built systems for wastewater and the rainwater drainage. As they did so, public health workers began their work, cleaning, sterilizing, setting fire to the homes considered irrecoverable, destroying furniture and any trash containers considered a health risk, vaccinating and revaccinating those who seemed too poor and much too likely to become a walking vessel of diseases inherited from the colony and the Empire, all of which it was imperative to eliminate without delay.

It didn't take much time, really, for Floriano to become completely convinced that the modernization of the country was priority, and if to accomplish that it was necessary to collaborate with the city's authoritarian elite, that was the price to pay for progress. And if everything comes with a price, did not progress, too? Yes, without a doubt, the modernization of the country came with a price. His dream country became a world that was spick and span, where progress could be measured with a ruler by engineers like himself. His enthusiasm regained, he was soon repeating "Now we shall become civilized, we shall rise to the challenge of humanity's progress!"

It wasn't long before other Brazilian capitals sought to follow Rio's example. Floriano was one of the technocrats invited to participate in plans to urbanize Salvador, the country's third most populous city, where the same discourse heralding sanitation and hygiene, the battle cry to make the city clean and orderly, was put into action. The conglomerations of houses in the city's central neighborhoods, immoral places overrun by the poor, were condemned as breeding grounds for disease.

Floriano, almost without realizing it, had become an ardent defender of the necessity of these demolitions and the effective means that ought to be adopted to accomplish them. That's how, with his vehement nature, he became a technocrat more than anything else, a stalwart for progress at all costs. The republic of his former dreams, his distant republic of the people, was buried without honors or glory in the same tomb as the fleeting dreams of his youth.

Diva, too, even if she never forgot the verses, never again sang "La Marseillaise." She dedicated herself entirely to her photos.

Through the world of photography, she had stumbled upon a fascinating path that was truly her own. She no longer photographed vegetables, flowers, and fruits in nature, as before. She began to isolate them, placing them against neutral backgrounds in her studio. The techniques she employed—photographing her subjects outside of their natural settings, in close-ups that were overexposed—brought forth, with rare force, the irresistible beauty and perfection of their natural forms. A handful of peeled pequi fruits against a neutral background, a single corncob, solitary on a flat surface, a bunch of tamarinds at rest, the lone flower of a blooming banana tree with a miniscule cluster of banana embryos, a composition of dry flowers from the Brazilian savanna: these were the serene still-lifes she captured with her camera.

By one of those coincidences that occur in the arts world, the work of Diva Felícia had many similarities to the work of British photographer Charles Jones, who lived at roughly the same time. Both of them, each in his or her respective country, were precursors, by a matter of decades, to some master photographers of the still-life who would emerge later. Unfortunately, the better part of Diva's photos was lost in the fire that destroyed the family mansion in the neighborhood of Flamengo, a fire started by her daughter-in-law, married to her oldest son, Eudoro, after learning the Botelho family had declared bankruptcy. But this is a story for later.

Diva and Floriano had two boys, Eudoro and Gaspar, and after a considerable gap, they also had a girl, Ana Eulália. But the couple's marriage was hardly a healthy one.

Floriano had changed in several ways, not only in the sort of republic he sought. By this point, his friends were the country's new businessmen and peddlers of influence, the so-called *arrivistes* of the Republic, whose goals were the rapid accumulation of wealth and the ostentation of their luxurious lifestyles. He had acquired an obsession for elegant dress and cultivated the conspicuous consumption of imported goods and works of art. He took a liking to the game of poker and to the casinos. Bit by bit, his marriage with Diva became a sort of front, indispensable to his position but lacking emotion and companionship. He spent his days involved in his projects, and at night went out with his new friends, whose company Diva did not care for.

She, for her part, set up her atelier and photography lab in one of the rooms of their enormous house, and there she spent a good part of each day; that is, when she wasn't walking around the city, absorbed in her search for new shapes, sizes, and lighting for her photographs.

She was considered an eccentric woman. She wore clothes that were unique; she had her own style, and refused to follow the latest fashions from Paris. She had no girlfriends, since she didn't care for the petty comedy that was Rio's social scene, and preferred to be on her own. For some years she had been part of a group of painters, but discord and rivalries overshadowed the tenuous commonalities between them. Her only true friend was an old painter, a solitary resident of the secluded Morro de Santa Teresa, with whom she would speak for hours about art and life and for whom she often posed nude, without her husband ever suspecting a thing. She missed her grandmother Açucena and also her aunt Magnólia, and ever since their passing she had never returned to the house at the foot of the mountains. She had practically no contact with her half-brother Dionísio, who had always treated her as a stranger, if not almost an enemy.

Her two sons and her daughter were away at boarding school, and she only saw them on weekends. The idea of boarding school had come from Floriano; she had agreed, thinking it would be best for her children.

Many people considered Diva too eccentric, too strange, even a bit off the rails. Perhaps she was. She had, it's true, led a very solitary life. She spent her childhood and her early adolescence with a sick and often absent mother, and a much older father, whom she idolized but who found it hard to converse with a child. The unforgettable short stays at her grandmother's house were nothing more than this, short stays, and could not make up for things that were missing in her daily life. Her time studying and traveling in Europe was always spent at the side of tutors who, no matter how kind they were, could not be considered equals or companions. Later came her marriage with the impetuous republican who soon became a technocrat much too self-involved. No matter how much she loved them, she could not demand of her children that they occupy the empty spaces that did not belong to them. Fortunately, she had her art and gave herself over to it with complete, and even satisfying, abandon. She was not an unhappy woman. She had realized herself artistically. Despite the voids in her life, she was fundamentally at peace with herself.

So she had a curious reaction when she discovered that Floriano kept a separate *garçonnière* for himself in the Lapa district, where he would rendezvous with known *cocottes* of Rio's bohemian nightlife. She obtained the key to the tiny apartment and, with her camera, began to inspect the location. Decorated with imported furniture, walls lined in light green silk, and curtains of emerald velvet, the place was certainly furbished in good taste, even if much too modern. She spent hours there photographing everything in detail. Then she went to the Mansions Le Ciel sur La Terre, which belonged to Mme Marie Lamber, and which housed the *cocottes* Floriano admired. She introduced herself to Mme Lamer as a photographer who wished to include the girls in one of her projects, and would pay, of course, for their time spent posing.

Diva wasn't exactly sure what her intent was. Hers was an almost instinctive reaction—to photograph the *garçonnière* and the *cocottes*. It was a sort of defensive attitude, a way to prepare herself for something, a decision that she intuitively knew she ought to take. She also wasn't very clear about the emotions that guided her actions. She felt neither sorrow nor resentment, since she had long stopped loving Floriano; nor was it some sort of rage at feeling her supposed ownership over her husband challenged, for she no longer considered him hers; nor was it some inexplicable feeling of humiliation at his betrayal, for she did not see their relationship in that way. Nor was it surprise at realizing how little she knew her husband, for she had also discovered long ago that it was impossible to truly know another person, any one person.

No, it wasn't any of that, but rather the shock of coming to the sudden realization that, from that moment on, one way or another, her life would have to change. It was the arrival of something unexpected, setting into motion something that had been stalled on account of a stability that made no sense, but which had existed for so long that it seemed impossible that she might still have the ability to change it. The abrupt rediscovery of this ability had brought her to that crossroads, not knowing how to proceed, but proceeding so as to be able to think the way she knew best: through the magic eye of her camera.

When she finished photographing the *cocottes*—a project that lasted weeks—she saw that she was in possession of material of startling originality. In the beginning, she had photographed them right there, in the bedrooms, from several angles and varying positions, taking close-ups, shooting at mid-range, their entire bodies, sitting down, lying on the bed, in the bath, laughing, crying, smoking, getting dressed, talking to one another. Soon, however, she began to take them out to pose in unexpected settings throughout Rio. Unlike with her work with the vegetables, flowers, and fruits she took from nature and isolated in her studio, she took the opposite approach with the women, positioning them nude or seminude as fruits of the earth, transforming them into one more element of nature, integrating them into the landscape. Legs and arms sprouted like branches from trees, bushes mingled with an unknown species, the foliage fused with body hair, bulbs revealing a certain resemblance to the women's breasts.

When Diva saw that her work with the *cocottes* was done, she also realized that she already knew what she wanted to do next. She wanted a complete change, to spend some time back in Europe, to visit old acquaintances in Paris, and then return to Brazil to lead a completely different life.

She explained to her children that she was going to Europe for a few months and left a large envelope for Floriano that contained all the photos of his *garçonnière* and a tiny note saying that she had gone to Paris and, when she returned, did not want to find him in the mansion that had belonged to her father. She took the series of photos with the *cocottes* to show her friends, together with an older series of vegetables, flowers, and tropical fruits.

She set out on that trip to rediscover herself, to reaffirm who she was and her commitment to her art. She saw the country that had rebuilt itself after the war and was certain that her life, too, could be reconstructed. Three months later, she thought she was ready to return home.

On the ship back to Brazil, Diva met a Brazilian painter, a captivating young woman who was also returning from Paris, and the two became fast friends. Despite the difference in their ages, they had many things in common: Diva, a photographer, a stunning and well-lived woman with white hair, and Tarsila, a painter who was equally striking and bursting with a sophisticated youthfulness.

Diva eagerly showed her new friend her series of photos, which fascinated Tarsila. When they said their goodbyes, Diva gave Tarsila two of the photos that had bewitched her: one, a close-up of a solitary, bulbous squash that looked as though it were standing at attention; the other, a close-up of a bundle of tiny wild tomatoes that looked like black pearls lit from within.

In one of the long letters she later wrote to Diva, Tarsila sent sketches of what she was painting and asked her to note how the shapes and sizes from the photos Diva had given her on the boat had helped her to conceptualize the shapes and sizes in her latest paintings. She was insistent in her invitations that Diva visit to see the exhibition she was preparing, and also invited her to exhibit her photos in São Paulo. She spoke of her friends there and of how she was certain they would share her captivation by Diva's work.

But Diva was unable to make the trip, though she had planned to do it soon thereafter. She returned to Rio to find Floriano's stubborn refusal to accept their separation, which would be a blemish on the Botelho family name. Their two sons and daughter all supported their father, equally unwilling to accept their mother's position. Despite her efforts, the force of inertia and the hypocrisy of her conjugal stability conspired to ensure her plans to separate did not come to fruition.

Diva, who had returned from Paris so certain of what she wanted and ought to do, was now confused. She hadn't expected this pressure from her children and, above all, the unhappiness she saw on the face of her youngest, Ana Eulália. She had never managed to understand her daughter's behavior and strange manners. In fact, when she'd been able to, Diva had tried to pretend not to see the scorn she long feared had lurked in Eulália's heart. She told herself she was wrong, that all adolescents were the same, but she knew deep down that one day she would have to face her daughter's disapproval of her lifestyle. How often we resort to magical thinking, this almost unconscious putting-off of an especially difficult situation, as though refusing to see it could make our problems finally disappear, or as though the attempt to put it out of mind would allow the necessary time for a solution to appear.

Diva maintained her habit of walking through the streets, absorbed in her task, her camera at the ready in her purse. These outings became her way to think. She was forty-nine years old and, unlike other women of her generation, thought herself entirely capable of anything; she loved life, the light, her art. Yet she was confused. She didn't know what to do, where to find an exit. She could return to Paris—but no, she loved Brazil, this was where her children were, this was where she wanted to live.

Her entire life, she had always been distracted. While she was out walking one day, an inexperienced young man driving an imported sports-car he'd just received from his father gave in to the desire to attain a speed completely unfit for the city streets. Diva didn't realize how dangerous Rio had become with the increased movement of cars and trolleys. Automobile accidents had wreaked absolute havoc in the city, which lacked adequate roads, signage, or transit laws. A luxury item, cars were seen as sporting vehicles whose ability to reach unthinkable speeds was the pinnacle of modern life. Running over pedestrians, even in cases of death, was met merely with a fine, and a tiny one at that.

The car sent her flying.

She hit her head on the asphalt and died almost instantly.

All that remained of her life was a brief moment, enough to see the incandescent glow that came over her to whisk her away forever in its phosphorescence, thus unexpectedly satisfying what, without her realizing it, had always been her greatest desire: More light!

ANA EULÁLIA
(1906-1930)

In the boarding school chapel, the mammoth building with soaring walls where she had spent most of her life, Eulália prayed and wept and wailed in misery. She prayed to God, asking him to change her life; there were so many things she didn't like! If her mother separated from her father, she would die of shame; she prayed for this not to happen. If her mother were to die, she would no longer have any problems; she would be sad, but she would have no need to feel ashamed. If her mother died, she would take care of her father and so many things would be better in her life! Dear Saint Rose, hear my prayer!

Eulália was born during a period of rapid change. Brazil was urbanizing, its landscape changing, a surprising series of events swept everyone along on an assembly line of turbulent and never-ending transformations.

When Diva told them—Eulália and her brothers—that she was traveling to Paris, she hadn't revealed her true reasons for doing so. She wanted to make sure her children learned of the separation in the right way and at the right time, and she had told them only that she needed to travel for a few months. But Floriano did not share the same opinion. On the contrary. He took advantage of his wife's absence to give them his version of events, telling them their mother was deteriorating, growing stranger with every day, and that she now had the immoral idea of separating. She wanted him, their father, to leave the house where they had lived as a family. He told the story in such a way that all of the children became disgusted with Diva's decision, especially Eulália, whose fervently Catholic, adolescent mind resembled a tightly wound skein of disoriented thoughts and desires.

She cried for days, feeling betrayed, rejected, scandalized, and she firmly took the side of her father, whom she also considered a victim of her mother's madness and insensitivity.

The news had, in fact, been the last straw in her troubled relationship with Diva. At home, she fawned over her father, whose elegant and pompous figure she had always fervently admired; at school, she strictly adhered to the rules and etiquette of the small, elite world in which the students lived. She began to form values that irrecoverably distanced her from her mother, whose behavior and attitudes, so different from those of her classmates' mothers, she viewed as excesses and eccentricities that made her feel awkward and embarrassed. So great was her rejection of Diva's peculiar lifestyle that she considered it an act of martyrdom to go with her mother on the days that she, and not her father, would pick her up to spend the weekend at home. She was overcome with an unspeakable and diffuse feeling of shame whenever she saw Diva dressed in a way she considered bizarre and reprehensible. The colors Diva wore, the styles, her gestures, attitude, and looks, everything about her clashed with the demure French elegance of the other mothers. Eulália would slink away, eyes on the ground, and, growing red, tug at her mother's hand so they could leave the school as fast as possible.

One afternoon, as the students were leaving for a trip to the beach in Botafogo Bay, Eulália recognized her mother atop an enormous rock out above the sea, completely absorbed as she photographed something. One of her classmates also recognized Diva and pointed her out: "Look, it's your mother!" At that moment, meanwhile, Eulália had begun practically shoving her classmates forward to get them to the other end of the beach, and struggled to hide her shame: "Who? My mother? No, you must be mistaken, that's not her. Let's get out of here, quick, this end of the beach is dangerous. Come on!"

But of course it was her mother, unmistakable in her thin dress with its luminous white glow—white was Diva's favorite color, practically the only one she wore, in contrast to the darker, more discreet tones the other mothers wore—and her fluttering silk shawl, also white, pure like sea foam rolling down her back, her long hair let out in waves like the sea beneath her feet, hair that she allowed to fall naturally in yet another staggering difference from the other women, who wore theirs in tight, orderly buns beneath their hats. Of course it was her mother—she recognized her mother by the wild hair that Eulália thought made her look like a savage. Fortunately, Diva was so preoccupied looking through the magic eye of the camera, which she never let out of her sight, peering at some shape lost along the rocks, that she didn't notice the group of students retreating to the other side of the beach at her daughter's command: "Let's go, let's go, Sister Alfonsina warned us not to come over to this end of the beach."

Diva's bold individuality was truly an unbearable burden for an insecure adolescent whose most intimate desire was to have a mother be as normal as the rest. She detested the photos Diva took. She thought them horrendous—Diva could at least take photos of something beautiful, but no, her photos only depicted things that were strange, spiteful, things that no one, only her mother, photographed! She hated her mother's camera and didn't understand its appeal, and she abhorred walking into her mother's studio the same way she experienced a palpable fear of the darkroom where Diva developed her photos. Eulália was a deep well of shadowed and heavy thoughts, in great contrast to her mother's easy and carefree radiance: Eulália was a font of confusion, jealousy, rejection, shame, hate, and an obscure desire for everything to be different.

When Diva was so stupidly run over and killed, Eulália reached the peak of her religiosity and dark thoughts, adding to her explosive cauldron of turbulence a painful feeling of guilt, remorse, and loss. Of course, it was all her fault!

She spent longer hours in the tiny chapel, mired in unrest—sobbing, blaming herself, asking forgiveness, doing penance.

What a combination! Oh, how she felt disturbed to the core!

I want to be able to say that this confusion of Eulália's was merely a passing phase, a case of adolescent troubles, but no. This plethora of disturbing and directionless thoughts accompanied her, in one form or another, for the rest of her life.

The famous boarding school for rich girls housed students who came from several states.

Among them was Adriana, daughter to coffee barons from São Paulo, who became Eulália's best friend. Adriana had returned from vacation that year completely taken with a gorgeous Italian she had met at her cousin's house in São Paulo, and with whom she had traded a few words and two or three smiles—sufficient, in the meantime, for him to become the constant topic of conversation, where he was described as a direct descendant of Apollo, except better, since, in addition to everything else, he had a dimple on his chin and two more that appeared in his cheeks whenever he smiled. As soon as she'd arrived back from vacation, Adriana had begun to write him formal and polite letters, as a friend, trying to muster the courage to declare her feelings.

The world of those young girls, regimented by the soaring walls of their strict boarding school, was leagues away from any real world. The identity of the young Italian, what he did or didn't do, had no part in their conversation, not by a long shot. Those privileged girls didn't have a single clue about how privileged they truly were, and it was as if the world outside was merely an extension of their own. In their eyes, the young man whom Adriana had fallen for was as well off as they were.

Except that he wasn't.

Umberto Rancieri, on the day Adriana first saw him, was walking along with his father, a tailor. They were on their way to deliver a suit ordered by the man of the house, Adriana's uncle, for a final fitting and to make any last adjustments. Umberto had learned his father's trade, served as his assistant, and was, in some sense, also his model and walking advertisement, for each time he donned one of his father's fine suits with an air of refinement, he became the physical manifestation of what it meant to dress well. This refinement, coupled with his natural beauty and dimpled cheeks, made all the society girls, little flowers full of illusions and naiveté, melt around him.

Adriana immediately fell for the figure he cut, that of a young god, and she needed nothing more.

In Eulália's mind then, given that she only knew the young man through the reports of her rapt friend, Umberto Rancieri was a young prince who soon inhabited her own dreams and who deserved a woman who would fight and even die for him.

During the long hours she spent in the chapel pouring out the feelings that disturbed her heart and mind, she began to pray that her closest friend's boyfriend would fall for her instead. Her sensuality exacerbated by a flurry of strong emotions, she implored Saint Rose to dissuade Umberto from responding to Adriana's letters.

Yet, despite her troubled mind and deep religiosity, the young girl was no fool and sensed that she couldn't leave real life matters up to the saints. And so, without her friend's knowledge, she discovered the address of the dimpled Paulista and began to write him letters of her own that were much more explicit and considerably less formal than her friend's. In addition, Eulália was able to steal some of Adriana's letters from the mailbox and, imitating her friend's handwriting, which she did all too well, added a postscript that dispensed with any ambiguity about how she, Adriana, was ecstatic and overjoyed with her impending engagement to a suitor from Rio, a good catch, a very handsome man with an inarguably promising career!

After this little ploy, Eulália's amorous playing field was wide open. All that was left was to meet the young man in person. Ana Eulália was so wrapped up in her romantic preoccupations that she found it neither strange nor worrying when her father told her he was removing her from school, bringing her formal education to an end. On the contrary, it seemed a natural and appropriate decision; yes, he truly could consider her education complete, which was just another way of saying she was now ready to marry.

In reality, though, things were headed in a direction the young girl could never have imagined.

The motive for her father's decision to take her out of school was entirely different from what she supposed. Two years after the death of his wife, Floriano Botelho had come to the realization—there could be no doubt—that he was one step away from bankruptcy, ruined, without anywhere to turn for help.

An entire lifetime of lavish spending, plus the fact that his two oldest children, Eudoro and Gaspar, dedicated themselves above all else to spending too much and earning too little, gradually chipped away at old Acioli's fortune. As an engineer, Floriano brought in a good salary, no doubt, but not sufficient to bank the lifestyle to which he'd become accustomed. What's more, while he may have been a competent engineer, he was terrible with finances: he had made two or three attempts to launch businesses with his children and some *arriviste* friends, which only served to whittle away at the paltry inheritance left him by his father-in-law. After the last of these failed ventures and mounting gambling debts, he'd arrived at his present predicament, one step from the street.

Floriano found this realization unacceptable. His mind for precise calculations considered it an inadmissible error, a shameful failure, a humiliating situation. His friends disappeared, one by one, like falling dominoes. Having become an individualist to the core, he was incapable of looking around and realizing the insignificance of his problems in comparison to the hardships that plagued the country.

The First World War had ended, but it had ushered in other surprising changes, like the Bolshevik Revolution and a general strike among the working class that had begun in São Paulo and spread to Rio. The country was changing rapidly, though not everyone noticed, and no one seemed especially satisfied, not even military officials— namely, a group of young lieutenants in São Paulo growing increasingly outspoken in their threats of revolt.

It was in the midst of all this agitation that Floriano decided to go to São Paulo to make a final play. It was 1924, hardly an ideal time for such travels, but Eulália saw in her father's intention her big chance to finally meet Umberto, and she insisted that her father take her with him.

She was about to turn eighteen, and carried in her heart the great secret of this long-distance passion.

Floriano, lacking the energy to consider any decision at length, agreed to take her: no one in São Paulo knew much about his financial situation, and perhaps his daughter could still manage a good marriage into a family of wealthy coffee growers.

It was June, and the sun danced in the sky as only it knew how on certain winter days in São Paulo. The unfamiliar chill in the air engendered a particular euphoria in the young woman who, as soon as she arrived, sent a letter to her elegant Italian with the name of the hotel where she was staying in the city center.

He immediately set off to meet her. He also introduced himself to Floriano, who barely spoke three words to him before leaving in a hurry, lost in his own personal abyss. Umberto invited Eulália to accompany him along the Vale do Anhangabaú and then to take tea at the creamery in front of the Teatro Municipal.

São Paulo was a peaceful, spacious city, with provincial airs. Much different from the nation's restless capital.

On that bright sunny day, Umberto held her parasol and admired her delicate figure and hungry eyes. Eulália quivered as she touched his arm and felt like the happiest girl alive, certain she was making every passerby jealous.

What would Adriana say if she saw them now?

The winter sun had warmed the afternoon, and a tiny drop of sweat slowly trickled down from behind Umberto's left ear. A tiny, glassy little drop that gave Eulália such a strong desire to kiss him right on that spot that her breath caught, and she let out a gasp as she was overcome with dizziness and the total and absolute certainty that she would love him forever.

Meanwhile, dissatisfaction was growing among São Paulo's young lieutenants. They wanted President Artur Bernardes removed, limits placed on the executive power, an end to corruption. In the barracks, soldiers were readying the revolt. Floriano's friends advised him to return to Rio, or to at least leave the hotel where they were staying. He accepted one friend's invitation to stay at his mansion in Higienópolis, a safe distance from the streets of the city center, which was overrun with soldiers.

But Floriano was unwell; nausea swept over him. Self-absorbed and shut off to all around him as he anxiously waited for the loan that he believed would save him, he wandered through the streets almost without noticing the frenetic activity, the warlike atmosphere that seemed to overtake the city, the pamphlets found wherever he went, the sidewalks barricaded. He appeared to see nothing, be interested in nothing. He walked along, Eulália at his side. The two of them had gone out, despite the tense atmosphere, because Floriano felt almost obligated to go out to the streets, as though he had something important to do, to flee the heavy weight of expectation regarding his loan and to make it appear in his host's eyes that he still had important friends and business matters that required his attention. It was early June. The two of them, father and daughter, strolled through the streets of Higienópolis.

Eulália, who hadn't wished to go out, noted that Floriano seemed to be wandering aimlessly, and she asked her father where they were going. She had arranged to meet Umberto and didn't have much time to waste.

Her father did not respond. The thought struck him, though without much clarity, that Umberto must be the young man who was courting his daughter. What family did he come from? He did not know the young man, he would have to learn more, but even the simplest tasks now required great effort on his part. Umberto was an elegant, well-dressed young man, he must come from a family of some means; perhaps his plan to marry his daughter to a rich Paulista would work after all. But his queasiness would not pass, and he felt a pain in his arm; he turned to look at Eulália, he wished to say something to her, but suddenly his voice failed him.

Floriano clutched his arm and stumbled, feeling the world buckle around him. He reached out to grab hold of something, turning a full circle before collapsing with his eyes bulging out of his head, in a desperate attempt to say something.

It was a massive heart attack.

When the people walking along the sidewalk stopped to help, Eulália refused to believe her father was already dead.

The following days fell like a fog over the young orphan girl. The city was bombarded by federal troops who sought to quash the revolt of the Paulista regiments. Her brothers weren't even able to make it to the funeral, since all lines of communication between Rio and São Paulo had been suspended.

War had broken out.

President Artur Bernardes's cannons struck the Praça da República, the Viaduto Santa Ifigênia, the Largo São Bento, the Largo do Paissandu. The terrifying thunder of the cannons was as frightening as the fire consuming the city center, the peaceful city that Eulália had only recently come to know. Buildings and homes were razed to the ground. Thousands were forced to evacuate. Hundreds died, thousands were wounded.

Whisked away by the family of her father's friends, who had also provided a quick and simple burial, Eulália took refuge on a farm a few miles from São Paulo, where she spent those days lost in her private fog.

At the end of July, the rebels abandoned the city, making their way northwest to the state of Mato Grosso. That marked the initial formation of the group that would later become known as the Prestes Column—named after their young leader. The group would march again months later, joining up with rebels from Rio Grande do Sul, and would cross a good part of the country over the next two years, always under pursuit.

The city center had been left in ruins. People walked through the streets, shocked at the destruction and the war whose motives they had not understood.

Eulália returned with her father's friends to their mansion in Higienópolis, where Umberto came to look for her. Everything that had happened to her, her father's unexpected death, the experience of war, the fear, the helplessness, the future that suddenly appeared like a dark cloud obscuring everything—it had all left its weight and mark upon her.

She was thinner, paler, and she had never felt so adrift.

Like all the city residents, Umberto and Eulália went to see the ruins wrought by the war. She leaned on him as she waded through the wreckage, the city's and her own, her world as turned upside-down and bombarded as the streets they walked, the gates and the walls collapsed, an acrid burning smell invading her nostrils, broken glass on the ground, cinderblocks exposed, singed, black, revealing the wounds of the devastated city.

That was no place for a lovers' walk and much less for a marriage proposal. But it was there, among the strange smells and ruins, that Umberto told her that he wished to marry her. He did not want her to return to Rio, but to stay there, where he would watch over her forever.

Umberto would later ask himself numerous times what had brought him to marry that strange girl whom he had barely known at the time. Perhaps it was a consequence of the nonsensical emotion brought on by war. Perhaps he had confused love with his strong desire to protect her, and the sort of compassion he had felt since the first time he'd laid eyes on her. But there was also his desire for the creamy softness of her milky skin, the longing to fold her up in a strong embrace that would take her breath away. There was also the vanity of knowing he was so loved, his pride at feeling the caress of a passionate gaze as fervent as Eulália's.

Back when he'd received her first letter, in which she'd introduced herself as Adriana's friend and said that she'd fallen in love with him from afar, he thought she was a bit flighty, a bit odd, but he had responded regardless, partly for the satisfaction of his conquest, partly from feeling so flattered, and partly for the adventure of it. When she continued to write him and even sent her photo, her delicate little face smiling lovingly from the paper, he again responded and, before he realized it, was anxiously awaiting the arrival of the next letters when they took too long to arrive. Her smile in the photo, the letters with thoughts and comments that lacked any sort of logic, the perplexity of it all—something about her began to stir something within him, even if he wasn't exactly sure what it was.

When he met her in São Paulo, he thought she was different from all the other girls he had known. Her delicateness, her skin so white and smooth, her somewhat ethereal manners; he would never forget when she had sat down on that bench in the square on that afternoon, the sun just a touch too strong for winter, and opened her mouth, revealing her small, white teeth. She looked at him with such intensity and desire that he thought, for the briefest moment, that she was about to faint. Ever since then, that briefest of instants, he knew that if it were up to him, he would never let her out of his sight.

When her father died suddenly, and in that period in which the city seemed to have suddenly transformed into some sort of hell, with her so alone in the midst of that nightmare, he felt even closer to her, as though fate itself, that mysterious force, was placing her under his wing. He could not and would not leave her on her own, and it was then that he asked her to marry him, in the middle of a city of ruins.

Umberto was an enthusiastic defender of the rebels, though his father—an armchair anarchist—had told him loud and clear that it wasn't worth taking sides in that fight, that neither one of them was worth a damn.

His father was a tailor with a steady clientele in São Paulo. He lived on the top floor of a small two-story house in Bexiga, with his shop on the ground floor. In addition to Umberto, the youngest, and his older brother, who helped out and learned his trade, he had three other employees, all men. The tiny room with its long tables and heavy irons smelled of clean, freshly pressed cloth, marking chalk, and sweat.

It was there that Eulália went to live after they were married.

The wedding took place not long after Floriano's death. When things calmed down a bit and Eulália was able to return to Rio, she was already engaged. She was truly in love with the kind Italian man with the dimples and, like anyone who is in love, didn't give much thought about her family's situation. She had no idea of the extent to which her new life would be different and, even if she had, she did not see much alternative. When she arrived in Rio, she found her brothers at each other's throats over their grandfather Acioli's modest mansion and its furniture, the little that remained of their inheritance.

Eudoro, the eldest, who had married a young society woman whose father was also in financial straits, had returned to his grandfather's mansion to live with his wife while Floriano was still alive. Gaspar, who had inherited the family's penchant for gambling and the night-life, was beginning to earn a living from a small casino he had built on a deserted beach in Urca; he finally agreed to take the furniture and works of art and to sell them, while Eudoro and Eulália stayed on in the mansion.

When Eudoro promised to sell the mansion as soon as possible and split the profit with her, Eulália packed her things and returned to São Paulo to marry Umberto.

Gaspar wished to accompany his sister and was curious to meet the family of Italians, but he was unable to leave his casino unattended at that time. He promised to visit them soon. As far as Eudoro and his wife were concerned, they didn't have enough money left over to pay for travel and lodging in São Paulo, and they feared they might be asked to help with some of the wedding expenses if they were to attend.

So Eulália set out alone to begin her new life.

The Rancieris welcomed her with open arms.

The changes, however, were too drastic for her. The handsome home inhabited by a small millionaire-bourgeois family was traded for a semi-proletarian house with few rooms and many mouths to feed: the couple, their five children, and their new daughter-in-law. The newlyweds took up one of the rooms, and the remaining four Rancieri siblings piled up in another. They were all men, which was one more reason the family welcomed Eulália as though she were their first daughter; the effusive and exuberant affection of the Italians, however, knocked her off course. She was more confused than ever, completely at sea. She sought any possible excuse to remain alone in her room and pray.

Where was she, she asked herself, where was she?

Her family had fallen apart; she was ashamed to seek out her school friends given her living conditions: one bedroom of a tiny neighborhood home. She would die of embarrassment because of her mother-in-law, an unsophisticated, fat, horrific woman who didn't even speak Portuguese, and who yelled all the time. Adriana, her good friend Adriana—had she tricked her, making her believe that Umberto was from a rich family? Had Adriana already known everything? My God, how she wanted to die! Or perhaps Adriana herself had died! If Adriana were dead, her shame would be diminished, dear Saint Rose! But if she hadn't, what could be done?

Nothing.

She'd heard of young women working as telephone operators. But her, work? What a hare-brained idea! How could she possibly?

And if she were to pass Adriana in the street, good heavens!

Adriana lived in São Paulo, so in the event she might one day run into her in the street, she would pretend she didn't see her—she would never, ever see Adriana ever again. Adriana no doubt knew she had married Umberto. Umberto with his dimples, such a handsome man!

When Umberto embraced her, she forgot everything. When they were together, things no longer seemed so dire.

During the hours she didn't lock herself in the room, Eulália would go to the tailor's workshop to be closer to Umberto. There she would stay, watching the burning red embers an employee placed inside a clothes iron, the sharp hiss of the bit of damp cloth when it met the heat of the piping-hot metal, the sweet smell rising from the ever-so-singed cloth, the laughter of the young men, and her father-in-law telling old stories of the anarchists back in Italy. Umberto, the measuring tape hanging around his neck, lowered his head to run the chalk along the thick wooden ruler to mark the cloth, allowing her to catch a glimpse of that glassy little drop of sweat rolling down his neck, filling her again with desire.

That masculine environment, there next to her handsome Umberto, was the only place she liked to be.

Her husband's family was from northern Italy, from the Veneto region. Her mother-in-law practically spoke only Italian and made polenta every single day, as though they were still in Italy and had no other type of food. Their neighbors and friends also spoke Italian, and they spoke it loudly, and all at the same time. Eulália felt ready to keel over, a bit dizzy; she couldn't spend extended periods amid all that commotion, and would eventually lock herself back in the bedroom.

Without realizing it, she began to drink. Only a little at first. She would drink one, perhaps two small glasses of her father-in-law's wine, and it was as if something came loose inside her. A knot was undone and her heart grew lighter, her valves and veins and doors and windows opened up. She took a liking to that sensation, and the first couple glasses quickly became four, five. Some nights, she almost felt happy, a sensation she wasn't used to and which left her a bit silly, laughing at herself and her life. She never had a hangover, and so the pleasure of drinking did not lead to her ruin. She remained intact, waiting for the next occasion to do it all over again.

On Sundays, her father-in-law would go out after lunch to meet some friends, anarchist sympathizers who were, however, not given to radicalism; they were professionals, craftsmen who little by little were managing to make a life for themselves in Brazil and who wanted the best for everyone, that no one would suffer so much *infelicitá, dio mio, tanta miseria!* It was a fun group of good-natured Italian men for whom the anarchist tradition was more a lifestyle than a political movement.

Eulália attended Mass with her Catholic mother-in-law; she would wrap herself in her black shawl so no one could recognize her. None of the men, not even Umberto, went with them. That's how it had always been in their family: the boys had permission to go to church with their mother until the age of seven, when their father would grab them by the neck and say: *Questo allora è finito! Basta!*, and their mother would continue with only the younger ones. But by that time the youngest son had already turned seven, and so Eulália and her mother-in-law went to church by themselves.

When the couple's first daughter was born, her father-in-law had a small room constructed just for them in the back of the house. Eulália chose the name Rosa Alfonsina. Rosa for her favorite saint, and Alfonsina for the nun whom she had admired in school and to whom she still wrote long letters about how everything in her life was just perfect, how God had been extremely generous with her, how it was as if her husband's family were her own, how they had brought a considerable fortune from Italy and how everyone lived in luxury in a gorgeous mansion in São Paulo where she anxiously awaited the nun's visit one day. And had Sister Alfonsina by chance heard any news about Adriana?

Despite her love for her husband, Eulália felt she could not handle such a life for much longer. Her hopes hung on the money they would receive from her family mansion, whose sale, meanwhile, her brother had repeatedly delayed.

Her husband told her that business was improving, that their clientele was growing, and that, in fact, her father-in-law had begun to build another house next to the existing family home, which would be entirely dedicated to the family business.

Nonetheless, Eulália was unable to adjust to the simple life of an immigrant family. She dreamed of her former clothes, the luxury she'd known, her mansion in Rio, the enormous bedroom that was hers alone, the thick curtains that fell smoothly and gracefully to the floor, enclosing the bedroom in a dark circle of warmth and comfort. Now, through the curtainless windows of the couple's miniscule bedroom, the cold seeped in and dug into her bones like sharp little daggers. She began to wear a wool coat even during the summer.

The knots of troubled feelings in Eulália's soul wound tighter and tighter.

Her excessive and somewhat distorted religiosity returned with absolute force and influence. Besides the wool coat, she began to walk everywhere with a rosary in her hand, praying, her lips opening and closing with her silent invocation; on the trolley, in the kitchen, seated on the tiny porch, in the bathroom. These prayers were her company, her refuge, her obsession, her way of life. When she prayed, she asked everything of Saint Rose. That her parents' fortune be restored. That her father-in-law fall ill and leave the business in Umberto's hands alone. That her mother-in-law drop dead in the kitchen like her father. That her husband's entire family return to Italy, leaving only her and Umberto and their daughter in the house. That her brother would tell her the mansion was hers alone, that she could return there to live with her husband. That Adriana would see her in the street next to Umberto and their daughter and think that she was very rich and happy. That Adriana would never see her in the street, but think that she was married to Umberto and that they were millionaires and happy and lived in a gorgeous mansion in Rio. Saint Rose, hear my prayer!

Eulália was pregnant for the second time when she received the news of the fire at the mansion. So great was her despair that she fainted in the middle of reading Gaspar's long letter recounting the tragedy in harrowing detail.

Albertina, Eudoro's wife, was mentally ill. Eudoro had been reluctant to send her to a clinic because he didn't want anyone to know about her illness, which he considered a stain upon the family's honor. Even Gaspar had known nothing. It's true that he barely visited his brother's house, but whenever he did he'd seen his sister-in-law, so pale, so thin, seldom saying more than "Good morning," "Good afternoon," "Be well." She seemed a bit sickly to him, but he thought it was merely a passing thing. It wasn't. She had violent episodes, and her husband would lock her in her bedroom, where he'd removed all the objects she might have used to hurt herself.

Such was their life during those years in the mansion, which grew more and more decrepit given the lack of necessary upkeep, cleaning, or maintenance. The only people living there were Eudoro, his wife, and an elderly woman paid to care for his wife. Things had remained almost identical to the time their parents had lived there, including Diva's studio and photo lab, with her photos stacked in piles of manila folders, all the liquids for developing and enlarging the photos in enormous bottles.

During her latest episode, Albertina had, by a stroke of fate, found the door to her bedroom unlocked. It was night and, lighting a candle, she began to wander through the sleeping house, stopping in the rooms that had been Diva's domain and setting fire to the curtains, the paper, the rugs, and the furniture.

In a short time, everything was incinerated. The entire mansion, with Albertina, Eudoro, and the old caretaker inside. The other two had been sleeping and hadn't managed to escape the flames in time.

When Umberto walked into the bedroom, he found his wife unconscious, letter in hand.

From that point on, she spent the rest of her pregnancy in bed, in a deep depression, lacking the strength to get to her feet.

As everything had gone smoothly with the birth of her first child, the complications of this pregnancy took the family by surprise. It was her mother-in-law who generally delivered the children in the family, and who had done so with Rosa Alfonsina, but this time, as soon as she realized that the child was positioned feet-first, she sent the men to call the midwife from the next neighborhood over. The midwife, older and more experienced, thought she could handle the situation, that the child would turn in time for a healthy delivery. As the hours passed, however, Umberto could no longer contain himself and decided to call a doctor.

But by the time the doctor arrived, there was no longer anything he could do for the child or for Eulália. There was nothing he could have done even had he arrived earlier.

It was a cold and dark winter night, with hardly a light in the sky.

Eulália was buried the following day amid a mist-drenched morning, dressed in her wool coat, her rosary in her hands. The tiny white casket with her son was buried by her side.

A
PROMISING
SIGN

ROSA ALFONSINA
(1926-)

Rosa Alfonsina flashed the cameraman from *O Cruzeiro* magazine her most beautiful smile. They'd placed a heavy cloak of smooth, navy-blue velvet trimmed with fur across her shoulders, a scepter in her hands, and a sparkling gold crown encrusted with diamonds over her dark, honey-colored hair, all in a careful imitation of luxury. She wore a handsome dress of white silk whose incredibly narrow straps were two gold laces; it was a stunning dress made especially for her by her father, the famous designer Umberto Rancieri. She was full of life on that, her day of glory: she had just been crowned Miss São Paulo and was smiling with demure delight to all who applauded her and to the shining lights that lit the runway along which she walked, magnificent and regal.

Rosa truly was beautiful, though she had inherited the wide hips of her father's side of the family, which over the years might make her appear wider than she really was. But not at that present moment. She was just fine with her hips and had been crowned Miss São Paulo, after a tremendous battle with her father and grandmother for permission to participate, who didn't even want to hear about such things, but now there they were, in the first row, proud as could be, wildly cheering her on.

Rosa was not just some pretty or silly girl. Not at all. She studied hard and was full of ideas; she had just earned her teaching certification and had completed a typing course like all the other girls at the time. She was full of dreams germinating in her little head full of dark-gold hair that cascaded over her shoulders like molasses slowly overrunning the edges of a spoon.

After her mother's premature death, Rosa had been raised in her grandparents' house. Her father, after a long and begrudged widowhood, eventually married an Italian woman who was no longer so young but who, besides being kind and caring, was also an excellent seamstress. They had no children, since Umberto—who had never forgiven himself for being unable to protect Eulália as he had promised her—managed to come to an understanding with his new wife that they would keep close watch on her monthly cycle and would take all precautions against her becoming pregnant. Together, they oversaw a considerable expansion to the tailoring business following the retirement of the elder Rancieri, transforming it into one of, if not the first, stores to sell haute couture fashion in São Paulo. They enjoyed their craft and had the instincts to guide them in making sure the texture and shapes of fabric fell perfectly over any body type—male or female, fat or thin, voluptuous or shapeless. The names of Umberto and Leda Rancieri became well known throughout São Paulo society.

After the euphoria of the Miss São Paulo contest had passed, there was a huge quarrel in the family, for while her father had permitted Rosa to compete for the title of municipal beauty queen, there was no way he was going to let her do the same for the statewide title, much less that of Miss Brazil. Deep down, he'd only consented—and against his wishes—because he thought that, however beautiful his daughter may have been, the cards were stacked in such competitions and she would probably get nowhere. His surprise and pride had both been considerable when he discovered he was wrong, but the whole thing had gone too far—so no more! *Basta! Basta!* Only over his dead body.

Rosa did what she could. She wanted to be Miss Brazil because it was electrifying and fun, and she liked to have fun. She was happy, uninhibited, and left all her doors wide open to embrace everything the world had to give, now that the Great War had ended in Europe and it was no longer necessary to mull over the suffering of distant countries. Faced with her father's refusal, she cried, screamed, slammed doors. She declared that the family was interfering with her happiness, that she would never smile again because hers was not a life worth living. She systematically cycled through all the standard exaggerations. But this time her father, with the support of her grandmother, was unshakeable.

Basta! Basta! Basta!

By a happy coincidence, on the same day of crying and empty threats, Rosa received a letter from a fan, a young doctor who requested permission to introduce himself and meet her. Written in an elegant handwriting on fine white stationery, it had been delivered by a young boy who stood there waiting on her response.

On any other day, she would certainly have hesitated and almost certainly would have said no to this daring stranger—the nerve! But in her moment of rebellion against her family, she decided she had nothing better to do than to immediately meet the doctor. She told the boy to reply that her answer was yes, she would wait for the doctor at her home at five in the afternoon, and then she went off to dry her tears so as not to greet her guest with a swollen face.

For the rest of her life, she would congratulate herself a thousand times for the wise decision to meet, on that gentle May afternoon, the great love of her life. Túlio Faiad, a young man with a tan complexion, who arrived to see her with a rose in hand.

Ten years Rosa's senior, he had graduated from the Faculdade de Medicina in Minas Gerais. The son of Lebanese immigrants who ran a small business in the countryside of Minas, he had come to São Paulo for a residency. With black hair and dark eyes, a kind and easy smile, he had seen Rosa at the contest and had dreamed ever since, night after night, of that young woman with voluptuous curves, the smile of a goddess, and hair like honey.

Rosa immediately took to Túlio. His kind and polite manners, his dream to use medicine to alleviate suffering in the world, the enthusiasm of a young man who has realized his dream to become a doctor and knows he is capable of pursuing many others, all of this together with his dark eyes and beautiful long-fingered hands made Rosa forget all of her ambitions to participate in other pageants.

Their courtship was brief, as was their engagement, since the impatient doctor and the impatient beauty queen were anxious to begin their new life together. Túlio's plan—which met with Rosa's unconditional agreement—was to move to the countryside, where the lack of doctors was considerable and he could be more useful than in the big city. After her father's blessing and her grandmother's endless sobbing, the couple moved to a small city in the countryside of Minas Gerais, at the commendation of a friend of the family, Doctor Juscelino, an older man who had graduated from the same medical school as Túlio and become something like a mentor, whom Túlio admired greatly.

Rosa Alfonsina was happy. She loved her husband and was proud of his work and his intelligence. She liked to hold his hand and discretely lift it to admire his long fingers, and the ring finger where the doctor's emerald ring glimmered next to his gold wedding-band.

In the town where they were going to live, a small community with a penchant for gossip, Rosa was initially received with curiosity and distrust. She was the doctor's wife, and came from the capital. She had different manners, big city manners, she would participate in the men's conversations, had her own ideas, wanted to assist her husband, became a practicing nurse, and was a quick learner. From the very beginning she also made her own good friends, unconditional fans who would support her in slowly gaining the trust of the rest of the city.

The region's health problems were more drastic than they had thought. The poverty of entire families left to their own devices was horrifying: they lived on plots of barren earth unfit for even enough crops to feed themselves, and stayed in mud houses infested with kissing bugs. Thyroid conditions were widespread, since iodized salt was still rare and expensive in that part of the world; the kissing bugs, carrying chagas, infected entire families with the disease. The biggest problems were endemic and required public health campaigns rather than sophisticated medical knowledge. The young doctor began to despair; he felt impotent before his task and would arrive home exhausted after spending the day on horseback beneath the strong sun as he sought to help those families out in the middle of nowhere, where the greatest ill—poverty—was neither within his reach nor ability to resolve.

He encountered so many unexpected situations, so many illnesses that should have been eradicated, so much suffering due to the same devastating cause, so much calamity, that he felt his mission had to expand: if he did not treat their social causes, he would never be able to put an end to the illnesses.

Together with some friends, the city intellectuals, a local school instructor, the pharmacist, and the dentist, Túlio began to print a monthly newspaper, *O Piston*. The pharmacist, Seu Matias, was a Communist sympathizer, but the others were not necessarily driven by ideology. They were merely people who saw what was happening around them, who found the poverty of the countryside unacceptable, and who wished to see their country move forward.

The newspaper's production meetings took place at Túlio and Rosa's home. Rosa, with great enthusiasm and energy, served coffee and biscuits, but also offered up ideas, participated in debates, and began to write short texts that were later published. She would write *crônicas*, short observations on everyday life, sometimes moving, sometimes playful, always with great verve. She was worried about the small town's isolation and sought to write about events in the rest of the country, but in a style that was intuitive and personal. She was one of the few people there who subscribed to national magazines, bought books through the mail, and was aware of what was happening beyond the town limits, far away, out there where the road to the big city began.

Her articles became one of the most-read and discussed parts of the small newspaper. Always using the everyday stories of people she knew, like the stories of her grandpa Rancieri, the old anarchist sympathizer, her writings spoke mainly about events beyond that world closed off to itself.

A *crônica* she wrote about her grandfather in 1932 became quite well known when São Paulo once again took up arms and went to war against the dictatorship of Getúlio Vargas, demanding the promulgation of a constitution. Her grandmother, Nonna Sofia, had sat in the window excitedly watching the troops pass by, and behind the troops young men, behind the young men young women, and behind the young women a group of children, as though it was nothing more than one big party, and she lamented: "*Dio mio, com tanta terra em questo paese, siamo fermati in quella in cui si piace di più far la guerra!*" She would close the windows and doors, grab the rosary to pray, and prohibit her children from going out into the streets.

But not Grandpa Rancieri. Taking care to keep it from his wife, he helped to prepare the "matracas," curious instruments made of iron and steel that emitted sounds like a machine gun when shaken and served to disguise the rebels' chronic lack of ammunition and guns on the front line. He encouraged Rosa, then a girl of six, and the other neighborhood kids to parade through the streets carrying flags and banging on cans as though they were drums; he would tell them they ought to learn early to do whatever they could to make the world a more just place. As a matter of principle, Rancieri didn't take sides; he thought that war was for rich men, an arm-wrestling match among those who had always been in power, a settling of accounts between American and British imperialism, that neither side was worth a damn and had nothing to do with them, the poor of this earth, anyway. But since he was viscerally opposed to dictatorships, he couldn't help but root for the rebels.

Another of Rosa's most discussed articles was one that told the story of Old Man Damasceno, who lived in her house and had become a caring and beloved figure in the town. How one day, an elderly black man in tattered clothes had knocked at Doctor Túlio's door, his feet infested with worms and an ugly wound on his leg. Raising the man's filthy shirt to examine him more closely, the doctor was surprised to find an enormous tattoo with the face of Christ covering the old man's entire back. The tattoo was well done, and the face of Christ crowned with thorns seemed to leap from the black man's ribs, his eyes full of compassion, facing forward with a steady gaze, and seemed to come alive with the movement of the old man's shoulder blades.

Damasceno explained to the doctor that he'd lived in Rio when he was a boy and had practiced capoeira, but had suffered the heavy repression of the police as they sought to modernize the city. Capoeira had been outlawed and those who practiced it persecuted, and soldiers would beat anyone refusing to leave their homes in the city center. Many of them had gotten tattoos with sacred images covering their bodies in an attempt to limit the beatings, believing the soldiers wouldn't dare turn their clubs on the tattooed face of Christ.

"And did it work?" the doctor asked.

"Not at all, doctor, they beat us all the same! The streets of the big city are like a poisonous beast. The only way out is to run. At that time, the police followed anyone without a job or a home, and who among us free blacks had work and a home? Nobody. They also gave a hard time to natural healers, witch doctors, and anyone practicing capoeira. They said they were cleaning up the city. With all that suffering, I ended up leaving there and found my way here. We're just as poor here as anywhere, doctor, but here the police don't come around to club us."

Damascento ended up in a small bedroom at the back of the doctor's house until his health improved. When he was better, he'd become so attached to Dona Rosa that he asked to stay. He became an adopted member of the family, a grandfather, a storyteller and guitar player, bringing joy to Túlio's and Rosa's children, who had recently been born.

As was to be expected, *O Piston* was big news in the region, where changes arrived at a snail's pace.

The farmers in the region enjoyed the apparent tranquility of a well-established power that was rarely questioned. After a quick pass from one end of their lands to the other to ensure everything was in order, they would bark out an order or two to their foremen before going back home to lie down in their hammocks and rest. When the sun cooled down a bit, they would stop off at each other's homes to have a hot coffee, eat cookies, and talk away the afternoon. A bit later, it would be time for the liquor and card games, hard-earned forms of relaxation.

Life brought few worries in that town: inertia had left the scenery the same for decades. The world had its natural laws, and one of them was the continued power of those already in its possession.

If anyone had any worries, they were with the natural world, which always sins, either by excess or by scarcity. Rare were the years when the sun and rain got along to the farmers' satisfaction and the crops grew as expected or the cattle grew as fat as they ought to. Either the sun was too strong and the rain scarce, or the contrary. Either the sun bore down, the water dried up, cracks began to appear in the earth like awful, dry scars, or suddenly it was all torrential rain, thunderstorms, rivers overrunning their banks and flooding the animals up to their necks.

They also enjoyed discussing the weather that year and in years past, and could spend hours talking about how nature had once been more reliable and predictable. For them, a change in climate was the most palpable sign that the end times were near. It was practically the only thing that changed, even if it had only become noticeable over the course of decades and centuries.

The wealthy landowners viewed the newspaper with unease and feigned disinterest. They pretended they had no desire to read such communist drivel, but deep down they were worried. Though not very much; there was nothing that caused anyone to lose any sleep. But the newspaper was a kick in the pants for each one of them. And also for the village priest. According to the priest it was all drivel from that group of scoundrels led by Seu Matias, an atheist who hated the clergy, everyone knew it. The priest would have to take a copy of the newspaper to the bishop to see what ought to be done.

But that was not the time to take any of that so seriously. Of course, there was an article or two that made them stomp angrily into the town saloon, ordering up a cachaça and practically yelling so everyone heard them when they declared that the band of no-good communists was in need of a lesson.

This happened especially when the articles Túlio wrote associated the region's poverty with the system of concentrated land ownership. He also blamed the wealthy landowners for evicting farmworkers from their small plots of land so as to leave them no choice but to work on the larger farms. Those articles made Rosa think about the cousins she'd met only a short time before.

She knew where her relatives lived because her father had told her that her mother's brother, Gaspar Botelho, owner of a casino in Rio de Janeiro, had once visited them in São Paulo. On that occasion,

Gaspar had told family stories and mentioned that his mother, Diva Felícia, Rosa's grandmother, had a half-brother no one had ever met. Gaspar, however, knew that this brother, whose name was Dionísio Augusto, had been raised by his grandmother Açucena, a landowner in the Minas countryside whose land, as far as he knew, had long been sold. Umberto committed the name of the city to memory and told it to his daughter who, many years later on a trip through that state, where she had since moved with Túlio, passed through the area and tried to find out more about her relatives.

What she found was an old house in ruins at the foot of gorgeous emerald-green mountain, whose slopes began to rise at the edge of the city.

She also found out that, of Dionísio Augusto's twelve children, only three grandchildren still lived on a small piece of what had been the great plantation of Açucena Brasília, the family matriarch. Rosa went to visit them. Two of them weren't home, but the third was.

The tiny house with its beaten-earth floor was spotless, and the aluminum pans gleamed as they hung on the kitchen wall near the wood-fire stove. It was the house of poor people, the home of honest folk. It was one of the grandsons of her great-uncle Dionísio Augusto who lived there.

He welcomed her affectionately and amiably, and as they drank the coffee promptly prepared by the man's wife for their visitor, he told her how the children had been forced to partition the land and then sell it, eventually leaving their heirs with that tiny plot of land, and even so he could see they too would soon have to sell everything because no crops would grow there. Herds of cattle belonging to rich farmers had overrun the crop fields, and as a result the people in those parts found themselves forced to move. The man's sons had gone to try their luck in the capital; his daughters had married men from the same town, all of them working on someone else's land, and the only child who still lived with him worked at the local butter and cheese factory.

At the end of her visit, when Rosa stood up to leave, he told her that he wanted to show her something: it was a grimy little box that looked as if it had once been a jewelry case. It had belonged to the matriarch, Açucena Brasília, but there it was, abandoned, and if Rosa wished to take it, he couldn't find any use for the old thing, though he also couldn't bring himself to get rid of a family heirloom.

Inside the box there was a pencil stub and a timeworn silk camellia.

When she opened the box, Rosa was overcome with a strange emotion, intense but fleeting, a gust carrying spirits from centuries past. She thanked him profusely for the present and took the box with her. She had it carefully cleaned, fixed the leather straps, and gently placed it on her cedarwood vanity. The man was right: it wasn't pretty. But she found it difficult to put her finger on the curious sensation of inner abundance she felt each time she opened it.

They were good and peaceful years, those that Rosa and Túlio spent in that tranquil town in the countryside.

Almost nothing happened outside the natural order of the era. Rosa became pregnant with their fourth child.

Their first daughter, Lígia, and her brother Lauro would play nearby. The third child, Leandro, still very small, still took afternoon naps. Rosa wanted him to be her last child. Earlier she had thought of having more, six or eight. But after the third, three seemed like a good number. Her family was already quite large, since besides her own children, she was raising two belonging to her brother-in-law, whose wife died after giving birth to her youngest child. Túlio's parents' family business had hit a rough patch, and Túlio thought it was important to make sure his nephews had the chance at an education, as he had.

When things had settled into a peaceful lull, the time came for the presidential elections of 1955, and one of the candidates was Túlio's old friend and mentor, Doctor Juscelino, who had already been mayor and later governor of the state of Minas Gerais. In fact, he had twice invited Túlio to join his staff, but the doctor enjoyed his simple life in the countryside and had no wish to leave it.

That year, the presidential campaign descended on the city with fury, sending everyone to the streets and transforming each citizen into a rabid defender of one side or the other. After all, this was the presidential election, the candidate was from Minas, and it looked like he was headed for a win.

Rosa and Túlio were enthusiastic participants in the excitement. Rallies brought the town squares to life, groups of women spent days teaching the poor how to vote, going door to door, farm to farm, plantation to plantation. The horses, the oxcarts, the carriages, everything that moved around the city carried the colorful flags indicating support for one campaign or the other. There were fundraising parties every night, complete with street fairs, raffles, and bands giving life to boisterous dances.

Election day turned into an entire day of revelry that, in reality, had begun some time earlier. Voters had been arriving from the countryside since the beginning of the week, carried in by cars and pickup trucks, a small, motorized fleet. The majority, however, came by horse, wagon, or even on foot. Large shelters were set up to house those who came, and the parties and dances and lines for food stretched long into the night.

The National Democratic Union also had its electoral "corral" set up, but the party's chances were poor; Juscelino was heavily favored among the city's voters, and there were none of the wild quarrels common in areas where the number of supporters on each side was roughly the same. The Social Democrats dominated the city, and Doctor Juscelino was an acquaintance and friend to many who lived there. What's more, he was from Minas, and the state had the obligation to vote for him.

As was to be expected, the vote count in town overwhelmingly favored their candidate. The celebrations stretched on into the night with news of their man's long-awaited victory throughout the entire country.

The townspeople would never learn about the frustrated coup attempt in Rio, where Carlos Lacerda sought to have the military stop the inauguration of those elected. Word of Lacerda's maneuvering never made it to their small town in Minas Gerais and the people went on celebrating, commemorating the election of their new president with resounding joy.

That election would radically change the life of the Faiad family.

This time, when Doctor Juscelino, now the newly elected president, insisted his friend take on a role as physician to the enormous construction site that had cropped up in the middle of the country's central plains, Túlio felt it was his obligation to accept. The construction of Brasília, which was to replace Rio as the country's capital, was too important, and the quiet doctor thought he could not forgo the chance to contribute to the project's success.

Túlio and Rosa packed their bags, leaving their house in the hands of Old Man Damasceno.

Rosa would always clearly remember the afternoon they arrived in the immense savanna that was to become Brasília, the gigantic swirling dust-clouds rising from the red earth and covering everything, including her hair, which she would only manage to clean—really clean—years later. They arrived during the most beautiful sunset she had ever seen and, as was her wont, she immediately fell in love with the sky of Brasília, the new city that was yet to be born in that barren land full of promise.

She felt herself overcome by an emotion almost like the euphoria of forging a new life: her children would grow up on those plains in the heart of Brazil and she was a content and fulfilled woman at the side of Túlio, who was laying a city at her feet.

LÍGIA
(1945-1971)

It was easy to see at first glance that Lígia was a determined person with her own inner light. Old Man Damasceno had certainly noticed it. He was filled with tenderness for the girl and was like a grandfather to her, always only too pleased to do everything she wished. It was he who taught her how to play guitar, master capoeira, and view spirits as a natural part of the world.

But one day he opened the little girl's tiny hand to look at the lines crossing her palm. He'd done it without thinking, almost joking, something the old man never did because he never read the palms of children and never read the palms of those he considered family, and Rosa's family was his family. But you tell me why people suddenly decide to do things they've never done before! It'll take you a lifetime to figure it out.

The fact is, the old man opened up Lígia's tiny hand and almost instantly closed it again, the small white hand between his fat fingers, and the smile that had begun to dance in his eyes, as it always had at the girl's side, departed for some faraway place.

Lígia asked him: "So, what do you see? What's my future?"

"Nothing, girl, I'm getting too old for that stuff! I can't see a thing anymore. I think I need to get me some glasses."

What is certain, though, is that after that he never, ever read anyone's palm again.

This had been before the family's move to Brasília. Until the old man died at somewhere around the age of 100 (no one knew his age for certain), Lígia always returned to spend school vacations in the old house, with the old man, his old guitar, and his stories.

Lígia had been twelve when the family moved to Brasília. She grew up watching as the city grew with her—and not just any city, but the most beautiful and modern city that had ever existed, the magic city on the savanna—and she grew up believing that anything was possible. It was possible to transform the country into a land with justice for all, it was possible to make men brothers to each other, it was possible to end poverty.

At the age of eighteen, she took her entrance exam for architecture school at the Universidade de Brasília, which had just been founded in the nation's new capital. It was 1963, three years after Juscelino had left office and exactly one year before the military coup that would depose President João Goulart.

At that time, Lígia didn't formally belong to any political group. She merely got together with friends to read about and discuss Marxism. They'd read *The Communist Manifesto, The Part Played by Labour in the Transition from Ape to Man, The Eighteenth Brumaire*, and had just begun to read *Capital*. They were young and enthusiastic at the possibilities opened to them by a knowledge that brought with it the need to understand the world and change it.

Soon afterward, in the tense days of early April 1964, a wave of arrests swept through the country, taking with it union leaders, students, professors, and workers. Radio stations, under heavy censorship, spent the day playing solemn classical music, spreading across the airwaves the funereal certainty that something very grave and very terrible was taking place. Troops were on alert in their barracks and no one went out at night; the cities declared curfews, everything was still. Then came the depressing period of the deposition of senators and deputies, visits from the secret police, and the first wave of Brazilians forced to go into exile.

It was the first time that the entire country, from north to south, had experienced the same atmosphere of repression and fear, the stifling air of a military dictatorship.

Lígia and her friends were perplexed by the events unfolding before them.

Since life always has the power to resume its course, no matter how improbably, things eventually seemed to return to a tenuous norm little by little. Classes resumed at the university and the students once again began to organize politically, and there was a rebirth of political parties and movements opposed to the military regime.

Suddenly it was as if the country was undergoing a flourishing and unexpected cultural explosion. Those were the years when the military dictatorship, preoccupied with destroying Brazil's political and economic life, instituted a sort of informal ceasefire, leaving some meager space at the margins that led to a burst of creativity. The result was cultural guerrilla-warfare, and those in film, theater, music, and literature harbored the illusion of living in a free country and began to make some serious noise.

At the university, Lígia was part of a musical group where she sang and played guitar. She had a husky, thick voice, and she both composed music and wrote lyrics. She participated in protest concerts organized by students throughout the entire country. Wearing a black shirt and long black pants, her hair straightened thanks to nighttime hairnets, her great big eyes shining brighter than headlights, her voice amplified truths so obvious and yet so denied, and she would sing for an audience as full of youthfulness as she was, as full of life as she was, as utopic as she was:

"Earth belongs to man, not to God, not to the Devil."

Chico Mata first saw Lígia in the university auditorium, just before a student rally was about to begin. She was leaning over to speak with someone sitting in one of the chairs of the packed auditorium; he was trying to bring a bit of order to the space, which was bursting with students, and tapped her on the shoulder with the intent to ask her to take her seat, as their *companheiros* were about to begin. When Lígia swung her head around to look at him, her hair long, her face framed by bangs that covered her forehead, he found himself before the largest, brightest eyes he'd ever seen. He was caught with his mouth literally agape at the size of those extraordinary eyes.

Lígia's eyes truly were that—extraordinary. There were some who thought them too exaggerated, bringing imbalance to the face of the doll-like young woman, who was petite in every other aspect. But there were those, like Francisco, or Chico, as his friends called him, who considered her eyes the most astounding and luminous they had ever seen on this earth.

But at that time, if someone had asked her what she most liked about her own body, Lígia would have said her hair, not her eyes. Her hair was the focus of her vanity, her private obsession. Ever since she'd been a teenager, she'd collected recipes for homemade creams and hair treatments, and spent her time trying the most varied combinations of eggs and olive oil, tea baths, and all sorts of other things. At night, she would brush her hair religiously before twisting it up around her head, tucking it under a hairnet—only then would she go to sleep.

Oh, that hair! It often caused her to enter a rather special sort of trance. When she went to the cities of Minas on a student tour to see the region's Baroque art, what most fascinated her about the works of the sculptor Aleijadinho was the wavy hair of his prophets, the curls he made fall with a curiously natural exuberance, delicately framing the severe expressions of the sculpted creatures. Lígia spent hours trying to reproduce the same waves with her own silky black hair.

It was also on account of these prophets and their hair that she never forgot the ruins of a tiny chapel she found in a little village, its few houses nearly all as abandoned as the chapel itself, where the family had stopped once when they left Brasília on vacation. The little village didn't even have a name, as they were told by an elderly man at the roadside tire stand, but it was known as Capela. They hadn't planned on stopping there, but were forced to due to some car troubles. While her father and the man from the tire stand fixed up the car, Lígia set out with her brothers to explore the locale.

They'd discovered the tiny chapel on the top of a small slope, its walls lined with shelves holding tiny statuettes of saints carved from blue-green soapstone, their white hair falling to their feet in waves. Lígia stood there for a good long while, completely quiet, admiring the statuettes. Oh, she could hardly resist taking one of those saints home with her! The chapel was practically abandoned, and it left the impression that other tiny statues had been taken from it as well; there were several empty spots along the wall, like ancient wounds, but Lígia—understand it if you can—didn't have the courage to go through with that petty but profane theft. For some reason she couldn't explain, though, she would always be flooded with emotion whenever she recalled those tiny images of the saints, and would regret lacking the courage to take one with her, since it no doubt wasn't long before the tiny chapel would be completely vandalized.

Chico Mata was also an architecture student. He came from the backlands of the southern state of Sergipe, the son of poor farmers, and had only made it to college out of great determination. A spindly boy, his skin tanned dark by the scalding Northeast sun, he was a backlander of few words and gentle manners. He'd invited Lígia to be part of a study group focused on the works of Lenin and Che

Guevara, and that's how the two began their relationship and their political activism.

Lígia liked Chico's quiet and reserved manner, his quick and expansive intelligence. She liked his legs with their knotty forests of curly hair. And his broad chest, where she could lay her head and dream.

Soon after graduation, they were both hired by the university as graduate teaching assistants and moved into one of the modest apartments on campus. Less than a year later, in 1968, Lígia became pregnant. The sight of her petite figure with its protruding belly was guaranteed in all the political marches, on all the outings to spray-paint messages of resistance on city walls and façades, in the distribution of pamphlets, in running from tear gas, police horses, and billy clubs.

Maria Flor was born under a full moon, and her birth coincided with the arrival of the country's darkest moment, AI-5—the Fifth Institution Act—ushering in a fiercer repression, the end of the cultural ceasefire, and the determination of the generals to eliminate any form of opposition to the dictatorship.

In their modest apartment on the university campus, the Beatles's *White Album* played until it almost split in two.

The posters and the graffiti seemed to age prematurely: "Forbidden to Forbid," "The Earth is Blue," "May a Thousand Flowers Bloom." Faces everywhere carried tense and somber expressions. From one moment to the next it became clear that the revolution could not be launched from the universities. The military dictatorship had adopted a harder line, the party was over, and the promise of tomorrow was no longer the same; it was and for years would remain overshadowed as the resistance was driven underground and a bloody fight to the death began between the status quo and utopia, between the injustice that was, and the thousand of possibilities yet to be discovered.

Between the military's professional killing machine and the improved tactics of the resistance.

Lígia rocked her newborn daughter to sleep with the same songs everyone was singing, still believing that the risk of danger, like all things on this earth, ought to be greeted with open arms:

"We need to remain alert and strong / We don't have time to fear death or wrong . . . / At every corner, danger lurks. All is divine, oh so fine. Watch out!"

Like thousands of young students, however, Lígia and Francisco saw no other option than to join the armed opposition to the dictatorship. The open war on students and left-leaning groups declared by AI-5 had escalated. In response, these groups became increasingly radical. Chico and Lígia, wanted by the Brasília police and unable to move through the city because they were far too recognizable, saw themselves forced to leave. They decided to flee to Rio de Janeiro.

It was painful to leave Maria Flor with her grandmother, but there was no other alternative at that point. Fugitives, subject to having their house invaded at any moment and being arrested without the possibility of leniency or appeals, there was no way they could bring a child who had just taken her first steps.

A revolution is no dinner party.

No.

A revolution most certainly isn't a dinner party—soon Chico and Lígia would know exactly what this meant.

In Rio, they underwent training in the armed resistance. It was, let's be frank, pretty amateur training; no one there was a professional soldier, they were just kids with the absolute and boundless conviction that they were doing exactly what they ought to be doing and that, if they opened the way forward, the Brazilian people—that group of their countrymen who, despite being nameless and faceless, had nonetheless assumed mythical proportions in the young revolutionaries' minds—would soon rise up to follow them. The starving Brazilian people, exploited right down to the bone—people without jobs, land, school, or futures—that Brazilian people would certainly follow them. It was only a question of showing them the way.

To her surprise, Lígia discovered that she had excellent aim and nerves of steel. She could make decisions quickly and was capable of confronting the police as though she'd spent her entire life doing nothing else. At times, in the midst of a special set of circumstances, moments beyond the typical unfurling of each day, we suddenly discover that we are capable of things we never even dreamed. The same Lígia who just a few years earlier hadn't dared to take a small, blue-green, soapstone statue from a crumbling chapel was the same woman who now robbed banks and expropriated property without hesitation.

There was just one thing: she didn't like to talk about what she did. In fact, it seemed that this was a rather common trait, and perhaps it is so in any war: the young freedom fighters preferred not to discuss their armed exploits. They were such monumental events that they belied description later. No one basked in his or her accomplishments, *I was the one who shot him*, or *I did this or that*. What they were doing was so serious; they were so young and inexperienced that taking part in a war of life or death made them appear nearly reverent before their task.

The young couple's life was now completely different from what it had been before, during their years at the university. It was a life lived in isolation, bouncing from safe house to safe house, a life spent on the move so as not to provoke the suspicions of neighbors. Their friends were limited to their comrades, their activities to the work of revolution: constant reading, studying, and discussion around Marxist texts and the situation in Brazil. They produced fliers and newspapers, to be distributed on the front doors of factories and other strategic locations. They underwent training, and laid plans for the requisition of cars and arms for their operations: expropriations of bank reserves to finance the revolution—which, as mentioned, was no dinner party and thus required considerable resources. They carried out kidnappings to secure the release of their imprisoned comrades and to ensure their revolutionary message was read across radio and television stations.

Every now and then, they went to the movies and had a beer to relax.

Described this way, it might seem that this was a barren, unhappy, and miserable life. But it wasn't. In all of this there was a higher calling, the participation in something much greater than the individuals involved, a collective project whose generosity and objective, however utopic it may have been, had the power to reach far and wide and create in everyone a sense of belonging and extraordinary achievement. As never before or indeed thereafter, it was a moment in time whose importance clearly transcended the daily lives of each of the group's individual members. Perhaps only those who've had the privilege to live such unique moments, when history appears to acquire its full meaning, are capable of understanding why and how an individual in such a situation, despite and against everything, becomes something greater, more fulfilled, more content.

Lígia, like her comrades, kept her utopic views intact. At times she perhaps even dreamed a bit too much: she would compose songs while she waited for a comrade she was to meet, wrote poems on the eve of important operations, brought her guitar to each safe house where she went to live.

And on the headboard of the bed where she slept, wherever she was, she always scrawled out a quote from Che: *Hay que endurecerse, pero sin perder la ternura jamás.*

On one afternoon while scattering fliers around Rio's city center from the top of an office building on Avenida Rio Branco, she unwittingly grabbed several pieces of paper with lyrics she had written as she grabbed a handful of fliers from her satchel, and tossed the lot out the enormous glass window. Poetry and fliers denouncing the political situation in the country rained down on those walking along the avenue that afternoon. Later, she returned to the site to see if she could recover some of the papers with her poems from the sidewalk. No such luck. The pamphlets and poems had been trampled by passersby and were now covered in mud, torn to pieces. Lost.

Time passed quickly, and not in the revolutionaries' favor. The dictatorship was growing stronger by the day, the net was closing in around them. Each day, more of their comrades found themselves in military prisons, where they were tortured, killed, or disappeared. Photos of Lígia and Francisco circulated throughout the city on wanted posters, declaring them terrorists.

The photo of Lígia was an old one, but she nonetheless found herself obliged to cut her long hair and wear fake glasses to gain some anonymity.

It was one of the saddest days of her life when she found herself before the mirror cutting her own hair, lock by lock; her beloved hair, which she had always treated with such care. Tears fell, soaking the wavy tendrils that also fell one by one, just as her comrades had fallen, one by one—imprisoned, murdered, tortured, disappeared. They became more isolated by the day, they were losing the war that had begun with so much hope and so much belief in mankind's ability to create good in the world.

It seemed increasingly impossible to reverse the path they'd taken.

One afternoon a few days later, Lígia and Chico went to gather information for an assault on a bank in the Madureira neighborhood. The couple opened an account at the bank, their pretext for visiting the locale to examine it up close. Later, Lígia had a meeting with another comrade, next to a newspaper stand outside the Jardim Botânico. She said goodbye to Chico with a strong, lingering hug— that's how it was in those days: each time they separated, they couldn't be sure they would see each other again.

It was a radiant, sunny afternoon, and she decided to walk along the Lagoa Rodrigo de Freitas, basking in the limitless exuberance of Rio's natural surroundings. She began to think about just how incomprehensible it was, the capacity beauty had to veil the injustice and cruelty that reigned only a few short steps away.

Lígia was also happy at that moment because it looked as if she would be able to visit Maria Flor in the coming days. She had been unable to see her daughter for months; her mother, the child's grandmother, was under constant police surveillance, and it was difficult for the two of them to leave Brasília without their noticing it. It would be a complicated operation, but it was worth the risk and Lígia couldn't wait to see her little girl. She opened her wallet and took out the last photo her mother had sent of her daughter, pursing her lips into a pucker as she blew her mother a kiss.

As soon as she stepped off the bus near the arranged meeting spot, Lígia felt a twinge. She had a strong intuition that something was wrong. The sharp jab of imminent danger landed an icy chill in the pit of her stomach. She took a few steps to get her bearings and decided to cross the street, without stopping, without looking around her, straight ahead, stiff.

Too late: she had been spotted.

Without turning her head, she saw some fuzzy shadows moving toward her out of her periphery. She tried to run between the cars, but an ice-cream vendor—an undercover cop—took out his gun and fired; she dropped to the ground, shot in the back. Cars slammed on the brakes and horns honked in alarm as Lígia was surrounded and pulled to her feet by four, five men, who put her in a car whose driver stepped on the gas, wheels screeching against the asphalt.

Everything happened so quickly that the passersby barely had time to see, much less understand what was happening before their eyes.

In the spot where Lígia fell, a blood stain soon turned black against the scalding pavement. After their initial shock, the cars resumed their impatient forward march. People on the sidewalk had instinctively come to a halt when they realized what was happening, but just as instinctively cleared the area quickly as could be. The city lived in a panic, and no one was looking to mess with the dictatorship's agents of repression.

The bullet had pierced Lígia's ribs. Unfortunately—and how—it did not kill her on impact.

Thrown across the cold hard floor of a tiny cell—in a brief respite from the torture, between the dark, red haze that enveloped her thoughts, which now zinged chaotically around her head, intermittent flashes lacking logic or reason—Lígia could see the tattoo of Christ on the back of Old Man Damasceno. The image had always disturbed her; she didn't like to look at it, but her brothers would spend all day asking the old man, always kind and ready to please, to lift his shirt to show them the disturbing face, but she did not look, she couldn't, as if she found the whole thing obscene. At that moment, she realized that the horror she felt when faced with the tattooed Christ had, in some way, been a premonition of what awaited her. But if she had such a tattoo of her own at that moment, she would have needed it to cover not only her back, but her legs, her breasts, her buttocks, her head, her vagina, her anus, all the places throughout her body that her torturers found to provoke cruel and heinous suffering. Like Old Man Damasceno, it would make no difference, no matter how many Christs were tattooed across her body.

She couldn't be sure how long she had been there, whether it had been hours, days, or years.

Again, she found Old Man Damasceno before her, he who had raised her. His fat fingers, his skin as dark as unlit charcoal cupped over the tiny white hand of a child, her hand, the contrast such that it made her skin shimmer. He tried positioning her childish little finger on the exact point where she was to press down on the string of his guitar. But soon, another image crosses her mind. A barefoot

Damasceno tossing her into the air to immediately pull her back to safety as he taught her capoeira, saying: "If you want, you can be good at this, my girl. But you have to learn to control every inch of your body."

Every inch of her body.

She had learned a great deal from Old Man Damasceno, much more than her brothers.

But what good had it done her?

It was just like in the story of Chico's that made everyone laugh. It had been at the burial of one of the resistance's leading intellectuals, an erudite man. Another comrade—a pragmatic fellow opposed to all the petit-bourgeois intellectuals who, according to him, were a scourge upon the movement—commented: "You see? He read *Capital* in its entirety, he read the complete works of Lenin, all of Engels, all of Mao, he knew everything, he'd read everything, but what good did it do him? He's dead anyway."

He'd read everything, learned everything, but what good did it do him? He died anyway.

Lígia's swollen lips tried to form a wry smile.

She was unable to open her eyes; all she could see were dark red blurs and shadowy figures, but in her mind's mirror, she could make out a vision of herself. In the vision in the mirror, she was fifteen years old and trying on her dress for her debutante ball; her grandfather made sure her coming out took place in São Paulo, in a gala celebration that occupied the ballroom of the Paulistano, the most exclusive club in the city.

Yes, it's true, her debut was at the Paulistano—it didn't get much more petit-bourgeois than that. She was fifteen and reading *Gabriela, Clove and Cinnamon* by Jorge Amado and *Wind, Sand and Stars*, by Antoine de Saint-Éxupery.

What sort of world was it that she found herself in at that moment?

Between the blood clots that had formed in her eyes, she could see the little body of her Maria Flor, walking toward her with arms outstretched.

No, no. Not that. She couldn't think about her daughter, she would be unable to hold out if she thought of her, she wouldn't be able to do it.

She focused on her white debutante dress. It was an elegant white dress made of organza and crepe, with extraordinary straps made from the golden lace that had belonged to her mother. She saw her grandfather's smiling face, her grandfather who thankfully was dead, he would have been unable to see her this way. His only granddaughter, ever since she was a little girl he had given her dozens of the most beautiful dresses to ever leave the shop of Umberto and Leda Rancieri. She always wore the latest collection of haute couture creations that they insisted on sending her. She was the best dressed of her friends no matter where she went, including political rallies and marches. Her nom-de-guerre was Chanela, given to her by a comrade in honor of the famous Coco Chanel.

The biting pain returned and she no longer needed to force herself to concentrate on anything. At least the pain brought her this much relief: it made thinking impossible.

Lígia died three days after being captured, after undergoing all manner of torture in the military police barracks on the Rua Barão de Mesquita in Rio de Janeiro.

Neither her capture nor death were officially acknowledged.

Her body remains unfound to this day. She is among the four hundred thirty-four Brazilians suspected to have been killed or disappeared during the military dictatorship.

MARIA FLOR
(1968-)

Blue like carbon paper, pink like infant clothing, purple like the cloak they threw over Jesus's shoulders: Maria Flor had dyed her hair all the colors of the rainbow, hair she always kept neatly trimmed to reveal the butterfly tattoo on her neck, opposite the tiny, dark triangular birthmark whose tip leaned ever so slightly to the left. These days, her hair was fern-green. She had two belly button piercings that made it quite plain which generation she belonged to, the generation living at the end of the century and the millennium, the generation of boys and girls who were born in the midst of the disturbing variety of infinite choices that modern life presented, who had been born into an avalanche of information and possibilities, but also of violence, poverty, calamity, traffic jams, new diseases, obsessions, stress, and the savagery of a world of haves and have-nots.

What a life!

What a life Maria Flor has!

Getting from her apartment in Flamengo to her studio in Santa Teresa can take her thirty minutes or two hours, depending on the day of the week, the time of day, and the whims of the traffic. If she's having a good day, she won't be mugged the way she has been some eight times while waiting at stoplights. Every one of her friends, in one way or another, has already been victim of some form of violence amid rising unemployment and urban poverty. To live in a big city in Brazil at the end of the millennium is to live in the eye of the hurricane. You feel oppressed and impotent in the face of so much misfortune, and your dreams become filled with the desire to move to another city, another country, or, if possible, another planet.

From the closed window of her car, she watches the young thief strolling down the sidewalk, the penknife in his hand concealed by the long sleeve of the shirt that is two sizes too big for him. During the unbearable summer, this is the official uniform of such thieves: an extra-large shirt, the sleeve pulled down to cover the hand that holds a weapon or drugs. She can still remember the first time she was mugged, the time she saw the filthy little boy rolled up in the shirt three sizes too big, his nose running, and how, before he drew close, she had naively asked, "What are you doing in a long-sleeved shirt, kid? It's hot out!"

Hey, kid! What are you doing?

She raises her eyes to the horizon to glimpse the sunset, dyed red on account of the pollution; the rays of light hit the billions of billions of billions of dirty particulates that, refracted, take on this fiery red tone that frightens her because it's so out of place, an unhealthy color that doesn't belong to the sun.

But Maria Flor is pregnant, and ought to think positive thoughts, and that she will. In Rio, this isn't so hard. It's enough to look around in any direction to distract yourself and allow the city's indestructible natural beauty to work its magic.

Maria Flor is good at distracting herself.

I mean, she is and she isn't. At some moments she is, at other moments, she isn't. It must be like that for everyone, she thinks. But she makes a mental note that this is a matter to discuss with Joaquim, her live-in psychiatrist, when he makes the next of his private visits to her home.

She manages to distract herself from big problems all too well.

The small ones, not so much.

But she's already had several worries that have weighed her down in the past, and which now are nothing but ghosts of their former selves.

One, for example, was her weight. A plump girl since childhood, for many years she felt she needed to spend her life counting calories, until one day she decided to view the issue from a new angle and convince herself that it made no sense to spend her life taking pills and going on diets to be accepted socially. She thinks back to this turnabout in her life with a certain pride. She remembers how she began to go after data about the multi-million dollar weight-loss industry and take note of how marketing did its best to try to convince her that there was something wrong with her body. What sort of oppressive system had they created at the expense of the overweight? she asked herself at the time. Why is the only acceptable body type for a woman a thin body? If I believe that my body can also be attractive and powerful even if it's a bit rounder and fleshier, I can be as desirable as one of these walking collections of skin and bones. If you don't feel well in your body, you won't feel well anywhere: this was her new maxim and certainly had much to do, later, with her future success in her profession.

Another worry of hers was money: like many young people of her generation, she thought money was certainly important in life, but contrary to many of them, she believed that the way you earned it also made a difference. She felt uneasy around her friends who measured their worth by the size of their bankbooks. Her great ambition was to do something she enjoyed and achieve a quality of life that she considered high. She wanted to live without stress, calmly enjoying whatever came her way, to live and let live. In other words, if things continued as they were in Brazil, she really would have to convince Joaquim to move countries after the child was born.

This country!

She considered herself incapable of understanding what was happening before her eyes and her disillusionment was so immense that she had trouble believing that Brazilians might come to have some sort of better and more just life.

On three occasions she had experienced the joy of belonging to a group that shared a cause and a collective will to change things, and on three occasions she looked on as everything stayed the same or grew even worse. The first was the era of mobilization for direct elections; she had just returned to Brazil with her father as a teenager, and she thought the most important thing one could do was bang on pans and participate in the enormous protests where she carried posters that read "Direct Elections Now!" in large bubble letters. The second was when the Worker's Party nearly won the presidential elections and she and her grandmother—yes, the great dame of education Rosa Alfonsina—handed out fliers with the photo of a smiling candidate Lula, during the remarkable campaign when it still made some sense to urge the people "Don't be afraid to be happy!" The third was the impeachment of president Fernando Collor de Mello, when she painted her face green and yellow and felt, at last, that the country had changed, that to finally remove a president for corruption meant the people had had enough, that they would never again accept anything like that.

But it was what it was.

Soon, there was greater poverty. Greater concentration of wealth. Greater unemployment. Greater violence. Greater deterioration of city life. A greater number of armored cars among the upper-middle class as they drove through the streets, where more and more unemployed families were forced to live. Greater corruption that became the currency of the daily newspapers, which she never read to avoid filling her head with such dark news.

Ah, this country!

She would speak at length with her father about her perplexity and ask him to explain why nothing seemed to go right here. But how was he to explain a thing like that? Of course, Chico had his theories, but, strictly speaking, no one could account for the predatory and perverse behavior of the Brazilian upper classes.

But now isn't the time for such thoughts.

She looks at herself through the rear-view mirror, retouches the striking red lipstick on her thick lips, and smiles to herself: she's pregnant! She's going to have a child! Isn't it a wonderful thing?

She gets a kick out of herself.

She gets a kick out of the way she would blow challenges out of proportion just a few years earlier. Her favorite response to a problem was always to create a mini-drama out of almost everything, as though by exaggerating her problems she could create enough distance to laugh at them and, who knows, reduce her burden. She would spend hours on the telephone with her father in the Northeast, or with her grandmother in Brasília; or with her uncles, one in Brasília, two others in São Paulo, giving them a report of her daily theatrics. Her telephone bill was always sky-high, it was her Achilles' heel when it came to budgeting.

She can remember how complex and tortured her choice of a profession was. Her grandmother had been the first woman in the family to have what they call a profession—that of an educator; Maria Flor, on the other hand, found herself facing myriad decisions: what did she wish to be? What sort of work would she like to do?

Her Uncle Lauro had given her a single bit of advice: whatever you decide to do, let it be something you truly like, that you can dedicate yourself to with all your heart. This is the most important thing and it will make all the difference throughout your life: to enjoy your work.

But she enjoyed doing so many things!

First, she had thought about film. No doubt influenced by her two filmmaker uncles, she had considered becoming an actress. She could try her luck in the theater or in soap operas. The problem was that, in order to be eligible for roles other than the chubby girl, she would have to diet constantly, and this did away with just about any desire to become an actress. Next, she thought about becoming a ballerina: she'd studied ballet from a young age and he'd always been told her pointe position was the most graceful at the academies where she'd danced. To become a professional dancer, however, she also needed to be thin, and would have had to make her decision earlier to have sufficient time to build her technique—or was she mistaken? Whatever the case, it was out of the question.

After that, she thought about becoming a singer. Though she had an interesting voice, it wasn't as good as Gal Costa's, for example. Maria Flor had Gal's bow-shaped mouth, and she was always wearing bright red lipstick, but her voice, though pretty, was nothing extraordinary. Never good enough.

When it came to science, she lacked all interest. She hadn't exactly been an enthusiastic student and had no desire to enter the research field, spend years and years bent over one invention to discover another. That wasn't who she was.

When it came to the humanities, she thought it was all a tad boring and a bit useless. She shared her generation's cynicism and didn't even think it was possible to better understand how societies functioned, much less change them. She thought that humanity's stupidity, cruelty, and selfishness were indecipherable and she maintained a distance from politics. Just look at what had happened to her mother . . . ! There was, understandably, no solution to her incompatibility with that field . . .

Architecture, law, journalism, economics—no, no, no, and . . . no.

Medicine, odontology, and other such professions—no way; she couldn't stand the sight of blood and had a strong tendency toward hypochondria, she had often found herself suffering the symptoms of any disease she'd learned the least bit about. In her head, she'd contracted practically all the illnesses that had sprouted up in recent years: extreme stress, depression, anxiety. She had developed a habit of self-medicating and had racked up reward points at the corner pharmacy, where she was a guaranteed client. There could be no doubt, she didn't have the objective distance to work in that field.

Business administration—NO WAY. She was horrified at the thought of business administration. She believed herself to have truly undergone a traumatic experience thanks to the field: the most disgusting guy she ever met had earned his degree in business administration. The third-generation heir was a poor imbecile who had thought that he could buy everything with his family's money and had tried to take Maria Flor by force in an episode that, however incredible a story it might make, she still prefers not to discuss. He was the whitest guy she'd ever seen, you could almost see right through him he was so white, a watery blond, with red eyes and white eyelashes: if you come across men with white eyelashes, her subconscious had told her, run the other way. Such men were ugly and repulsive—they likely had tiny dicks and were premature ejaculators. Actually, she was so disgusted by guys like that at the time that she imagined some obscure motive for her feelings, something she wasn't aware of, but which, in some form or another, was there, deep inside her mind, always ready to appear at any moment.

One day, as she was telling her grandmother about her disgust for men with such white skin, reddish eyes and white eyelashes, Rosa Alfonsina recalled a detail from the time she would make desperate trips to military offices in an attempt to have some news of Lígia. She had no desire to expose her Maria Flor to this frequent torture and had never taken the girl of three or four with her to such places. One day, however, there had been a sliver of a chance she would be admitted. Along the way, she was going to leave Maria Flor with a friend, but there was misunderstanding and her friend was not at home. Already late and without anyone to leave the girl with, Rosa was forced to take her granddaughter with her.

It was all for nothing, as it always had been; on that day, as well, she was unable to discover anything about Lígia's whereabouts.

Her hopes had been raised by the fact that the person who answered her phone call was a general she had known from the early days of Brasília, Antonio Camargo Garcia. He had been very friendly on the telephone, telling her that he did indeed remember the little Lígia who played with his children amid the gigantic machines carving out what would become Lago Paranoá. And, of course, he remembered Rosa Alfonsina quite well, the exuberant wife of Doctor Túlio. He would see what could be done.

The busy general wasn't certain what it was that, against his principles, compelled him to look with certain deference at the case of the young disappeared woman. He sat thinking about how he'd remembered Rosa Alfonsina because she had been a pretty woman toward whom, at one time, he'd looked with the hungry gaze of a starving dog.

He couldn't know—and would never know—that it was something in his blood that caused him to remember her and her daughter, the little girl with her short little bangs and extraordinary dark eyes, who he'd seen laughing and playing with his children one day. Something in his blood that had the same origin as the blood of Rosa and Lígia: he was a descendent of Gregório Antonio Garcia, brother to Clara Joaquina.

But the vestige of such an old and, in the end, distant relation was incapable of swaying a general of the military government for longer than a few moments. When he learned that the young girl suspected by her grandmother to have been disappeared had in fact died under torture at the hands of police in Rio, General Garcia preferred to avoid a meeting. He asked his assistant to inform the kind lady in his waiting room that there was nothing he'd been able to find out and that he was too busy to receive her personally. If she wanted, she could reschedule for another day, perhaps she'd have more luck then.

As she'd left the ministry, Rosa had been unable to contain her tears, and Maria Flor, standing at her side, noticed. There was more: they had been followed by the assistant to the general, the strong, tall, and blonde fellow who had been watching them in the waiting room.

He was the type of guy with a loud and grating voice that, as he told Rosa that the general could not see her, repeated, after each of his clumsy justifications, "You understand, don't you, ma'am?" as though he suffered from some nervous tic. "The general is a very busy man. You understand, don't you, ma'am? He needs to dedicate his time to his priorities. You understand, don't you, ma'am?" The fellow had followed them quite some way and surely the girl had noticed her grandmother's jitters and tears. Well, as it so happened, this guy met her granddaughter's exact description of the abject man: a tall, strong man who almost glowed he was so white, with watery blond hair and horrifying white eyelashes! Yes, her granddaughter was right: there was no doubt he had a tiny dick and was a premature ejaculator.

Maria Flor had spent almost all of her early childhood with her grandmother and uncles.

The house where they lived was always filled with the sound of boys, Lígia's brothers: Leandro, Lauro, and Laércio. All of them were studying at university, and though they all supported the Left and participated in student protests and marches, none of them took up arms as their older sister Lígia had. Leandro and Lauro loved movies and wanted to change the world and the Brazilian people through their films and their art. Laércio, the youngest, was a bit more suspicious and cynical than his brothers, and though he agreed that everything was wrong, he saw no solutions on the horizon, whether near or far. He kept to himself, looking on, without committing to anything. He was studying economics.

Maria was the apple of their eye, the little girl who they stuffed full of candies, lollipops, and chocolates.

Rosa Alfonsina had become a widow in the most unexpected and premature way. Túlio had barely reached fifty when he died in a single-propeller airplane crash during a tropical storm, one of those downpours that darken the sky without warning and seem to signal the end of the world. A doctor, he had been summoned to an emerald mine a few hours outside of Brasília, where a malaria epidemic had taken hold. He had gone to have a look at the situation, spent a week there, horrified by the conditions in which those men, women, and children lived, digging trenches in the earth gray with schist in search of the glimmering green stones. He saved many lives that week, including that of the son of one of the big mining bosses, who insisted on giving him a pure emerald in return, nearly the size of a quail's egg, a stone later discovered inside his clenched hand and which Rosa wore around her neck to that day, dangling from a gold chain she never removed, not even when she took a bath.

Following Túlio's death, Rosa's life changed in several ways. The most important, perhaps, was that she began to work. As luck would have it, Brasília was a city that created jobs in those years of growth, when the transfer of the nation's capital gave rise to all sorts of tall tales that caused the government workers in Rio to sell their souls and anything else they did not have to move to a city without the sea and—what was even stranger—no street corners! The city with no corners was the terrible nickname that stigmatized Brasília during its first decades of life, scared off many people, and left many posts across government organs vacant, given the requirement that government workers move from Rio to the new capital. The utopic vision that had given birth to the city was so unreal and disconnected from modern life that for many, it became incomprehensible and unbearable. Meanwhile, for others, like Rosa, it was exactly for this same reason that the city wielded fascination and seduction.

It wasn't difficult for her, wife to one of the pioneers of Brasília, to find a job in the Education Ministry, despite the fact she'd never worked before. There she could stay without being bothered, as though the job were merely a way to pass the time, as though she were a prop, or a furniture support, one among the countless employees who find in government work the means toward an easy life. Rosa, however, was not a woman to sit still.

At the time, it was widely believed that at forty years of age, women started down an irreversible path toward old age. But Rosa didn't think so. With all of her forty years, she felt alive, more world-weary, much wiser and more beautiful than on the day she'd paraded around as a beauty contestant with her cloak, her scepter, and her crown. She had four precious children to raise and was not about to allow their lives to be filled with sadness just because fate had robbed them of a paternal shoulder. Túlio had been the most incredible and beloved person she had known, but, if she had been given more time to live, live she would.

Rosa began to work with remarkable diligence and creativity for someone who had never worked before. She unearthed from deep within her memory what she had learned in her teaching courses and sought out the latest books on education, found intensive courses and conferences at the university, went back to school, to get informed, to figure out what needed to be done. Over time, she gained prestige in the education field. Her purpose was to combat the easy optimism that reasoned that every underdeveloped country would naturally develop, as though it were following its own necessarily unique path toward progress. To Rosa's mind, a country—any country—confronts problems, conflicts, and obstacles that it may or may not manage to overcome and take a step forward. It was imperative that people worked toward that goal, and she sought to be one of those people.

She became a bit meatier, the wide hips that were a family trait grew wider, but her exuberance and joy remained the same. She had several suitors, but she had a habit of repeating that she would only marry again if she fell in love one day, otherwise, she would remain as she was, she was fine just as she was.

During the years of military repression, when her house was constantly monitored by the police and she was followed on the streets, Rosa had just begun working at the Education Ministry. As she'd always had many friends, ever since the time when Brasília was just one big construction site, she knew absolutely everyone, including several colonels and a few generals.

At the beginning, when things were still very much a student movement, she had obtained, through her personal contacts, permission to visit a friend of Lígia's who had been imprisoned and of whom no one had received any news, or learned where another jailed student was to send him clothes, food, and other such things. As the situation worsened, though, this crack in the door became increasingly less accessible. People she had known from when the city was scattered with tents stopped greeting her. Wives to military men, women who just a short time earlier had made frequent visits to her house to ask her to share the recipes for which she had become known, suddenly pretended not to notice her.

When Lígia disappeared in Rio, Rosa's trips from military precinct to military precinct in search of news of her daughter, where she was and what condition she was in, rendered no information. At times she would spend entire afternoons day after day waiting to be seen in the waiting rooms of some colonel or other she knew, only to be sent away with a thinly veiled rudeness. She was eventually prohibited from entering any of the military ministries or other precincts throughout the city.

Those were dark days, hellish days.

Arriving home, after one more day in the useless pursuit of news, Rosa would sit Maria Flor on her lap and tell the girl everything she knew about her mother. She would show the girl some of Lígia's photo albums, would speak in detail of even the most insignificant events of Lígia's childhood, what she was like as a teenager, how she had dressed, what she liked, her favorite foods and colors, everything one could say to the daughter about the mother she would never know.

Maria Flor remembers well these hours spent on her grandmother's lap listening to stories of Lígia, those were her favorite stories, much more than any tale of fairies or princesses. Later there came the stories her father told her, of the country that he and her mother had fought to change, why they had engaged in the struggle, what had happened, why Lígia died the way she did.

Maria Flor has only two photos in which she appears with her mother: one from the hospital from the day she was born, and the other in her parents' arms, taken on the day they left Brasília.

In the photos, Lígia is thin, petite, with long hair and hypnotic eyes like headlights that light up her face.

There was a time when Maria Flor often compared herself to her mother. The two women are rather different: for one, Maria Flor is tall, likes to cut her hair short, and the only thing she inherited from her mother is the dark color and the long, dark eyelashes. She's nowhere near as beautiful as Lígia was, she's sure of that. Her grandmother used to tell her she was wrong, that she was every bit as beautiful as Lígia, but her grandmother was the queen of saying such things, and the fact that the old woman thought so didn't make it true. And anyway, she actually wanted her mother to be more beautiful, it gave Maria Flor one more reason to admire her.

There was one other aspect, at that time, in which Maria Flor felt she was different from her mother: her mother was thin, the line of her collarbone well defined. At the time, Maria Flor still cared about such things, she had just returned from France and was heavier than she had ever been.

Today, Maria Flor has mixed feelings about the years she lived in France with her father.

She had liked being at her father's side, but she sorely missed her grandmother and her uncles and hated the dark European winter. She hated the dull, wet cold, which had caused her to curl up in a ball and chatter her teeth. She also didn't like the kids at the school she would attend during the day, boys and girls who entertained themselves by pulling her hair, calling her "latina," as though it were an insult, and stealing the chocolate bars that she had a habit of carrying in her pocket as a form of consolation. Her only friends were, like herself, children of exiles, children who, for the most part, formed a group that, despite the best efforts of the adults, felt weighed down by the heavy cloud of their past, of denunciations, of suffering, of sadness. These elements were a constant, in the adults' conversations, in the news coming from Brazil, in their plans to return, in the stories they told, in the vague darkness that clouds the future of any exile.

After Lígia had disappeared, Chico could no longer stay in Brazil. He decided to go to Chile, exiled like thousands of other Brazilians in his situation during those years in which the dictatorship expelled wave after wave from the country.

For a long time, he held out hope of finding Lígia, of finding that she was merely imprisoned in some unknown but very real location, of her reappearing one day. Curious how in the space the human mind allows for irrationality when in the depths of our desires there shines the tiny light of "if," however miniscule and entirely void of reason, entirely nuts, entirely blind—yet there it is, shining its light. Until his return to Brazil following the general amnesty, this insane little light still glowed within him, though it eventually dimmed and flickered only intermittently, the light he hoped to find in Lígia's unsettling eyes as he turned a corner, the solemn voice he hoped to hear when he picked up the phone.

He had been preparing to bring Maria Flor to Chile when there was suddenly a coup against Allende. The horror of the days that followed replicated the horror of earlier events in Brazil. Chico was imprisoned in the soccer stadium, along with Chileans, Brazilians, Argentines, Americans, Europeans, people of all nationalities who had gone to Chile to change the world. From there, he was exiled to Belgium, and from Belgium he went to France.

Only in France, after some time, was he able to send for his daughter. Maria Flor lived there with her father until just before her teenage years. After the general amnesty law, they returned to Brazil, Chico married a woman from Pernambuco, and went to live in Recife. Though she loved her father and the beaches of the Northeast, Maria Flor hadn't wanted to follow them. She preferred to stay with her grandmother in Brasília, where she completed high school and soon embarked on the tiny drama over what to do with her life.

Flor enjoyed drawing human figures in several outfits and always had a genuine interest in the human body in all its aspects. She was vain; she liked to dress up and put on makeup, and given her uncommon nature, she always designed her own clothes and accessories. There was even a time when she designed, and quite successfully, the costumes for her uncles' films. She knew better than anyone that the right clothes help to build the profile of a character.

Hovering on this thought and its ramifications, she made a decision: she was going to be a stylist. She would work with fashion, like her great-grandparents Umberto and Leda Rancieri.

As soon as she made this decision, Flor became another person. She forgot about her post-modern illnesses, her doubts and anxieties, she adopted the maxim that "she who isn't comfortable in her own body can't be comfortable anywhere," and off she went: she moved to Rio, rented an apartment with some friends, and set to work with fervent dedication.

She considered clothing an integral part of a person, her character, and her personality. It could add or subtract from a person, change their way of seeing the world and the way the world saw them. It could lend, or take away, charm or a certain gracefulness. It was capable of attracting, or repelling, admiration and interest. It was a trigger. A first step. A magnet. After that, the rest was up to them.

She was happy with her choice and was soon in high demand. She made costumes for the movies, the theater, and TV soaps and had a studio with a view in Santa Teresa and all the bells and whistles. She would research new materials and come up with brilliant ideas. She earned prizes for her work, such as that which she won for her black, slim dress made of a soft synthetic fabric that she'd help to develop, without anything, anything at all, but her grandpa Rancieri's straps of gold lace. She lived her life amid the colors, shapes, and beauty that she so loved.

But there were times when she still found herself in the midst of a tiny drama over her choice of a profession. Like the day when one of those mean and cruel little people that infest humanity managed to get close to her—which was rare, because in general Flor surrounded herself with people who were as friendly, warm, and affectionate as she was.

Thinking it over, wait a second! What I just told you couldn't possibly be true. No one is able to surround herself with kind, warm, and affectionate people alone. The fact is that Flor wasn't exactly an expert in reading people and liked to think that others were as sincere as she tended to be. She considered herself a skeptic, a woman who knew a thing or two, experienced, someone who knew the ways of the world, but deep down, she had a tendency to be naive the way most kind, affectionate, and warm people tend to be these days.

And this little person came close only to ask Flor whether she thought that her mother, who had given her life to the revolution, would have liked to see her dedicate her life to something as futile and vain as fashion.

Flor had arrived at home in tears.

She had never thought about her profession that way, and luckily she had Joaquim, her psychiatrist boyfriend, at her side, a man who understood the human heart and who understood hers even more fully. As a result, he was able to help her digest and rid herself of that tiny but damaging dose of venom. He listened attentively to what she had to say: First (Maria Flor was one of these people who liked to organize her thoughts and she preferred to think things through by classifying them, placing everything in its proper place, ranking them—first, second, third), her mother was her mother and, whatever sort of person she was, she would have accepted and loved Maria Flor as she always had loved her. Second, each person's beauty and well-being might be considered a side-point, but they weren't "futile and vain." They were part of things called "imagination and entertainment," which, though not (this she recognized) basic needs in the way a home, food, health, and education were, were nonetheless an important component of one's happiness. And her work was concerned with people's happiness, exactly the same ideal for which her mother had died. Third, she had never given her vote to any of the horror-shows who made the daily lives of Brazilians torture: all those unscrupulous politics had been elected without any contribution on her part, and so she couldn't make herself feel responsible for what was happening.

Those were more or less her thoughts on the matter and she could even have continued until she reached a ninth or tenth argument, because whenever Flor wanted to reason things out and classify them, she went all in. But she had already begun to feel calmer and more secure, and Joaquim thought it better to end their session.

Flor had met Joaquim Machado, the psychiatrist three years her junior, at drinks following the release of a book by a mutual friend of theirs. He came from a family from the state of Amazonas, had studied in Rio, completed his residencies in France and the United States, and had just opened his practice in Rio when they met.

Over a glass of white wine, they struck up an animated conversation that continued with a glass of prosecco in a restaurant that was all the rage. But it didn't stop there, either—they continued their conversation at his apartment over other things. The initial remark that set off this intense process had been the age-old theme of differences between the sexes, but in this case, fueled by genuine curiosity on both sides, it had been capable of sweeping them through the night.

Both of them had found themselves in the midst of a discussion during drinks where one of the male participants, surely for lack of a better subject, had raised the question over whether women had a smaller brain, proportional to the size of their bodies, to which another woman in the group, also in an attempt to overcome her boredom, had responded: "But with a denser distribution of neurons, of course," and so went the conversation until Maria Flor asked her new acquaintance and psychiatrist at her side another question, merely with the idea of making sure the conversation did not die out into awkward silence.

"But where on earth did men get this idea that women don't need to have as much sex as men? What's all this about men being more promiscuous by nature and women being more interested in stable relationships?!"

As the question had been posed directly to him, after one of fate's masterstrokes had placed him next to Maria Flor, the young psychiatrist also began to speak directly to her. Thanks to the old art of chemistry that often intercedes in such cases and keeps the world spinning, the circle composed by the others disappeared from their sight, and in no time they moved from idle chatter to an exhilarating tête-a-tête on a variation of the same theme: how men had repressed women and then later believed that the result of their own work was a legitimate product of nature, how startling it was that, to that very day, the proper attention hadn't been given to the fact that the clitoris was the only human organ whose exclusive function was to give pleasure, while the penis, with its role serving two masters as a conduit for urine and semen, lacked such a refined specialization.

Given the theme they discussed with such passion, it should come as no surprise that the conversation they had that night continues, in a certain sense, to this very day.

Both of them, each in their own profession, are doing pretty well. They more or less like the same things—music, movies, nice restaurants, new computer programs, conversations about the third millennium, the stupid things people do, and the prospects for a better future for the country and the world. In soccer, one of them roots for Fluminense, the other, Vasco. One of them takes care of a Siamese cat, the other a stray dog. They enjoy dancing and vegetarian food at home, but they're no fanatics. They spend hours on the Internet. While one of them goes to the gym, the other receives acupuncture sessions and gets shiatsu massages.

Flor likes Joaquim's sensitive and nervous fingers, and he likes her ballerina feet.

They've lived together almost since they've met, and more recently, they decided to have a child. Maria Flor is thirty-three, an age that seems about right to her, and Joaquim also thinks it's time he figure out what it's like to be a father.

Whether by talent or by luck, or because they know the right people, or for all of these reasons, Maria has become a media sensation. Though at first she was a bit startled at her fame, which took off at a wild pace—the pace of the fashion industry in the age of globalization—she's now earning relatively good money and she intends to use it to fulfill a longstanding desire.

An old and mysterious desire that started the time she vacationed on a rather unknown beach in Bahia, and which has only increased now that she's pregnant: the desire to live on the edge of the sea, where the mornings glisten beneath golden rays, the sun's true color when there is no pollution. She thinks perhaps, who knows, she'd like to live in some place like that, open a *pousada*, divide her time between there and Rio, with Joaquim. She also thinks the idea is a bit crazy, but she knows she could make it work, at least for a time. What is life made of, after all, if not exactly this: stretches of time, some longer, others shorter, all of them finite, finite moments that form our brief histories here on earth, composed of several layers, yesterday this, today that, tomorrow—who knows?

Deep down, she wants a rest from her chaotic life in the big city, where the worst of Brazil seems to parade on display. She wants to give things in the country time to improve.

She wants to run barefoot along the beach with the very same sand where perhaps one day other feet had tread, feet belonging to someone she never knew but who she knows existed and may well have tread that same spot. It could have been her mother, or her mother's mother, or her mother's mother's mother.

Now, as though in a fleeting mirage, she hears the sound of laughing and light footsteps racing along the sand. She can taste the salty seawater and luscious fruits, the flavors of the forest, she can smell the wind, she can hear bare feet trudging through the mud, the murmur of river waters, their pure gold, rippling silk, there's the smell of roasted meat, the whisper of sugarcane in the fields, and bright sunny mornings. She can feel the weight of the impossible silence that belongs to the backlands and to the darkness, she hears a voice echoing through the woods, the melancholy chords of a piano and lament of violins. Horses galloping and livestock mooing, gunshots, feet running, blood, blood, and more blood, the taste of red savanna dust, the heights of the jatoba tree, and the warm scent of a woman.

All this, she knows, is a taste of the past in disguise.

A taste that is fleeting, ever-changing, but which she somehow feels is a part of her. These things belong to her, she carries them within her, as will the children who are soon be born.

Children.

Maria Flor parks the car in front of the building where she lives. Pregnant, her hair now the dark blue of a raging sea, she is coming home from the doctor's office with Joaquim. At first, the news they have just received left them perplexed, almost worried: how could they have guessed what fate had in store for them after so many years using birth control?

But now, they laugh at the news, thinking about all that remains to be done, their thoughts and energies directed toward the unexpected future that is now theirs: in Maria Flor's latest ultrasound, they learned that they are going to have not just one child but twins, a girl and a boy.

The two of you.

Can you hear them laughing?

And so, we've arrived at the end of our story, and the hour is near. The genetic codes of both of you are already processing information, and the proteins that will form your own memories have begun to reproduce. And that's how the distant memories of time will continue to live within you and in your children, the children and grandchildren of Maria Flor.

Tomorrow, April 22, will be a full day, the first of all of the days of your lives.

A cloud floating outside in the nighttime sky, on this night with its full moon, a night on which babies like to begin to be born, will soon have moved on. Tomorrow will be as beautiful as April days centuries ago.

The sky will be bright blue, for there are still special days when it manages to display this color; a small and sudden gap in the pollution will open in the sky, a pleasant breeze will blow through; the noisy traffic will unexpectedly pause and the street kid will put away his penknife for a moment of rest.

But don't take it from me.

Extraordinary things await you both.

ACKNOWLEDGMENTS

I would like first to thank the many hardworking professionals who have dedicated themselves to researching and writing about the history of Brazil: their works were of immeasurable value as I wrote this book. The wealth of historical writing today is extraordinary, thanks to the serious and skillful research that now has covered nearly all eras of the country's history. Perhaps there is still much to do, but our historians have already been on the job for some time, and have delivered exceptional work.

I would like to acknowledge here the origin of three episodes in this book: the story of Hans Staden, of which Tebereté's tale is one of many versions already written; the story of the soapstone, which can be found in a report by Yeda Brandão about one of our common ancestors, and which was sent to me by Dulce Pedroso; and finally one afternoon in 1970, when Maria Lúcia Torres, without realizing it, tossed her poetry, together with fliers protesting the military dictatorship, from the top of a building on Praça João Mendes in the historical center of São Paulo.

I would also like to thank several friends for reading this manuscript, and for their valuable suggestions and encouragement: Maria Lúcia Torres, Peg Silveira, Neide Rezende, Rodrigo Montoya, Alípio Freire, Virginia and A.C. Scartezini, Laura Duque, Maria Lucia Alves, Maria Luiza Torres. To Octavio, Px, Flavio and Denise, Jacinta.

And especially to Felipe who, "from the end to the beginning," made this book possible.

.

Maria José Silveira is the author of ten novels, including the prize-winning *Her Mother's Mother's Mother and Her Daughters*, the film rights to which were sold to TV Globo.

Eric M. B. Becker is editor of Words Without Borders and an award-winning journalist and literary translator. He received a PEN/Heim Translation grant for his work on Mia Couto, and has also translated works by Lygia Fagundes Telles, Noemi Jaffe, and others.

**OPEN
LETTER**

WWW.OPENLETTERBOOKS.ORG

**OPEN
LETTER**

WWW.OPENLETTERBOOKS.ORG